Eternal Night
of the
Northern Sky

Anne Bellows

Content Warning

Dear readers, this is a content warning for graphic violence and adult themes. This book contains mentions of assault, self-harm, and suicide. Readers should take the utmost care for yourselves when approaching this book. Thank you.

Contents

To my younger self—

We did it!

Map of the North

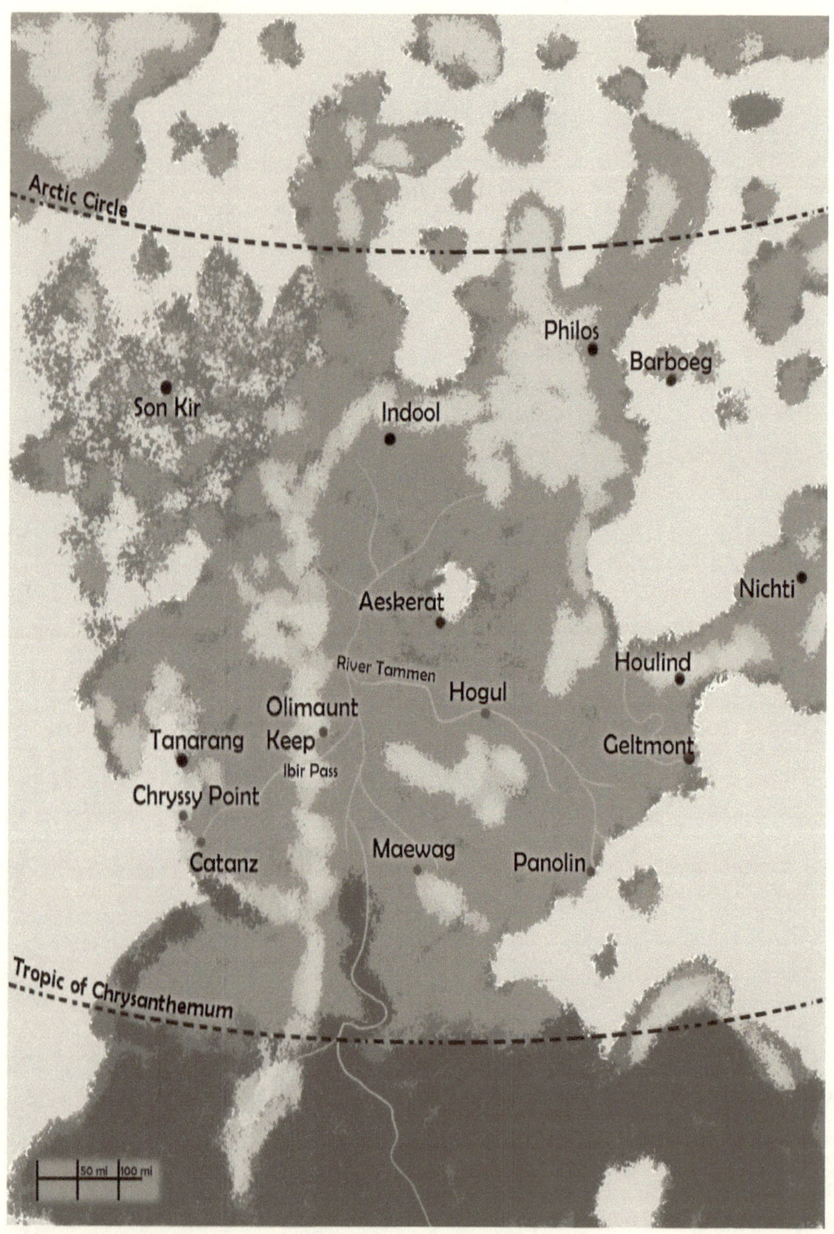

Chapter 1:
We're Alive and They're Not

B eneath the snowdrift of the longest blizzard Elias has ever endured, the last vampire in the dungeons finally succeeds in taking its own life. He doesn't hear of the incident until it trickles through the stone tunnels of Clan Maewag three moons later.

The last vampire has died, their blood has burned off, and the clan must either risk a hunt, or freeze.

Now Elias counts the last of their stores of dried meat and frozen broth when Netto shares the news, grinning wide and absolutely vibrating with excitement. He's already picked out his favorite spear. Elias keeps taking inventory by the dun light of a seershroom lantern, jotting down the barrel counts without once looking at his cousin.

"When's the last time you went outside?" Netto whines. He pokes at Elias with the blunt end of the spear and scrunches his face. "Come *on.* You've already finished anyway. If you didn't miscount the first four times, you won't the fifth."

"Your ability to enjoy the surface is entirely independent of me joining you," Elias remarks idly, finishing his count anyway without looking up. "I'll join you after the storm passes."

"You say that every time, and then another storm comes and you never keep your promise." Netto pouts and curls his fist under his chin. Then he bounces and pokes Elias again with the spear. "I'll tell Auntie you're a liar and she'll force you to come."

"Will she?"

"Uh-huh." Netto bobs his head and leans against his spear. "She'll take your charcoal away so you can't write anymore."

Once. His mother tried that only once. Elias won the war of attrition when he still refused to go outside *and* the ledgers never got done. Chief Yarren had to step in and overrule her.

"Elias." More poking. "Sissy. Eli. Elio—"

"Netto, *please*." Elias resists pinching the bridge of his nose. It's always like this, always guilt-tripping and whining and begging. Elias doesn't need to see the surface. It's bad enough he can smell it, the spill of icy wind that blows through the door at the mouth of the cave, clean and cold and empty. Either it'll be exactly like he pictures, an immense white wasteland, or he'll catch Misha's wanderlust and find himself at the bottom of a crevasse.

Netto's ability to tear up on command doesn't work on him, try as he might.

"Auntie needs me here," Elias reminds him. "Ulira's sick, and if she dies, so will her calf. I'm on watch duty, and hunts are never shorter than five moons."

"She's dead anyway," Netto mumbles. He burrows deeper in his furs. Above them, the warning bell clinks and Netto gasps, sprinting away with his spear and a rushed goodbye before the hunting party can leave him behind.

Elias collects his inventory list and locks up the pantry vault, the only door that locks in their entire cave system. The rare thieves among them still think they can get away with pinching crumbs *just this once.* The clan can't afford to dole out harsh punishments befitting the crime of threatening their precarious food supply, only the silent treatment. Elias himself has been subjected to cold shoulders and stinkeyes simply for having this job. He's spent more than half his life doing it and long since stopped taking it personally. Long since embraced that Keeping is a lonely life.

Yarren wordlessly stops him in the main atrium and takes the inventory list. He doesn't have to tell Chief Yarren what the whole clan already knows—Ulira's going to die, sooner or later, and if they come back without fresh game, it won't be the Freeze that kills them.

Yarren shifts to stand between Elias and the wind, grunting in disapproval at their dwindling inventory.

"Nobody eats but the children until we get back," Yarren orders.

As if Elias alone can enforce that. He nods anyway. "If you don't?"

"I trust your judgment."

The party of six makes for the surface, snowshoes and weapons strapped to their backs for the climb. The door is far above, but still, when it opens, a bitter cold breath steals away the stale warmth in the cave. It drifts down in icy fingers across Elias's skin. The cave always smells stale, but the outside air of nothingness is bleakly sterile. Elias shivers and cinches his clan belt tighter, almost choking himself with his furs. He inhales one last gasp of outside and then, mercifully, he's left to finish his chores in peace.

The rest of the clan thinks his a boring, if necessary, job. Elias appreciates that it gives him an excuse to be left alone and not dragged into droll conversation everyone else finds funny except him. There's much to do and ample time to do it, and now he can work in blessed silence, the light math and monotony keeping his mind busy, without Netto tripping him up at every step.

The kid's cute, eager, honest. He's just enamored with the hunt and hasn't yet seen the dangers of when they have to track down vampires. Elias hasn't either—the last one they caught had been theirs since he was young.

Elias stops at the intersection of tunnels, where down one dead end is the hold for vampires, the only section of the cave that Elias has never seen. He's not forbidden, but he has never wanted to gaze upon a beguiling face that must look so alive while hiding a monster underneath. All he knows is that they take every precaution they can when the hold's door can't lock.

Their vampires have less freedom than their cattle. It's not like they need space to move or freshwater or enrichment. They don't even need a corner to relieve themselves in—they're dead. But all those moons spent trapped in one room, bereft of conversation and companionship... Elias supposes it can drive even those undead leeches to bitter ends.

He'd be impressed at this last one's fortitude, if his clan's survival hadn't been depending on the vampire's continued miserable existence.

Elias's seershroom lantern casts dim shadows on the tunnel walls, chain squeaking softly as it swings in his grip. Their garden is finally recovering after a blight nearly wiped out the colony. The one in his lantern, pillowed in a bed of protective moss, is one of the few original survivors. Fat cap glistening with milky spores, it's as bright as a candle flame. Elias never lets the soft little light out of his sight, even sleeping with the chain around his wrist lest anyone try to take it from him.

The rest of the revived colony sprouts around the roots of the Takkha Tree that stretch from ceiling to floor in the temple. The roots are older than the Great Freeze, wound through fissures in the rock when only a dead stump remains on the surface. The roots endure, as Clan Maewag has, and should be honored, or so the rest of his clan members think. The only value Elias sees is precious wood to burn.

The temple might be the eeriest cavern in the network of thirty-odd chambers, far and away from the main atrium where a rogue ember from a hearth could set the ancient wood aflame in an instant. The cracks in the rock, barely wider than his wrist, continue down into a black void where other sounds echo up from below. Trickling water, squeaking bats, falling stalactites.

Get drunk enough on *schninir*, and the screech of the bats starts to sound like the voice of Takkha themself.

Elias sets the lantern down to count their stockpile of emergency wood bartered from other clans. The same amount as last moon, save for one precious log sacrificed in the hearth fire to pray for good fortune on the hunt.

No thieves, not anymore. The last one's skull grins down at him from a notch in the Tree's roots to remind everyone of the consequences. He counts the wood thrice, and then finds himself in the garden counting the colony. The snowmelt that makes survival in the cave possible pours down from high above in the cavern. It continues on down as an underground river far below where their network of tunnels ends.

Ulira bays and moans in her pen across from the garden, dying slowly of starvation like the rest of them. Elias's mother lies with her and her calf in the dirt, singing lullabies. He pockets his inventory and leans on the shallow stone wall. If he doesn't come to see her, he doesn't see her at all.

Morjanot is the calf's and its mother's last defender, taking it upon herself to stand guard as the rest of the clan clamors to use Ulira's meat while it's still on her bones before there's nothing left for her to give. Everything must serve the great circle, or it's no less a burden on the world than the plague of vampires.

"You didn't want to go on the hunt?" his mother asks wearily, scratching behind Ulira's ears. Elias has had to bring her last six meals to her, yet the irony of where he gets his stubbornness eludes her even now.

"I'm not good at it, and it's still snowing."

"There's more to life than lists and counts, *bimpet.*" She lifts her head, purple bruises underlying the sunken eyes from her ceaseless watch.

"And if I go out there with dreams of greatness and fall into a crevasse?" He doesn't mean to be rude, but they've had this conversation before. Round and round in circles they go. "Ambition gets you killed."

"If it did, the North would be a dead world, and still we endure."

We do, he thinks. *Misha didn't live long enough to enjoy it.* "I can endure in the safety of the cave."

His mother tries to smile, but it wrinkles into a grimace. "We endure so that one day, we might not have to live in the safety of the cave."

No one remembers what the sun looked like since it disappeared. The last soul in the North who did died twenty-two generations ago. Elias rests his chin on his arms and watches the weak calf stumble around on knobby legs. She bumps her snout against her mother's flank and snuffles. Ulira flicks her tail and nothing else.

"Would promising that I won't live and die down here make you happy?"

She answers with a *hmph.* "Don't make promises you can't keep."

He did have ambition. Once. Then the hunting party came back and told him his brother died. Felled not by beast or monster but by not watching where he stepped. If the gods were real—if any of their prayers to the Takkha Tree mattered—then Misha wouldn't have died such a pointless death.

The Tree keeps people from going crazy. It gives them something to blame for their misery other than each other. It tells them they have a purpose, enduring up here in the Great Northern Waste, instead of the reality: They were too stubborn and afraid of what was out there to pack up and move to warmer climes.

"I can matter in other ways," he argues, because he's not Misha or Ulira or the calf on knobby legs. He's not already dead and going through the motions. "I Keep. It's not glorious, but it matters. I still serve the circle."

Morjanot only nods, because she's heard this before, too. Never satisfied with his contentment. Never eager to have her last son always by her side. Twenty-six generations of Clan Maewag hiding under the ice, and she'd had her eldest convinced he'd be the one to lead them all to the promised land.

"There's nothing out there but snow and darkness," he mutters, then leaves her to her dirges.

Overmoon, Ulira passes without ceremony. His mother doesn't shed a single tear, assisting the butchers stone-faced. They burn more precious wood smoking the meat and use every last joint. Elias updates his inventory count and moves on.

They make the most of her passing and feast on whatever won't keep while enjoying the rare fire while it burns. His kinsfolk, fifty-two in all save the hunting party, dance and sing and add Ulira's silhouette to the atrium's wall.

Elias claims a drum as an excuse to avoid the dance circle, dully keeping rhythm with Bini and Loric. Beside him, a dancer dresses down beside the heat of the flames, painting himself with blood and ash before joining the rest of the group showing off skin and dancing provocatively.

"If you like that sort of thing," Bini muses. Then she's pulled into the circle herself and strips down her furs with the rest of them, hooting and howling and tugging fistfuls of her hair.

It ends how events like these always end. Bini smiles coyly and kicks Loric's drum aside to drop into his lap, both unmindful of the audience around them. *We're alive and they're not*, the dance cries. *We're alive and they're not, so let's enjoy it.*

Elias found himself a partner only once, but his clansman had gotten drunk on seershroom liquor and thrown up all over Elias, remembering none of it once he woke. Bringing it up to him at that point would have only earned Elias a cheap apology. Better to avoid the *schninir* and spend the aftermath of the party drawing even if it will garner relentless teasing. *We're alive and they're not, and this is what you do with it?*

Elias retreats to the garden as couples and trios trot off to get lost in each other at the first convenient place. Ulira's unnamed calf cries for attention as Elias passes. He loops a lead around her neck to let her join him in the tiny seershroom meadow.

"Just don't eat them, you'll go blind," he warns.

No one would care if he took an extra jar of ash and soot from the fire, but Elias tiptoes back into the main atrium to pinch a few handfuls. He sketches with his fingers on the exposed rocks in the empty spaces around his previous work. The Takkha Tree and the calf's predecessors, fanged faces or what he thinks they look like.

The calf shivers and nestles right beside him, and Elias sketches her likeness—big eyes, floppy ears too large for her head, dappled fur.

"I'm naming you Dapple," he decides. "You'd better live long enough to learn it."

Sickness took the rest of her tiny herd, and it was his mother's insistence on taking Ulira to sleep with the rest of the clan in the bedding chamber that saved her life.

Music still echoes through the tunnels from the dregs of the party—what might be their last if Dapple can produce no babies herself. The great and defiant clan of the North, bested not in battle with vampires or gored by beasts on the hunt but crippled by starvation and the Freeze.

If the six who left don't bring back a mate or surrogate mother for Dapple, if they don't bring back some of the scant wood that remains on the surface, if they don't bring back a vampire to battle back the Freeze, Clan Maewag will leave no greater mark on this world beyond finger paint on the walls. A thousand years from now, when the humidity from the garden has seeped through the tunnels and rotted away all their furs, when the Takkha Tree and the rest have withered away and been consumed by the seershrooms, some curious soul might wander in and think, *Oh. A savage lived here once.*

But they've been teetering on the edge of imminent doom since the sun disappeared. Going mad about it is a waste of energy. So, Elias falls asleep with ash on his fingers, sharing Dapple's warmth on the rocks to the sound of the snowmelt trickling into oblivion.

The six return as three. No meat, no wood, no livestock, no Netto. The cold that sweeps in from their entry lingers. Underground, they can't insulate without suffocating. The bedding chamber is lined along the walls and the floor with pelts, but the massive entryway that lets in fresh air to combat all that's consumed by the clan's sleeping bodies nips at whatever warmth they can create. It doesn't matter how deep they dig or how many fires they burn, the Freeze has come. It ices their furs and reddens their faces, threatens their toes and noses and fingers.

Clan Maewag holds a vote on whether to burn more wood. Yarren intends to head right back out after they warm and eat, leaving it up to the clan to decide in case they don't return. One can't anticipate the valley of their darkest hour and no one will judge the clan should their resolve break and they burn through a log minutes before Yarren returns with fresh livestock.

Elias, along with two-thirds of the clan, raises a hand in favor of using what they have while they have it. They have the wood, it should be used. They have rendered-fat candles to cling to during the worst of the chill, but a single flame won't save an appendage.

Elias stands stiffly beside Yarren as he rattles off their dwindling inventory. He avoids the dozens of hole-boring eyes, staring instead at his feet. He doesn't envy Yarren at all. He's made it clear to Yarren that if he dies, Elias isn't taking his mantle. They'll hold a vote, as decorum dictates, and the clan will pick someone far more charismatic to make the tough decisions with Elias's input as Keeper only.

After, his mother leads the clan in song, all hands linked. The unnatural Freeze comes when they lose hope, lose strength, lose ambition. All the burning wood in the world can't revive that warmth. So even on this moon—especially on this moon—they crowd the Takkha Tree, the petrified roots of some ancient perennial long since swallowed by the earth, and pray. In this, Elias joins, so no one can say he didn't. He echoes the rest of his kin as softly as he can until Chief Yarren's hand descends on his shoulder.

Yarren nods toward the door and Elias tiptoes around the others, following him out of the Tree room.

Yarren's nose is permanently red and deformed, two fingertips missing from his left hand. He doesn't smile much anymore. When he does, his lips bleed. He commands but does so softly, even now.

"The lists are done?"

Elias folds his arms tightly. "Ulira's meat will keep and we'll have more candles in the stockpile."

Yarren nods and claps him again on the shoulder. "Pack some jerky. You're coming with us."

"Wh—*me*, Chief?" Elias backpedals. "I've never been to the surface, I'll just slow you down."

"Aye. But everyone better is too fearful or cold to be useful, and now the lists are done." Yarren starts to lead him farther from the Tree room as if he might try to flee. Elias swallows and tries not to drag his feet.

The two Yarren returned with, Lalo and Minira, are already waiting, two axes, a chain, and four spears between them.

"I don't need another spear," Yarren explains. "Only a lookout."

Lalo spins Elias around to saddle his shoulders with snowshoes and a cumbersome travel pack before he's uttered a word of consent.

"You'll be tethered, not to worry," Yarren assures, then nudges him back toward the Tree room. "Go say your farewells if you've got any to give."

The first face that comes to mind is Dapple's, not his mother's. He can imagine his mother's excitement that he's opening up, branching out, seizing the day. One or all of such unwanted platitudes. He's not Misha, and he's not joining the hunt for any reason except obligation.

"No," he hears himself say. His hands have gone tingly and his body moves on instinct, adjusting his heavy gear. "No, let's go before they freeze." He should be terrified—they're going to get him killed up there—but it doesn't feel real yet. Any moment now he'll wake up drooling in Dapple's fur.

Only the four of them. Not six. If six weren't enough, how would four be? He doesn't ask what happened and Yarren hasn't said. *They've given their ends to the circle. Not the undead.* There is no more explanation than that.

They begin the long climb up the slope to the surface, passing the old lift that broke before he was born without the resources to repair it. More wood he could have added to the list. Leaving it there helps the clan feel not so buried alive, but the time for faith is at its end. There's wood to burn, fires to keep.

He's out of breath barely halfway up, weighed down by the pack and the grade of the climb. Keeping doesn't demand strenuous activity, and the cramped tunnels don't offer much space for exercise. He'll be useless out there. Tether or no, he'll fall into a crevasse or flat on his face. He'll fall and leave his party vulnerable to attack.

At least he knows, in theory, how to wield spears and axes and short swords with the brittle training weapons bartered from other clans. Lalo's axe had lost its handle, the replacement now a curved rib of an unearthed skeleton. Minira's dagger is from the same bone. Elias has no weapons to call his own. Minira hands him a spear. It's as long as he is tall, and while Lalo can transform one into a seamless extension of his arm, Elias scrapes the cave wall with a metallic squeal and thrusts it back at Minira, red-faced. Saying nothing, he pulls goggles from his pack.

They have reached the doors, heavy thatched panels thick as his torso. They're slathered in insulating mud on this side and, he wagers, covered in frost on the other. Elias wants to expect daylight, snow so blinding white he'll have to squint for the first time in his life. As it is, he won't even be able to smell fresh air beneath his fur mask or see the darkness in its full might behind his goggles.

They've all been taught how to brave the snow, should the cave collapse or burn or force them out. Lessons and grand stories painted on the walls by the fire, however, are no match for reality. When the doors open, the winds from the blizzard are still blowing, the snow piled as high as his hips. If he stretched out his hand, Elias doubts he'd be able to see his fingertips. No tunnel in the cave is wide enough where he can't touch the walls. Yet never in the cave does he feel claustrophobic. He always has a seershroom to see by, knows the layout of all the tunnels even in pitch darkness. The cave is home. This wide-open wasteland is crushing. Elias flails in a panic at the empty nothingness around him.

This is what Netto wanted him to see so badly?

Yarren leads at the front of the tether, booting up with his snowshoes without care for the bitter wind. Elias can't move, numb already to Lalo securing the tether around his waist. Lalo knocks on his goggles and Elias brings his fist to his forehead. *I'm ready.*

Courage or no, the Freeze sinks its teeth into his soul the moment they leave the cave. The surface isn't the bitter nothingness he thought it was. Even the wind is hungry for his death, a boulder against his chest buffeting him back. Every step feels like there's stones on his ankles. His mask, heavy and thick with frost, might as well be mud. Frost coats his goggles, too, as fast as he can scrape it off, the tether tugging at his hips his only lead. Elias clings to it with aching hands, focused entirely on putting one foot in front of the other before he spirals. The only thing grounding him is the crunchy snow beneath his boots and the tugs on the tether.

How long or far they walk eludes him. Elias sweats beneath his furs, parched and delirious and sore from coiling his every muscle. He's walked further on this trek alone, this single straight line, than he has his entire life. Noises don't echo without the closeness of the cave. He could be leagues from any form of cover.

When they do stop, the wind has died down enough that Elias doesn't have to brace to stay upright. He rips off his goggles, yanks down his mask, and gulps down icy air. It burns his throat and tongue and stings his eyes, forcing them closed. Lalo's shouting, but he can't make it out over the wind, and then Lalo tackles him to the snow and drags him by his ankle.

The wind dies completely, and he finally opens his eyes to a shallow icy shelf that now shields them. Lalo lights a candle to warm his fingers, and the light is more than enough for Elias to see by.

Whorls of purple and blue marble the solid ice, the colors transfixing. It once existed in paint they can no longer make on the walls of the atrium, in plants that no longer grow so far north in the Great White Waste, in the few books held together by hair threaded through broken bindings that taught him how to read.

He brings his fingers to the vein. Is this what the Southern sky looks like? The ocean, too, on a cloudless day? Some of his kin have blue eyes, but in the darkness of a cave only ever lit by seershrooms and flames, he's never seen them in natural light. This must be what they're supposed to look like.

Elias notices Lalo and the others staring but can't bring himself to be ashamed of his wonder. He grins softly, stretching toward the veins of color above his head. Ash piles litter the ground of the shallow alcove. Old camps from past hunts.

Yarren has already dropped his pack, digging out more candles from a notch in the shelf for their hands. Outside, the wind rages, a thick current of flurries. It's so *loud*. He's used to air whistling and whispering through cracks in the stone, but this storm howls as if a horde of monsters hides beyond the white veil. Elias keeps the icy wall to his back and takes a deep breath. The air still burns, but it's *clean*. Nowhere in the cave can he escape the smell of mildew, smoke, dirt, or the consequences of an entire clan in close-knit quarters.

The surface smells like nothing at all, just cold.

"The storm will pass soon," Yarren says, flexing his fingers around a flame. "We march onward once it does."

"How do you know?" This storm could rage for a lifetime and Elias wouldn't think it strange.

Yarren passes him a single strip of jerky, fatter than the rest. "We hiked back in the eye and it was moving south. For now, eat, drink, recover your strength."

Despite his hunger, Elias's stomach is churning too terribly to eat. Instead, he takes a candle. It isn't much, but it warms his fingertips—and his nose when he goes cross-eyed bringing it up to his face.

Minira chuckles. "Careful, Keeper. Wind burns are bad enough without adding real ones to your skin."

His chief pats him on the back. Elias smiles gratefully. He's outside, on the surface, and he hasn't died yet by falling to his death. Elias still doesn't know if Misha died on impact or if he froze to death slowly, trapped in a hole with nothing to think about except his inevitable end.

"Chief?"

Yarren gnaws on a strip of jerky, at ease with Lalo and Minira up here on the surface. He inclines his head with a distracted *Hm?*

"What happened to Netto and the others?"

"Fell."

"But if you were tethered..."

"Kort thought he heard something growling," Lalo says flatly. "He freaked out, cut himself loose, and started running. Netto and Ulric went with him. By the time we found them, they'd fallen down a slope into a ravine."

"We're alive and they're not," Minira mumbles. "Rest, Keeper, or you will be, too."

Chapter 2:
The Grove

The storm does finally pass, leaving the sky clearer than Elias ever thought possible. He hurts his neck craning it to examine the endless starry night. Minira tells him the blotchy purple expanse arching above is where the gods live, and when he asks how many stars there are, she huffs a laugh and says, "More than all the grains of sand in the world." Elias doesn't say that he has never seen sand, nor that he doesn't know how much sand that is. Lalo tries to show him constellations, but even following his finger, Elias is hopeless to see them and finally nods in faux understanding. They're up there, that's all that matters.

Both moons are out, too. Lumbering yellow Gellen dwarfs the little rock that looks almost like another star, Dania. They're nothing like the illustrations with faces and silver swirls in his books—they're *better* because they're real.

Without the blowing wind, the Great White Waste spreads before him in frigid clarity. No more trees grow without the sun. It's only snow, glaciers, and mountains, a land as sterile and empty as the moons.

"We're moving out," Yarren orders brusquely, rolling up a map painted on an old hide. Real game hasn't been spotted in months without anything for animals to eat. Any game left up this far north has long since figured out how to live underground like the clan, feasting on whatever mosses or mushrooms or lichen that grow in a world without daylight. They're smarter than his clan, he thinks, toughing it out without having to resort to using the undead leeches to survive.

"Do we have anything to barter with the other clans?"

They don't produce anything except candles and seershrooms, and no one's pack is large enough to be carrying a trade worth a whole animal. With the loss of Ulira, he'd thought finding fresh meat as vital as finding a replacement leech.

"No, we have weapons."

That kind of barter, then.

They march over the fresh white snowfall, still tethered should the ground collapse beneath them. With the mountains so far in the distance, never seeming any closer, it's impossible for Elias to tell how far they walk. Snowy plains slowly fade to ice pillars that Lalo tells him hide a petrified forest. Long bereft of branches and leaves, the trees look nothing like the ones in his books.

Still, the old forest stands thick enough to force them to backtrack and take a circular route around it. Gaunt trunks jut like stalagmites, the same in every direction in a disorienting maze. Elias's cumbersome snowshoes and awkward gait leave his legs achy, and without a destination to look forward to, he starts to question what young Netto ever saw in leaving the cave.

Minira clicks sharply and they jerk to a halt. Elias holds his breath, imagining everything from a crevasse open before them to a lone corpse. She crouches, studying a path of hoofprints in the snow. They're downwind of the animal's path and hopefully not too far. It's alone, wandering for one reason or another. Silently, Minira points where the prints lead with her dagger. Lalo tightens his hold on his weapon. Yarren had told him they needed a lookout, not an extra spear, but proceeding empty-handed while they brandish their arms feels absurd.

They strip their snowshoes, which should have made moving easier, but now every crunch of their boots risks scaring off the game.

Then they find it—or, rather, smell it. Wet fur. Moments later, Elias spots a mass of black fur shivering in the cold. A calf, wandering in circles, crying out for a mother that isn't coming. Maybe she died protecting it in the storm, else they got separated. A calf isn't what they came for, but it's too lucky a find to pass up and hauling a calf back alive is a far easier prospect than dragging an unwilling bull or cow. A boon, Elias thinks. The cave will be better. It'll be warm, and this calf will have a friend. They couldn't have asked for a greater gift. When Minira says she'll take Elias with her to escort the calf back to the cave, it's the best news he's heard all day.

Minira whispers a plan to flank it. They split up, Yarren with the chain and the three of them with spears to block its escape route. Elias's only job is to keep the frightened animal from running past him. He can do that, no problem. He takes his position, spear at the ready, and waits for the others to circle around.

The calf either hears them or smells them, going rigid on its knobby legs. Elias licks his chapped lips beneath his mask, and toes forward. The calf trembles in its exhausted circle, crying louder, red-rimmed eyes wide with terror. Elias knows they're not going to kill it, but the animal doesn't. Minira coos and clicks her tongue, sliding ever closer. Yarren hefts the chain. If he manages one good leap, he'll be able to tackle it to the ground. It's not going to be a difficult fight.

Elias backs off so as not to get in the way, too focused on the calf to notice the movement above them until it's too late.

An arrow sprouts from Yarren's back—so sudden Elias didn't see it fly. The chief howls and drops to his knees. Elias freezes, feet stuck to the ground, joints stone. The calf rears and escapes past him. Minira screams *"Vampire!"* before another arrow finds its mark in her chest. She drops with a choked cry. Lalo throws his spear wide. The vampire doesn't miss.

As Lalo falls, Elias drops his spear and throws his arms up, screeching, "I surrender!" Eyes closed so he doesn't have to stare down the arrow meant for his heart, Elias waits and waits and hears a soft *thwick*. An arrow whistles past his ear, fletching kissing his cheek before it embeds in the ice pillar beside him. He flops back, staring at the arrow impaling the pillar. It's entirely made of ice.

How didn't it shatter on impact? Some kind of magical permafrost? Perhaps it's simply a rare pale wood that only looks like ice—*Oh, it doesn't matter!*

The vampire's on him then, standing there wrapped in white and black seal leathers, bow in hand. If it wanted to kill him quickly, it would have.

He's going to be food.

Elias is not above begging for his life, so he gets on his knees, presses his hands together, and does just that. "I'm just a Keeper, I'm not a hunter. I'm only out here because there was no one else. Please, please let me go, you already have the rest of my party. I swear we won't come after—"

A boot shoves him flat on his back, the sharp end of the bow's limb at the hollow of his throat, forcing him to look up.

Elias isn't sure what he expected. Something more monstrous in stature, to be certain. Blood red eyes, a black mouth spilling with fangs, claws or talons, even a tail for all he knows. But it is plain brown eyes that look back at him from beneath plain brown hair held back in a complex weave of thin braids. The only way he can tell the being before him is a vampire is its unblemished skin, untouched by the bite of frost and less sun-starved than his own. It's so...

Normal.

Those eyes fall from his face to his belt, and it juts its chin. "I have not seen that stitching before," it says, with a light accent he can't place. One of the old ones, that's all he knows. "What clan are you?"

"M-Maewag."

"Your hunters were yearling fools, Maewag, and you do not have the supplies for a long journey." The tip of the bow digs into his jugular. "You don't leave your cave much."

Elias swallows the admission of why they're out in the Great White Waste like a fist in his throat. "We weren't expecting, uh, our cows got sick. We only have the one left, we were just looking for replacements."

"I can see that."

Behind it, Yarren moves sluggishly. Elias, refusing to drop his gaze, rambles to keep it busy. "It was a blight, you know? In the seershrooms. And it just—well, it cascaded from there, and you know, I just keep the records. I count them once and twice and—"

With all his strength, Yarren surges up onto his knees and spears the vampire from behind. It gasps, spine arching, but the hit isn't good enough. The wooden shaft isn't close enough to its heart. The vampire stumbles forward, slipping the spear from Yarren's grasp.

When it turns to finish him off, Elias sees his chance. He lost his own spear, but he yanks the arrow free from the pillar and launches off his knees, aiming at no spot in particular. Just one lucky hit so Yarren can kill it for him. One good hit.

He finds his mark as Yarren is knocked again to the snow, burying the arrow in the vampire's kidney and falling with the full force of his weight on its body. He doesn't let go. The creature grunts and wriggles but can't buck him off. Elias is thankful for this small blessing, sure he'd otherwise lose his head. He holds tight, waiting for Yarren to get up and miraculously save him or for the vampire to brush him off and snap his neck. When neither happens in the next moment, Elias looks for something, anything. The spear shaft has cracked, he notices; its other half lies in the snow beside him.

He can—he can do this. He can kill it permanently and... and...

And what? Without Yarren or Minira or Lalo, Elias can't navigate all the way home. If another storm comes, he'll get lost and turned around. Fall down and never get back up again.

"Chief Yarren," he whispers, unable to tell if he's dead or alive under his furs. "Chief?"

No answer.

He straddles the vampire, deliberating. The calf ran off. Lalo and Minira haven't moved. He has all the food in their four packs, but how long can that last? How long can he last battling the winds and the elements alone?

He comes to a horribly stupid decision and snaps the fletching off to pull the arrow through the vampire's side.

It hisses, face scrunched in pain.

Elias hesitates before removing the spear. "I'm saving your life," he says. "You owe me now."

Once it's out and tossed aside, the vampire curls in on itself and grits out, "We do not hold ourselves to the same constricting honors as your kind."

True, he supposes. The vampire could have its choice of meal in his clansfolk. It could heal and leave him behind and Elias will likely die anyway. He backs off and keeps the broken spear close, for all the good it'll do. "I hold myself to that honor. If you don't attack me, you don't die this moon."

It struggles to its feet and collects its arrows from Elias's kin, then kneels beside Minira and feasts. She does not flinch in pain—she's already dead, Elias knows—but watching it is no less disturbing. It fists her hair and holds her head to the side, draining all that remains of her, and when it's had its fill, it stands without issue. Head on, now on guard. Elias's little stick won't even touch its skin if it comes for him.

Eyes locked with his, it licks the blood off the arrows before returning them to its quiver.

He's supposed to be numb to death. Minira and Lalo were never his friends and Clan Maewag learned long ago that the dead can't hear the living mourners. A candle lit in their honor is better spent warming hands. Yet seeing it—seeing death itself staining the snow before him—rakes a different kind of cold over his heart.

Misha fell in a stroke of misfortune. Lalo, Yarren, and Minira weren't looking up. If Takkha exists, they must find this existential struggle to survive in a land no longer meant for the living incredibly amusing.

Elias looks away from his dead kin and huffs. "If you're going to kill me, get on with it."

"Mister Altruist, he thinks," the vampire chides. "You didn't spare me for honor, you spared me because you're lost, Yearling. You will die out here anyway."

"Do you always play with your food before eating it?"

It crouches before him, head cocked to the side as if daring

Elias to try it, to see what happens. "Very well," it decides. "I will repay this debt."

He startles, fist around the spear going limp, the wood dropping to the snow.

The vampire doesn't wait for him.

"Wait! Wait, let me at least grab my pack." He scrambles around his fallen kin, taking all their provisions since they won't need them anymore, and the rest of the spears.

The vampire arches a skeptical brow at this last. "I won't be caught surprised twice."

"I know. Wood burns." But just in case he also takes Minira's dagger.

Ten steps from the final resting place of his kin, Elias stops. They're going in the wrong direction. It's less shock that he's going to be food than at the audacity of the vampire to think he'll willingly walk into its teeth.

"Vampire," he asks through chattering teeth, "where are you taking me?"

"I have a name." The vampire sighs. "And I'm taking you home."

"*Your* home." Elias glares. "As if I'd happily follow you into a nest that'll make a meal of me." He rubs his arms but can't burrow any deeper into his furs to abate the unceasing cold. Without a fire or a spit of vampire blood, Elias has to keep his head and his resolve to combat the creeping Freeze. *I will not die out here*, he declares to himself. *I* will *survive.*

The cold bites a little less.

The vampire holds up a small metal spile, lifted from one of its victims. "If I take you to your home, I end up a meal myself. Apologies, Yearling, you won't win this one."

... No, he won't. "My name is Elias, not Yearling."

"And mine is Dorian, Yearling. Now walk."

Elias knows he's being led to the blood farm in the vampire's nest, but his hands aren't bound, he isn't blindfolded or gagged or dragged by a chain. He's free to keep gazing up at the stars and all the cloud formations—the puffy ones, the hazy ones, the rows of wispy ones.

"Which ones are storm clouds?"

A moment passes before the answer comes. "The tall ones."

They've been walking through the frozen forest, a crystalline labyrinth as dizzying as the limitless plains. For all he knows, they've been going in circles; the endless repetition of frozen spires look no different ahead or behind them, save for the direction the wind has blown the icicles.

"Can you touch them?" Elias imagines reaching skyward and standing on his toes to do just that. Brush his fingers against the lid of the world.

"No. They're like fog."

"What's fog?"

The vampire stops short. It turns, looking at him like he speaks in tongues. "How old are you?"

The undertone is clear. As if Elias should feel shame for never leaving the cave. This hunt proved exactly why doing so was a terrible idea. "I don't know."

"How can you not know?"

"My clan counts in lunar cycles, not years," he defends. "I could tell you that I've survived a bit more than two hundred, but the exact number no one knows nor cares." What happened more than two lunar cycles ago rarely matters and planning more than a few cycles into the future is a waste. They live for the present, their only guarantee. "We don't have yearly harvests, and the North has no seasons. What's the point?"

It frowns, head cocked to the side. It might've been Elias's age when it turned—too old to be treated like a kid anymore, not old enough to feel prepared to raise its own.

When it speaks again, Elias finds himself disappointed that its fangs have retracted, one less degree of monstrosity to separate them. "You scrape out a frightened, miserable existence in the North, and you can't even enjoy it. What's the point in your lives at all?"

"Who says we don't enjoy it?" He keeps walking, fearing that if he doesn't, he'll join the petrified forest as another lifeless spire covered in snow. His toes are numb in their boots and even without the wind, he pictures each breath coating his lungs with frost. "I'm a Keeper—I Keep. I draw. I tend to the livestock and the seershroom garden. I've had many chances to leave the cave. I choose not to."

Until today. Which makes him wonder... "Were you hunting that calf, too?" Elias knows vampires are stronger than they look for their size, but it would have had to carry it dead or struggle with it alive the entire hike back alone.

"You are not the only person with hungry mouths to feed."

"You mean your livestock."

"Pots and kettles, Yearling." It starts toying with an arrow, cleaning dried blood from its fingernails with the tip. It wears leathers, but not so heavily like Elias must. Every bit of the vampire's outerwear is tailored to fit. Sleek and sturdy boots, a luscious white and black-speckled fur cloak. Even its braids, a dozen or so arranged artfully through its hair and draping over its temples, serve as decoration rather than utility. Elias has never had anything sewn just for him, and all of it, even the shiny bow, looks new and well-cared for. More... the word *expensive* sits wrong on his tongue. Designed with intent. To look the part, possibly, of something not-undead, or camouflage against the snow.

Elias's garments, by contrast, pile atop him, oversized and passed down from other bodies that no longer have use for them. Holes and bald patches litter his furs. Blood and dirt and soot stains them everywhere else. His belt, all manner of rusty brown now, barely keeps it all together. Its cracked leather bears his clothing's only flourish, a bit of extra stitching in interlocked geometric spirals that designates him as Clan Maewag should he die out here and get discovered.

"You are staring, Yearling." The vampire smirks. "Mister Keeper never dirtied his hands with us before?"

Elias scowls and rolls his eyes. "We all have our roles. Handling the livestock wasn't mine."

"*Wasn't?* For someone who has never left his cave, you seem quick to accept that you'll never go back."

"I don't think it's hit yet. Maybe I'm hallucinating as I bleed out in the snow."

The vampire has no provisions, he notices, unless more weapons are hidden under its cloak and leathers. Only the bow and quiver. It's not out of breath like he is, not thirsty and hungry and sweaty and sore like he is. About the only indication that it's not dead inside is a visible puff with every exhale. It could have traveled for thrice as long as his party had from its nest without batting an eye.

Meaning they could be walking, the two of them utterly alone, for a grave long while.

The forest slopes upward into the mountains until cutting off sharply beneath the purple peaks. Every step of the climb leaves him short of breath and the vampire isn't patient. It takes Elias's pack off his back and threatens to drag him by the chain more than once.

Elias drops to his hands and knees, gulping down air too hard to retort. Being dragged sounds relaxing compared to the slog of scaling the rest of the mountain. The higher they go, the faster warmth seeps out of him, the louder the wind howls, and the colder his soul gets.

Until he doesn't feel so cold anymore, panting for an entirely different reason and careening off into the trees when the path ahead melts and swirls. "How's it so hot up here?" he wheezes, pawing without dexterity at his furs.

The next time he falls, his face hits the snowy rocks and the chill is divine. He wants to shovel the fresh powder inside his furs, snuggle into the icy blanket.

He's moving, he thinks. Or, being moved. The steep slope levels out, and the whistling, ringing wind quiets. His waterskin is pressed to his lips.

"This is the last of it," the vampire warns. "I have more melting, but it won't help you yet."

Elias sucks it all down and takes far too long to realize that it's not horribly dark wherever they are but that his eyes are closed. They can stay that way for now. He can't remember how to open them.

Being cold in the cave is far different than out here in the open. He's never alone in the cave. All the noises of his clan, all the smells, are a comfort. Out here it's all wrong and confusing. Gravity might be holding him down, but he can't say which way is up.

Strong fingers grip his jaw, and the smoky, salty scent of clan jerky hits his nose as a strip of meat bumps his teeth. He's not panting anymore, not shivering either.

"Eat, before I cram it down your throat."

He would, but he can't remember how to chew.

The vampire curses in some harsh language, all teeth and thick consonants. The jerky disappears, and something sweet and tangy hits his nose. Silky skin mashes against his chapped lips, and a hand at the back of his head forces him to drink.

Elias knows the taste of vampire blood, more addictive than any *schninir* they can brew. It splashes onto his tongue, spiced and warm and viscous. Feeling returns to his extremities, first in a tingle, then a burn, then a roaring ache.

He's finally able to open his eyes to the frustrated vampire glaring at him, like it's his fault he can't stand the winter its very existence forced on the North. He hums and presses its wrist tighter, taking more than he should, but he doesn't care.

A single shot once every couple of moons staves off the bitter chill. Elias slurps down more in one gulp than he's had in an entire lunar cycle. He could climb a whole mountain at a dead sprint now.

He's still no match for the vampire's strength when it wrenches free, but Elias chases after the drops that hit the ground before the wound closes.

"I was going to let you rest," the vampire chides, "but since you're all better now, we're moving on." It tosses his pack at his feet with a cold indifference.

They'd stopped beneath the cover of a crack in the mountain, barely enough space to lie flat if he tried. He licks his lips, still chapped, whole body still sore from the hike, and thinks resting is a wonderful idea.

The vampire won't leave him behind, no matter what it says. It'll get hungry eventually, and Elias is the only food around. He still isn't upset, but he should be. Upset that he got caught. Upset that he was right all along.

It stops when Elias still hasn't moved, arms crossed. "You *have* had a taste before, haven't you?"

Elias ignores it, staring out above the sloping foothills at how far they've come. It's been clear since the storm, yet the edge of the petrified forest is barely visible at the horizon. The snowscape glows faintly purple beneath the night sky and it's hauntingly mesmerizing—it keeps *going* until it bends with the curve of the world. Somewhere southward, there's daylight, and the vampire keeps dragging him farther and farther away from it.

"This isn't what I pictured. It's so... peaceful."

He can imagine his mother happily saying she told him so. Elias snorts to himself and turns away. If he starts thinking about her, he'll start thinking how she'll inevitably accept that he's not coming back. She'll burrow back into herself like she did after Misha. If the clan mourned everybody who died without ceremony, they'd never stop grieving.

"I can't let you go," the vampire says, as if it's so terribly unfortunate, as if Elias had commented on some horror instead of the strange beauty of the expanse before them. "You'd freeze to death before you found your way back."

Freezing to death admiring this great white wonderland doesn't seem so terrible now, especially when the alternative is dungeon walls. But no. He'll die an emaciated husk and take many moons to do so. In a panic, he'd only bought himself more time to stew in anticipation.

"They won't miss me anyhow. It's not our way." That's what hurts, even as he knows not to expect any different. Clan Maewag will find a new chief and a new Keeper and all that will remain of him will be some soot sketches in the garden. "Sing for the living while they can still hear it, but the dead are gone."

"You're not dead."

"I am to my clan. You left three bodies of much more capable fighters and drained one of them. If anyone comes looking, they'll figure out I was taken, and won't risk more lives on a suicide mission." Elias stands, almost warm enough to not need his furs. The pack is still as heavy, but now he doesn't mind as much. "How much farther?"

"A while."

The vampire turns to climb a worn switchback path, and Elias digs out Minira's dagger. The sharp edge rests against his own throat, an empty threat. The vampire hears and turns, unimpressed. Elias stands there anyway, swallowing thickly. "If I asked you to make it quick, would you? You could move faster without me, and I'm bound to get annoying."

It smiles thinly and closes the distance between them. "I can hear your heart beating steady. You won't do it."

Maybe so, but he wants to convince himself that he isn't going quietly. He wants to threaten his own life until the vampire forces the blade out of his hand, ties him up, has to drag him. He wants the vampire to prove itself the monster it's supposed to be.

His hand trembles. A shallow cut stings in the wind.

The vampire's eyes drop to his neck and back up, voracious hunger absent, practiced restraint unchallenged by monstrous instinct. Elias wets his fingers with his blood and smacks the vampire, smearing red on its cheek, lips, and chin.

Do it! he shouts in his mind. He waits for its pupils to dilate, for its fangs to appear, for need and desire to best composure and will. The monster resists as easily as the grove has stood the test of time.

Elias's hand wavers, knife tickling his skin. What will it take to anger it? Threatening to gut himself?

Elias whines when he means to growl, trying to stab it. The

vampire leans out of his reach once, twice, toying with him even as its face remains impassive. Every punch and slash misses, and when he tries to kick its shin, Elias loses his footing on the slope. He skids and bangs his knees, scrapes up his palms.

The vampire stands there and watches.

It aches and stings and he hisses, easing off his gloves to assess the damage. He didn't even break skin. He slumps and bows his head and can't even say he's been defeated because it was never a contest or a fight.

"You are a coward, Yearling," the vampire says softly, neither mocking nor patronizing, but stating fact. "That is why you live and your chief does not. Cowards inherited the North. Cowards are too afraid to leave the known caves for the unknown South. Cowards don't try to rescue their kin or mourn their dead. Cowards endure, only because they're too afraid to die."

"Until you get hungry. Then I'm meat." He doesn't look up from those expensive boots with proper treads for mountainous terrain, toothier than the vampire's stupid, smug face.

"Would tying a chain around your neck like a slave help you feel better?" This, now, is patronizing. "Must you play the unwitting victim to feel stronger?"

"No," he whispers, rising to his feet. "Let's just go."

Chapter 3: Tanarang

They stop, but not because Elias's muscles have turned to putty and every step feels like stabbing glass into his feet. No, the vampire smells something unfriendly on the wind, and its grand plan is to lie prone in a snowbank. There's a gap in the ice, and Elias thinks he'll slip and slide down into black oblivion, but it's cramped enough at his feet that they brace against it. He's so exhausted from their relentless pace that even sleeping here sounds as good as his bed back in the cave.

Elias whispers, "What's out there?"

The vampire shushes him and throws its cloak over him, sealing them in, ear pressed to the rock. They're flat on their bellies for minutes on end before it curses again. "They must smell you. Move."

It punches out the snow shield and drags him upright. "You will say nothing and not look them in the eyes." A chain winds loosely around his neck; it's working feverishly fast to beat whatever's after them.

Chain secured to its belt and bow readied but not drawn, the vampire composes itself and gets them moving again at a leisurely pace. Snuffling reaches Elias's ears with seconds to spare, and he can't help but gawk at the approaching rider.

He wasn't aware vampires could turn animals until the rider arrives on its frosty steed. The horse is too twiggy and lean, lacking the shaggy coat critical to survive the cold. Yet the ice coating its legs seems not to bother it one bit. Neither does the leech in its saddle.

This vampire looks the part of the monster he pictured. Blood makeup streaks beneath its eyes, head shaved except right down the center where it's piled high with thick twists, teeth and finger bones tied there like jewels. Its leathers are unmistakably pale, and when it smiles, fangs shine in the starlight.

"Tanarang," it mocks, "you're too far east. Running away with your pet?"

"I'm a scout, and I have blanket permission to wander your lands as you do mine, Aeskerat." Dorian looks so normal compared to the other vampire, Elias forgets to keep thinking of him as *it*.

"The pig doesn't." The mounted vampire looks Elias over, eyes narrowed. "Where did he come from? Aeskerat land?"

"An avalanche washed out Ibir Pass. We'll be out of your territory without delay." The chain clinks softly as Dorian turns to leave.

The rider draws a long, icy sword, and Elias can't help but wonder if they've been wrong all this time thinking wooden stakes were the only sure weapon against the undead scourge. It doesn't dismount, only moves into their path.

"He reeks of mildew and seershroom pollen." It sits back in the saddle and smiles toothily again. "Tanarang doesn't take blood slaves."

What?

Dorian scoffs, annoyed. "Well, *he* didn't know that. Now you've ruined it. And he was behaving so well."

Now it dismounts, dropping heavily onto the gravely snow. "You're trespassing all the same. Pay the fee, and I'll let you go. What's yours is mine." It struts forward and breathes in deep, crowding Elias's space as it giggles. "You haven't claimed it yet? Allow me."

Dorian shoves Elias forward onto his knees without a moment's hesitation, leaving him too shocked to protest with more than an aborted noise. Those teeth are too sharp and too close, and this one doesn't seem the type to refuse a free meal. Elias breathes short and shallow, spine arched as if any extra distance, however small, can help him.

"We still have a long journey," Dorian says blandly. "Do make it clean."

Is Dorian *serious*? Elias gulps, silently imploring his traveling-companion-slash-captor to not kowtow so easily. Dorian does nothing; the other vampire chuckles as it unlinks the chain.

"Your journey is not my concern, Tanarang."

Elias glances back. Shouldn't Dorian want him all for himself?

Dorian moves slowly sideways as if every crunch of snow beneath his boots is a quake. *He's going to stop it*, Elias hopes, and in the same thought, *No, no, he's not.*

Elias flinches away from the sharp graze of fangs at his neck, taking their sweet time savoring his racing pulse. His so-called savior doesn't do anything to stop those teeth from breaking skin. He presses futilely against an unyielding chest and a hand tangles into his hair.

Metal scrapes his cheek, slicing between him and the rider. Dorian yanks, the chain tight around the rider's throat. His arms strain from the force, holding fast despite the elbows rearing back into his chest.

"Stake!" Dorian grunts.

Elias scrambles for the broken spear, raising it over his head before hesitating. "What if I hit you?"

"You won't."

"But—"

"Do it!"

Elias tries, hammering down with all his might. His hands slip down the wood. The rider's leathers, layered armor thicker than it looks, absorb the impact. The rider gurgles in triumph despite still clawing at the chain blotting its pale skin red.

Elias looks on helplessly and goes for the bone dagger instead.

With a yell, Dorian shoves them both to the ground, grabs the other's head, and twists with a horribly loud *crack!*

Elias doesn't breathe, staring at the body limp on the gravel. "Is it dead?"

"Not yet." Not until the straps of its armor are undone and there's nothing left to protect it from the stake Dorian drives home. "Now she's dead. You're weak, Yearling."

"It's a stick!" Elias yelps. "Not even pointy at that end!"

"It was pointy at the other half of the spear, yet you went for the stick," Dorian mocks. "You're weak *and* stupid."

Oh. "I—yes, that would have been the smarter option." Elias holds his neck. Blood beads but doesn't gush. "But you said stake, not spear." Saved by a vampire, *again*, and still not made a meal. Yarren and the other hunters talked like the beings were mere slaves to their bloodlust.

Dorian glowers, fangs poking free in a flash before they're gone again. He searches skyward and grumbles about the lack of any cloud cover to hide the smoke from a fire. "Help me bury her in the snowbank. Others will catch her scent, and I can't have

Aeskerat declaring war on us over *you*."

Let them pick a fight, Elias thinks. The fewer vampires in the North, the better. Like rabid wolves, the lot of them, wearing people-shaped skin. Do they not have better ways to spend eternity than petty slaughter?

Still, Elias lifts the legs and scoops up the snow and gravel that it bled on for good measure. Its mount never ran, busy biting off the tips of icicles as if no gory fight occurred. For a prey animal so twiggy and fragile, its skittishness must've died when they defiled it with vampirism. Dorian bites into his palm and lets the horse nuzzle and lick to its heart's content.

"What are you doing?"

"Letting her claim me," Dorian says. "Unless you'd like to continue walking the rest of the way."

He holds his neck again, aghast. "Am I claimed now? Whatever that means?"

"It's an archaic tradition that should have died with the last sunset in the North," Dorian explains, bundling the chain to shove it back into Elias's pack. "Let me see."

"Archaic, yet you did it with the horse."

The vampire doesn't poke or prod. "You got lucky, you're fine," he mutters. "The bite leaves your scent on whatever you claim, so all other vampires know it's yours. If you're Aeskerat, or like many others, the claim is law regardless of the circumstances under which the bite was given. That lack of context makes them no better than animals."

Dorian pets the horse's striped muzzle and smiles sweetly despite the harshness of his words. "Can you ride?"

"No." Elias huffs and squares his shoulders. "But I can learn." He takes an embarrassing amount of tries getting his foot in the stirrup and then swinging his leg over. Then he scoots back, thankfully without falling off the horse's rear, to leave room.

The vampire, of course, mounts fluidly.

"Be loose in your hips and hold onto me, and you won't fall."

Elias sighs into the speckled fur of the vampire's cloak once they get moving, suddenly cocooned in steadfast warmth. "I owe you an apology, vampire."

"I forgave you for the stick."

"I thought you were going to let her eat me," he mumbles, "and save yourself the trouble."

Dorian glances back over his shoulder. "If I'm going to sacrifice you to save myself, it won't be to a damn Aeskerat."

They make good enough time through a valley under the light snowfall that Dorian finally lets him sleep in the ruins of some old outpost. One tower still stands, stones slick with ice, the rest of the once-grand structure littering a courtyard with its slowly eroding chunks.

"Olimaunt Keep," Dorian explains wistfully, as if he used to live here. "Survived a hundred sieges and fell to its mad lord's paranoia. They say the whistling wind through the ruins is his wailing spirit, still searching for traitors."

Elias tries to recreate the Keep's walls in his imagination and fill it with people but it instead fills with ghosts. "Are you trying to give me night terrors?"

Light snowfall dusts the vampire's hair and eyelashes delicately, while Elias's furs are caked with it, his nose numb and raw. Dorian leaves their horse to wander the ruins freely and juts his chin. "This way. There should still be oil lamps in storage."

"After all this time?" Elias follows, slipping on the ice twice and scowling at the vampire's back when he snickers.

"We don't get cold, and your kind don't wander this far into the valley."

The Keep extends into the mountainside, and Elias hasn't felt as safe the entire journey as he does now with rock and stone pressing in on all sides. He might be cornered in the cave, but he knows that the only exit is also the only entrance for whatever might come to eat him that isn't immune to the fear of getting crushed like he is.

The deeper they go, the less reach the elements have, and when they turn a corner, the late lord's possessions greet them. A blood-red rug, fancy candleholders in alcoves, paintings of landscapes. Elias moves closer to one, frozen by it.

Dorian lights one of the fancy candles and doubles back when Elias doesn't follow. "That's green, right?" Elias asks, looking at lush rolling hills covered with fuzzy things. It's more color and detail beneath one thumb than he's ever seen at once.

"The grass is green. Those small bits are pink wildflowers."

Pink, Elias thinks. He takes the candle closer, the soft color even more brilliant. "Have you seen green before?" He forgets they're not supposed to be friends when he asks, distracted by his desire to touch the canvas and absorb the color into his skin. He's seen the subtle pink of a drunken flush on his kin, but this pink is much happier. Warm, whimsical.

"I have, and this painting doesn't compare. Not anymore."

The rest of the paintings are as foreign and no less dazzling. A ship tossed about in ocean-colored hues of blue that Dorian calls *teal* and *aquamarine*. Sunlight shining over grain fields. He's familiar with yellow, but the omnipresent liquid gold spilling over everything it touches is mesmerizing. Elias does bring his fingers to the painting now, wishing it as warm as it looks. "Does the sun make a sound? Do you remember?" He can't bear to look away as he asks. "I hope it roars."

Dorian doesn't answer beyond a noncommittal shake of his head.

They're not friends, Elias reminds himself. He's food, and the vampire will get hungry eventually.

"The larder's this way."

The food stores have long since disappeared from the larder and been replaced with a rusted weapons cache and assorted other tools, plus the oil lamps. Elias pools together a nest of abandoned brown cloaks embroidered with the crest of a tree and two sliver moons; at his feet and head he places a lantern. Dorian keeps his distance. He will, he says, allow Elias only this one rest before a long and winding ride through the mountains to his new home on the other side.

"Do you sleep?" Elias finds himself asking despite his droopy eyelids. *We're not friends!*

"If we want to," he replies evenly. "We don't dream, though. Dreams are for the living."

"Do you remember dreaming?"

He takes up a seat on a long table before reconsidering and tossing his cloak to add to Elias's pile. "Sleep, Yearling, otherwise I'll have to gag you the rest of the way to stop your complaining."

Elias tucks Dorian's cloak up to his chin. It's every bit as warm as it looks.

Dorian busies himself repairing the holes in his jerkin from the spear and arrow. Elias's breathing and heartbeat never slow, but if he ignores him for long enough, surely the yearling will finally pass out and give him a break from his constant noise. Hopefully,

Elias sleeps long enough that he can mend his shirt, too. Elphaba will scold him for being so careless.

He works by the light of the candelabra, stitching with a methodical precision. On the third hole, Elias's breath catches with unspoken questions, too loud to ignore. Dorian vows to fulfill his threat to gag him. "What is it?"

Elias rolls to face him in his nest, head propped on his fist and wide awake. "The Axelskat vampire—"

"*Aeskerat.*"

"What did she mean when she said Tanarang doesn't take blood slaves? You have to eat, like everything else."

"The blood that sustains us is given willingly and paid for."

Elias snorts, incredulous. "You can't expect me to believe your prisoners happily bear their throats to you whenever you get peckish."

"Do I need to define *slave* for you, Yearling?" Dorian resumes his stitching. "It is our way, whether you believe it or not. I won't waste my time arguing when you'll see soon enough."

Elias sits up straighter, dwarfed by his grand nest. "So—what? I just happen to have been captured by a scout for the only coven of vampires in existence that thinks itself benign?"

"Had I been Aeskerat, you would have died with your companions or indeed been chained and dragged for their amusement." Sparing this obviously incompetent fighter of the group had only been so he could question him. If his chief had better aim, neither of them would be here.

Elias grows haughty in his familiarity, crossing his arms. "If you think your prisoners haven't been beaten into submission, you're wrong. No one happily bears their veins to monsters."

"Indeed," he counters. "I was to be *your* replacement blood slave, wasn't I?" No one would so foolishly brave a storm that severe unless starved for sustenance. They were as desperate for warmth as for meat, and the way the yearling's heart skipped at the sight of the spile earlier gave him away.

He scowls like a child now. "That's different. We need it so we don't freeze, and you don't die if we take too much."

Dorian hadn't wanted to argue and now here they are. He sets his jerkin aside and braces his hands on the tabletop. "You need it? No one is forcing you to stay in the North."

"You took the sun away!"

"To survive!" The audacity of the living... "Is your claim to a pile of rocks so important that you can't leave it behind for warmer weather and better lives?"

"If we leave, we get eaten," he snaps back. "The entire North isn't yours to claim. You stole it and told the rest of us to run, hide, or die."

Dorian stops himself from letting this devolve into a nonsensical cycle of insults. "We had nowhere else to go," he says, as calmly as he can. "We were facing extinction, and we refuged in a land we'd assumed no one wanted anyway."

"You should be extinct," Elias sneers in a bout of brashness he likely only risks because Dorian isn't showing his teeth. Maybe he's been too lenient. Selling him to the Aeskerat for her horse would have saved him this headache. "You don't respect the circle," the yearling continues. "All you do is consume. When you die, you can't even bother to rot and feed the fungi."

The table legs squeak against the floor as he shoves off it. Elias's scowl melts to fear. Dorian is on him in three strides, pinning Elias more easily than a wriggling babe. "None of us is innocent nor our survival here bloodless. My kind doesn't play the victim, justifying our cruelty because we're too proud and stubborn to leave where we're not wanted."

Elias swallows thickly beneath the arm against his throat. The yearling wants him angry, Dorian knows, even as he's afraid of the consequences. He wants to be proven right, wants a reminder that any shred of kindness is a lure, that closing his eyes is all the opening a monster needs to pounce.

And *oh* is it tempting.

"You are young, Yearling. I won't punish you for believing the teachings of your bitter kin, but mark me." He presses a little harder, and Elias's face tints. He winces and squirms. If he were strong enough, trained enough—Dorian knows he's not that much heavier—Elias could put up a respectable fight, but he doesn't. His limbs stay stiff as a dead beetle's. "Become more trouble than you're worth, and I won't hurt you or bite you. I won't give you the satisfaction of being right. I will leave you in the snow and not even linger to watch you freeze alone and unmourned, won't even remember your name by the next moon. And you'll have no one and nothing to blame but yourself."

He relents, and Elias coughs and hacks, eyes watering, whole body wracking. Living bodies, such *messy* things. Their noses run with snot, their skin bruises and infects and rashes, they reek of sweat. Before they leave Olimaunt Keep, he must scour the place for new clothes to replace those filthy furs.

"Why?" Elias rasps, and it's an impossibly vague question. Why what? Why would he leave him in the snow? Why won't he prove him right? Why won't he remember his name? "I thought your kind wasn't bound by honor. So why bother? Does changing my mind mean that much to you?"

"I lied." Dorian rocks back and off him. Now's the perfect time to go searching for those clothes.

He knows the Keep well enough but never paid mind to the details, only ever using the crumbling, musty halls to shelter from storms. All of the bed chambers line the exterior walls of the Keep, which had allowed occupants access to windows. Most of what's left behind, though, is useless—rusty weapons, faded scrolls, cracked pots, fancy silver and jewels. He does find a gilded chest of dresses and only takes them because the horse has saddlebags. He knows a few bright faces that will be overjoyed playing princess. Any food stores left behind have already rotted away, but as he digs, he finds two sealed pots embossed with bees, and smiles. The perfect treat for the little ones.

He finds a book, *A Written History of the Lords of Olimaunt*, and thinks it'll work as kindling, as will the handles of the junk weapons. He's not giving Elias more blood unless his fingers start falling off, unless he grows out of his impertinence, so fire and new clothes are a must. The outfit he finds for Elias, simple brown leathers perhaps from a pageboy, might be snug—he can't tell his shape under all those filthy furs—but with one of the cloaks, he'll be fine.

It's still snowing lightly as he ventures out to load up the saddlebags and ensure they haven't been boxed in by avenging Aeskerat. But Elias is so deep inside the Keep that even Dorian can't smell him, and his own blood wasn't spilled in the fight. The snowfall has already covered their tracks as well. It's the best they're going to get, but finding a deep hole to dump that fledgling in would have left no trace. He walks the perimeter of the Keep, an arrow nocked, and senses nothing but the wailing wind.

Elias is still asleep and snoring when Dorian decides they've rested long enough. The break in the weather won't linger forever. Elias startles with a shout when the bundle of clothes drops onto his face.

"Get dressed and leave that filth for me to burn and bury." He is halfway to the door in an attempt to give Elias privacy before the Yearling stutters out a plea for him to wait.

Dorian turns to see him staring helplessly at the jerkin. "How do I put this on?"

Sweet mother of the moons, cave squatters really are savages. Dorian undoes all the laces so he can get it over his head. He's thinner than Dorian expected, all twiggy limbs and barely any musculature, as if he's lived his life perpetually hungry, never knowing a full belly.

Elias squirms and hugs himself once it's on. "I still feel naked."

Dorian tosses old leather gloves his way. He couldn't find any boots that weren't falling apart, and the lumpy bundle of furs will have to stay behind. "Take one of the cloaks and deal with it."

Elias hugs himself tighter and flushes. "I need to relieve myself, too."

Messy, messy, messy. "Can't leave your scent here. Come with me."

He dumps the furs beside a well, ignoring Elias's shivering, then waves at the pile to do his business.

Elias squawks. "There's an entire castle!"

"I can't burn the castle."

Elias grumbles, cheeks aflame, refusing to budge until Dorian moves away, and really, he hardly wants to stand beside him and watch. Elias mutters all the while, big words like *degrading* and *humiliating* and *plight of the living*. It could be a chain around his neck and a gag in his mouth, but this here, *this* is degrading.

He complains even as Dorian tosses the furs into the well, setting them on fire. He's still complaining when they mount up, almost too stubborn to hold on until they start moving and he nearly topples off.

"I hate you," Elias mumbles, a petulant child.

"You're welcome, once again, for saving your life."

Chapter 4:
House of the Whale

Elias had been impressed with Olimaunt Keep, but he refuses to gawk at the castle nestled on the oceanside cliff ahead of them, a thing of stone skinned in ice. The craftsmanship of the outer wall isn't intimidating, the skinny, towering spires not at all magnificent, the glowing ice certainly not ethereal in the moonlight.

"Castle Tanarang," Dorian says, as if it isn't obvious. "Your new home."

Beneath every lookout on the wall, they'd carved a crest of a... wrinkly thumb? Whatever animal it's supposed to be, outlined in thick soot, he can't place it. "It's a...?"

"A breaching whale," Dorian explains, not without dripping condescension. "You can see them from the ramparts and the western windows."

The ramparts, as he points out, aren't empty. Motionless shapes up in the gloom stand at even intervals on the wall and shout to open the main gate, a set of massive ribs.

"Whale bones?"

"Perceptive."

The gate begins to close before they've even passed through. Inside, three adjoining walls protect a courtyard and steeply pitched little buildings backed against the ocean where freshly caught fish and sharks hang. Three people work on untangling a single massive net; another polishes harpoons. Seal furs and meat add a shock of red and silver against the greenish greys. It's more bustling activity out in the open than Elias has ever before seen.

Another vampire with a less elaborate braid arrangement than Dorian's but cloaked in the same black-speckled fur runs up to them. He eyes Elias critically. "Ibir Pass?"

"Impassable. The last merchant ships had already left by the time I reached Panolin." Dorian dismounts and pats the horse's neck. "Picked up an Aeskerat horse."

"I can see that," the other vampire deadpans. "What happened to yours?"

"Stake pit in Clan Hogul territory."

Elias tenses, still astride the horse. Maewag traded seershrooms with Hogul for fish until Hogul decided seershrooms weren't valuable enough and wanted little girls they could turn into mothers instead.

"And Clan Hogul?" the other vampire asks, brow arched.

"Probably still digging their way out of a perfectly coincidental cave-in," he answers blithely. Dorian starts unloading the saddlebags and carries on his polite conversation like Clan Hogul's demise means nothing. He took out an entire clan over the death of his horse... and let Elias live after he'd stabbed him with an arrow? "Markus, tell—"

The other vampire coos at the new horse and pets the white stripe down her face.

Dorian snaps his fingers. "*Markus.*"

"Hm?" The other vampire, Markus, blinks owlishly.

"Tell Sascha that Kymiria gets to name this one." Dorian wordlessly waves for Elias's pack, even already ladened with the saddlebags.

"Dorian, are we going to have an Aeskerat problem?"

"She was a fledgling, never seen her before. I'd be glad to be rid of the nuisance."

Markus nods and takes the reins, looking at Elias expectantly. "Are your legs frozen?"

He almost falls off in his haste.

Nose wrinkling, Markus leads the horse away. "Get that one a bath before he stinks up the place."

Does he smell that bad? His musty, stolen clothes have got to smell worse than he does. Still, he follows Dorian numbly across the courtyard, past an ice sculpture of a whale escaping the frothy waves, and looks back to count the vampires on the wall alone.

"How many vampires live here?" he asks as they approach the doors adorned with more bones arranged in wave patterns against what looks like a thickly packed kelp surface. One vampire opens it for them, braids simpler even than Markus's. Elias studies Dorian's leathers again compared with the lowly doorman's. "And where do you rank among them?"

"One hundred and thirteen," Dorian answers like the population should impress him, and it does. "And we don't care for petty labels when we live forever."

"Right, but this is a castle and you clearly aren't the stableboy." Good goddesses, he'd stabbed the lord or the heir-to-the-lord of the castle with his own arrow, hadn't he?

"Yearling, lines of succession are wasted on beings that aren't related and never expect to die." He drops the saddlebags in the entryway. "I'm a scout. That's my job, I'm good at it, and I need not be more than that."

"Master Dorian's home!" A gaggle of children, five in total, comes screeching and sprinting down the hall, swarming the vampire and pulling him to the floor. The youngest toddles after them and launches himself atop the pile, and Elias has a moment to feel utterly horrified that these so-called honorable vampires have turned children.

But they haven't. Otherwise Dorian wouldn't be gawping at how big they've all gotten while he's been away. The kids—the *living* kids—climb over him and themselves, pulling at his hair, vying for his attention, talking over each other to share all that he's missed. "I brought a surprise," he interrupts as they grapple for a little clay jar tucked inside one of the saddlebags. "Now you have to get your parents' permission, okay? *Okay?* If you don't say *okay*, I'll eat it myself."

The eldest, or tallest at least, a girl in a fluffy pink dress, pouts and agrees, and the rest follow suit, calming down to echo a promise that they'll behave. That all vanishes when Dorian produces the jar of... where'd he find *honey*? They've cracked it open and have all shoved greedy fingers in before Elias realizes he must have found it while he'd slept.

Dorian doesn't try to stop them, only warning that it's sticky and urging, "*Please* don't spill it all over me."

Elias steps back and almost knocks into the wall. They're living, breathing children, completely unafraid of him. He wants to convince himself this is all a grand illusion, that the children are good actors, that it's all to lower his guard, but he doesn't matter to the castle or its inhabitants one bit, so why would they bother?

Dorian frees himself to distribute the rest of his gifts—

dresses and jewels that even the little boys fawn over to claim for themselves.

"That's it, I'm afraid. Now how about you go and take your new clothes to Elphaba for a good scrubbing—and keep your promises!" They're already running off as he threatens vague horrors should he find the jar in any of their rooms. He rolls his eyes and stands, and pulls a second honey jar from the bags to hand to the doorman. "Tokh, can you please take this to the kitchens. Be certain it arrives unopened?"

The other vampire looks older than him in the face, a gathering of faint smile lines peeking out from under a short, silver-speckled beard. He nods and agrees, tacking no fancy title onto Dorian's name but rushing off with the saddlebags in tow as if issued a proclamation by his lord.

He notices Elias staring with what is surely a funny look on his face. "Yearling?"

Elias clears his throat and tugs the sides of his cloak tighter.

"This way."

Every archway they pass under bears crossed whale ribs, and Elias can't imagine how many have had to die simply to adorn the place. "The architecture's... quaint."

"We don't murder them." Dorian, who must have caught Elias's pinched expression, sounds insulted. "We find their carcasses washed up on the shore."

The deeper they go, the warmer it gets. Frost gives way entirely to intricately carved stone, and Elias stops seeing his breath. Fancy candles dot the walls, all lit, but they're hardly enough to be the cause.

Elias unlatches his cloak and folds it in his arms, studying paintings much like those in Olimaunt Keep. They're far and few between, the intricate ones. Some bear shapeless splatters and handprints, juvenile drawings and less-than-perfect portraits, renditions of the castle wall, the stables, the cliffs.

He bites back compliments on the vampire's home because this is still weird and mind-boggling, and he's still waiting for the illusion to drop. The air still warms with every level they descend, and curiosity once again wins out. "How is it so warm in here?"

Dorian smiles cryptically. "You'll see."

The answer turns out to be steaming freshwater pools in a spacious cavern bursting with seershrooms and other lichen and mosses glowing where they grow on stalactites. Elias gasps, and it echoes. Water drips in soft *plinks* from above, the resulting steam a hot balm on his lungs after the frigid air outside.

It's not empty. Three other bodies scattered across separate pools glance at him, greet Dorian, and turn away. Towel racks and dividers sit on the paths between the pools, and he even spots a little bar with fragile glasses hanging like bats from their racks.

"Well?" Dorian nudges him forward. "Nothing will nibble your toes."

Elias eyes the nearest pool, water clear but refracting the natural stone's pewter grey and too deep for his tastes. Metal steps and benches line the flat stonework pools, so they look less like holes in the ground, but still.

"I—um. I can't swim." The deepest water he's ever been in was from the cave's underground river, an overflow in a shallow plateau that covered his ankles, a cold and miserable experience.

"That's what the ladder and benches are for."

"Right. But—" Elias winces and wavers on his feet under Dorian's unblinking and unyielding stare. "Right." He struggles with the stupid laces on the jerkin once again with no excuse of numb fingers this time. He longs for the dividers folded up nearby but says nothing, not that Dorian can't hear his fluttering pulse.

Dorian turns his back, not offering to help him into the water. Which is good, yes, but if he slips, falls in, and panics when his head goes under, he's going to be mortified. Elias grips the ladder with all his strength, easing down one rung at a time.

Hot water is a whole different experience than sitting in front of a fire. Where a fire warms only the parts of him it faces, the water surrounds and consumes. It's hot, scaldingly so, and has him awkwardly rising up and back down to get used to the temperature. It takes ages to finally feel secure on one of the six benches arranged like steps around the edge of the pool.

"Okay. I'm in."

He cups his hands over his lap under the water when Dorian turns and wheels a cart over and tosses him a little jar of pale paste and something squishy. "It's a sponge. Scrub yourself with it. Wash your hair if you can. I'll be back."

Elias clings to the support for the bench. "You're leaving?" The prospect of being left alone is worse than having Dorian standing here watching him.

"I need to find you proper boots and better-fitting clothes. And you're not alone." He leaves no room nor time for argument, gone before Elias can claw at his ankles to keep him close.

Elias stares after Dorian's shadow until it disappears, then he drops his forehead on the stones, defeated. He's not about to sit here unmoving until Dorian comes back. It would be nice to get the smell of horse off his body.

The sponge is a strange, scratchy texture that leaves his skin rubbed raw. Too afraid to submerge his head, he cups his hands and tosses water over himself instead.

Once he accepts that nothing's going to worm out from the

depths and swallow him, it's... nice. Relaxing. He tips his head back and even lets his eyes close, but the patterns on the cave ceiling are too mesmerizing to ignore for long. Swirling stars of white, blue, and green. Seershrooms have nothing on such a sight. He didn't die alone in the Great White Waste. He didn't die to fangs at his neck either. He survived to see *this*.

By now, his clan will have realized that something went wrong. They're probably debating on how to use the last of the wood, electing a new chief. Elias scowls, having completely forgotten about them for a glittering castle and too-kind vampire captor.

Though... except for his mother, they will have more quickly forgotten about him than he them. If his clan mourns anyone, it's Minira. Lalo. Yarren. The actual hunters. Maybe Dapple misses him.

Really, for all Elias knows, he's alive and they're not.

Dorian returns with fresh clothes, a deep blue fabric he calls velvet, and a pristine white shirt Elias will surely stain within the hour. It has buttons instead of ties, and Elias ignores what might or might not be wry amusement on Dorian's face. Elias's skin is tinged pink from the warm water, an even line across his chest, and even when he stands on the stones to dress, the warmth lingers.

The pampering doesn't end there. Dorian takes him to a new room—*Elias's* room, one he and he alone will occupy.

"Until you adjust," Dorian explains, "unless you want to board with the others."

No windows, but he's used to that, and not all that big, only enough to fit a skinny bed and a wooden case Dorian says is his wardrobe. His pack has been emptied onto its shelves.

Elias drops onto the lush bedding in disbelief. "So this is it?"

"What's it?"

"I stabbed you, and you take me to your home and treat me

like royalty." He balls his fists loosely in the sheets. "All so I'll feel indebted enough to bare my neck in gratitude? *Master* Dorian."

Dorian rolls his eyes and lets the door shut. "They do that no matter how much we tell them they don't have to."

"Sure they do."

Dorian lights the candles on the walls—sconces, he recalls—and tells him there's always extra candles and that he need not be frugal with burning them. "No one here is forced to sustain us. No one is permitted to until they're old enough."

"But?" Elias crosses his arms, letting himself feel a little smug when there is indeed a *but*.

"However, Mister Keeper, everyone must contribute to the well-being of the house."

That's not... unfamiliar. Everyone had their role in the cave, too.

"No one will hold you down and bleed you, but your attitude won't win you any friends and I won't protect you, especially if you don't contribute in other ways."

He *hmphs*. "So you won't force me, you'll simply make me feel terrible until I'm compelled to do it lest the cooks spit in my food."

"Something like that."

"If it's so wonderful here, why would they care if I resist?"

Dorian smiles thinly; Elias still can't succeed in truly angering him. "They're protective. Grandmothers were granddaughters in this castle, and to some, this is the only home they've ever known."

"And if I want to leave?"

He shrugs and heads for the door. "You weren't and still aren't a prisoner, but if you couldn't find your way home less than a moon's walk from it, you won't find it from Castle Tanarang. There's worse than Aeskerat scouts between here and there."

Just because there aren't shackles on his wrist doesn't mean he's here willingly. If the choice is servitude or death, Elias doesn't see the difference.

"You're free to explore any door that isn't locked, but know that should you attempt to stir dissent in this house, your kind has a unique penchant for cruelty and will police themselves."

He leaves, and Elias flops back onto the bed that's still a little too perfect to be anything less than another trick in a grand illusion.

Elias keeps track of the lunar cycle in charcoal marks on his wall. Five moons pass, and he still hasn't given in to complacency. He meets more people than he can remember, all of them ready with a funny look and never lingering to answer his questions.

He learns from the matriarch of the living, Elphaba, that there's seventy-eight members of her little clan, soon to be seventy-nine. She's got bony hands and silver-white hair and saggy arms, and can lift more on her hip than Elias weighs, even while bustling around the kitchens. She cooks, she delegates her people to keep the castle in order, she mends clothing and scolds the vampires that rip her hard work, and she babysits her twelve grandchildren whenever she can.

And she tolerates absolutely none of his attempts at *pot-stirring*.

"I don't have a problem with servants. Such is the way of castles and any complex society—there's always going to be those above and below," Elias argues once again, careful not to pause kneading dough for her because if he stops she whaps his knuckles with a wooden spoon. He hasn't found a job that accommodates his stubborn refusal to submit to being livestock, so she works him to the bone, and when he hides, she sends her grandchildren, banging pots and pans relentlessly, to sniff him out.

"Yes, yes, I know what you have a problem with."

"Then why don't you have a problem with it? I get that it's the only life you've ever known, but do you understand how insane this is? Do you want your grandchildren growing up calling vampires their master and bearing their veins?"

"They are the masters of the house and should be addressed as such."

"That's not the point—"

Elphaba pulls another rack of fresh bread from the ovens and wipes sweat off her brow. "Child, I'm afraid you are the insane one here. Look at the luxuries we have. This castle had sunless winters long before the rest of the North, yet we don't freeze. We don't know the pain of starving, of wondering if the storms will smother us. We don't fear other clans or covens."

"But you have to *bleed* for it!"

He won't deny the luxuries. They have more than enough food to last until trade routes are passable again in several months, and there's more variety in Castle Tanarang's storerooms than Elias imagines exists in the entire world. But *he's* not allowed to eat any of it until he *contributes*, stuck with bread and water, Elphaba's orders.

The kitchens alone had astounded him when he first saw them, so much empty space dedicated to the singular task of cooking. His clan was bound to the size of the caves carved by nature's hand, and a cavern this big wouldn't have been wasted on a kitchen. They would have converted it into more stables, routed river water through it to cultivate a more productive fungi garden.

So this entire castle lives in excess, yes. Elias has come to terms with their fundamental differences on that and much else. But serving themselves up as food will never sit right with him. They have to see that.

Elphaba rears the wooden spoon but wavers and pockets it in

her apron. "Rinn, dear?"

One of her granddaughters, who had been dutifully shucking a giant bag of dried peas in her new dress from Olimaunt, looks up.

"Don't let the bread burn." Elphaba smiles at her and snags Elias's wrist in an iron grip in the same breath. "Why does this bother you so much, child?"

"You're not prisoners here, you nearly outnumber the vampires. What would happen if you all rose up and declared that you won't feed them anymore?" There's only one answer. He knows the leeches wouldn't shrug, pack up, and leave their castle behind. They disappeared the sun to keep what they considered theirs.

She leads him through the halls he hasn't had a chance or desire to explore. "Why would we? We have a perfect relationship."

"Humor me. Tomorrow, for whatever reason, every person living behind that wall decides, no more feeding. What happens?" He doesn't pay attention to where they end up, only noticing that Elphaba stops him before a set of double doors.

"They would be justifiably upset," she answers plainly. "They would ask in what way they've been insufficient hosts and defenders of this castle, our *home*, and how they could right this wrong. And, child, should the hour come when compromise fails, I suppose they would send us away and start over."

"So someone has to be livestock, exactly—"

"But that won't happen," she implores. "Never. It is the way of this world, and should we leave, far worse horrors wait out there in the cold. They didn't ask to be what they are, and for shelter, food, warm beds, safety, and a fulfilled life where I might see my first great-grandchild? A little donation here or there is an insignificant show of gratitude."

Elphaba opens the doors to a lush room filled with cushy furniture, pillows, and furs. Six vampires sprawl wherever they please, fangs buried in wrists and necks and wherever else they fancy.

Elias jumps back, scalded.

"You must see, child." Elphaba doesn't force him to enter, waiting in the doorway with breadcrumbs on her apron and flour dusting her cheek. "See."

He follows her stiffly, making sure the doors remain open, and sees Dorian for the first time in five moons, partaking with the rest of them. He's got blood in a fancy cup and is mid-chat with its donor, some man who probably has kids he's raising to do the same. Elias's lip curls.

Dorian looks up, fleeting surprise crossing his features, then carries on, propped on pillows and listening intently to whatever the man's going on about. He sips the blood like wine, not missing a beat, the only one not gnawing on someone's neck or limb.

Perhaps that's why Elphaba bustles his way, Elias compelled to follow if only to avoid watching the feast surrounding him.

"Master Dorian, may I borrow you?"

Immediately, Dorian looks indignant, rising to stand at her side with a scant apology to the man. Elias thinks he's mad she's interrupted, but *no*. "Has he done something?"

Does no one see the insanity here?

"I'm sorry to tear you away from Castor's, I am sure, riveting story. Your esteemed guest requires a demonstration. He's driving me quite mad with foolish ignorance."

Dorian downs the rest of his glass and sets it aside with barely tempered disappointment. "Castor, may—"

"No, I insist." Elphaba holds her arm out, drawing the attention of the rest of the room. "The needle, please."

Dorian hesitates but buckles under Elphaba's stern look. The needle comes from a drawer of dozens, then is passed through a candle's flame and screwed into a curved tube. "Hand or—"

She presses the crease of her elbow, skin spotty with age and littered with faded burns. "Here."

"It will bruise, Elphaba," he warns. "Castor?"

Castor rushes right over, voice dropping to a whisper to scold her for being so stubborn. He presses his hands to his chest, pleading. "Mother, I'm fine for a few drops more."

"He must see, or he must leave."

The stares from the rest of the room singe Elias's soul. Dorian relents and finds a vein in three seconds, the needle piercing her skin. Elphaba doesn't so much as twitch, rolling her arm so the tube can trickle into Dorian's glass enough to re-wet the bottom before she tells him to stop. He looks like he doesn't know what to do with the glass, the tube still draining in it, until she stomps on his foot and demands he not let it go to waste.

He passes her a tiny square of cloth, then drinks, and places the empty glass on top of the cabinet. "Press hard," he mumbles. "You've made your point."

"Have I?" She gives Elias an expectant look.

Castor looks like he might impale the needle in Elias's eye if he doesn't say exactly the right thing.

Elias swallows and folds his arms. "How does that work?"

"It's a thin, hollow needle that doesn't make a mess." Dorian hands him another. There's nothing special about it up close.

"Why doesn't everyone use them?"

Castor interjects, lip curling like Elias isn't worth the mud on his boots. "Some prefer real teeth to metal ones. Small veins can be tricky to find. Regardless, we all have a choice, and it remains ours, not theirs."

Elphaba rolls her sleeve back down, and Castor steers her toward the door. Their departure doesn't lessen the heat of the glares from others, living and undead alike.

"You've attained many enemies in an impressive amount of time, Yearling." Dorian ushers him toward the door as well, but Elias roots himself in the fluffy rug.

"I asked her, and I'll ask you the same: What would happen if they all decided not to feed you anymore?"

Dorian cocks his head, gaze searching. "Why do you hold us to a standard higher than any other being in this world? We're predators. We need to eat, and we manage to do it without slaughtering anyone. Can you eat the flank of a cow and expect it to keep living happily, Yearling? Can you wear its hide without skinning it?"

Elias's nostrils flare. Every time he gets in Dorian's face it amounts to nothing, but he's obnoxious and infuriating and missing his point. "Animals aren't people. Now answer my question."

"You don't deserve an answer you won't respect," Dorian says idly. "I'd hate to see your opinions on the dungeons of other covens or on the living slavers who take not blood from their victims but all honor, hope, and dignity."

"That's different, that's—"

"You're wrong, and you know it." Dorian's voice softens, dancing the razor's edge of patronizing and pitying. "And you're too stubborn to admit it. I promise we won't laugh and say we told you so even though your bratty attitude justifies it. Play nice, or Elphaba will send you packing and I'll lock the gate behind you myself."

He leaves Elias unheard and muttering curses after him. He's *not* wrong. He's the only one who sees the truth, and soon enough they'll all know it.

Chapter 5:
Black Sheep

"He's so boorish," Kymiria complains, stretching her arms out along the edge of the pool. "It's not even fun to watch him skulk about, it's annoying. *He's* annoying, Dorian. And useless."

Dorian doesn't need her to tell him that. He runs a comb through her damp hair and starts separating it into sections for her braids. The baths are empty aside from them, and music plays from Kymiria's Southern halophone. She'd been humming along, dancing her fingers through the air, entertained by their idle wonderings about how much money it would take to invite an entire Southern orchestra to the castle to play for them.

Then she'd brought up Elias, and here they are. "He didn't know of the color pink," he says, as if that explains everything.

Kymiria tilts her head back and scrunches her nose. "Is he colorblind?"

"No." He hadn't asked though doubts that's the case. "He's insulated by his clan. Have you heard of the Maewag?"

"The who?"

"Exactly. I've never seen one of them before, yet Elias says they've been in the same cave for nigh on twenty-six generations."

Kymiria hums, steam curling around her face and along Dorian's dancing fingers. She can braid her own hair, but he likes doing it and she likes him doing it so it's a comforting symbiosis. "Twenty-six... does that predate the Great Night?"

"It does, even if their mothers bear children at fourteen."

She hums again. "He could be lying. Or stupid."

"He could be. Point is, yes, he's an infuriating ignoramus, but it's not entirely his fault. Ties, please."

Kymiria tosses the wad of ties beside his knee and puffs her cheeks. "You got sloppy out there. Speared and stabbed. *And* you lost Poppy."

"I did," he laments. "I know you loved her, I'm sorry. The pit was well hidden, but even in her panic, she bucked me off so that I wouldn't fall with her."

"Because she was good." Kymiria hugs her knees and lets water droplets drip from her fingertips. If his hands weren't knuckle-deep in her hair, she'd probably turn around and splash him for being so careless. "Your yearling is not only stupid, he's a hypocrite. There's a rumor going around that his clan would have made a blood slave of you. *Savages.*"

"I can't disagree with you there."

"Then he should be punished," she insists, waggling a finger. "Kindness won't persuade him, so pain must."

Dorian sighs and abandons her hair to rub her shoulders instead. "He is being punished. No one talks to him. They pretend he's a ghost, unheard, unseen."

She chuckles and rocks her head back against his shins. "That's not what I meant. He disrespects this house and its matriarch. It's not enough."

"Have there been ominous rumblings in the halls?"

"Many," she sighs. "Talks of beatings and lashings and nights spent locked out in the snow. And one I won't name who'd like to pitch him over the cliff on a bungee." Now she turns and folds her arms on the stones beside him, eyes glittering with desire of a less violent sort. "Join me?"

"Does talk of torture excite you so?"

Now Kymiria does splash him. "Waste not, as they say. You're already wet."

Enticing as that might be, Tokh marches into the baths, heels clicking primly on the stones. No matter his age nor how long the list of vampires his junior, Tokh, a dedicated steward in life, hasn't shaken his sense of duty in his new eternity. Never improper, back always straight, hands clasped behind him. He wears his one braid as a badge of honor, and no one in Castle Tanarang, no matter the many more dozens of braids atop their heads, begrudge him for it.

Never does his gaze wander, ever firm on his feet as he bows to Kymiria. "My apologies, Kymiria. I'm afraid Dorian is needed in the Grand Hall."

"Oooh, you're in trouble," she teases, chin on her fists, then she smiles wide at Tokh. "Do you want to help me finish my hair? Dorian surely knows the way to the Grand Hall without escort."

Tokh blusters, cheeks tinting. He seizes a robe off the cart, nearly wheeling the thing into the pool in his haste to hand it to her. "It would be highly improper."

Kymiria doesn't take the robe, drifting into the center of the pool on her back. "Dorian's unfortunately busy now. Whatever shall we do to rectify my situation?"

Tokh looks at Dorian beseechingly. Tokh isn't the youngest nor was he young when he was turned, but he still hasn't mastered the subtleties of being a vampire or hiding all his tells. Neither has Tokh yet embraced the idea that eternity is an unforgivingly long time to be chained to one person.

Dorian shrugs and sympathetically pats his shoulder. "I'm not her keeper."

"Sir?"

If Tokh could still sweat, Dorian imagines that a single bead would be trickling from his temple. He grins. "Kymiria, do be gentle with our friend."

She titters and water splashes.

He'll bet his next three meals that Tokh staunchly attends only to her hair, no matter what tricks she pulls, but life is too long to never answer *what if*.

The Grand Hall is a racket he can hear even from the caves. Table legs scrape and chatter abounds over how to arrange decorations for the imminent arrival of new life in the North. They spread pink and red candles, and Dorian wonders if Elias has emerged from his sulking long enough to appreciate all the colors everywhere that had enchanted him in Olimaunt.

The head table is still the place for most meetings—out in the open, transparent, in earshot for the whole host of the castle. Taking up half the chairs are Tanarang's two grandsires, as well as Elphaba and her second-born, Dorotea.

Dorian dips his head in greeting and remains at the bottom step. Maybe he really is in trouble. None of them looks particularly happy. "This is about Elias, isn't it?" After the yearling's insults toward Elphaba, Dorian would be shocked if this ambush had another occasion.

The matriarch gives a bone-weary sigh. "I know you meant well, Master Dorian, but he is a nuisance, and he's upsetting my grandbabies with his insensitive questioning."

Dorotea smiles kindly but fragilely, hopefully here to help temper her mother's quick tongue. "Mother wants him thrown out into the snow to fend for himself."

"I'm not going to claim he wouldn't deserve it. He's causing the dissent I explicitly warned him against." He had hoped, however naively, that Castle Tanarang's atmosphere and kindness would soften Elias's bitterness. It would, at least, have softened the surprise of him. He couldn't warn ahead that he was bringing another mouth to feed in the dead of winter. Another mouth that keeps insulting and rejecting their ways of life. A clansman with kin responsible for countless vampire deaths in the name of vindication. "If that's the will of the majority, then so be it, but if it were already decided, you wouldn't be sitting up there."

Amaranth, forever baby-faced, laces her fingers. "We understand this attitude stems from extreme sheltering. I don't want to see the boy punished for crimes he hasn't committed, but he's dangerously close to committing plenty of others every hour he remains."

If he'd been a warrior, a true threat, Dorian wouldn't have spared his life. Elias is exactly who they expect him to be, no more.

Amaranth's brother, Hyacinth, stands with his hands braced on the tabletop. His voice, belonging to a body perpetually trapped in between childhood and maturity, squeaks and catches as he talks. "You're the only one here he marginally respects, so we charge you with explaining to him his choices so that he might believe we are serious."

Neither of them believes in violence for violence's sake, but he can see on their faces that Elias's options won't be pleasant ones. "And those choices are...?"

"A sincere public apology to every wronged party is mandatory," Amaranth decrees flatly. "Then he may either commit to a single lunar cycle of hard labor or join the guard on the wall. Whichever he chooses, he must also take a vow of silence until and unless he has only kindness to speak."

Oh, he won't like that. Dorian dips his head and assures the terms will be heard.

The vampires of the house can't partake in food, but they still join in polite conversation with their living comrades during meals. Dorian doesn't participate on every occasion—the living are incessantly hungry beings and eat far more frequently than he must—but he hasn't seen Elias in the Grand Hall with them once. Despite his insistence that Elias has the freedom to roam the castle, the yearling, as far as Dorian knows, has gone only between his room and the kitchens.

That's where Dorian finds him, taunting himself by staring at stores of food Elphaba forbade him from eating, stomach grumbling loud enough to hear from the door.

"I'm beginning to think you have a lust for pain." Dorian joins him on the other side of the worktable, but Elias doesn't give any sign he heard him. "Oi, Yearling." Dorian snaps his fingers in his face.

"What do you want?"

"Your bratty attitude has consequences, and today you reap them." He lays out the options and non-negotiables, and Elias still doesn't react. Maybe he would if Hyacinth flogged him against a post, but that's not their way, no matter how badly Elias may want to witness otherwise.

"What kind of hard labor?"

"Lucky for you, vampire horses don't defecate." More than half the castle doesn't need chamber pots, in fact, which means Elias has gotten a better deal in servitude here than he would most anywhere else. "But tending to our mounts' needs and pens might be part of it. As might scrubbing the floors, shoveling snow, bussing dishes, wall duty. Whatever else we feel like, really."

Elias wrinkles his nose and folds his arms on the tabletop. "You've seen me fight, and I can't use a bow. I'd be useless on the wall."

Dorian smiles and raps his nails. "How long do you think you can weaponize your incompetence and get away with it? You will be trained in swords and archery. You will *not*, however, be given vampire blood to stay warm unless your limbs blacken, so I'd suggest keeping yourself moving up there." Relaxing on top of the wall counting snowflakes doesn't fit Amaranth's idea of hard labor, even if no one expects to have to use their weapons.

Elias's discomfort mutates into an irritated scowl. No one has lingered on his chosen hill as long as Elias in a long time. If he doesn't thaw his stubborn soul, Elphaba will get her wish, and dying cold and alone is no way for anything to leave this world. There is another option, if the yearling can tolerate the horrible, terrible, no-good monsters he'll have to survive here first. Dorian doubts that he will last that long, but maybe the promise of gold fields and pink wildflowers will be what sways him. "If, once the merchants return in five months' time, you're still miserable here, I can see about letting you join the party south. I escort them every year." Most of their fresh blood comes from the South, when Elphaba's gaggle of eager learners befriends strangers and convinces them to come back to Castle Tanarang.

"South?" The word slips from his tongue as if more enticing than all the forbidden food in their stores. "Really?"

"You have to be a decent and respectable member of the house the entire time, on your best behavior." Amaranth and Hyacinth won't let him escape his hard labor even so, but all the better to make amends. The ride across Aeskerat territory to the other coast is tedious enough without an entire party bickering and resentful of someone who didn't earn their spot. "There's no guarantee I can work this out, but I will do my best if you do yours."

The prospect of leaving brightens the yearling's mood, and Dorian smothers a resigned sigh.

"Will you be training me?"

"Nope. I'm needed elsewhere." He stands, happy to leave Elias to pick his poison.

Elias chooses cleaning duty instead of the guard, unbothered that it might make him look like the coward he is. In the cave, he always had something to keep him busy, and he'll take scrubbing dishes in the warmth over standing one frozen post for hours on end. Either way, he expected the resentment of his teachers, whether weapons' masters or other cleaners. He didn't anticipate those teachers to be the children.

They take potshots whenever they can, whispering blatantly within earshot about how selfish and ungrateful he acts. How mean and ugly he is to the amazing and wonderful Master Dorian who saved him from the Freeze.

He's accepted that this whole place isn't a trap waiting to spring, but now, even after many moons of laboring without incident, as he stands before the entire host of Castle Tanarang for his public apologies to everyone he's wronged, he can't bring himself to mean any of it. He's already lost his cave, the furs of his clan that were the only clothes he ever knew, the only job and the relevance of the only skills he ever before needed, and every one of the familiar faces that surrounded him since birth. He's not Elias of Clan Maewag anymore. He doesn't think he deserves his given name anymore. He's walking around in a body that isn't his anymore.

It's not pride that has him refusing to embrace his new reality. It's the last piece of himself that he can still find in the mirror, the last bit of this world he can say is his. Surrendering it would be the last betrayal against his people, and he can't bring himself to commit it. If he gives it up... then who is he?

So, he won't be mean and spiteful, but if he's leaving in five months so long as he behaves, then there's no need to find happiness here. Dorian said he had to be respectable and decent. Dorian did *not* say he had to be friendly or interested, and that's the line he'll walk. There's no need to explore the castle and fall in love with the library, no need to appreciate the undead hospitality. If he's going to smear his identity into something unrecognizable, he'd rather restart in the sun of the South than find that, in five months' time, he doesn't want to leave Tanarang at all. Twenty-six generations living in fear and cold and darkness because of the selfishness of the vampires that took the sun away—and he finds himself in the company of the only coven in existence that calls all of that into question? No. No, Aeskerat is still out there. Had his party not crossed paths with Dorian exactly when they did, Elias would never have known such contradictions exist.

He stands now in the middle of the Grand Hall and can only tell the living and the undead apart by which ones wear braids, the weavings all ajumble and rarely divided into neat sections. Elphaba helped him rehearse and memorize all the names he'd have to call out, but he's never stood under the magnifying glass of this many eyes before. It leaves his hands sweaty, his heart racing, his mouth dry. Elias balls his fists to stop their trembling.

Two child vampires have hair down past their hips and about a hundred braids between the two of them, all in different arrangements and thicknesses, and he hasn't met them but knows they're Amaranth and Hyacinth, and that by offending Dorian and the five other vampires in the feeding lounge, he offended these grandsires of the house. Still, he can't get a read on either of their expressions because they are also children Netto's age. It's also *creepy* knowing they're the oldest beings in the castle.

He still doesn't understand the ranks or the politics beyond more complicated hair equates to higher status. Half of them speak in a multitude of languages he doesn't know. And though they're all united by the braid arrangements, there's skin tones and hair textures and eye colors he never thought possible. He goes down his list as each offended party steps from the crowd to hear his apologies.

Elphaba, for repeatedly interrupting her work in the kitchens and compelling her to give blood when apparently no vampire out of the hundred and thirteen in the coven would dare. Castor, her son, for upsetting his mother. The other five vampires and living residents who were in the lounge, whose names he fumbles through with his cheat sheet, for disturbing the peace. Dorian, for... well, he has an entire list of slights. Elias stares at Dorian's knees instead of his face as he details their journey and all his attempts to goad the vampire into attacking.

The hall is silent up until they hear the details, likely for the first time, and Elias's voice drops to an intelligible mumble. It's ridiculous, this whole thing. He doesn't mean any of it and they all know it. This punishment is purely to embarrass him, and it's working.

Dorian thanks him and returns to the fold next to a lady vampire glaring at Elias like she plans to rip his head off.

Then, finally, he apologies to Amaranth and Hyacinth, for—again—disturbing the peace.

Amaranth speaks next, her loud voice commanding for her size. The luscious purple furs around her shoulders and lining her purple dress look fit for royalty. "Elias has voiced his transgressions and apologized for them witnessed before this host. The opportunity to air grievances has passed. Now"—she spreads her arms and smiles—"let us feast."

Surely public humiliations like this aren't the glue keeping this glittering utopia together. If someone had a problem in the cave, they dealt with it between the affected parties quietly and bluntly. None of this... pantomiming.

He doesn't have the luxury of letting his imagination wander, rushed around to serve bread and refill chalices and clear plates. He doubts Amaranth's simple *No one's allowed to snark at Elias anymore because I say so* will amount to anything, but even the glaring lady vampire treats him cordially, if coldly. He takes away empty soup bowls and catches snippets of conversations— vampires asking how it tastes, what the texture's like, what spices and herbs Elphaba and her army of cooks used in the soups and grand displays of fish, squid, and sharks—salivating despite himself at the vivid descriptions filled with words Elias has never heard before. After dinner comes a round of desserts so vibrantly colored they look fake. Elias tells himself it's all fake, that he's hallucinating all the spices, the sugary aromas. That his stomach isn't growling traitorous protests.

Several of the children—he recalls them as the ones who swarmed Dorian for the honey pot—stage a performance, reenacting some old folktale with hardened kelp swords and practice bows. One of them crawls around wearing leather antlers and bleating.

Elias backs himself away from the tables to watch the rest of the performance and the gnawing feeling in his gut is as much hunger for all that delicious food as it is for a seat at the table.

He's present with the rest of them—arms sore from hauling dishes, voraciously hungry smelling all the food he's still not allowed to have—yet he might as well be watching the feast unfold behind a thick window of ice. He doesn't know the story of the play, doesn't know the names of the children beyond Rinn, Castor's daughter, the girl who'd separated the peas. He doesn't understand why the vampires taunt themselves with the meal or why they don't join in by tasting their tablemates.

Dorian, cuddled up next to the lady vampire with their fingers linked, pressed together shoulder to hip and enthralled by the performance, doesn't look his way once. Amaranth's word might be law, but she can't force her coven to be polite where she can't see.

Elias tries to figure out if Dorian was older than himself when he turned, to decipher what kind of realm a man with such rich copper highlights in his hair originated from. The maps Elias kept were limited, only detailed with what was useful for their hunts and no further. He thus doesn't know the names of any lands in the South or of any clans beyond the ones that traded with Maewag, but he imagines that with hair that shines in the candlelight like the amber veins in the cave, Dorian must've come from a very sunny place.

Elias's dull, mud-colored mop hadn't ever seen a comb more complex than his fingers until he found one in the bathing cart. He'd gotten frustrated with the nipping pain trying to sort out all the tangles and finally tied it up only so it didn't catch fire in the kitchens. He curls his fingers now in his loose strands absently until it stings, wishing that he had done something more. The lady vampire beside Dorian has pale yellow curls fit for the finest tapestries, Amaranth and Hyacinth's ember-red even more so. All their hair, even that of the living, looks soft and well-cared for and fed.

Them in all their fancy, rich leathers and dresses and jewels from all across the world.

Elias scowls and takes his dinner of a whole seeded roll in his room once Tannys, another of Elphaba's brood and the coordinator of the magnificent feast, tells him he can go. Free bread had impressed him for all of five minutes when it had been such a luxury in the cave. It's still delicious, but it's not what's behind the pantry door or spread out on all the tables, tantalizing him.

The castle doesn't moan with echoes from distant, unreachable caves, cracks in the rock that seem to split the world to its core. Someone had built these walls, laid all these stones and the whale bone archways. They didn't fit themselves inside a hole that already existed, curving with natural tunnels. They'd picked an idyllic plot of land and scarred it with every brick. The clan never wanted for more than necessity and all this pomp and preening is the luxury of being vampires or protected by them.

Elias finds a mirror in a fancy room filled with little tables and pieces of dresses strewn everywhere and more primping accoutrements. He yanks the tie around his hair free and pulls at the greasy strands, knowing that's himself staring back at him even though he's only ever seen his reflection in the rippling water of the cave, the warping metal of a spoon. Imperfections and blemishes he's known only by touch trace an irritated red path along his jaw and nose and temple. He pokes at them and they ache in protest, and when he scoffs, his uneven teeth sneer back above stubble growing in uneven wisps.

None of this mattered before. It's not like he's the only one with crooked teeth, but he *is* the only one with skin that suffers from a life in a cave, and he hates that the people in this castle throw it all in his face by virtue of merely existing in the same space.

Castle Tanarang isn't, and won't ever be, his home. He lasted his entire life in the cave. He can last five months among these strangers, playing nice, letting them dress him up in *respectable* clothing because his furs mark him a savage.

Five months, then he's gone.

Hard labor demands Elias learn the layout of the castle, and every time he thinks he's found every dead end, there's another to uncover. All the different rooms have names he has to learn in all their different degrees of redundancy.

The fancy room with all the mirrored tables and the dresses is called a parlor, its desks—*vanities*—intended for frivolous habits like primping and prettying. There's an armory with forges heated by the same forces that warm the bath waters, but the smiths in them don't craft weapons. They forge blood needles and kitchen tools, decorative metalwork, and tin toys for the children in the absence of an abundance of firewood.

Bigger performances occur in an actual theater built into another cavernous room that doubles as a library. Elias doesn't care about whatever's on stage, as it varies from singing to a single storyteller to instrumentalists and acting groups. He thought his vow of silence would be more inconvenient, but it gives him a reason to not engage with anyone and sneak glances at all the books. He gets the chance after his chores are done, and the first five he pulls are illegible to him. He spends all his time meant for sleep gazing at the illustrations—fancy lords and ladies in ridiculous headwear and vibrant colors—and trying to piece together what the words say.

Someone who must be Castor's older brother or father by the strong shape of his nose and identical pinched expression finds him among the shelves. Elias braces for a reprimand even though he sped through his allotted tasks thoroughly.

"Can you read that?" asks the man, draped in black robes, a

big medallion with the whale crest on his chest. He folds his arms inside his sleeves, the candelabra set in a nook beside them limning him eerily.

Elias shakes his head. "I like the drawings."

A knobby finger points past him. "You might try your luck in a more familiar tongue."

He can't tell if it's a dismissal or suggestion but reshelves the book he'd been holding anyway. *Kindness,* he reminds himself. The only condition by which he may speak. "Thank you, Mister...?"

"Zeon." His eyes crinkle with a smile. "You're the yearling."

Elias can only nod. It's the first he's heard someone else use the term. Is it supposed to be an actual designation and not an insult? Zeon was no doubt in the Grand Hall watching him humiliate himself during his amends, so why bother asking?

Zeon leads him through the shelves, shuffling along like he's got bad knees. "If you like drawings, I have an atlas here that might interest you. First edition all the way from Miníge."

Elias has no idea what an atlas is and figures the next book he finds should be one that can help him not look like an uneducated simpleton every time he's spoken to.

The atlas turns out to be broader than he is, worthy of its own pedestal and filled with intricate maps.

"Never forget where you come from, but don't let it define where you're going, yes?" Zeon's eyes twinkle and he chuckles to himself. "And don't forget to put that back where it belongs when you're done."

Zeon leaves, and the warping of the gold-edged pages is horribly loud in the silence. The ink the mapmakers used holds a metallic shine, and every spread is detailed with wave patterns in the oceans, feathered pen-stroke forests, and pinpricked snowy mountaintops.

The map of the whole world folds out beyond the binding of the book, four great landmasses and all the islands in between. The map must predate the Great Freeze because most of the North is covered with deep green forests.

He finds Aeskerat first, stretching its claws across mountains and rivers and valleys. A tiny star next to a massive lake reads *Castle Aeskerat*, standing farther north than the forests even back then. To its southwest, Tanarang is tiny by comparison, hugging the coast like the runt about to be kicked off the bottom teat. North of Tanarang, the land belonging to Son Kir, a stake of what seems a thousand islands.

Elias scowls. The vampires have carved up the North, nine houses marked by sharp fangs beside their names. The mapmaker included no labels for clans, and Elias can't tell where Maewag would be beyond vaguely southeast given the path their journey took. He does spot Panolin on the other coast. Whether it's an entire city or a tiny port, he can't tell. In five months, though, he'll know.

He studies the atlas for hours, committing what he can to memory. If Dorian doesn't take him, he might finally have the tools to take himself.

Chapter 6:
The Damned

Elphaba's thirteenth grandchild comes into the world screaming beneath a quarter and a new moon, and her mother names her Lidya. Dorian doesn't get to meet her until the festivities in the Grand Hall. Wispy hair, tiny fingers curled into squishy fists, black eyes that look exactly like her mother's peering up at him briefly before closing again. Lidya's drowning in piles of gifts—socks and caps and blankets newly knit by vampires who don't have to sleep and can focus on a singular task for a week without stopping. They churned out more tiny mittens than Lidya can hope to wear before she outgrows them. Dorian has been here for the last twenty-three of twenty-nine births in Castle Tanarang. It never gets old.

Lidya doesn't linger long around all the commotion, but the ensuing party drags on long enough that he forgets about the stubborn yearling until he's headed outside to relieve the guard and runs into him carting dishes to the kitchens.

"Do you want to learn how to shoot?" he blurts, gesturing vaguely toward the wall. "Even the children have their lessons."

Elias stops up short. "I have chores," he deflects, not meeting his gaze. He then goes right on rolling his cart like he's chained to it.

Dorian winces. The yearling's not banned from what should be a happy occasion for the whole castle. If he wants to continue skulking around without attempting to befriend anyone, that's his prerogative, but his vow of silence explicitly applies only to nasty comments. "No one will complain if the dishes sit for another hour or two, and if they do, I'll shoulder the blame."

The constant reminder that there's a warm body under the same roof determined to stay miserable sours other moods like a contagion. Teaching him how to defend himself could prove he's not a prisoner here once and for all. And it's all Dorian could think of on the spot.

"Come, we can do target practice." Dorian repossesses the cart and wheels it to the kitchens himself so that Elias has no excuse to dawdle, then throws the yearling a cloak and a pair of gloves.

Elias fists the gloves, a hard set to his otherwise miserable face. "If I asked you to take me home—right now—would you?"

Dorian examines the expression behind this question but finds no clarity there. "I thought you wanted to go south?"

"South isn't a guarantee." Elias drops the cloak and the gloves and crosses his arms. "You can't expect me to embrace a world entirely alien to me, a world that goes against everything I've been taught. Throwing me into the river when I don't know how to swim. I understand that you have responsibilities and I'm not one of them, but yours is the only familiar face I have, and you spare the time only to tell me what I've done wrong."

The pink indignation on his face is the most emotion Dorian has seen out of him since his fit in the mountains. He's tense, shoulders up and lips twitching, ready to beat back whatever comes out of Dorian's mouth next.

Dorian cocks his head. "I was under the impression you hated me."

"I've been saved by you thrice. I've been humiliated in front of the entire castle kissing your boots, been taunted and teased and treated like a fool with no one defending me," he nearly shouts, stomping closer. "Then you show up out of nowhere when it's convenient for you to pay attention to me and still patronize me. You never apologized for shooting my kin, by the way."

Apologize? Dorian scoffs. "Kill or be killed, Elias. If it wasn't me, yours would have been found by that Aeskerat scout and gifted far slower deaths. If I didn't shoot first, you would have speared me and dragged me back to your cave as your blood slave."

"It's the principle!" Elias stomps his foot with a great huff, yet he doesn't deny that that's exactly what would have happened.

"Keeper or no, Yearling, you've drunk from unwilling donors to stay alive like any vampire," Dorian snaps. "At least when I do it, I stare you in the face. I told you, none of us is innocent, so get over yourself, or we will throw you out into the snow."

Elias rolls his lip and heaves a long-suffering sigh. He closes his eyes, slowly, and opens them with a little less childish indignation this time. "I can respect your way of life and not like it," he says, "but if you do want me to like it, could you show even a shadow of interest in helping me adjust?"

"Whenever I'm nice to you, you throw it back in my face," Dorian claps back. "Whenever anyone is nice to you, you go out of your way to ruin it. I haven't been hiding. You could have sought me out at any point." Dorian can acknowledge that he did leave Elias to sink or swim in deeper waters, but Elias has put forth a valiant effort to bite helping hands. "I'm a vampire, not a mind reader. By all appearances, you're tolerating us and self-sabotaging until the seas unfreeze and your imagined shackles unlock. Why should I help you adjust when you've treated this home like a pit trap in the snow waiting to swallow you?"

Elias glowers and crosses his arms high, again a child in an adult body. He's a mess of contradictions and oxymorons, saying one thing and doing another until doing the opposite suits him. "I don't want the chance to go south to come, only to wind up convincing myself against going because I'm starting to like it here."

Dorian huffs and rolls the cart past him to stack up the dishes with a clatter. The wall is waiting for relief and clearly Elias doesn't want to join him. "To answer your question, no, I can't escort you all the way home. The only reason I ended up near it was because I lost my horse and had to throw off any potential Clan Hogul pursuers."

Elias has no rebuttal because of course he doesn't. He can't make up his mind about anything.

Dorian stores the dish cart and throws his hands up. "You know where to find me."

The promise of target practice to take out his frustrations has him running to the wall. Quinn must see it on his face because whatever complaint she has, tapping her foot at the top of the stairs waiting for him, promptly dies.

"I'm sorry for the delay," he says, rushing past her to take her place.

Quinn shrugs, lingering on the stairs. "I don't usually see you this agitated."

"I'm fine," he deflects.

"We can just let him go," she says. "Give him a map and leave him to his own devices. You don't have to save him, Dorian."

He grabs a quiver, pretending to struggle with buckling it to his belt. "Never said I did."

Quinn hums knowingly. "Some people don't want to be saved. You tried." She shifts her weight and folds her arms. "Just... don't blame yourself if he wants to leave. We worry."

Dorian hesitates, biting back a snappier retort. "I know what I'm doing," he says instead.

Quinn nods, lips pursed, and walks away.

Dorian rolls his eyes and counts his arrows. He doesn't have much to shoot at that won't shatter them on impact outside the wall, so he settles on trying to draw a pattern on the ground by aiming upwards and predicting each arrow's arc back down. He's emptied an entire quiver in the vague silhouette of his late horse, Poppy, and is squeezing through the gate to collect all his arrows when he spots Elias coming to find him. He takes the icy stairs one at a time like a child who's never seen ice before and—

And that's exactly what he is.

Dorian sighs and picks up an old, shredded target of bundled black kelp from along the wall. If Elias wants archery practice after all, they'll start simple. It's the least he can do. Elias is his responsibility, and he's been treating him like the Southerners who arrive at their gates—educated and prepared for life with vampires. Not like someone ripped away from their small world and everything they know.

He finds Elias atop the wall, waiting.

"I'm sorry," the yearling begins, seeming to fight his tongue to get the words out.

"No, I am." Dorian tucks his hair back and folds his arms. "I know what it's like to be in your position. I thought that since we're not Aeskerat, that since we're kinder, fairer, it would be easy for you, and it's not. So I'm sorry for leaving you to drown. I'll do better, starting now."

Elias studies him, like Dorian has ruined some prepared speech and took the wind out of his sails. "How could you know what it's like?"

It's a question, not an accusation. His cloak and long sleeves hide all his skin except his face and his hands, but Dorian holds them out and arches a brow. He's tanner than Elias, than Kymiria and Amaranth, but not as dark as Markus. Not anymore. "Do I look like a Northerner to you?"

But then, Elias wouldn't know anything about what born-Northerners are supposed to look like.

Elias shifts his weight, though, seeming to understand. "Apology accepted," he mutters. "Back home, I kept to myself, but I wasn't—at least, I don't think I was mean. It's hard to do it intentionally." He keeps his distance, bundled up in his cloak.

"Dare I ask the obvious of why you'd intentionally be mean to people who've done no wrong to you?" Elias isn't entitled to their kindness, but he doesn't have any idea how good he has it here compared to what it could be. Because they're not Aeskerat. Yet he's still convinced they're monsters.

"I already told you, I don't want to get comfortable and complacent here."

Dorian nocks an arrow because if this *apology* is going to become more assertions that they're all wrong and delusional, he doesn't want to hear it. Elias flinches when it hits the target. "Five months is a long time for a creature with such a short lifespan to waste being unkind because he's afraid he might"—Dorian gives a mocking gasp—"actually start to like living with vampires. For shame, Yearling."

Elias toes closer, perhaps mustering some daring, and eyes the outer wall. "The only thing I have left of who I was is my beliefs and my name, and I haven't heard you use even that once. You burned my furs and the belt of my clan. You've brought me to some place that might as well be on one of the moons for how hopelessly lost I am."

Dorian lowers his bow and toys with an arrow. Elias's words haven't honed his attention, but his voice has. It's soft, vulnerable. That's real pain in his shiny eyes.

"If I disrespect the foundations of our way of life, then who am I? Beyond me, I don't know that Clan Maewag still lives." He waves over the wall and shivers as the gentle wind penetrates the gap in his cloak. "Without vampire blood, without a mother to nurse our last calf, without our chief and our best hunters, they may have burned through the rest of the wood and wasted away. They only exist now, for certain, in me and my memory, and every time I catch myself being nice and invested in the ways of their mortal enemy, I'm betraying that memory."

Dorian taps the arrow against his palm in thought, then points it at him. "Do you know how vampires are created?"

Elias frowns, brow pinched. "A fever. Too much vampire blood kills you, and you wake up rabid."

"Too much can kill you, yes, and it is a fever that does it, but you only wake up a rabid wither if it's not done properly. It can't be left to burn away the self. The *you*." He can't say he's met a wither, more encountered them. All long-fanged and clawed and eyes bleeding red, just a sharp mouth and soulless mind, as hungry for vampire blood as they crave the living. "But even withers, Yearling, aren't monsters. They're wounded animals that can no longer know better."

Elias's frown deepens and he shifts his weight, shaking his head. "Okay, thank you for the lesson, but—"

"Did Clan Maewag know about us Tanarang?"

"No," he grinds out.

"You're right, you have no guarantees there are any left of Clan Maewag except you. We can stand here arguing over the merits of remaining in a land without plentiful game or trees to burn or sunlight and warmth to grow crops." He unbelts his quiver and offers it and his bow to Elias, who takes both skeptically. "But instead I ask, is it a betrayal of their memory to break bread with us when we are not, in fact, the enemy they'd thought us? If their commitment to that memory is what got them killed, would it honor their legacy to die the same way?"

Elias's grip tightens on the bow. He stares over the wall like all his answers float beyond. "Do you think we could—if they're not dead—I know you can't escort me home, but what if you brought all of them back with you?"

A laugh surprises its way out of Dorian. "We can barely convince you to keep from whittling your own arsenal of stakes." Letting Elias keep a stake of his own would upset the coven, otherwise Dorian would let him have one as a security blanket. "An entire volatile clan acting like you won't be welcome here."

Elias sighs in resignation like he expected that answer and simply needed to hear it. He studies the bow and quiver and tries to stand properly, body bladed. He nocks the arrow but it won't balance, slipping off his thumb before falling to the stones. "This is harder than it looks."

"Would you like me to teach you?" Dorian holds his hands out.

Elias finally meets his eyes and holds them in his gaze. "Yes."

If Elias had any fantasies about suddenly excelling at archery by willpower alone, his first few lessons are a rude awakening. He doesn't have the strength in his arms to draw even the children's practice bows back enough to reach the target, much less to aim.

Dorian tries to encourage him by saying most of the big bows are designed to be drawn by beings far stronger than mortals, but the children have no issues with theirs and the pitying assurance only worsens his mood.

He's not absolved of extra duty—he still won't let himself be bled—but with Dorian's help, he's treated less like an invisible ghost by everyone he works with. He gets a proper tour of everything he hasn't seen in the castle and is shocked at how many individual bedchambers there are for beings who don't sleep.

Dorian shows Elias his room, one he occasionally shares with the golden-haired lady vampire, Kymiria, and it too has a bed, a giant thing framed by posts of crossed whale ribs. Elaborate tapestries hang on the walls and a pile of knitted socks and blankets balances precariously on a woven kelp chair. The bed, though, Elias can't comprehend. A couch or one of those loungers, maybe. Not a bed that takes up half the floorspace.

"They're comfy," Dorian says with a light shrug and no further explanation when Elias continues eyeing it. When he asks if Dorian and Kymiria are together, the vampire shrugs again and says, "Sometimes."

All of it can't hold a candle to finally being permitted to eat with everyone else now that he's stopped his complaining. A part of him had wanted to remain obstinate, to refuse to reciprocate kindness, simply to spite Amaranth, but he couldn't eat another bland bread roll. Elias doesn't care about the salacious noises he makes at all the textures and flavors he's never had before. He gets sick eating too much, too fast, and mourns the loss of the first properly full belly he's had in recent memory.

He pays attention to the nightly stage performances but keeps having to whisper questions to Dorian to several hissed *Shhhs* before they move to the empty library balcony. But Dorian doesn't seem to mind answering them even when his questions tend to drift away from the acts on stage. Obvious questions that eat at him, like "If someone goes south and wants to stay there, what happens?" *We let them and leave the door always open to their return,* Dorian had said. *Most visit, some don't.*

There isn't always a performance to interrupt. Elias finds comfort in all the books and drags Dorian into the library when it snows too hard for archery lessons. They're there now, a lantern on the floor between them and a blanket around his shoulders. "Do you ever turn the people here? Do they ever ask?"

"Kymiria is one of Elphaba's aunts," Dorian answers with an amused smile. "And Quinn came back with Blane from the South to escape an abuser. She came all the way here to be turned."

"Which one is Quinn?"

"She's got the ribbons in her hair? Dark skin? Almost always up on the wall?"

Elias frowns, picturing the only vampire he's seen with the ribbons Dorian describes, but... "She?"

"She," Dorian confirms. "She says she's a lady. Who are we to question her?"

Elias purses his lips. "Gods are the only beings without definition."

"Then I guess Quinn's a goddess. I'll be sure to let her know of her first devotee." Dorian smiles cheekily and arches his brows. Elias swallows a rebuttal.

About a third of the living here, Dorian explains, escaped the limiting laws of the South, nonsense rules that Clan Maewag never respected to begin with. Laws over women and the impoverished, children born out of wedlock, men who love men, women who love women. Many shed entire identities to take new names once they pass through the whale-bone gates.

"What we were in life matters not in death," Dorian says. "Vampirism can be a blessing even more than it is a curse."

One of the performances Dorian drags him to features figures he recognizes but a story he doesn't. He knows this story, but not *this* story, and dares not speak of the version he grew up watching retold around the fire in his cave. Elias misses the first half, distracted with other musings, and recalls another rendition of a vampire falling for one of the living and eventually turning them, only this one turns it on its head.

Rinn dresses up in a grand gown, stars on midnight fabric, commanding half a stage of frightened vampires against half a stage of vengeful living wielding lanterns on poles, a mock sun.

"Queen Chrysanthemum," Dorian whispers. "The last grandsire of the united covens."

Rinn steals away from the battle to confront a girl in rags and broken shackles, two bundles held to her chest as she lies dying. The Queen weeps as the battle fades, pleading with the dying girl to let her turn her, but she refuses, instead pushing the two bundles into Chrysanthemum's arms.

"They will be punished," the dying girl says. "Protect them."

Elias glances at Dorian for an explanation, but the vampire's face has gone stony along with the rest of the audience.

The Queen watches another battle rage and end with the vampires either dead or captured, both bundles tight in her hold. She hides them, then drifts onto the battlefield, checking motionless bodies for life. "This cannot persist," she proclaims, skyward, "or the world will soon know no more of either of us."

The Queen sheds her starry cape and drops to her knees, pressing her forehead to the stage. She prays to the moons, to all the gods she doesn't believe in from distant lands, to the sun herself.

"Grant my people sanctuary from the warmongers among the living. We will take the crumbs no one wants, pay whatever price is owed to endure in this world that is as much ours as any other's. We seek no vengeance for the thousands lost, only peace. There must be a way. Tell me!"

A boy in all gold and a girl in spring green donning a cape of moss appear. The girl snaps her fingers, and an actor in full silver brings out two children as the golden boy raises a wicked dagger.

"Choose," they say in unison. "The living or the damned."

Elias gapes. Choose? Choose what? To murder her own kids or sacrifice her entire race? It's not the version he knows, not at all. It wasn't only two kids, it wasn't *her* kids.

The Queen, distraught, accepts the dagger and hides it behind her back, beckoning the children forward. "Come," she says sweetly. "Come to Momma!"

Elias watches through his fingers as the kids eagerly hug her, unaware of the dagger poised above their heads. The Queen nods to the gods. "The damned," she declares. "Protect them, and I will hold my end of the bargain."

The gods disappear, and the Queen huddles the children close, bids them to drink from her wrist, and instead of killing them, turns them both.

Fake lightning flashes and drums pound. All the sun lanterns blow out, all the prop trees tip over, cut down, and fake snow pours from the rafters.

The Queen wails. This isn't what she wanted.

"You broke your oath," the gods say. "Now the world will know no more of the living or the damned. It will begin anew."

The Queen flies about the stage in a panic, and Elias forgets it's a performance when Rinn's anguished cries cut to the bone.

She begs the gods to stop the creep of the endless winter with her death, and stakes herself.

In the corner of the stage, a single lantern flicks back to life. The curtain drops.

Elias, the only one still sitting amidst the applause, stands abruptly. "I need to go."

He trips over Dorian scrambling to the aisle and almost throws up his dinner again in the hall. He slumps, sliding down the wall with jelly knees, ignored by the rest of the audience leaving the theater. Amaranth and Hyacinth regard him cooly, staring into his soul, and drift right past like he's a stain on their rug.

Dorian finds him like that and toes at his shins. "What's wrong with you?"

"The mother," he asks hollowly, "why didn't she want to turn?"

Dorian offers a hand, but Elias can't bring himself to take it. Dorian gets him up anyway, a guiding arm at his back. "She had been a slave in life. Some think she saw an eternity unable to die a natural death as a different kind of prison. No one knows for certain."

"Vampires... you could have had the entire world to rule." He knows he's being walked to his room but keeps stride with Dorian only on instinct.

"Yes. An entire frozen, lifeless world, where the living would starve or freeze or turn, leaving the vampires to waste away, forced to kill ourselves before we lost the strength to do even that." Dorian gets his door open and leads him to his bed.

Elias sits but doesn't unlace his boots or make any effort to prepare for sleep—how can he? "If Chrysanthemum had kept her oath, had killed the kids, what then?"

Dorian shrugs again. "No one knows what that would have looked like either. It might've granted us immunity to the sun, or a great wall to keep out the living. That is not what she chose. That's all that matters." He cocks his head and sets his hand on his hip. "It is all that matters, right?"

"It's... not the story I know," Elias admits. "There was no queen, no slave mother. Only an army that swept over the North and left a massacre in their wake so bloody, you could see it from the moons."

"It was bloody, yes. On both sides."

Elias shakes his head. "I learned it was an offering to court Dania and Gellen. They were so impressed, so empowered by all that sacrifice, that they frightened the sun away. She was too ashamed to ever come back."

Dorian says nothing. Elias chances a look over at him. He's not silent with rage or judgment. "Maybe we're both right." Dorian shrugs and rubs his arms. "Either way, the North, and the North alone, is ours, and what's done is done."

He leaves, and Elias falls back on the mattress, staring up at the ceiling with his boots still on until the bells chime for breakfast.

Elias was never big on stepping outside his comfort zones of Keeping and tending to the garden with his mother. He compliments Rinn on her performance the first chance he gets and she beams, and it's as if all bad blood between them evaporates.

She had been sorting through a box of recipes for mushy baby foods when he'd shuffled over but has abandoned it and is now gushing about how, when spring comes, she has a spot in the next caravan to the South to study in a professional theater.

Elias thinks that's the end of it but then she asks him if he knows how to skate.

"Skate?" he asks, giving her a puzzled stare.

"Yeah! Sometimes they freeze water in the courtyard. You glide around in these boots with blades on the bottom and it's really fun." Rinn drags him along to the room she shares with two others and busts out her pink skates. They look like a catastrophe waiting to happen. Her cousins watch from the door, all piled atop each other as she demonstrates, hobbling around her room.

She introduces him to all her siblings and cousins and friends, and because he has Rinn's approval, it seems he's good enough for everyone else. They pester him with questions about life in a cave. If it was bigger than the castle, how many horses they had. Elias concocts vague little white lies to entertain them, out of his depth with a curious child now underfoot anywhere he goes.

Dorian can't teach him archery all the time. He's gone on a mission with a team of other vampires to recover what they can from a whale carcass washed ashore at the bottom of the cliffs. Elias's private lessons get lumped in with the kids' classes taught by Neire, the most robust woman he's ever seen, vampire or otherwise. Her sleeveless arms bulge with muscle, dark skin littered with old nicks and burn scars. She keeps her braids tied back neatly beneath a bandanna, stitched with little whales that betray her stern attitude. She has zero patience for show-offs and heroes, whapping her bow against anyone she catches talking out of turn, not paying attention, or disobeying her rules.

They practice by shooting more kelp targets, fingers protected from the chill of the Northern ice with slim-fitting gloves. Kids scream and cower when someone dry-fires their bow, sending wood splintering in every direction. The boy who did it stands motionless, arm still outstretched with a piece of broken bow in his fist. Neire assesses no critical injuries, only an eye that will surely swell up on the boy—the bow had smacked him hard enough to leave a fat red line down his face—and goes on a booming tirade about the weapons, *not toys*, they're training with.

"What if your bow splinters had struck me in the heart, Gilan? Your favorite teacher."

He looks like he might burst into tears, lip wobbly. "I'm sorry, Master Neire. I'm sorry!"

She picks up the largest splinter and displays it for all to see. "You can't rely on shattering your bows to defend yourselves should the day come when practice becomes combat. So what do we do against a dangerous vampire?"

"Shoot them!"

"Aye!" She twirls an arrow and presses her thumb to the tip. "But that won't put them down for good, now will it?"

"No!"

"So what do we do?"

Every child whips out a thin sliver of wood from their boot, each no longer than their forearms. They charge the targets with high-pitched war cries, stabbing gleefully.

Elias's jaw drops. Neire pins him with a frigid stare. "I said, *what do we do*?"

"Uh. I don't—I didn't know we were supposed to bring stakes."

She whaps him with her bow. "You should always have it on you! Sleep with it under your pillow! Stakes remind the whole castle that we are symbionts, not parasites. So where is yours?"

Elias backs out of her reach and hides his vulnerable wrists under folded arms. "I don't have one."

She quiets, *hmphs*, and folds her arms behind her back. "That will be rectified. Pick up a piece and join your classmates."

He doesn't get the same enjoyment the children do stabbing kelp, earning a splinter in his thumb for the effort. Class ends, and

Gilan runs for the infirmary, holding his eye the whole way and only crying once he's dismissed to do so. Neire sends Tokh to get Tannys so she can comfort her son and mutters to herself, picking up the rest of the shattered bow in the slushy snow.

"Can I ask a question?"

"You just did," she grunts. "What's your second one?"

He twirls an arrow. Touching its frigid head without his gloves burns his hands. "How are these made? And why do you use them if they're less effective than wooden arrows?"

"They're chiseled from the ice," she answers simply.

Elias balks. "What ice is this strong?"

"Northern ice. The Great Freeze?" She tuts at his blank stare. "Do you see ample forests to turn into stakes? No. The gods decreed that we could have the North, but at a great many costs. This ice grows like trees and is harvested like wood."

"But not as effective as real wood."

Neire tuts again and hands him the largest splinter from the bow. "It incapacitates if struck true, and that might as well be a death sentence for us vampires if the assailant can finish us off. The pain, though?" She smacks an arrow against her palm and shows him that nothing happens, then drags the tip against her skin hard enough to cut, and the blood that wells up freezes on contact. "The pain is worse, even if it does not kill."

Elias perhaps owes Dorian an actual, sincere apology for stabbing him with his arrow. Before Elias can begin drafting it in his head, Neire pats the broken chunk of bow. "Sand it, smooth it, make it yours, and always keep it with you."

"Isn't it dangerous? Arming your food source?"

Neire gives him a funny look and scoffs. "If any of us finds ourselves staked by our own house, I'm certain it will have been deserved."

By the time Dorian's team returns, hauling the frozen salvage of whale carcass, Elias can reliably hit the target, just never in the spot he's aiming for. He resumes his private lessons and keeps the sanded stake in his boot like he's supposed to. It should reassure him. Instead it leaves him uneasy, like at any moment he will have cause to use it.

Dorian helps him hone his form, tilting his elbow and correcting his lean. The stake snags like a hangnail every time he catches himself staring at Dorian, looking back after a good shot for the vampire's praise and approval, messing up his form so Dorian will make his adjustments.

He's at least as old as the Great Freeze, no matter how young he looks or how lively his emotions. Elias hangs on that praise anyway, on the way Dorian flips his hair back, how he deftly twirls his arrows, grants him all those cheeky smiles. That Dorian is dead and a monster is a thought that grows quieter and quieter and quieter in the back of his mind.

They're in the middle of practice, not a cloud in the starry sky above them after a snowstorm. The kids have taken sides in the courtyard, building snowy walls of their own to stage a snowball skirmish. He sees it out of the corner of his eye—a sprawling game of chase—when Rinn slips, hits her head on a shovel's blade, and doesn't get back up.

The whole host of the castle stands motionless for all of a second before springing into action. Elias only watches from a distance. The rush to get her inside, to warm her without vampire blood, to wake her up. The commotion passes in a blur. He's still on the wall, the spot where she fell right below.

He drifts inside and can't get close to her room with the hall as crowded as it is. He picks his way through camping vampires and all of Rinn's relatives. Amaranth sits at her bedside, along with

Elphaba, Hyacinth, Zeon, and Castor.

She's awake, propped up on pillows, and pale. He can't hear what they say, but Amaranth hangs her head, immortal form barely older in appearance than Rinn herself.

Her gathered cousins all mutter about whether or not she'll turn. No one wants to let her die so *of course* she'll turn, Elias thinks. She's bleeding inside her head and there's only one way out of it in the time that they have.

Elias, because he's not needed and is still an outsider where it matters, returns to the kitchens to cook for the people who still have to eat, who are unable to waste away waiting for Rinn's decision.

Dorian comes to find him later to tell him he's welcome at the funeral, and it's all so sudden Elias wants to believe he's joking. He wasn't close with Rinn, but she was just out there laughing and playing with her friends and in here dragging him around the castle and she's gone.

"Why didn't she turn?"

"She was fourteen. She asked Amaranth what she would have done if she had a choice, and Amaranth told her the truth." Dorian shrugs, voice hollow. "We have to respect it."

"But she's gone." Elias looks at her stool, still pulled out from the table where she always sat to help cook. "She just slipped."

Dorian gives him a heavy look and he *knows*. He knows. Everything is all mixed up and backwards now.

They send her body out to sea. Elias watches with most of the castle from the cliffs. He's never witnessed a funeral without the words *We're alive and they're not* echoing in his ears.

We're alive, he thinks, as the pale shape of her raft drifts away, *and she's gone.*

Chapter 7: Lighthouses and Shadows

Elias naively assumed that the lounge Elphaba dragged him to for hungry vampires was the only place for their meals until he's picking up dishes left outside the many bedrooms and comes face-to-face with a vampire freshly fed. He recognizes her vaguely only by her short sandy hair—Amity or Amnesty on the tip of his tongue. She grins back through the doorway at the lanky beanpole in his bed covered in sanguine-stained kisses and bites, trills her fingers in a teasing wave at Elias, and skips away. Heat floods his face and he stammers his excuses, collecting the dishes with a loud clatter.

Maybe they're less aware of him, less on their guard now that his attitude has tempered, but the more couples he *catches* in various acts of intimacy the more it seems a little too convenient. Vampires with other vampires in between bookshelves in the library, vampires with their meals in the watering caves.

If it is on purpose, it's increasingly annoying and more than a little creepy. He can accept that this is a group of people happy to bleed for the world's most charitable monsters, but their finding said monstrosities attractive is unnerving. Less so, though, than watching the living hold casual conversation about training with the guard while a vampire sips away at a chalice of their blood. Doesn't it bother them? Isn't that weird? If he sat across from a cannibal dining on his severed fingers, he'd be disturbed. That blood replenishes isn't the point. It's not as if their faces morph into anything hideous when they feed, lips to stein or skin, but that's even worse. There's no separation between a body that was once like theirs and the monster that now haunts it.

Those thoughts stay with him when he's outside the castle walls with Dorian so that he can teach him how to ride alone during a particularly placid break in the weather. It's breezy and his face is still red from the chill as he saddles up and adjusts his cloak, but it's not a soul-crushing cold, not like in the cave. There hasn't been soul-crushing cold since Olimaunt Keep, if he thinks about it.

Dorian warns against bringing their horses side by side, as they like to race. Dandy, coat snow-white and grey across her flanks, prances about like she's just waiting for the chance. Dorian's coal black horse, Lily, seems to egg her on.

The mandatory distance spares him from conversation, but lagging behind means Elias's eyes trail too easily onto Dorian. It doesn't bother him until he realizes that it should.

It's easy to forget what Dorian is, easier to forget the longer Elias stays and the more they interact, and this, too, *bothers* him. Not because he expects Dorian to try anything at this point, whether that be pounce on him or abandon him if he falls off his horse. No. He's bothered because he's not afraid, and he should be. He's not disgusted, and he should be. Dorian had offered him blood before they left the castle as casually as he'd asked which color horse he wanted, and yet Elias didn't care. Dorian has countless decades of experiences gained over him and is far older than he looks, and yet

Elias doesn't care. And he *should*. Forget that Dorian is a monster. He's dead! Vampirism is only a stay of execution until something finishes him off.

Dorian hasn't done anything. He hasn't commented on Elias's lame excuses for needing help with his archery form. He apparently gives everyone else as much attention as he does Elias. But damn if Elias doesn't *feel* like the exception. Part of him knows that whatever tangle his emotions find themselves in is tainted by facts he shouldn't ignore—namely, that Dorian is still several lifetimes older than him with worldly experience Elias can't catch up to. But a part of him that's far less easily silenced doesn't care.

That part wants to run his fingers over those delicate braids, wants all those cheeky smiles to himself. That part's been neglected in the corner of the cave his entire life and now doesn't know what to do with itself under the eager exuberance of a handsome monster's undivided attention.

A handsome monster who doesn't seem to notice or reciprocate anything. Elias is his archery student, his riding buddy, his ward, but damn it if it's impossible to hope for more when they're alone like this.

"Dandy can smell fear, you know."

His hands are sore from clenching the reins so tightly, his legs achy from holding himself secure in the saddle. But he jumps at Dorian's sudden words, still not convinced that he can't read minds. "You all can smell fear," he finally thinks to say.

Dorian has taken them the long way around through more frozen forests and prickly spires of ice like stalagmites stretching skyward. Elias dismounts to poke at one that smells faintly of sulfur and rust. It's streaked with browns, yellows, and reds, and stands taller than the castle wall. "How are these made without a cave ceiling?"

"Tiny geysers," Dorian says, unimpressed with a world he's explored for centuries. "Same phenomenon that fills and heats the cave pools in the castle and sustains the kelp forest."

Elias asks him question after question that he doesn't have the answers for and wants to sit and wait for the geyser to burst, but Dorian promises more exciting sights ahead.

Whatever exciting is, it doesn't include the collection of scorched stone walls that used to be houses. Only the tops poke up out of the thick snow, their lonely chimneys their own petrified forest. It doesn't smell like smoke anymore, but rust and metal hang heavy in the air, itching his nose. Elias stares at the frames left to brave the elements. Buildings are so *fragile* compared to the cave. Whether Maewag lives on or not, the cave certainly does. A home can burn down like it was never there. "What happened here?"

Dorian steers Lily right along past. "Withers."

"I thought you said they were little more than animals." Elias nudges Dandy after him.

"They are. We started the fire." He shrugs and wraps his cloak up tighter. "They wander the wilderness, usually too weak to be a threat. Enough of them catch your scent, though"—he nods to the chimneys—"doesn't end well."

Elias twists to glance back as Dandy lumbers forward. "Can't you wipe them out? There can't be that many, can there?"

"Irresponsible Southerners continue to make them," Dorian chides. "Some of us try to exist among the living down there." He clicks his tongue. "Doesn't end well."

In the middle of the ruins, blue ice sprouts, streaked with rusty red swirls. Elias cranes his neck to check that it's not a trick of the light. Lalo had told him of the frozen, petrified trees. But the sickly blue sapling sprouting up from the snow with its frosty, prickly branches is everything the lifeless spires were not. "That's the kind of tree Neire was talking about."

Dorian stops again to follow his gaze. "They grow at sites of great bloodshed—*don't* touch it."

Elias freezes, half out of his saddle. "Neire says that's how you craft your arrows."

Dorians shivers and nudges Lily along. "That one is too fresh. Leave it be."

Elias watches the frosty sapling until it disappears behind the ruins, the metallic tinge in the air vanishing with it.

They eventually loop back to the coast, and Dorian stops them at a lighthouse. The beacon itself, Dorian tells him, hasn't been lit since before the Great Freeze. Chryssy Point marks the southern border of Tanarang land, the juncture between vampire territory and the plains of the Great Waste.

Dorian ties up Dandy and Lily, and kicks away the snow gathered around the door. "The view isn't any better up top, but I think it's still worth the climb."

The tower is one great skinny spiral of stones with a small house for the keeper beside it. In its decay, the windows have shattered and snow has blown in over the stairs. Maritime wind whistles and moans through the gaps, and Elias finds it less magnificent and more unsettling amid the hypnotic helix of the steps. "Was this built by you, or the living?"

"By monks of a religion that no longer exists." Dorian lights sconces as they ascend, his heel-clicks on the stones warning Elias when ice slicks the stairs that have no guarding rail. "They got sent here for some kind of test of commitment. All alone, hand-copying texts, trying not to go crazy from the isolation."

Elias shivers, eyeing how far they've climbed and how far they have still to go. "That's not a comforting image."

"The North isn't for the faint of heart, Yearling. Don't worry. I'll protect you from the lonely keeper spirits." Dorian grins.

Elias's cheeks tint from the attention, but Dorian's already gone up farther.

He can't be imagining this, can he? Unless Dorian is just being friendly, adhering to some custom Elias is unfamiliar with, in which case he should stop digging where there's no riches to be found. Elias doesn't know what he wants anyway. Dorian's attention? Yes. A vampire's attention?

... No.

These paradoxical desires occlude each other at the basest provocations, and it's exhausting. They're not here on anything more than a training excursion, exploring Tanarang land. That's it. Elias scolds himself and climbs after Dorian.

The view from the top is, as promised, no more impressive than from the ground—the grey horizon looks the same—but the tower's narrow, a daring precipice over the edge to the choppy sea. Elias keeps his distance, a new respect for heights searing itself into his bones. Dorian doesn't seem to care.

But then, Dorian wouldn't stay dead from the fall.

The vampire sees him clinging to the ice-slick remnants of the lighthouse's crown and all joking smiles fade. "We can go now."

Elias keeps himself talking on the way down for something else to think about other than the drop. "Vampires can feed from each other?"

Dorian glances back in mild surprise.

"I saw it," Elias defends stubbornly. "A few times now."

He shrugs. "We can, but we don't do it to sate hunger. It just feels good."

Elias scrunches his face. Teeth sharper than knives and thicker than splinters can't, in any way, be pleasant. Can it?

Dorian sighs lightly, taking the stairs with far more reckless abandon than Elias. "The line between pleasure and pain is blurrier than you might imagine. We're dead, Yearling. Feeling of any kind can be good. It reminds us we're still here."

Elias blames his loose tongue on his nerves when he asks, "You're dead, but you bleed. Do you have a heartbeat?"

Dorian takes his hand for the last three slippery steps. He doesn't let go after, instead pressing Elias's fingers to the side of his neck for his answer—a strong, rhythmic thumping. "All the blood in my veins is taken from another. When we heal, it's not replenished. That pulse slows as we starve."

But starving will never kill them, Elias knows. It only brings them ever closer to a perpetual non-death. He imagines a heart unable to die, pumping the last dregs of blood as thick as tar through a cold body.

"The last vampire we kept in the cave killed themself," Elias hears himself say, as if Dorian couldn't have guessed.

Dorian's expression sours as he snuffs the candles out. "Vampire blood slaves might've earned their place to your kin by virtue of what we are, but unlike the living, we can't count on the hope that a hungry predator will take too much."

Elias can mount Dandy now in one fluid motion but sits awkward and heavy in the saddle watching Dorian dote on Lily with an icicle treat. "Can I ask why you turned? When?"

"Some other time perhaps on the why. As for when?" He grins cheekily. "A while ago."

"How long after the Great Freeze? Can you tell me that?"

Dorian hums, tilting his head this way and that in faux deliberation.

"Before."

"Wait. The play about Chrysanthemum—I thought Amaranth and Hyacinth were the oldest vampires in Tanarang?" He'd presumed this mostly on the grandsire title, but why wouldn't vampires respect age above anything else? Years are all they have.

"The grand in grandsire isn't like in grandmother. It means only what it says—grand." He waves dismissively, like this should have been obvious. "Other covens respect age, but wisdom comes with experience, not years. And when you get this old, what difference does a hundred years make?"

They don't turn around, leaving the vague safety of Tanarang territory to tread closer to the water and a black pebbly beach. Now Dorian pulls Lily side by side with Dandy, chiding the both of them into behaving.

"Is this the part where you tell me you were, in fact, a lord when you lived? Heir to such and such?"

Dorian snorts and shakes his head, side-eyeing Elias. "I'm from Kenoa. Have you seen it on your maps?"

The name doesn't sound familiar, but Elias hadn't been able to put an image to hundreds of places within the atlas pages. "Can't say that I remember it, no."

"It's small. A little group of volcanic islands. I wasn't heir to anything except the house I was born in and whatever earnings my parents would have left when they passed." Dorian lets Lily wander into the lapping waves, where she chases little white crabs with her hooves. "My mother made pottery, my father was a cobbler, and my sister and I spent most of our days in the vineyards, stomping grapes for wine."

"Sounds idyllic."

Dorian hums noncommittally. "It was simple."

As the weather turns out at sea, Dorian turns them back home. He talks all the while about the colorful plants and eclectic wildlife native to his islands, the scents of all the fruits and nectar, the acres upon acres of wine grapes.

Elias forgets that all these memories date back hundreds of years ago. Dorian talks about them with such vivid detail and open expression, gestures grand, voice colored with fondness and longing for a sun-showered home to which he can never return.

"I don't miss the sun," he says, "as much as I miss the smell of those grapes in the summer heat. I can't dream, but sometimes, when I wake, it's there like a phantom limb. A whiff and then gone."

The door to ask after anymore shuts quietly but firmly. Dorian gathers his reins and tells him they're going to try for a canter, then a gallop, if he's up for it, all the way back to the castle.

He agrees, an image of the atlas in the library an imprint on his mind, the need to find those little islands called Kenoa a hunger he's never known.

For all he thought the whole host of Tanarang was trying to tease him with its promiscuity, when he tries to observe and participate in castle life, he's unwelcome.

Castor takes pity, showing him how they feed the horses. Elias had forgotten that vampire horses rely on living blood as well. Elphaba's son is in good spirits, at least as far as he can tell. Elias had offered his condolences for Rinn only once, and Castor had seemed to accept, even if to be polite.

"They're like pigs," Castor says. "Best not to fall off and scrape yourself up when they're hungry. They don't have restraint."

It's Tokh who disperses the pails filled with shallow but

substantial donations.

"You took a simple creature that eats grass and transformed it into an immortal leech."

Castor hums. "The Son Kir coven rides moose."

Elias is not amused.

"I guess it might look strange to an outsider, but this is how it's always been here, like other things."

The vampires do have partnerships, Castor explains, and a predictable rhythm. With that comes the unfairly upsetting revelation that Dorian has a regular—or *regulars*.

Castor only laughs at the frown Elias fails to hide. "Yeah, it's usually me and Cera. I've been told that more iron tastes better, like a finer aged wine," he jokes. "I think he likes our company. Why? You want my spot?"

"No," he answers too quickly. "He said, at least between vampires, that it can feel... good?"

Castor scratches at greying stubble along his neck, and shrugs. "I s'pose. I'm gettin' too old to think about enjoying it like that anymore. You grow up with those same faces never changing and they start to feel like living statues. Doesn't feel good or bad, just *is*."

Outside the stables, a freezing rain has formed an ice sheet suitable enough for skating, and though Elias wasn't invited to join in the festivities, he wouldn't have known how to partake either— Rinn never got the chance to teach him. So here he stands with Castor, watching undead horses lap up the last drops of blood like it's liquid sugar.

"I understand the agreement you have, but you're still treated like servants."

Castor folds his arms on the stable wall and gives Elias a knowing look. "Are living lords so much more fair and just? Elphaba has an equal seat at the table and when she's left this world, my sister will take her place. Elphaba is an unmarried crone. Where else in this world could she enjoy so much respect and authority?"

Elias sighs and rolls his eyes and *no*, Castor still doesn't get it.

"This castle can't exist in the middle of nowhere. Where're the villages and towns they once lorded over? There must at least be vacant buildings?"

"Elias," Castor implores, "you've seen what surviving up here looks like. That's not the way we want to live."

"Then go south—"

"You don't know them." He waves at the gathering crowd, an intermingling of vampires and living people, all wrapped up, much bulkier in their layers. Quinn and another dark-skinned vampire skate with a chubby little child holding their hands. She laughs and swoops the kid up in her arms, blowing a raspberry on their cheek. Elias would have had no idea that she's not the kid's mom. That she's a better mother to someone else's kid than Elias's own mother is to him, even with centuries between them, doesn't sting. Not at all.

"This is our home, Elias. We don't want to abandon it any more than you do yours."

Elias gathers up the empty buckets licked clean by the horses and sets to scrubbing as Castor lists all the weak reasons he and the other willing captives accept this life. "They hunt when we can't because it's too cold and dangerous. They defend this castle so we don't have to. They tend to our every want and need and when we want to leave? They send scouts to protect us on whatever pilgrimage we must brave to cross the continent to the port towns. All they ask in return is to be fed. I can't think of a better deal than that."

Elias wishes he could, because he can't either. Not truly. He's clinging to what he knows only on principle now, only because it's what he has, while still waiting for someone to legitimize his concerns. Still it never happens.

The children here adore the coven, whether born at Tanarang or relocated here from the South with their parents. That had bothered him—parents packing up their kids and ripping them away from a sunny world filled with the living... to come here? Most of the living aren't related either. Elphaba only has three grandchildren by blood, but she cherishes them all, wherever they come from, as her own. Rinn, he'd also learned, wasn't Castor's child. She'd pilgrimaged north with her late mother, and chose to stay with the friends she'd found here rather than return south alone. Her three adoptive cousins, Dorotea's sons, have never left the castle. With every passing moon, Elias starts to see why.

Castor has an entire family within the castle walls and more important places to be than standing in uncomfortable silences with Elias. He's got little nieces and nephews sniffing him out of the stables like hounds, each demanding he pay attention to their incredible twirls and twists on the ice.

Elias still prefers his room at the cost of being polite company. If not his room, then the library floor, sketching copies of the maps and the splotchy shape of the Kenoa Islands he found in the atlas. He doesn't have to ration his charcoal and has better tools now to draw with—pencils of different grades and thickness, as much sketch paper as he wants since it's used so rarely.

It's not that he's still behind a wall of ice—he's able to join and converse at dinner freely now—but there's stories he doesn't know, more than half a castle of faces without names, inside jokes that fly over his head. Dorian can't be at his every beck and call and he should branch out and try to make nice with the other vampires, but breaking into conversation is like trying to catch frozen breaths with his fingers. Once he tried, and the two vampires in his sights switched languages without sparing him a glance, so *no*, he's not trying that again.

He heads up to his room for his bundle of parchment and a few pencils, only to head back out to sit on the wall and draw the hustle and bustle on the ice. He squishes this small sketch between depictions of the archery targets and the horses and his various pieces portraying the castle, patiently waiting for Dorian to show because the kids love him. And he doesn't disappoint.

On the ice, the vampire glides around with Gilan on his shoulders and two others grabbing at his legs for a turn. Elias, too far away to capture his likeness with any detail, draws abstract motion that could be mistaken for anyone else. He's been waiting to get Dorian alone but preoccupied so that he can sketch a candid in peace but without the pressure of Dorian wanting to see the result. He doesn't get his chance until after the ice rink has been scratched to oblivion.

He's sitting in the lounge by the fire, a tightly compacted seaweed-log mixture that doesn't smell the best but warms his toes, as he draws the stonework around the mantle. Dorian's voice startles him, mid-conversation with a woman wearing thick spectacles and talking animatedly about her studies in the South. Cera, he realizes, and she's brought her own work with her.

Their conversation quiets too low for him to discern. Cera stops Dorian from going for one of the chalices, tapping at her journal and rucking up the poofy sleeve of her blouse.

Dorian shrugs and lets her lead him to a sofa. He takes her forearm gently and waits for permission before starting. Cera writes furiously with her free hand as if she's penning some dissertation on the nature of vampire bites, else she's so deeply unbothered by the task at hand that it doesn't even interrupt her work. The former, he decides, when Cera nudges Dorian back, but not before he can lick the wound closed. She loosens her high collar and nods once, then twice, then a third time.

Elias starts sketching on a new page. Cera, furious writing ceased, head tipped back and eyes closed. Her pencil drops, forgotten, to the floor, and Elias's stills in his hand, only vaguely defined shadows on his parchment.

Cera looks... happy. More than happy. She's not smiling, but at peace. Serene. *The line between pleasure and pain*, he thinks as her hands move to Dorian's hair to keep him firmly at her neck.

Elias toes the line between eavesdropper and voyeur uncomfortably. It's a public room and he's not the only one privy to the sight should anyone else wander in, but just because he can stare doesn't mean he should. He goes back to sketching, head tilted down but still glancing up through his lashes, changing Cera's form to one a little more vague but sharpening Dorian's that's draped over it. Elias stares at his drawing, at the figure that is but isn't Cera, little more than a shadowy head, torso, and cradling limbs. He imagines himself in its place.

This is—this is dangerous. They're monsters. All the sun-starved desire in his chest doesn't know what's good for him.

He's gone before either of them can notice he was there, smudging the distinctive braids with a clammy thumb the moment he reaches his room.

The feast thrown for Gilan's sixth birthday is as excessively opulent as every other occasion. The kid doesn't stop smiling for hours, showing off his missing front tooth. He opens his gift from Amaranth, an intricately detailed knight atop its horse carved from coral, and runs right up to her for an ecstatic hug.

Amaranth lets him drag her into the gift pile with the other kids amid his little army of other knight figurines. She still sits like a lady, straight-backed and proper, but she smiles and laughs like the rest of them, and Elias forgets that she's dead.

The grandsire lingers until Gilan's attention drifts to the sweets both baked fresh and imported from the South. She returns to her place at the high table with her brother and maybe it's the way the light falls on her face, but Elias thinks she looks disappointed.

He continues his rounds, refilling glasses from a pitcher of spirits, and when he returns to his spot in the shadows, she's waiting for him.

"What did you gift him?"

Elias smiles with a quiet huff. "A drawing of the castle with him and the other kids in the courtyard."

Amaranth laces her hands behind her back and tilts her chin. "You like to draw," she says, matter of fact. "Some subjects more than others."

If it's a condemnation, he refuses to let it bite. "Some faces are more familiar than others."

The corner of her lip quirks, and that might be the best he's going to get from her. "I've heard that you'd like to join the party to Panolin for the voyage south. We've sent many scholars over the years to study, and I can arrange a letter of recommendation for the vocation of your choice."

Elias blinks, startled by the generous offer. "Oh. That's very kind of you, but..."

Amaranth cants her body, managing to look down her nose at him despite not reaching his shoulder in height. "Do you not want to hone your artistic skills? If funds are an issue we can arrange for something to get you started."

"No. It's only that I haven't given any particular study much thought," he admits, no purpose in mind for his life in the South beyond living someplace sunny and out of reach of the leeches of the North. "I thought my mark on history would amount to being the Keeper of my clan."

"That it remains," she says idly.

Elias smiles anyway, pretending not to hear the insult, simpleton that he is. "Maybe I'll take you up on that offer, if there's no conditions to your investment?"

"Do you know," she begins softly, "that I speak nine languages? Hyacinth, too."

"I did not."

"I can weave baskets and tapestries, raise livestock and children. Paint, sculpt, and carve. I can fight with every weapon in this castle and beyond. I can read the stars and the weather like a book, dance in any court I might find myself in." She sighs deeply, soft smile turning wry. "I learn these things, however impractical, because eternity is a very long time. What was meant as a gift begins to feel like a curse if all I do is simply exist."

Her tone is light and she watches over her coven as she talks, so he can't say if it's purely a story or another jab at his character. If it's the latter, it's one he's heard before, but inspiration is difficult to find in a cave with little light.

Something catches Amaranth's ear across the din of conversation. She rises up on her toes and nods, then regards him coolly. "Should you wish to practice your skills in the interim, I'm sure many faces here would love to see their portraits." Then she's gone, a ghost drifting between the tables.

Elias doesn't wait around to see Gilan find his gift. He leaves and doesn't think a single soul notices and that's perfectly fine by him.

Chapter 8:
The Holdfast

The Aeskerat emissary arrives amid a light snowfall when Dorian's on guard. Jacobi is alone, hands in the air as he rides directly toward Dorian as if he knew exactly where he'd be on the wall.

Quinn jogs over, bow in hand. "I can send two around to check he's alone."

"If Jacobi's lackeys aren't within sight, then they're not here at all." He wants all the attention to himself at all times. Dorian stows his own bow and regards his kin down either stretch of the wall. "Keep this quiet. I'll go out to meet him."

Jacobi stops his horse before the ditch at the base of the wall, looking up calmly. They found the body. It's the only explanation. They've found the body, and they know it was a Tanarang vampire. Jacobi is here for justice. Aeskerat often lets Jacobi ride out to play at diplomacy before things get bloodier than necessary.

Dorian cocks his head toward the eastern edge of the wall. "If Elias wanders out here, distract him. Send somebody to alert Amaranth discreetly that she should meet me at the Holdfast."

Quinn purses her lips and nods, then takes off toward the western edge of the wall. Dorian repeats his orders to the remaining vampires he passes: Keep this quiet, Jacobi means no harm, presume nothing about his presence.

The wall ends at the sheer cliff of the mountains, both an impenetrable barrier against attack and escape. The days of infantry mounting attacks on Castle Tanarang came long before Dorian, but scars from old battles litter the rocks. One road in and out, blocked in by the cliffs on one side and the deadly drop to the frigid ocean on the other.

"Markus, at ease. He means us no harm." Not yet anyway. A fellow vampire of the South, Markus still looks like he never left, all fluffy gold hair and tanned skin poised calmly to aim at the intruder.

"Aeskerat always means us harm. You going down there?" Markus doesn't take his eyes off Jacobi, toeing at the whalebone ladder stored at his feet. "Alone?"

"He came alone. You can cover me from up here if that helps you feel better."

"It does." They hoist the ladder up and over.

Jacobi, now dismounted, casually holds a spear adorned with teeth and tiny bones like the ones decorating him and his kin. He dips his head in faux politeness. "Dorian, pleasure to see you again." His blood paint scrunches with his brows as he eyes Markus up on the wall.

"Old habits never die," Dorian says. "I can't say it's nice to see you. You never come with good news."

Jacobi smiles, an aslant thing, and returns the spear to his saddle. "I like to think my coming at all is good news. When I leave empty-handed, *that's* bad news."

"What do you expect to leave with, Jacobi?"

He *tsks* and sweeps his braids back. "Aren't you going to invite me in?"

"No. Your warpaint scares the children." Dorian waves off Markus and takes the horse's reins. "This way."

"I know the way." Visibly miffed, Jacobi snags the reins and follows him around the rock to the Holdfast, its entrance guarded by grimacing towers of icy faces. A smoothed stone table sits at the center beneath the threat of Northern icicles. Dorian pays them no mind, watching the narrow door to the castle at the top of the narrower stairs for Amaranth's arrival.

Jacobi, though, can't be patient and respectful. "I'm parched," he says, voice echoing around the alcove. "Shall we share a drink to our mutual interest of avoiding carnage?"

Only because Amaranth isn't here to scold him does Dorian engage. "You're Aeskerat. Just because you think yourself better doesn't mean you aren't in bed with them."

Jacobi laughs shrewdly, stretching his legs from the long ride. "I'm loyal to my kin as you are to yours. That doesn't mean I agree with everything we do or the means by which we go about it."

"But you do, if not by direct action. You are complicit. Or is that warpaint on your face not from a blood slave?" Or the finger bones and teeth that crown his head and dot his furs not from the same? The leather of his pale armor? Jacobi's far more polite company than anyone else they could send, but anyone else doesn't pretend they can walk on water.

Dorian lights the candles around the alcove, illuminating walls covered in handprints that mark old treaties—agreements with other covens, clans, and kingdoms of the dead and living alike. They're all dull red, indistinguishable.

"They are lesser creatures, Dorian. Limited. They think

themselves the gods' gift to the world."

Dorian suppresses an eyeroll at this pontificating, no more profound than the first time he heard it.

Amaranth's muffled footsteps approach from the tunnel and he couldn't be happier to hear them. Dorian stands at attention and mutters, "If the gods loved anyone, they wouldn't have bound us to the night."

Amaranth's not alone, but it's Castor, not Hyacinth, behind her. Dorian doesn't blame him. No one at Castle Tanarang mocks Hyacinth for his voice, but he doesn't command a foreign audience well when it cracks and squeaks no matter how strong he wants to sound.

"Jacobi," she greets, sweeping down the stairs in her dress with Castor at her heels. "What an unwelcome surprise."

Jacobi chuckles and dips into a shallow bow as if she cares for such flattery. "Lady Amaranth. Your name matches your dress."

"How observant of you." She nips her hand and offers the beading blood over the stone table. "May every word spoken around this table be true." Her blood drips and stains the rock, joined shortly by Jacobi's. "Dorian," she orders.

Dorian complies, eyeing the Northern icicles and empty sockets from liars past above them. He backs up next to Castor and shoves his hands under his arms.

"Are you famished, Jacobi?" Amaranth's smile is as fake as Jacobi's as she beckons Castor forward. Playing politics like this is exactly why Dorian happily remains just a scout. No one in the castle would have volunteered, and that Castor must've done so, however reluctantly after losing Rinn, has Dorian biting his tongue until it bleeds. He glares daggers at Jacobi behind Amaranth's back, politics be damned.

Jacobi simpers courteously and shakes his head. "I don't expect to be here long."

"Why are you here?"

Dorian has room to doubt the obvious reason until Jacobi sets the broken spear shaft stained with the fledgling vampire's blood on the stone table. "I am here seeking answers, Lady Amaranth, and justice. This was found in Janneah, young by our standards but smart. She knew the land as well as your scout here."

Hardly. I have hundreds of years on her.

Amaranth isn't fooled by his attempts at earning sympathy either. "Clearly not, otherwise she might've avoided a fatal encounter with a stake."

Jacobi doesn't miss a beat, waving at the murder weapon as if he stands before a gullible jury. "We tracked the scent on the wood west of Olimaunt Keep, and the only settlement west of Olimaunt is Castle Tanarang. It reeks of the living. I can smell it still. All over your scout."

He turns a cool gaze toward Dorian, nostrils flaring, daring him to deny it.

"She was murdered on Aeskerat land, her body left to discover in a snowdrift instead of given the respect that might have come if you'd informed us yourselves." He pantomimes tragedy like he's lost a child, but it doesn't reach his eyes, an overly dramatic performance that only mimics strangers he's watched grieve. "Provide us the horse you stole and the guilty party, and all will be well between us."

"Castor," Amaranth says, not taking her eyes off the intruder. "You may leave, thank you."

Castor huffs quietly and gives Dorian a sympathetic frown as he passes.

"The horse is yours. Your bold accusations against my scout

and my ward are another matter." Amaranth laces her hands behind her back and Dorian smiles.

Jacobi cocks his head. "Do you call me a liar, Lady Amaranth?" He turns a pointed look up at the hanging ice.

"I'm calling you misinformed. Dorian, please explain to the interloper what caused the death of their wayward fledgling."

"I killed her," he says simply, waiting for Liar's Ice that never falls. "She accused me of trespassing when I held permits. I defended my ward and stole the horse to expedite our journey back."

A tic ripples Jacobi's jaw. His smile cracks like plaster. "I see. Since this was so clearly done in self-defense, why did you fail to report it?"

"You would have come here anyway shouting the same demands. With you as my witness, I'm not lying, so take your horse and go. I'll fetch it myself to be rid of you." Dorian steps one pace away from the table before Jacobi finds his footing and clears his throat.

"Did you claim them? Have you claimed them in the months they've been here?"

Dorian spins on his heel. "As you well know, Tanarang doesn't recognize the laws of the claim."

"But Aeskerat does. Even our fledglings respect it. She would not have attacked if she smelled a claim, and if you hadn't established one, then your ward was fair game on our land. So did you, Dorian?"

Damn the sacred space of the Holdfast. "No," he bites out. "I didn't."

Jacobi's sharp smile returns. "Has anyone? Have they taken the oath of your house?"

"No."

Jacobi shrugs, his smile all slimy and crooked when he says, "Well, in that case, you harbor a fugitive. The responsible leader would hand them over. Justice served."

Amaranth, her steel grip coming down on his wrist, cuts in before Dorian can say anything else incriminating. "Dorian alone killed her, and he has taken the oath of this house. An attack on him is an attack on this coven. My ward is no more than a witness," she declares, all the weight of a thirteen-year-old in her voice sluicing right off Jacobi's smarmy face.

"A witness?" Jacobi *tsks*. "No, I think they're... what's the word, Dorian? Complicit." Dorian bares his teeth, held back only by Amaranth's grip on his arm.

Jacobi holds his hands up, offering a nonchalant shrug. "Since we can't have you, since *you* didn't trespass, we'll take the next best thing. Surely you're not so attached to a stubborn vagrant who won't even bleed for you that you'd risk conflict with Aeskerat over their skin?"

It's not even about Elias, he wants to say. It's this slick, putrid parasite's arrogance. It's his disrespect for their ways that he'd happily trod over with his horse. It's Aeskerat feeding off blood slaves no more than skin and bone all because they can't think further ahead than their next meal.

"Dorian, get the stolen horse and make no detours," Amaranth orders quietly. "I can handle this." She lets him go and shoves lightly at his back.

"Yes, Grandsire." If he doesn't leave now, he'll take them both out with a Liar's Ice.

Jacobi gets in one last dig anyway. "In case you're considering claiming them now or securing an oath, remember the last time Tanarang stole a fugitive from Aeskerat."

That debt was paid, and words to that effect twist in his throat.

Instead, he musters all the strength he has to stalk away, forgoing the ladder for the main gate. He'd snap it in half with the itch, hot under his skin, to break Jacobi's bones.

Markus meets him at the gate, and Dorian utters a *You were right* under his breath in route to the stables.

"What happened?"

"Amaranth is handling it." The horse had taken Poppy's stall, Poppy's nameplate replaced with one bearing Clover's name written in Kymiria's hand. If Jacobi expects the Aeskerat saddle returned, he can jump with all his ridiculous demands into the frothing sea.

Dorian pats Clover's muzzle and loops a woven kelp lead around her neck. "You're going to your old home, I'm afraid. You'll grow reaccustomed to its discomforts in time."

Markus frowns. "Kymiria just made that sign."

"I'll find her a new horse."

"Are we going to fight Aeskerat?" Markus keeps his voice low but not low enough to go unheard by the scant vampires in the courtyard. Despite his orders, Dorian is sure word has spread to the rest of the coven at least.

"I don't know, Markus," he snaps, harsher than he means to.

"'Cause we'll win," Markus insists, fangs slipping free with a hunger for combat. "No one's taken this castle in a thousand years."

"I'm sure that fact will be enough to deter them. Please resume your post."

"Dorian." Markus lingers at the gate, gripping the latticed whale ribs, a deep furrow trenching his brow. "What happened?"

What happened? "I messed up."

Markus doesn't follow him. Dorian returns to the Holdfast,

Clover in tow, and Jacobi is still smug, Amaranth is expressionless, and neither is speaking. He all but slaps the lead into Jacobi's hand, and Jacobi steps on his cloak, arresting him there.

"I am parched," Jacobi says, feigning hurt. "Be a good host and correct that oversight?"

"*Jacobi.*"

The interloper moves his foot at Amaranth's word and resigns himself to the travesty of feeding off his returned horse instead. Dorian didn't steal Clover with the intent to rob Aeskerat of her, but now he wishes he had.

"Didn't claim this one either," Jacobi muses.

"Get out. You got what you came for."

"Actually—"

"Dorian, come here, please."

Ice slithers down his spine. He looks between them, understanding too late that Amaranth's careful mask is for him, not Jacobi. She hasn't actually agreed to Jacobi's demands, has she? She couldn't have. Worst case, they send Jacobi home with nothing and leave his grandsire to come negotiate himself. Bowing down to *Jacobi*? Unacceptable.

Back turned to the Aeskerat, Dorian sends his grandsire a questioning look.

Amaranth keeps her chin high, hands laced in front of the dress that matches her namesake. "We're giving him up."

Kymiria isn't the last vampire in the castle to hear about Jacobi, but that she's not first might as well make her last. She finds Dorian in one of the cave pools to hear it from the source. He's sulking, wasting a dry robe by wearing it in the water with his head on his arms.

"Do you want company?"

"If you want mine."

Kymiria sheds her leathers but keeps her shirt so they match and slips into the steaming water behind him. She starts working free every tie in his hair, combing the braids loose with her fingers. "Amaranth won't change her mind?"

"I offered myself in his place since I'm the one that killed the fledgling."

Her fingers still. That he's still here and sulking means Amaranth didn't accept his proposal. "Are you surprised she declined?"

Dorian shrugs. "She said the entire host of Tanarang would blame Elias for being free, blood unshed, while I suffered to protect him."

"I'd have a hand in his doom as much as anyone, certainly." Kymiria cups her hands and trickles water over his head. Dorian twists to stare like he's actually shocked. "It can't be the yearling you care so much about."

"It is him and the promises she forces me to break," he mumbles, dropping his forehead on his arms. "It would be one thing if he was still a miserable lout, but he's not. I guaranteed him sanctuary, I gave him the conditions under which he could stay here, and he's kept to them, yet we're trading him to those parasites to keep ourselves safe. How does that make us look?"

Kymiria hugs him from behind, cheek pressed to the burgundy silk shoulder of the robe. "What would you have us do when all they ask for is one little boy?"

"And Clover. He's taking Clover."

And she'd only just hung the nameplate. Jacobi would pay for that. He would. But she would not see Tanarang pay for the boy. "Your yearling still resents what we must do to survive, what we must do to protect the other children here. Unless you'd prefer more funerals like Rinn's."

He turns in her arms and nudges them away, shoulders up high. "Amaranth fought for me."

"She did," Kymiria agrees. "But as I recall, you took your oath in the Grand Hall prepared to let Amaranth drink you dry. And were a vampire when you did it."

He tries to turn away again, shaking his head like they're not completely different circumstances.

Kymiria turns him right back. "You've saved his life how many times now, have proven the world over that we are not them, and still he holds out. There are consequences, Dorian, and you alone are not expected to bear them all."

"They'll kill him," he whispers, as if speaking too loudly will chisel the future into stone. "Not quickly or painlessly or mercifully. They'll break his body and his spirit and his mind until he wears his collar like a brand of honor, unwilling to trade it for sunlight even if they drowned him in it."

Kymiria has never seen inside the decrepit halls of Aeskerat or the other covens, but she's seen what comes out of them. "They don't break everyone."

"He's a coward."

Indeed. "His is not your weakness to atone for." Kymiria nips her wrist and gives a knowing smile at the blatant hunger that overcomes his features, brown eyes blown black and fangs poking free. She prods at his chest and chides, "You're hungry, *eliyre*."

He never eats when he's upset, as if abstaining from Castor or Cera will solve anything. Dorian doesn't take much more nudging to latch onto her wrist. It's not as potent as living blood, but it doesn't come with guilt, and Kymiria will shield him from as much of that as she can.

Elias is scrubbing dishes by candlelight when the note arrives via one of Rinn's friends. The child bounds in, hands it over with a close-lipped smile, and bounds away. He dries his hands so as not to smear the ink and unfolds the paper. *Paper*, he thinks, for a simple summons of all things. A blasphemous waste back in the cave, but not here.

He reads the note over and over again, committing the swooping penmanship to memory. *Come see me in my room when your chores are done. D.*

He speed-walks the whole way there on a break, imagining all kinds of spontaneous notions for what Dorian might want. When he gets there, the door's closed. Elias smooths his clothes and knocks.

"It's open." Elias deflates at Kymiria's voice but eases the door open, watching his feet in case she's not decent.

"I'm sorry to bother you. I was looking for Dorian."

"The note was mine. Dorian's not here."

He looks up and sees her lounging on the bed, wrapped loosely in vibrant floral silks. "Oh." Swallowing his disappointment, Elias steps inside and wrings his hands. "May I ask why?"

Kymiria waves her hand. "Shut the door."

The latch clicks resoundingly.

Kymiria sits up and fluffs her hair, yawning as if she's just woken from a glorious nap. "You want him."

Elias nearly chokes on his tongue. "W-what?"

She rolls her eyes and shrugs. "I can smell the arousal on you at the mere thought of a clandestine meeting."

Elias's face heats down to his neck, try as he might to will it away. He scowls and crosses his arms. "I think I'll leave now, if you only called me here to tease."

"On the contrary." Kymiria reaches the door with graceful speed, holding it shut with her fingertips. "I'm here to spare you further heartache."

He couldn't move her if he wanted to, so Elias huffs and steps back. "Jealousy looks ugly on anyone, immortal or otherwise."

Not to be baited, Kymiria simply remains blocking the door. "It does." She twirls a lock of hair around her fingers and kicks off the door to glide past him. On the bedside table rests a chalice of blood and she absently swirls it, perching on the edge of the furs. "There is a phenomenon by which the likes of us regard the likes of you. But all those epic romances the children stage only happen for fledglings and those far older than either of us, Yearling."

"Who said anything about—"

"Don't interrupt." Kymiria sips from her chalice, tapping her nail on the glass in thought. "It happens to those who are still too attached to life and those who forgot it centuries ago, only to be blindsided. Otherwise? The living do not compare. You're unclean, you're knobby-kneed and weak. You're *limited.*"

Elias leans against the bedpost and shrugs halfheartedly. "If you're trying to scare me off, it's not working. He doesn't think that of me." And if he does, he's not afraid to speak his mind to Elias.

Kymiria smiles ruefully. "Oh, but he does, Yearling. You're a puppy, a kitten. He can shower you with praise and attention because it's adorable to watch you putter about discovering your world. He can love you and your inevitable death will break his heart. But he does not see you as an equal. He can't. He's both too old and not old enough." She sips again and leaves the rim at her lip. A drop of blood escapes, and she wipes it away with a huff. "I know this because he treats me the same. He was here the night I was born, and no matter how much he loves me, he won't ever love me like I love him. It's the way it is. You aren't special. You aren't unique. And you aren't a vampire. So what's the point?" She sneers then, teeth bared. "You're not even a puppy. You're a fish in a bowl. The audacity you have to think yourself so important."

The chalice slams down, and she's on him in a single lunge, crowding him against the bedpost. For someone who claims she isn't jealous, her face betrays her. Elias bites back his retort, lest she lose her temper and stage an unfortunate accident for him at the bottom of the stairs.

"If he wants me gone," Elias says, pleased when his voice comes out steady, "he's old enough to tell me himself."

"He's too enamored with his little fish to risk killing it with hurt feelings. And what? You think you can handle a vampire?" Kymiria laughs humorlessly. "You despise us. Even now your blood remains untainted even by your savior. What exactly do you fantasize about with such a chasm between you?"

Her forearm against his neck suffocates, and on a roll now, she doesn't let up.

"We can't eat your food, can't get drunk on your alcohol before it turns to ash in our mouths. We can't enjoy the sun or dream while we sleep. We're stronger and faster and more durable than your paper skin or anything within it. You have nothing in common, cave rat."

Her fangs, still extended, muddy her words, and it might be funny if it weren't so terrifying. At any moment Kymiria could snap and he could do nothing to stop it.

"You don't know him, Yearling. What makes you think your

body has anything to offer him that he can't get without the sweat and stink of the living?"

There is one thing he has that she doesn't—she or any of Dorian's other vampire suitors. Elias raises his hands and waits for her to let him go, which she does, but not without one last shove to threaten his throat. He coughs and swallows roughly, adjusting his collar where it digs into his jugular.

"I won't tell him we spoke," he rasps. "You are jealous, and I understand why. You've known him thrice as long as I've been alive, and here I come, a fish out of my bowl, stealing all the attention."

She snarls, nails biting into the bone bedpost like it's taking all her strength to remain anchored to it. "You're nothing, Yearling."

"I'm something," he argues, "otherwise I'd be dead now. I'm something even to you. You're sparing me here, now, because you care about Dorian. And if you do love him as deeply as you say, you will also leave who he courts his own decision." He edges toward the door as he speaks, reasonably confident but not certain that she won't rip his throat out with her teeth and justify it later. "You shouldn't have anything to fear, though. After all, I'm a fish."

Kymiria doesn't follow him out the door. He speeds toward the castle wall as fast as he can, forcing himself to take deep breaths, convincing himself he can pretend the altercation never happened.

When he steps outside, he can't help the feeling that there's more eyes on him than usual. Elias draws his arms in and gives the spot where Rinn fell a wide berth. It's not stained with her blood and the stones aren't cracked from the impact, but to step on the ground as if it is unchanged doesn't sit right with him. He'll never forget exactly where it happened.

Quinn stops him halfway up the stairs and they're hardly friends, but there's something heavy in her eyes he can't place.

"He's not up here."

"Can you point me in the right direction?"

"Elias!" There Dorian is, running out from the stables of all places. It's only when Dorian reaches the bottom of the stairs and asks what he's doing out here that Elias registers the change.

"You said my name."

Dorian frowns, looking past him to Quinn and back. "What?"

"My name," Elias repeats dumbly. "You said Elias. Not Yearling." An awkward pause sets in and he rubs his neck. "Um. Never mind. I need to talk to you. Alone."

Dorian glances at Quinn again, then shuffles out of Elias's path down the stairs. "Sure."

"Is something wrong?" Whatever it is, he hopes it can wait.

"Always," Dorian mutters. "Come, it's warmer inside."

Inside turns out to be the library. Dorian fidgets the whole way, asking nonsensical questions about which book is his favorite and if he's learned anything new in them.

"Dorian." Elias cuts off another question about whether he's discovered any new colors he's fond of in the tapestries. "You're jumping at shadows. Did I do something?" Did Kymiria get to him first?

His face pinches and he searches the rafters, cursing in that curly foreign tongue. "Jacobi of Aeskerat is here. They found the body."

Oh. Elias swallows and tugs his cloak tighter around himself. "Do they want an explanation?"

"They have that. What they want is blood." Dorian drags a rough hand down his face and holds his jaw. "I've been ordered to tell you nothing, but I can't abide by that just to keep the peace. Amaranth has agreed to give you up to Aeskerat as payment for the dead fledgling."

Elias can see Dorian's lips moving and hear the noises that come out but can't make sense of the words they form. "She's selling me as a blood slave? When? Now? Tomorrow? I didn't do it!"

Dorian claps a hand over his mouth and presses him back against the bookshelves. "I know that. You're trying now, but it's too little too late no matter what I say. I'm sorry."

So—what? If he shouts, the vampires will swarm to deliver him early? Are they all hoping to let him walk around for his last peaceful night and deliver him completely unknowing so they won't have to face him?

Elias pulls at Dorian's fingers and he warily removes them, eyes pleading for him to stay quiet. "Why should I have to go if it's not your wish? You have a castle—defend it."

"Lives would be lost if Aeskerat attacks. No vampire here is willing to die for you, and after Rinn, Elphaba's family is in no shape to lose anyone else to avoidable tragedy." Guilt crumples his face, and he tears away from him as if burned. "I'm sorry," he says again.

"But I didn't do it."

"I know." His voice cracks.

Elias slides down the shelves and braces his elbows on his knees. The walls close in as he shoots down ideas as fast as they form. He can't run because he still doesn't know how to find his way home. Even if he did, Aeskerat would be after him the whole way.

"Wait." Elias rucks up his sleeve. "Do it now. Claim me and I get to stay, right?"

"I can't." The words are a whisper but they feel like a shout.

Elias surges to his feet. "You made me a promise and I respect that, but I'm releasing you from it now. *Do it.*"

"Elias, I can't." Dorian's eyes shine and he blinks hard. "Doing it now would be a declaration of war."

"It's a claim, right? You said they respect it, it's sacred."

"In this case, it's theft."

"How can it be theft if I was never theirs to be stolen?"

"Because you've been promised by Amaranth!" Dorian hisses, flinging his hands in desperation.

"I held my end of the deal!"

"Like a living lord's servant. Not where it matters, not now."

Where it matters. Elias quiets, stiff shoulders slumping at the thought. "Would it have mattered? Would your coven have defended me if I'd bared my veins from the moment I got here?"

Dorian huffs and gives a staunch, "Yes."

So be it, then. Elias nods, lips pursed. "What if you turned me now?"

Dorian gapes, horrified. "You don't want that."

"I don't want to be a blood slave," he snaps. "Would that be enough?"

"I—" Dorian cuts himself off to think, pacing in a tight circle. "Amaranth would respect it, we all would, no matter your reasons for turning. But we'd still be at war, and you'd be the first boots in the snow. You would still die before Amaranth sacrificed anyone else."

Naturally. Respect it, they must, but she couldn't force them to like it. In that case...

Elias pulls his sharp new stake from his boot and doesn't miss the split-second flash of fear in Dorian's eyes at the revelation of it. "Would you be at war if I died? Is that my way out?"

He offers the blunt end of the stake when Dorian doesn't answer, and the vampire scoffs. "I'm not killing you."

"This is merciful."

"I'm not doing it."

"Why not?"

"Because!" Dorian yanks the stake from his hand and tosses it to the floor. "Because Aeskerat doesn't break everyone. Because you'd never seen green until some painting in an abandoned keep. Because cowards survive, and you're too young to die never seeing those wildflowers with your own eyes."

Silence rushes in like winter wind. This deep in the castle, it almost feels like another world, warm and rich and stolen away from the bitter white waste, except it's not. Elias *hmphs*. "A fish who never left his bowl for the sea." Kymiria would kill him if he asked, he thinks. He could never do it himself. "I don't think he was meant to," Elias utters. "His bowl was quite safe even if it was small."

Dorian frowns and it is comforting to know for sure that he didn't put Kymiria up to that conversation. Among his every *because*, none of them was *because I care*, so Elias supposes that answers that question, too. He can't have expected better than that and he shouldn't.

Still, it's worth a shot, if only to silence that stupidly naive, childish desire sprung from not being ignored and cast aside for once in his life. "Dorian?"

Elias isn't totally certain on the mechanics, he's only done this once and was quite inebriated in the attempt, but it can't be that difficult. He leans up and threads his fingers through soft hair, and Dorian's more than strong enough to resist or pull away or shove Elias back and he doesn't.

A month ago, Elias might've imagined kissing a vampire to be like kissing a cadaver with ice-cold skin. Poisoned lips and teeth sharp enough to draw blood with a graze. Dorian doesn't kiss him back, but he isn't at all a corpse. He's soft. Warm.

Elias isn't bold enough or confident enough to throw himself fully at Dorian with no hint as to whether or not he's even good at this, but the idea sounds nice. A parting gift to remember fondly. He steps back, his hand falling away.

The watery look Dorian gives him has him reconsidering if something desperate might have merit after all, but Dorian has all the opportunity in the world to drag him back in or flinch in his direction and he doesn't.

Elias gives a resigned nod and swallows. "It's not because I'm a man, is it?"

A sad smile crinkles the corners of Dorian's eyes. "It's not."

Well. That's something, at least.

Elias rolls up his sleeve again and offers his wrist. "I know the claim won't work," he says before Dorian can say it for him. "I'm not planning on using it like a shield. But I don't think anyone in Aeskerat will be gentle, and I don't like the idea of some smug vampire calling dibs when it's all nonsense anyway."

"It would be an insult even if you didn't mean it as one."

"Oh, I absolutely do."

Still, Dorian shakes his head. "Amaranth would smell it on you."

Elias gives a broken laugh. "What more can they do to me?"

A dark fire burns in Dorian's eyes and fresh fear rolls in Elias's gut. *A lot*, that look says.

Elias retrieves his stake and silently holds it to his own chest once more. "Then don't let them."

And again, Dorian robs him of a quick end. "You haven't considered that I might be able to get you out," he whispers, composure solidly returned like the icy wall of the castle. "If you want to die so badly, I can't stop you, but I won't help you."

Fate decided, Elias holds out the impotent stake to Dorian. It's not the sketched portrait that he's too cowardly to offer, but it's all he has. Reluctantly, Dorian takes it, and it disappears beneath his cloak.

"I get one more chance to rest?" How could he, though? He almost wishes Dorian hadn't told him because now all he can do is stew in anticipation.

"As far as I know."

Maybe in the morning he'll have the courage to ask Kymiria to end this. Wildflowers sound like a wonderful dream, but they're just that—a dream.

Dorian offers to escort him back to his room, and he stands there seriously contemplating one last way out—nicking Dorian's blood and killing himself and then fighting tooth and claw for his place in the coven. He's not battle-hardened, he knows. He'll get out there and brave a dramatically unspectacular end. But at least it would be on his feet.

Kymiria dashes those hopes. She slinks into the library, all dreamy smiles.

Dorian frowns, stepping away from him. "Kym?"

She doesn't break stride, bringing her hands to his face like she means to kiss him and snapping his neck instead. Dorian drops in her arms, and Elias stands frozen beside them.

"You'll forgive me," she whispers.

Quinn blocks his only exit, unless he jumps over the railing to the auditorium below for a fall that would break a leg and nothing more. But Elias hasn't moved in either direction before Quinn's on him, pinning his arms back, shepherding him to the door, unyielding to his struggles. "Kymiria! Kym—wait, *wait*, Kymiria!"

Quinn doesn't stop to let him beg, and Elias nearly tears his shoulder from its socket trying to lock eyes with Kymiria. "You want me gone? Kill me, *please*. I know you want to. Please!"

She ignores him.

"Have some self-respect," Quinn mutters. "Act like a child, they'll treat you like one."

He digs his feet in, yelling at Quinn, at whoever's listening, voice shrill with panic. "I'll fight for you, I'll turn, please! You're supposed to be an honorable house!" The entire castle has disappeared on him, all hiding, all closing their eyes and plugging their ears.

Elias stops up short and rears his head back into Quinn's nose. She curses, grip loosening enough for him to wrench an arm free, spin, and sink his teeth into her hand.

Quinn yells and kicks his knee with a sickening snap.

Elias cries out and crumples. "Turn me," he pleads through a clenched jaw, leg throbbing fiercely, her blood staining his teeth. "What you're subjecting me to is worse than death. If you have any respect for me—if I mean anything to you at all—*please*, Quinn."

Her face scrunches and she looks away. The last thing he sees is her hand fisting in his hair before his head collides with the wall.

Chapter 9: Grandsire of Aeskerat

Vampires don't dream. Hours spent sleeping feel like seconds when the only tell is stiff muscles. Dying, though…

Dying is a grey horizon, one where Dorian can't focus on any one immutable point over another because it all slips in a continuous stream through his fingers. Each thread of thoughts frays quicker than it can braid together, leaving him to forget how long he's been floating with no sky or ground or anything more tangible than a formless mist devoid of warmth. His sense of touch returns first, slowly. A softness beneath him, a tickling on his face, the pads of someone's fingers on his skin. Kymiria, her scent present now. Warm cream and candle smoke.

"Shhh," she whispers, backs of her fingers tracing his cheek. "Easy does it."

Dorian's neck throbs where bones and sinew finish knitting back together, and he winces, eyes squeezed shut.

"Does he need more?" Castor's low voice. The faint smell of sweat and sea salt. The metallic tang of blood. Kymiria's fingers gently prod his neck and he flinches away. The grey horizon opens a black pit beneath him that swallows him whole.

He sees her wry smile first. Sees her hand resting beside his hip on the bed. Castor leaning on his elbows. Dorian swallows, lips sticky with Castor's blood.

"No," she decides. "Thank you, Castor."

Dorian's numb hand clasps hers. "You could have been gentler."

"I wanted it clean and painless."

"You knew." Is he that obvious? Quinn must've immediately run to get her to stop him from doing something stupid, but that wasn't their call to make.

Kymiria sits back and shrugs guiltlessly. "You're too kind for your own good. He doesn't deserve it, and he's done nothing to earn it.

"He's a person. He doesn't deserve slavery either."

"I wasn't going to let you sell yourself to Jacobi to save a cave rat. I'm sorry for the way it happened but not for what I did."

Castor pointedly looks between them and backs off, and Dorian is in no mood to argue with her. But what they did, what this whole castle did by doing nothing, was wrong.

Kymiria sets her jaw and searches the ceiling. "I'm more than happy to share your attention. You know that."

"I do." That's why they work so well together, especially when he's gone for months at a time scouting across the continent. She doesn't get jealous or possessive or suffocatingly protective. This is new, and as her heart hammers defiantly in her chest, he tries to think about their roles reversed, to think about Kymiria vanishing for a fragile soul she just met.

Vanishing into the untold horror of Aeskerat.

Still. He wouldn't have done it this way.

"But he's not good for you," Kymiria argues. "He can't love who you are and still deny your nature." She takes a breath and clasps her hands. "He's not Amelie's replacement either."

Heat flushes across his skin. "Amelie has nothing—"

"She doesn't?" Kymiria crosses her arms and sits back. "Elias isn't a nine-year-old but he might as well be with how little he knows about the world. The North is bitter and cold and pitiless. Elias isn't special and he doesn't get a free pass. Name one thing, *one thing* he's done for you, one thing to deserve you martyring yourself to Jacobi, and I'll take it all back."

Dorian closes his eyes and tries to come up with something beyond Elias *not* killing him when he had the chance. Her argument isn't fair. Elias never had an opportunity to do anything grand for him, but he knows what she'll say. *He still refused to accept what you are—what* we *are.* She'll say it's not about blood, it's about respect. The coven takes care of its clan, and the clan takes care of its coven in return.

He knows better than to wait for a false apology, but even sympathy eludes her. So instead of giving her the satisfaction, he changes the subject. "How long was I out?"

She helps him upright. Unsympathetic Kymiria may be, but she's not gloating that the nuisance is gone. "Does it matter? At the speed they push their horses, he's long gone."

"We could at least have turned him, given him a chance to fight and die as a person instead of as property."

"You would have caused a scene if we hadn't intervened, and they already know he means something to you. Did you want them sending his tongue in a box to spite you?"

No.

"If I may, Dorian," Castor interjects gently. Dorian almost

forgot he was in the room. "Aeskerat wouldn't have been satisfied with that. And he had his multiple chances to convince us he was worth fighting for."

Dorian hangs his head and holds his sore neck. He knows, of course, that Castor is right. He knew when Elias begged him to do it. "What happens if Aeskerat still isn't satisfied?"

"Amaranth is confident they will be." If he hears a little guilt in her voice for her part, she deserves it. "At least enough to stave off open war. You know them. Not a one would dare lose their immortal life unprovoked."

"Yes, we endure by Aeskerat's will alone." He stands and invites Castor to the door.

"Dorian." Kymiria balls her fists in the bedspread. "What would you have us do?"

"I don't disagree with the decision," he says. "That doesn't mean I can't be upset about it."

If they haven't already cleaned out Elias's room, Dorian will do it himself. The faster all traces of his presence are gone, the faster they can all move on. He'll strip the sheets and scrub the smell of him from the walls. Sweep up all the stray muddy blond hair and smear all the oily fingerprints he left on their books.

They should have killed him and had it look like an accident, or better yet, like the insufferably noble Tanarang host exacted their own vicious justice for some unspecified crime. He'd have stopped Elias's fragile little living heart himself before they mutilated his body enough to convince Aeskerat he hadn't died quickly.

No. Dorian should have exacted the claim before that fledgling got her teeth anywhere near him. Then she would have lived. She'd have gone home disappointed but alive. Disaster averted.

No. He should have shot the coward with his kin before giving him the chance to beg for his life. Look at what good mercy has done either of them.

Elias's room hasn't been touched, his charcoal tally marks mocking him from the wall beside his bed. They don't account for Elias's entire stay, stopping, Dorian thinks, after their trip to Chryssy Point. The musky smell of him is overpowering. It bleeds from every surface, from where it's seeped into the stone.

Dorian flags down Hilda, dusting in the hall, and she shies away from the snap in his voice. She's one of the newer residents. One of those who insists on calling every vampire *Master* after they plucked her off the streets and gave her the first shoes she'd ever touched in her life.

"Please hunt down every scented candle you can carry and bring them back here," he orders. "And the incense."

Hilda scampers off, and Dorian reminds himself that if they'd gone to war with Aeskerat, innocents like her would have gotten caught in the middle. She doesn't deserve to suffer for someone else's mistakes. She came for sanctuary, and only after Hyacinth ensured that Hilda understood staying was a choice did they let her bleed for them.

He has the sheets dumped in the hallway by the time she comes back with an entire cart laden with different candles and incense, a conflicting jumble of aromas that will surely give rise to a horridly pungent air.

"Master Dorian," she asks, wringing her hands as he nearly breaks the broom sweeping the floor, "can I do anything else?"

"Soak the bedding and be sure it's clean, please, then the rest of your night is yours."

She brightens and bounces on her toes. "Gladly!"

When Dorian lifts the mattress to flip, he spots a kelp-bound bundle hidden beneath the bed. The mattress falls to the wayside as he unties the twine holding everything together.

It's all of Elias's sketches, some more detailed and intricate than others. The castle, the kitchens, the Grand Hall, hands and faceless poses and two pages of eyes, various objects that struck his fancy and scenes he sat out enjoying to observe.

Then. Two figures on a sofa, one smudged, their positions unmistakable.

Dorian knows it's him—Elias wouldn't have gotten away with drawing anyone else like that—and it's not the only one. None captures his face head-on, only from the side or looking down or turned away completely, all rough and many incomplete, drawn over the two months Elias spent here.

Dorian never noticed. He knows Elias likes to draw but never caught himself as his inspiration, and now he doesn't know what to do with them. Burning them would be a shame, but the pages reek. He resolves to find a spot to tuck them somewhere in the library, where they'll collect dust with the rest of the books, then goes about lighting some forty-odd candles and incense to cleanse the room.

Unbidden, Dorian's fingers touch his lips, the feel and taste of Elias long gone from them. That... that naive *fool*. The last thing Dorian wanted was for Elias to come around by some warped sense of gratitude or indebtedness. Worse, for him to start negotiating with himself, twisting his wants and needs around in service of whatever he thought his captors wanted to hear.

It's the only explanation Dorian has for how Elias's feelings evolved so dramatically, or... or he's forgotten what it's like to live beneath the boot of marching time. He can't say.

As soon as the wax starts to melt, releasing vanilla and sugar and spices of all kinds into the air, he blows out the wicks so it's only the pungent smoke left behind, and leaves, closing the door to let the room marinate until all care for Elias has fled the castle like the last dawn to grace the horizon.

Elias imagined bloody dungeons, slaves living in their own detritus, stale bread for his one meal a day, a thick collar around his neck and chain between his ankles.

He didn't expect how clean it is. It's dark, so dark he's blind to his hands in front of his face in some halls, but it's not dirty. No finger paintings or lavish decorations for the slaves' quarters. If they had existed once, the coven must've stripped them from the walls. He's used to endless bland stone, though—aside from the faintly smoky, leathery smell.

The castle may belong to vampires, but it's just another cave to Elias.

Elias's hair is the first to go when he wakes in the Aeskerat keep, followed by his Tanarang clothes. What he's left with leaves his neck cold. It's long enough still to grab, to drag him around by, but too short to hide behind.

They move him like an oversized glass doll when he still can't walk from Quinn's kick, and tend to his wounds in the dark. They shave his stubble and bathe him despite his protests, and dress him in fresh, warm furs. When the chains do come, he's given socks to spare his ankles from chafing.

This, the idea of *socks* to keep him comfy even as he knows it's really so he doesn't get sick and die on them, is better than his clan gave their vampire. It's not a cell, not a spile in his neck. Tanarang won't be coming to save him, but if this is the worst Aeskerat can do to him without risking damage to their food, then this isn't so bad.

He's left on a board of a bed with his knee propped up when light finally comes, the lone candle bright enough to make him squint and look away.

"Skittish already?" the new, buttery voice asks. "I was told you'd grown used to vampires."

A weight drops beside him, and Elias gets a good look at the vampire with harsh shadows across his face. A strong, smooth jaw, sleek black hair held back with a headband of molars and incisors from a variety of animals, a choker of teeth around his neck to match.

The vampire smiles, resting the candle on his thigh, and it's neither cruel nor hungry, just polite. "I'm Gregori, Grandsire of Aeskerat."

"Elias," he greets warily. Gregori, like the fledgling he met, has blood-red face paint on his forehead and cheeks. Unnerving, yes, but Elias expected a more intimidating figure to lead a coven that scares all the vampires in Tanarang so thoroughly. His deep voice betrays him, because without it, Elias might've guessed him a lady with the dainty decorations.

Gregori pats Elias's uninjured knee and sets the candle out of the way on the floor. "Have the good hosts at Tanarang given the wrong impression of us?"

"You did almost declare war with them over a fledgling and one contested meal."

Gregori chuckles humorlessly, and when he sits back and the light hits his furs, Elias thinks they might have belonged to a bear, all thick and coarse. No—they certainly did. The boxy metal carving of a bear's face clasps his cloak.

"Jacobi is very good with words, I'm afraid, and our reputation precedes us. I would not throw my family against those gates over one tiny meal," he goads, "but little Amaranth doesn't know that."

Elias's eyes narrow. The rest of Tanarang might've been all too happy to buy their peace with his life, but he believes Dorian's fear of this coven. "You got what you asked for."

"Indeed." Gregori's grin widens, and the candlelight flickers on his fangs. "Two rules, remember them well. The first: Waste not. Winters are long and bitter in the North, and we only bleed when necessary." Gregori waves to his socks like they're woven gold. "The second: Only make promises you can keep. Hold to yours and my coven will hold to theirs, but break yours?" He *tsks* and waggles a finger. "Your word is precious. Waste not."

Gregori stands, arms folded behind his back. "Filthy livestock breeds disease, disease breeds sickly blood. Cleanliness, then, is paramount. No dirty soles, no grime under your nails, no crumbs between your teeth. *Clean*, little piggy, before every meal. Fresh breath, scrubbed skin, and *no* smelly leftovers from doing your business. If you can't maintain my standards, it will be done for you."

Gregori's heels click as he bounces, leering over him. "Am I clear?"

Elias swallows dryly, shying away from him. "Yes."

"Yes *what*, piggy?"

"Yes... Master Gregori." The title tastes sour on his tongue. Elias manages it nonetheless. It's a word, nothing more. He doesn't have to mean it or believe it. He knows a bite is coming too, but still, this is it? Gregori can't hurt him beyond repair. They can't hurt any of their slaves. He'll get it over with and carry on. Gregori can take all the blood he wants, but he's never going to earn Elias's respect. *This is the worst you can do.*

The vampire leans close and inhales deeply, huffing in disdain. "You still smell of Tanarang." Sharp nails dig into his jaw, brown eyes rake over him like he's a prized cow up for bidding, then

Gregori smirks, thumbs rough on his lip. "Let's wash away that blight, shall we?"

The vampire shoves him onto his back, his hold an anvil on his chest. Elias pictures Cera with serenity on her face and assumes she must find serenity in pain because Gregori's teeth in his neck wrench a whimper from his throat. His hands aren't bound but they might as well be for all the good they do fighting back.

Gregori's slimy tongue on his bleeding neck, the suffocating weight of his body, the horribly moist slurping right beneath his ear—it's all too much. The vampire doesn't let a drop escape, and the healing passes of his tongue give Elias a full-body shudder. It is a claim, in every definition. It burrows itself into his brain, a diseased tick, and he has nothing pleasant to squish it with.

"Hmm." Gregori sits back, hands on his knees. "You're iron-deficient. Pity."

The vampire sweeps to his feet and Elias rolls onto his side, scrubbing away the leftover saliva slicking his skin with his sleeve. The movement jostles his knee and he hisses, curling into a loose ball.

"Oh, and in case the noble Tanarang didn't explain the claim to you, you're mine now, piggy, and no one else's." His clicking heels fade away.

This, he resigns to himself as his grip on his courage splinters, *this isn't even the beginning of the worst they can do.*

Elias cries.

Dorian spends more time with the guard than he used to, watching the moons once again grow fatter and thinner in a parade of monotony, and if anyone has anything to say about it, they don't say it within earshot.

Amaranth, Hyacinth, and Elphaba ordered him not to stage a rescue attempt—for his coven's sake, for Elphaba's family's sake, and for Elias's. If his plan were to fail, Elias would suffer the consequences, and since he can't take Castle Aeskerat alone, Dorian stays put. All he can do is hope that Elias isn't depending on help that isn't coming, and guard the wall.

Markus is the only one who neither acts like Dorian needs to get over himself nor walks as if on cracking ice. The Southern vampire challenges him to archery trickshots to break up the tedium of the watch and talks about whatever catches his interest, whatever the topic may be.

They're separated by almost one hundred and seventy years, plus two days' sailing on a good wind—Markus is from the mainland that dwarfs Kenoa on most maps—but he's the closest Dorian has to home.

Markus catches Dorian staring eastward and asks bluntly, "Are you upset that he's gone, or upset that you couldn't stop it?"

"What's the difference?"

"One is his fault, one is yours."

Dorian glances back at him. He knows Markus isn't the most attuned to emotional turmoil, but... "Is there no one in this castle who cares that we sold a person on a gamble for a crime he didn't commit? *I* staked the fledgling."

"We didn't sell him for a crime he didn't commit," Markus argues. "We sold him to protect everyone else from a fight they didn't ask for."

Dorian folds his arms on the wall and scowls. "If we'd sent Jacobi home to tell Gregori that I'm the guilty party, they would have taken their horse and been done with it."

"Or they wouldn't have, and Tanarang blood really would be

on your hands."

Dorian gnashes his teeth, unable to find a worthy rebuttal. Fledgling or no, Elias was a... cheap price to pay in the grand scheme of things. He sighs and pinches his brow. "It's not Elias," he mutters, "it's letting Aeskerat get away with this."

Markus hums. "Maybe he'll prove as unsavory to them as he did to us and his death will be quick."

Which is not as comforting a thought as Markus likely thinks it should be.

"Can we not talk about this anymore? I'm not going after him. I don't need a guard to keep me from doing something stupid."

Markus doesn't answer and Dorian looks back, watching his head cocked in thought. Dorian expects some profound philosophical statement on the nature of life and death. Instead, Markus digs through a little pouch at his hip and offers a pressed strip of congealed blood. "It's a new recipe."

Dorian takes the jerky. Markus doesn't bring Elias up again.

Instead, he goes on about his experiments on the limits of what they can taste before it turns to ash. He's been relying on Dorian as his taste guru of late. "I have blood pops," Markus offered once, showing off frozen red skewers, and though they're edible even a while longer than fresh blood left to sit and fester, vampires are rarely patient enough to wait around for novelty when it comes to food.

Still, the new texture on his tongue from the way the ice crystals melted was a treat.

Animals, too, have been fair game, but in their experience after the Great Freeze, keeping animals alive and healthy is more effort than they're worth. Beasts of burden without fields to plow sit around, constantly needing attention and food to stay healthy, and they can never be tamed enough to bleed calmly, even with the needles.

Snow flurries blow by, and they're bored enough to try finding identical snowflakes until Markus muses, "Do you think we can eat people? Like, carve out a liver and munch on it? Would the entire thing turn to ash, or the tissue, and which tissue?"

"You could probably munch on a vampire liver," Dorian says, hardly wanting to try but what else are they supposed to talk about? "And it would grow back. I think the Son Kir coven dabbles on occasion."

He raises a hand, pointing skyward. "I could try eating my own, just to check." But then he shies away. "No, that's stupid."

"Vampirism is a curse," Dorian reminds him. "You eating yourself would be a worse punishment than that. It wouldn't be a reliable control for your experiment either."

"Hmm, true." Markus gasps. "Could—"

"No."

Markus joins him, Quinn, and Blane down to the water to collect some of the kelp washing ashore in droves. Quinn's black braids, interwoven with thin strips of blue silks and satin and pearls they found on the rocks, reach her knees. She piles them up in a scarf atop her head, safe from and far above the stinky brine.

Blane, half a world away from the cattle prairie lowlands he'd called home, drops a tangle of kelp down the back of her jerkin. Quinn squeals in an un-Quinn-like manner, squirming and dancing about as Blane cackles. Dorian gives the ensuing splash battle a wide berth.

Markus watches the two of them with rapt attention, head cocked like he's collecting mental notes on who to prank with his own seaweed spider. Quinn socks Blane in the shoulder hard enough to knock him on his ass, and all's forgiven with soggy hugs and an apologetic kiss to her neck.

Quinn, for her part, had pulled Dorian aside to apologize, but only for letting Kymiria convince her not to talk to him first. "We can't help who we care for," she'd said, "but we can help what we do about it."

Above, the guard lower and raise baskets along the wall, doing most of the heavy lifting while they splash through the shallows. Markus carries on with his musings. "Do already fanged animals grow a second set when we turn them?"

Dorian almost trips, tangled up in a stalk of kelp. "Like, what? Cats?"

"Snakes."

"I think they keep what they had, like we do."

Markus *tsks* in disappointment and trills his fingers on his chin. "I will find one someday. Do you think you can send for one from the South once the merchants return?"

Dorian smiles to himself. That Markus turned for no more profound a reason than to see what death feels like continues to feed his hunger for answers even these decades after his death. "I'll see what I can do."

Markus grins and gives a soft *Yay* and carries on with their task. When he's not flitting about with spontaneous curiosity on a path impossible to follow, he's pleasant company. Markus never utters words like, *It'll all be okay over there*, or any variation of such attempts at placating him. He fills the silence with everything else. Dorian doesn't care what anyone else thinks—Markus has much to say, if they'd let him talk.

"Do you think anyone remembers us?" Markus asks a few moons later, lounging on the wall with one leg dangling as he whittles more arrows out of Northern ice. "Do you think we got headstones?"

"We might have." Kenoans used to paint plates for the dead and mount them on the walls of their homes. For all he knows, the whole house he grew up in is gone, his plate with it.

Overhead, a meteor shower rains streaks of platinum. Markus sings a jingle to himself in his own language, then asks how many other people Dorian thinks are watching the same sky.

He doesn't judge Dorian for using the guard as a distraction. He seems to understand that Dorian isn't giving anyone the cold shoulder. He's not hiding, everyone knows where he is. He doesn't blame Kymiria, but he knows they don't agree and doesn't want to argue with her. A month since Amaranth sold Elias to keep the peace, half as long as Elias's entire tenure at Tanarang, and he feels like a blip rather than a whole person against his four hundred years of existence watching so many other blips come and go.

Selling Elias like livestock without giving him the respect of telling him, though? They could have done better. Should have done better. So no, he still has nothing to say to Kymiria.

She's kept herself busy with other partners, and far too many of them gossip not-so-subtly that they're *over*—not to be malicious, he thinks, but for their own idle entertainment, as annoying as it is. Henri, one of their younger kin, has his own opinions to share as they shave and whittle Northern ice from the Holdfast one cloudless evening. Henri makes more arrows. Dorian makes a fawn.

"She's probably doing it to get you jealous," Henri suggests.

Dorian doesn't bother looking up, trying to get the skinny legs right without snapping them. "She's not. She can have whoever, whenever she wants, as can I."

"But you're together. Doesn't that defeat the whole purpose?"

"What purpose?"

Henri shrugs sheepishly. "Of... being together?"

"We have an eternity ahead of us. Why should either of us limit each other to exclusivity?"

"But she was jealous of the yearling."

It's then that Dorian notices exactly what he's carving, and Henri gives the fawn a pointed look. "She didn't resent Elias stealing my attention. She just didn't think Elias deserved it."

Henri *hmphs*. "She's not wrong. Cave rat didn't know how good he had it here."

And with that, Dorian gets up to find Markus, who grabs his own ice chunk and asks how to carve a cat.

When Dorian does take a break, because they both need to feed eventually, Markus waits for him at the door of the lounge. "I want to try something," he says in that studious way he has. Markus needs spectacles for reading but rarely wears them, yet still pushes the bridge of his nose where phantom frames rest when he thinks.

The *something* turns out to be an invitation to Markus's room, and there Markus finds his reading lenses. He's got more books and apparatuses than space for a bed, his sheets and pillows tossed in a corner. "You like sex, right?"

Dorian's cheeks puff with a laugh. Markus asked in the same tone one might offer extra cheese as a garnish. "With people I care for. Not strangers, and not often."

Markus blinks owlishly at him, an open book pressed to his chest. It's an anatomy book, title partly hidden by his arm. "Am I someone you care for?"

Dorian shrugs. "In a friendly way. But if this is an experiment, what did you have in mind?"

"Sex."

He laughs again and rubs his face. No minced words, straight to the point. "I meant the mechanics you have in mind. You have done this before, yes?"

Markus wrinkles his nose and answers with a cryptic and dissatisfied *yes*. "I'm not all that fond of it. It's quite a lot of work." Whatever's on the pages he's peeking at pinches Markus's face further. "But I haven't bothered with anyone I cared about before, and now the opportunity presents itself. And I know you won't tease."

No one better have made fun of him or Dorian would shove a Northern arrow where the sun's never shone.

"I have a bed," he offers.

Why not? If it's bad, it's not about him anyway, and that Markus sought Dorian out of the entire castle to trust with this is, admittedly, flattering. "A bed would improve the comfort of things, yes."

"Change your mind anytime you want, no jokes."

It's not... well, erm, *good*, but half the time it's not ecstasy anyway. Markus is picky and indecisive, and if Dorian were anyone else, he'd probably kick him off the bed to stop wasting his time. Markus bows out completely halfway through with flustered apologies and promises of *It's not you, it's me.*

They return to their posts like nothing happened.

The gods robbed the North of the ephemeral liquid light that graces the sky near the pole, but at the right time of year, on a clear night, a silver-purple cloud of stars arcs overhead.

Markus shows him a stack of star chart scrolls and points out different constellations invented by the culture that wrote them. Neither can read the language, but the charts need no explanation. He traces a hare in the sky and Dorian tries to follow his finger.

"You are the closest friend I have here," Markus says out of nowhere. "I don't think many others have the patience for me."

"We're immortal," Dorian says. "All we have is time to be patient."

Markus sits right next to him at the next lavish birthday party to grace the Grand Hall a week later. "I would like a do-over," he says, shy but determined. "A proper follow-through this time."

"You owe me nothing," Dorian insists, yet they duck out early.

Markus seems to intend to fulfill his promise by moving as quickly as possible, an unpleasant experience for them both. Dorian figures it's not the mess, it's the overload of stimulation, the too much too fast of it.

"Can I?" Dorian asks once Markus has calmed down, resting a cautious hand on his thigh. "Just my hand. If you still want to do this."

Markus gnaws at his lip. "There is a way to enjoy this. I will figure it out."

"There's a way for your body to enjoy it, yes, but your mind isn't obligated to agree. Nothing wrong with that." That Markus does want to enjoy it, though, and is trying hard to force himself, is what keeps Dorian musing on a different approach instead of trying to convince him he's perfect the way he is.

"Do you want me to leave?" Markus picks at his thumbs, voice rough like he has something to be guilty for.

Dorian expected to have a degree of detachment. Markus is his friend and this is scientific exploration. Sating curiosity. Markus doesn't *do* wooing and fluttery feelings. But while it might've begun as an impulsive venture, Markus's gap in understanding himself is troubling.

He removes his hand and fixes both their clothes in lieu of an answer. "No, of course not. I want to help you figure this out."

"Can we just…talk? For a while?" *A while* takes on new ambiguity when they're both dead and timeless and the cycle of morning to night is broken. Markus leaves to gather his favorite books and comfort objects to fiddle with, arranging them deliberately, like a doll collection around Dorian's bed.

They talk, and no one comes to drag them back to the party or the wall. Markus isn't one for pretty descriptions and poetry, bluntly spiraling around different topics. Growing up in Balekesh. Studying under stodgy, self-important doctors who only experimented to confirm their hypotheses instead of from a desire to learn and be humbled. How the church hated the *defiling* of the dead for *science*.

Markus starts to get technical, impassioned, as he criticizes his old teachers and points emphatically at diagrams in his books, and most of it goes well over Dorian's head. While Dorian can't completely follow the conversation, he interjects with helpful comments like, *Oh, absolutely, of course they're asinine,* and Markus eagerly agrees.

The way he talks, Dorian can listen for hours, chin propped on his fists and feet swaying behind him. Markus keeps pushing his lenses back in place when they slip, missing the bridge half the time and smudging the glass. Dorian will take them, clean them on the sleeve of a satin robe hanging off the bed post, and set them back on his face.

The last time he does it, Dorian's fingers brush his cheek, and Markus's steady stream of words stutters to a halt as if he's remembering only now he's here for more than talking. His cheeks tint, an apology on his lips that Dorian doesn't give him the chance to voice.

"Can I try something else?" Dorian asks, gently moving a stack of books aside to scoot closer.

"Like what?"

"Well, most of these dalliances do begin with a kiss or two. You jumped straight to the big stuff."

Markus keeps hold of a silvery tool that looks like tiny tongs clutched to his chest, his gaze drifting over Dorian. He nods and slowly relaxes, lying back with a hunger in his eyes. He tugs a little too hard on Dorian's hair and jams a knee against his side twice, but Dorian ignores it all, trailing kisses down his throat.

"Do you like compliments? You're very good at this—it wasn't in my books."

"I might not have a fancy formal education," Dorian murmurs against his neck, "but I like to think I make up for it with my four centuries of experience."

They do end up finding things Markus likes in small doses. With half a dozen confirmations that touching is okay once he starts to enjoy himself, it doesn't end in a half-finished disaster like last time. Markus's voice turns light and breathy, body all boneless on the bed.

"I don't love it," he decides, "but I like that it's you."

"That's okay, too."

Markus doesn't snuggle or cuddle or get all mushy with his feelings. He doesn't care if Dorian finds a different partner when such inclinations arise, which they don't. But when the other vampire stands a little closer sometimes, when he makes sure Dorian's quiver is always full and his arrows always in immaculate condition, when he saves him a spot in the Grand Hall and occasionally fiddles with Dorian's braids, it's *something*.

Elias doesn't cross his mind until they're passing by his old room on the way to the lounge, its door propped open with a broom and dustpan. It still smells like the cocktail of smoke, and the wave of guilt for forgetting about him stops Dorian in his tracks.

Markus waits a few paces ahead. "Dorian?"

"I forgot about him."

Markus drifts back over and glances inside the empty room. "By your tone, I know you're upset, but I don't understand why."

Why? Dorian laughs humorlessly and steps away. "I abandoned him."

"But you didn't."

"Yes—"

"Not getting killed in a suicide mission is not the same as giving up," Markus insists. "If you switched places, how would you feel if he got himself killed, or started the war that sacrificing you was meant to prevent?"

But Elias doesn't know that. Dorian shakes his head, still at a loss with himself. "I can't believe I forgot."

Markus moves the broom and dustpan aside and lets the door close to a crack. He wrings his hands and stutter-steps forward. "I am not the best with these kinds of things, but you seem happier lately. What happened to him was unfair and undeserved, but if you can't do anything to fix it, and truly, it wasn't your fault, I think your guilt is misplaced."

"Misplaced?" He folds and unfolds his arms, then shuts the door the rest of the way. "I'm here with you while he's suffering as a blood slave, or dead, and I forgot about him."

Markus frowns and worries his lip. "Do you love him?"

"No." Dorian huffs and holds a hand up. "*No.*"

"Are you sure?"

If he thinks about their short time together—compared to the decades with Kymiria and even this shorter time with Markus, so easy to connect with because he's uncomplicated—he's independent and clear-headed and isn't wrought with the turmoil of a clansman who's never seen the sky before. Elias is messy and, more importantly, mortal. It was never going to work. *But does that mean I didn't love him?*

"I loved... who I thought he could become." And that's it, isn't it? "Not who he is. And that's not fair to him or me." Elias had potential—*has* potential. Expecting him to live up to it or waiting around for him to fulfill it was never a basis for love.

Stiffly, Markus reaches for his hand and squeezes. "You're allowed to mourn what could have been, but not if it means neglecting what is. You're happy—with me? I hope? Happier, at least? Eternity is a long time to always eat last."

Dorian *hmphs* and squeezes back. "You said you were bad at this."

"We can hold a vigil," Markus suggests, rising up on his toes. "For what almost was. Would that make it better?"

... Yeah. Yeah, it would. Dorian kisses his cheek. If they switched places, he would want Elias to have this. Maybe Elias wouldn't. Elias probably hates him now for not coming to save him, would probably rather see him bitter and guilty for another decade as penance. *I did try*, Dorian reminds himself. Elias's biases got in the way.

"Food first."

"Can I sit next to you? Tannys said it was okay." Markus laces his hands and holds them beneath his chin, like his whole week would be complete if Dorian agrees.

"Of course you can."

Markus beams.

Elias wishes he could turn, if only to keep Gregori out of his nightmares. Most of the time, the Grandsire of Aeskerat is all easy smiles, a level head, and casual conversation. The castle is depressingly cold, and when he shivers on his bed in the dark, the chill nips at his skin like Gregori's teeth.

There's nothing to fill his ample free time except sleeping or staring at the walls and the snowfall. Time passes above the ground as indistinguishably as it does in the cave. His hair grows enough to tickle his eyelashes, the only gauge of spent weeks he has.

The coven leaves its livestock to fend for themselves more than Tanarang did. They have their own kitchens and quarters in the servants' wing. But there's no mingling, no relaxing, no whiff of any vampire getting comfy with the pigs unless it's there to feed or satisfy carnal need.

One of Gregori's lieutenants, Julian, doesn't care what time it is or where he is, having his way with whomever he wants. When that means taking over the baths and forcing Elias to scramble out of the way lest he bear witness, Julian goads him with a sardonic laugh. "How else am I supposed to spend eternity if not reveling in the only hedonism that won't turn to ash in my mouth?"

None of his partners seems unwilling, and perhaps Julian cares as much about their pleasure as he does his own which is... not terrible. Or they're all fantastic actors who know the price of not pretending like he's the best lay they've ever had. Elias won't volunteer himself to confirm.

He's loud, though, hooting and howling, and there's not a corner in the castle Elias has found where he can't hear it.

There is no lounge, no meal schedule. Some follow their masters around like shadows, snacked on whenever a vampire desires. He's grateful in some ways that Gregori seems to tolerate having his piggies around only by necessity, not for entertainment or indulgence.

As far as he can tell, Gregori is the only one obsessed with cleanliness, but because he's in charge, everything must be scrubbed raw even if it goes nowhere near him. Elias gets no warning to prepare before Gregori comes sniffing out a meal. None of them does. It's an expectation that they're *always* ready, no matter where they are or what they're doing.

For fear of things getting worse, Elias does everything he can to meet those standards at the cost of regular meals and sleep. He befriends none of the other skittish blood slaves, even as he tries to offer commiserating smiles. Rarely do they speak. There's always eavesdroppers with better hearing. No secrets exist between them, no loyalty. If Elias screws up in the kitchen, he's ratted out before the mess can hit the floor. The reminder of why, as bitter as he grows, is displayed around the castle grounds. Skeletons hang in all manner of horrifying ways within view of every window, dead blood slaves robbed of their teeth, fingers, toes.

Elias has seen firsthand the consequences of falling short of Gregori's expectations. Luni, afraid of her own shadow, got pulled away from nursing a newborn with sick all over her chest by Julian. She was his claim, not Gregori's, but they happened to be in the same room when she arrived. Gregori lost his mind over the mess, and the demonic screech that thundered through the castle walls still keeps Elias from ever finding peaceful rest. He hid with his hands over his ears like everyone else because there was no helping Luni. When he had no excuse to keep hiding, he found that Luni had joined the skeletons outside. He doesn't know if Gregori killed her or if she threw herself off the highest wall, but there she hangs still, her infant passed off to someone else.

So long as he plays nice, Gregori is... not *kind*, but he's not violent. Unnecessary roughness runs the risk of infection, and Castle Aeskerat hungers for resources of every kind, medicine nonexistent. *Waste not*, the vampire reminds him incessantly. He takes what he needs, licks the wound closed, and sends Elias away.

If he wants to escape, and he does lest his body decorate the castle grounds for the next century and beyond, he needs information. The most important piece of which? Whether all of Castle Aeskerat is loyal to this maniac.

Amaranth enjoys universal respect from her entire coven, despite her age, despite her size, despite her stature. She'd earned it. There's no way every vampire here isn't at least annoyed by Gregori's fits, but if he keeps them safe and fed, their borders unchallenged...

Well, they're the ones spending eternity with him.

Gregori doesn't talk to him. He's never present in any meetings and the vampire doesn't go on long rambling monologues when he's hungry. Feeding, for him, is a chore, not a relief.

So if Elias is going to figure out which way is up in this place, then, he reasons, he needs something better to offer than blood.

He's dragging himself from the baths back to his pile of furs on the ground that constitute his bed, when Jacobi practically melts out of the shadows in the corridor to leer at him. Elias gasps and hops back, arms pinwheeling as he trips over his cloak.

Jacobi chuckles. "Little rabbit."

"S-sorry. I didn't see you there."

"I know."

Elias smacks his lips and sidesteps. "Don't let me keep you."

"Have you been outside?"

"Outside the building or outside the wall?" Either is a stupid question. Yes, he's walked between the main castle and the rest of the grounds. No, of course he hasn't been past the wall.

Jacobi smirks like there's some secret third option that he's not privy to. "I'll show you."

As far as Elias has gathered, Jacobi is Gregori's other lieutenant. Him, Julian, and possibly a quiet lady vampire who likes sharpening knives around the other blood slaves. The scrape of her whetstone is always annoyingly loud.

Jacobi leads him outside, and normally Elias picks his way around snow piles and slush. The vampire doesn't, treading toward a guard tower straight through a heap of fresh powder in his comfy boots.

Elias refuses to give him the satisfaction of discomfort. No, the cold biting straight through his socks doesn't bother him at all. The steps aren't slippery with ice. Imaginary thorns aren't pricking his toes by the time he reaches the top.

It would be a nice view, purple mountains sleeping giants stretching all the way to the west. Tanarang is on the other side somewhere.

"Janneah didn't have to die, you know." Jacobi digs around in his pockets for a little paper tube and a match. He lights one end of the tube and sticks the other between his teeth, breathing in smoke.

"Who?"

"The fledgling Dorian killed." Jacobi leans on the stone all chipped and eroded, the swirls once chiseled in it barely defined. "If he'd subdued her, this whole mess would have simply been about a stolen horse, and we all would have had a grand laugh at Janneah's stupidity."

Uh-huh. "What is that?" Elias points at the smoking tube.

Jacobi blinks and chuckles, nearly losing it over the wall. "Doesn't do a damn thing for me anymore, but it's already ash and smoke." Jacobi offers it, balanced between his fingers.

Elias shakes his head and debates sitting on his cloak to spare his aching feet.

Jacobi shrugs and blows more smoke. He is, for all his schmoozing and self-importance, hard to pin down. He, like Gregori, doesn't seem interested in bedding his slaves—or he finds the living too nauseating to even contemplate. He just seems cranky when he's not posturing, and what a miserable eternity that must be.

"Makes you wonder, doesn't it?" Jacobi asks. "If he did it because he hated her or because he cares about you. 'Course, you two'd just met, so I doubt it."

Elias rolls his eyes. No, he didn't wonder at all about Dorian's intention with the violent fledgling, and Jacobi's attempt to drive a wedge between them is laughably transparent. "If that's all, can I—"

Jacobi fists his tunic and, in a blink, has Elias dangling over the wall.

Elias clings to his forearm, numb toes scrambling for purchase on the lip of the stone as his chains rattle. "Jacobi—"

The vampire cocks his head. "Quite arrogant for a pig. Think yourself *oh* so important, don't you? Thought yourself safe because Dorian didn't eat you. Safe because only Gregori has eaten you. Safe because tradition demands I can't eat you."

"No, no, I don't. I'm sorry—"

Jacobi's fist relaxes long enough for Elias to squeal and claw into his arm, eyes squeezed shut. "Overconfidence is a killer no one ever sees coming, no matter how smart or important or special they think themself."

Elias nods rapidly. "You're absolutely right."

Jacobi scoffs and deposits him back on the walkway. "Go get warm before you lose your toes."

Elias hobbles back inside and tries to push Jacobi from his mind. What he said might be true, but if he'd thrown Elias off the wall and told Gregori he fell trying to escape, Gregori wouldn't believe it... would he?

The next time Gregori wakes him up for a meal, Elias tests the waters. The vampire notices immediately when, afterward, Elias doesn't commence his usual quick escape. "What is it?"

Gregori's lavish room, the tower's highest quarters, is the only thing about him that reminds Elias this monster used to be quite like him. Paintings of cityscapes and silky tapestries and statues, rugs and wallpaper and bedding with the richest colors he's ever seen. "Can I borrow a book?"

Gregori's brows shoot to his hairline. "You're literate?"

"I was my clan's Keeper."

The vampire waves at the small bookshelf dismissively. "Don't touch the pages with your greasy fingers."

"Yes, Master."

The book he picks blindly is some religious text with froofy language and handwriting that he can't decipher, but the border illustrations intrigue him. Big cats and deer-like creatures with sleek horns and stick legs.

The drawings remind him of Dapple. The calf wouldn't be fully grown yet even if they found a mother to help feed her. The persistence of his clan remains unknown, and with each passing moon, the ache twinges a little less. If alive, Maewag would feel similarly. His mother would have mourned and buried herself in the garden with the seershrooms, Dapple now her only legacy. All his soot sketches would have washed away in the humidity, and they never kept paper records. By now, the new Keeper would have erased his old markings and started over, nothing left of him in the cave but memory.

He returns the book in immaculate condition, and Gregori surprises him by letting him borrow another. "What clan were you?"

"Maewag."

"Hmm. Don't know that one."

"We didn't get out much."

This book is old milling ledgers, and a ludicrous idea strikes him. Can Gregori read? Or does he pick the books for the same reason Elias does—because they're shiny and colorful? The ledger is covered with a rich green leather and gold ink, eye-catching despite its dreary contents.

The bites sting less as Elias grows used to them. He debates on pretending to like them, to try to seduce Gregori even, but one misstep could earn him a spot next to Luni.

Seduce him with his body, no, but with his mind...?

Elias risks a misstep for a blind leap, nursing his sore wrist. He's on his fourth book now, run through Gregori's tiny collection. Gregori hasn't let his guard down, but he doesn't keep the disgust off his face. Or the discomfort. "You don't seem to like this very much," Elias ventures, indicating his bitten wrist, "or at least the cost of having it."

Gregori lounges back on his massive bed, his furs spread beneath him lest they get stained with his meal. "A minor inconvenience that keeps the piggies in their place."

"Sure," Elias ventures. Kymiria's snide remark that she could smell his arousal rings in his ears as Gregori can no doubt hear the skip in his heart, smell the beading sweat as he draws in on himself. "But maybe not an unavoidable one."

The vampire tilts his head, dark eyes narrowing. "You're growing rather bold."

"Not at all," Elias assures, waving his hands. "I just—I might have a solution that helps the both of us."

"Why would I want to help you?" Gregori asks frankly, as if the notion of taking his boot off a claim's neck for even a moment is simply preposterous. He's listening, though, because he hasn't thrown Elias out the door yet.

Elias scans the room for something to draw with and comes up empty, so he clears his throat instead and tries to smile. "The Tanarang are insufferable, yes—"

"Flattery and false commiseration will get you nowhere, piggy," Gregori chastises. "I know they treat their livestock with a looser leash."

"Loose enough to send me here when the bathwater got a little too warm," Elias counters. Gregori smirks and waves for him to continue like he's watching one of the children's hyperbolic performances. "They have their ways. One of those lets them feed without ever touching their livestock. No need to taste their skin or lick the wound closed."

Gregori still doesn't throw him out, foot tapping impatiently.

Elias clears his throat again and rucks up his sleeve to press at the crease of his elbow. "A hollow needle, right here. The blood pumps out and into whatever vessel you want, and it leaves behind a scant drop before it scabs."

"To avoid the claim?" Gregori asks skeptically.

"Why does it matter if you get what you want out of it?"

"It's less painful for you, yes?"

"Yes," Elias agrees. "I think. I didn't actually try it, but I watched it done to an aging woman. The rest of your coven can keep doing as they please, they need not know. I'm already yours."

Gregori mutters under his breath and sweeps to his feet. Elias, clearing far out of Gregori's way, catches only one word. *Elphaba.* He knows her? Elias tries to picture him mingling with Tanarang, or Elphaba reprimanding him with her wooden spoon. She's got several decades on him, and if the Tanarang matriarch has always been so assertive and unimpressed by coven drama, Elias can imagine their first meeting. It almost makes him snicker.

The vampire sets his hands on his hips, tapping his foot once more. "A hollow needle?"

"Yes. Someone learned to craft them in the South. I can draw—"

"Leave."

Elias recoils, staring at Gregori's back. He swallows thickly and complies, even as a *but* sits heavy on his tongue. He never waits for the vampire to ask twice. "Yes, Master."

He thinks that's the end of it, that he danced too close to the candle and got the doors shut in his face. The next time he wakes, though, a thin slab of stone and stick of chalk rest at his feet.

Chapter 10:
King of the Hill

"This is an urchin, from the coast. Will its spines suffice?"

Elias had been given a rare respite while Gregori disappeared from the castle without any entourage. When he returned, the vampire ordered Elias to his quarters and locked the door, presenting the purple-black creature in a cloth.

Elias reaches now to inspect the strange animal and Gregori slaps his hand back. "Careful," he warns, "it's poisonous."

Elias nods and gently works a spine free. It's not as thin or sleek as the metal ones, but it does look hollow. "Possibly," he mutters. "There was a whole apparatus attached that I don't know how to recreate, and it might be too thick."

Gregori plucks the spine from his fingers and loosens his sleeve. "I am immune. Test it on me."

Elias blinks in surprise and nods shakily. "I haven't tried this before. Do you want to sit so I can see?"

"Piggies and your terrible vision," Gregori mocks, then joins him on the bed. His pale skin should mean it's easy to find a vein, but Elias only has candlelight to work with. He squints and prods at Gregori's arm from wrist to elbow, squishing a tiny bulge of a vein beneath his thumb.

"It might take a few tries," Elias warns. He tilts his head and sticks his tongue in his cheek as he concentrates, pricking Gregori's skin thrice before blood spurts weakly through the spine. He huffs in relief and presents his work. "A cup or a bowl—"

Gregori ignores him and uses the spine like a short straw, sucking up his own blood before pulling it free. "It's quite tedious," he says, "when I am made for this."

"It takes practice, and the metal ones seemed more efficient."

"The ports are closed, and I'm not asking Tanarang to sell me anything." Gregori stands and discards the spine next to the rest of the urchin, thin shell snapped by his fingers. He regards the blood on Elias's hands and waves. "Waste not, piggy."

"W—really?" Gregori gives him a woefully flat look and Elias ducks away. The spicy warmth of vampire blood has his toes curling in his socks. Better than any furs or blankets or weak candles.

"Now leave."

"Yes, Master."

Elias finds food for himself, a rye roll that doesn't compare even to the scraps from Elphaba's kitchen. Julian chases another conquest into a dead end and Fawn squeals once she's caught. Elias clears out before they can get involved with each other right on the table.

Gregori is a monster, yes, but he could be worse—which is a problem. If his own coven doesn't see him as worth replacing, there goes any chance Elias has at escaping in the chaos.

Where he would go still eludes him anyway. He remembers where Castle Aeskerat sits on the map, impossibly far north and even farther from where he suspects his home cave to be. Tanarang isn't an option either. They'd never open their gates, and they'd hail Aeskerat to retrieve him themselves to avoid a fight. He wouldn't make it any farther alone now than he would have splitting off from Dorian when they first met, and he isn't about to become a blood slave of a third coven. There is no escape, but accepting that means accepting defeat.

He can... he can flee to the port towns and wait out the next two months until the ports open and smuggle himself south? He can bide his time with Gregori, lower the vampire's guard, and flee when the merchants return?

Yes, he thinks, *there's still hope.*

Any plans he has of eavesdropping on careless vampires are dashed time and again. Half the time they don't converse in words he understands, and those he does understand never amount to anything of import, no convenient, juicy gossip he can use. Once, he spies Julian staring up at Luni's corpse. Elias can't see his face, but Julian stands out there motionless and utterly alone for too long to simply be lost in thought.

Julian only bites those he's claimed, but he'll lie with anyone he wants—which is ridiculous and leaves the whole *claim* thing entirely up to semantics because sex surely leaves the same stink behind—and Elias *almost* offers himself up if only to try and get inside the vampire's head.

He goes as far as seeking Julian out to assess if he'll snap like Gregori, and the vampire turns him down before he can say a single word. "You, get out of here," Julian dismisses, batting the air. "Gregori will pitch a fit if he thinks anyone dares sully his claims." The dramatic roll of his eyes doesn't hide the discontented scowl on his face.

He's not the only one, either, the more Elias searches for it.

Jacobi masks his with backhanded praise. He's *too* nice, always agreeing with his grandsire whenever Elias does catch snippets of conversation.

Gregori wants to change up their scouting patterns to cover more land with fewer people? *Splendid, my thoughts exactly. It's terribly redundant.*

Gregori wants to send a party to raid a nearby clan for food? *Of course, when should we leave?*

Elias might be impressed with how blatantly obvious Jacobi's tactics are if Gregori cared one iota about his underlings stroking his ego. Whatever has Jacobi even bothering to butter up his grandsire, it seems like an exhausting waste of effort. Jacobi's kiss-assery grates on his ears and his slimy smile makes Elias irrationally irritated, and neither is ever directed at him.

Gregori rewards Elias's good behavior by unchaining his ankles, though he claims the scraping sound of the metal on the floor irked him. Elias gets sore striding up and down stairs and stretching out on the floor with his new freedom. He's not the first slave with the privilege—Luni and Fawn had earned theirs—but it's tangible progress, and being able to sprawl, such a simple act, might as well make him invincible.

The vampire takes him along to a balcony ringing the castle courtyard—a huge square surrounded by high walls that has been turned into a fighting ring. *Waste not* apparently doesn't apply to vampires gutting each other for fun. It's anything goes short of killing each other permanently. Elias is numb to the blood and gore now, numb as he can be watching it from a distance. He's now seen plenty of eyes and tongues clawed out, guts spilled over the ground, bones splintered through skin.

When a victor emerges, they take their spoils in teeth from their opponent, holding up bloodied molars and incisors victoriously, and stealing two from their collection. Elias eyes Gregori's impressive trove in the headband and the choker and his leathers.

Gregori's lieutenants have plenty of their own, but not as many as him.

He's not the only one who brought a snack to the spectacle. The latest loser limps away and tears into his meal to start healing himself. Elias wrings his hands, waiting for someone to challenge Gregori, however foolishly. Whether a vampire wins or loses, they have a manic bloodlust in their eyes, rough and needy with their fangs. Gregori chuckles and goads him. "Relax, Piggy. I don't lose."

As if that brings Elias any comfort. The losers might take out their humiliation on their blood slaves, but the winners still revel in their victories, and none has walked away unscathed.

Elias stands dutifully at Gregori's side, no mention of the needle project between them since the disappointing urchin, watching the fights unfold. After hours of this, vampires facing off with increasingly impressive fortitudes, Julian wins the last round and smiles up at Gregori like this is all routine. The grandsire raises his arms, longsword drawn, and rouses the crowd before jumping into the ring and landing like a boulder.

One of Jacobi's claims brings out a shiny new Northern ice spear. He wipes the blade with a cloth, tosses it to Julian, and the fight begins.

It's bloody. Like all the others. Gregori's light on his feet, toying with Julian, who toys equally with him. Elias imagines Gregori will win with cunning over brute strength. He doesn't have the build for a fight, if that still matters with vampires.

They lop off fingers and take eyes, nick ankles and legs, exploit every crack in the other's armor. Gregori snags Julian by his longer hair and slams his head into the ground so hard, Elias is surprised the other vampire's skull doesn't crumple on impact.

It's a speed and a strength he thinks neither Tanarang archers can compete with nor the children with their little stakes. These are vampires who fear no pain, sacrificing their own limbs to throw off their opponents. Tanarang... They use their courtyard for ice skating with the children. Aeskerat could have taken the castle whenever they wanted even if, as far as he can tell by the size of the crowd, Tanarang has the numbers over them.

So why haven't they?

Julian rises sluggishly, and though Gregori's prancing around gloating, he's not blinded by bravado. He kicks Julian's head back and the lieutenant flops hard with a choked groan. Gregori ends the massacre stabbing him through the eye and leaving it there. He's still gloating, bathing in the cheers of his coven, but there's something... off. He walks with heavier feet, shoulders pinched with agitation despite his victory, and doesn't take his prizes. He simply leaves.

Elias slips away to find him braced against a wall. "Master?"

Gregori shoves off the wall and holds the remainder of his own missing eye. "I told you, Piggy." He doesn't make for his chambers, heading to the baths instead. Elias follows at his heels. At his entrance, the scattered slaves scramble to give the grandsire reign of the room.

They're not heated, not like the natural pools beneath Castle Tanarang. Aeskerat's baths are dark and decorated sparsely with browns and reds, a far fall from the luscious mosses and lichen blooming over the pools. Every time Elias has to bathe, which is sometimes twice a day to satisfy Gregori's standards, he hates it. The water is merely melted ice and snow from outside and always leaves his skin red and joints achy from the cold.

Gregori limps toward one of the big basins, pulling at his leathers.

"Here, I can—"

"I don't need assistance." Still, he struggles, cursing under his breath.

"Waste not," Elias sasses, and does it for him. Gregori left his furs so they wouldn't get soiled in the fight, but his leathers are practically dyed red.

Gregori, unbothered by the cold, slips into the water with a hiss. His hair falls in his face, now free from the headband, and the choker joins the pile. An ugly old scar underlines his ribs, silvery pink and ragged. Vampires with scars isn't a notion Elias ever considered. Obviously, Gregori got it when he was alive, but it looks nasty enough to have been deadly. The vampire catches him staring and arches a brow.

As if.

Elias offers his wrist and huffs. "Waste not, until you try to slaughter each other, that is."

Gregori gives him a goading look. "It's not easy ripping tradition away from vampires who were alive to create it."

"But—"

"I've tried," Gregori says sharply, "but it's seen as weakness. I take the grandsireship only to outlaw the Aeskerat way of obtaining it? No."

Elias rolls his eyes. "Have you even tried democracy?"

Gregori twists and pins him with a one-eyed stare. "If Aeskerat were a democracy, Jacobi would be in charge and we'd have thrown ourselves into relentless war with the other covens. A leader must make the difficult choices even if they are unpopular, otherwise they will run out of people to lead. I happen to have the strength to enforce my rule and am not bound to the whims of ever-changing opinions."

Jacobi as grandsire... Elias shudders. He still can't forget that Gregori murdered one of their blood slaves, a whole person, over a little mess, but... is he the lesser of two evils? Thinking about the politics between centuries-old vampires hurts his head. Elias had been sprinting at breakneck speed down the path of usurping Gregori at any cost, and now it's not so black and white.

Elias lowers his voice to say, "Jacobi did something to Julian's spear."

"I'm aware," Gregori mutters, cradling Elias's forearm.

Gregori must be starving, the bathwater is already cloudy red from all his wounds, but he doesn't drink with any more ravenous hunger than usual. Elias winces and hunches beside the basin. "I thought you were immune to poisons."

Gregori lets him go and drops his head back, face pinched as his wounds slowly close, as missing tissue regrows. Elias wraps up his wrist with a shred of a stained shirt sleeve, surprised still that he hasn't taken more. "Urchins aren't the only poisons," he grumbles. Of course, Gregori won't tell him what poisons would work. Can't give his slave any ideas. "I'm aware of their scheming. They don't have the numbers to mutiny without ripping Aeskerat in two."

Don't they? Elias tries to recall the reactions of the crowd during Gregori's fight with Julian, which ones cheered sincerely, but it was all a gory mess. "Then why do they live?"

"They may hate me, but they hate the other covens more and they're useful in maintaining our borders." Gregori's lashes flutter, eye regrown but filmy and milky. He sinks to his chin in the bloody water and closes them both.

"For now," Elias mumbles.

Gregori hums. "Afraid for your safety if I'm not around to protect you anymore?"

Hardly. The chaos is exactly what he's waiting for—but at the right time. If Gregori gets stabbed in the back before winter ends, there goes his chance of fleeing in the madness. Once he's gone, Elias reminds himself, he won't care who's grandsire or what wars they start. "Can you blame me? You have your vices, but bedding your pigs isn't one of them."

Gregori's nose wrinkles in disgust. "You're very good with your words. Always know exactly what to say."

Elias shifts to sit on his legs despite his knee's protest, and shrugs. "I was a Keeper. I maintained ledgers and took inventory and was never the center of attention, so I got to listen."

"Is that what got Dorian to take pity and shed Aeskerat blood for you?" A brown eye cracks open, peering over at him.

Elias holds his wrist tighter, shoulders up. "You know him?"

"I'm old. He's old. All old vampires know each other."

"Know *of* each other, or *know* each other?"

Gregori chuckles. "Like I said. You're good with your words." He stands laboriously, red water sluicing off him. Elias averts his eyes so Gregori can scrub the red tint off his skin in a clean basin.

"What makes you so sure Jacobi and Julian don't have the numbers?"

Water splashes and trickles, and bare feet pad around on the flagstones. "Immortality puts death into a new perspective. The unknown of when your day might be due is perhaps scarier for us than it is for you. Most don't want to risk their immortal lives dying in a battle when they can choose to never die at all—"

"You just said they're the last line of defense—"

"When they have clear heads." Gregori *hmphs* and shakes his head. "Hunger makes you short-sighted. Vampirism makes you overconfident."

Gregori drapes little more than an embroidered sheet with a

neck hole cut out the middle over himself, cinching it closed with a sash. He orders one of the other slaves back in to clean his leathers spotless, wounds still puffy but no longer bleeding. "But make no mistake." The vampire's voice drops. "I still fight for what is mine, and I don't lose."

Elias follows him back up to his chambers, and Gregori trades the thin slip for different leathers with the growling bear over the heart. "Now then. I'm still famished and you're still bleeding."

Elias swallows a sigh. "Yes, Master."

There's that hunger, knocking the wind out of him when his back hits the bed. Gregori goes straight for his neck, ignoring his wrist entirely. It stings, a sharp ache dancing on his nerves, but it's different this time. The wet ends of his hair tickle Elias's skin and he does his best not to squirm.

His body betrays him, shivers tingling up and down his spine, and *no* he's not at all supposed to be enjoying this. Maybe it's the gusto with which Gregori drains him leaving him lightheaded. It must be. He's not thinking straight.

Elias mewls, tingly fingers tugging at the vampire's hair.

Gregori pulls back and frowns like it's Elias's intention to make this horribly, embarrassingly awkward. He rolls his eyes, now both clear and dark. "Roll over."

"What?" Is he—

"Roll. Over."

Elias does and gets smothered by the furs. Gregori goes right back to his neck. On his stomach, Gregori's weight on him, Elias can't so easily grab at his hair or squirm against him and *oh*. Oh, Gregori doesn't want to deal with the squirming or any further betrayals of his body.

At least losing all this blood solves that other problem. His vision goes fuzzy and his body goes cool before he's aware of the weight leaving his back.

"Sleep, Piggy." His voice echoes, and Elias drifts off without protest.

Elias watches life outside the castle through Gregori's tower window on a bright night of full moons. Aeskerat's castle sits in a wide valley with a lake to its northeastern corner, a whole lot of open nothingness that he can't reach. He sketches the outer wall on the stone tablet merely for something to do as Aeskerat scouts come and go.

Seeing the horses reminds him of his ride to the lighthouse with Dorian and he looks away, smearing his work. They didn't have to fight for him; they just had to turn him and he could have fought for himself.

He doesn't dare to hope for rescue or ransom, but he studies the riders as they come and go from a distance. Dorian won't come for him, he knows. Amaranth won't let him. Amaranth doesn't think Elias is worth saving.

They didn't know he'd end up as Gregori's. He could have been Jacobi's or Julian's and in a much more horrifying situation. They sold him without hesitation. He didn't get the chance to plead or beg in the Grand Hall or negotiate, and his only would-be defender got his neck snapped for disobeying orders.

"I can hear your pulse raging," Gregori says. "What is it?"

What is it?

Elias hasn't shared one word with Gregori's two other blood slaves, each in their own separate sleeping quarters. That is something he'd noticed, the physical divisions, as if this coven of immortal monsters has something to fear should all their slaves gather in one place. He's seen some weaving or knitting their own clothes in silence, but there's no singing, no birthday parties, no feasts. It's quiet in this castle. Too quiet, filled not with plays and theater, only mindful silence. The entire place is one big cell and under Gregori's boot, the living don't seem the only prisoners. Or the vampires are far better at discretion and keeping quiet here than Tanarang. Gregori is their grandsire. If they hated him enough, he wouldn't be. They like the bleak silence, or they don't notice or care what they're missing out on.

Elias does know what he's missing, and staring out at the snow he can't touch, the world he can't reach, the life he could have had if Amaranth fought for him, is worse than never having known at all.

Elias huffs, breath steaming the window. "Nothing, just… bitter."

Gregori hums, toying with a playing piece between his fingers. He's playing a game with a circular board and little whittled pieces alone, yet he won't teach Elias the rules because he's been playing for centuries and can't be bothered with a novice. "The best revenge is letting go and living well."

"Living well?" Elias echoes sardonically.

The vampire shrugs. "There are no illusions in this castle. You know your place intimately. Amaranth can play house all she wants, but in the end, they are still masters and livestock beneath their makeup and pretty dresses."

"Do you really believe that?" Elias sets his tablet aside. "That we're livestock? You were alive once. Were you happy to be a piggy before you turned?"

Gregori takes one of the darker pieces, swapping its place in the ring for a pale one, and casts the loser aside. "I was never a piggy, *Piggy*."

"How'd you turn, then?"

He smiles and moves the board to his bed, waving invitingly at the open space across from him.

Elias takes the spot as Gregori resets the pieces with practiced fluidity around the outer two rings of a big bullseye bisected by a thin line across the fold of the board.

Gregori taps the circle in the center. "The game is called *King of the Hill*. You battle your opponent for the highest-scoring pieces, up to three, to hold the center defenses."

Elias nods and grabs the tablet to take notes on the point system of all the pieces. Which outrank others depending on the rings they sit in, which can jump and move backwards. "Did you change the subject or are you going to answer me?"

"Patience." Gregori moves first, capturing one of Elias's pikemen with his own. "This is not the original Castle Aeskerat, you know. It used to be Castle Selimini, the country estate of the Khoul royal lineage."

"I did not know that, no." Elias turns the same move on him, dethroning one of his archers. "Selimini wasn't on any of the maps I've seen."

"It was a long time ago. Most maps that would have included it are now inaccurate." Gregori props his chin on his fist. "It fell to vampires long before the Great Freeze, so long ago that the battlefield still had grass to fight over. Trees, too—big evergreens—and meadows of widow's lace. Dandelions, I think they're called now."

Elias lets a piece get taken right from under his nose. "How old are you?"

"I was a child when this castle fell and our banners burned. I'm *old*."

"And you never learned to read?" Elias almost slaps his hands over his mouth. He can't breathe.

Gregori only huffs a laugh. "I'm older than books. Not letters, but books. They're quite dull, the ones I've had read to me, and tell me nothing I don't already know."

"You've been Grandsire of Aeskerat this entire time?"

Gregori smoothly takes three pieces at once—two archers and a mounted knight—and keeps one in his fist. "I was eighteenth in line to the throne of a kingdom that died so long ago, I'm likely the last who remembers its name. This room"—he waves, melancholic—"was my uncle's. It only became mine a couple centuries ago. I was like you, saying all the right things and biding my time. My… *quirks* entertained them and kept their teeth from my skin."

Elias snags a knight for himself and Gregori falters, amused. "You would not have survived one moon with my clan."

Gregori's eyes glitter, and he knocks out the rest of Elias's meager defense in the next attack. Then he resets the board, letting Elias take the first move. "Aeskerat grandsires fight for their place. It's not an inheritance."

"I gathered as much from the show."

"No one expected much from me. I threw my fights, sacrificing pride to learn the weaknesses of those in my way. Eventually, there were only two left I hadn't faced." Gregori smiles wistfully. "I have an ex–blood slave to thank for the demise of one. The other only took me one nasty defeat to decipher. And now here I am." He raises his hands and lets them fall in his lap.

Elias thumbs over the little figure holding only a scroll and a horn. "The strongest muscle doesn't equal the brightest mind."

"That's why Julian and Jacobi are still my lieutenants and not spearing each other for this room." Gregori keeps beating him in six moves or less but doesn't seem to tire from his lack of progression.

"Do not be bitter. Your life is too short, the world too small."

"Is that why you won't attack Tanarang? It's not worth it?"

Gregori shrugs again and twirls his king piece. "It's not, no. Other vampires are not the enemy. Your ilk is, and we'd all be wiser to remember that."

"You seem to lord over us without much effort." Clan Maewag kept a record of every soul they lost to vampires, and throughout Elias's tenure as Keeper, that number had been frozen at a hundred and thirty-six. *One-thirty-nine now*, he amends. "What about us scares you so?"

Gregori smiles wryly. "Vampires depend on the living to survive, and all we have to offer you in return is a phantom hearth to ward off the Freeze. My people endure in this bitter prison of our own creation because hunting us to extinction isn't worth the effort of marching into this wasteland. Someday, it might be."

What a glorious day it would be when vampires are eradicated. "In my clan, we're taught that vampirism breaks the circle of life and death. When vampires die, they give nothing back to the world that they spent their existence leeching from."

"Indeed."

Elias checks his little cheat sheet for all the possible moves he can make. Gregori surely only left an obvious opening to go easy on him. He moves a cavalryman to the circle, enough points by itself to count higher than Gregori's two lances. Now if he can hold that position until Gregori runs out of moves to overwhelm the little horse figure, or to land another piece in the circle...

Elias licks his chapped lips and sits back, satisfied. "And yet vampires exist nonetheless. So you must give something to the world, even if it's just keeping the living in check." The gods created vampires for a reason. The argument his clan and their books always gave—that the damned immortals represent those who stray off the virtuous path and nothing more—isn't as comforting as it used to be. And never was it quite sensible.

Gregori taps his nail on the king's crown and smiles. "I do appreciate the irony of Dorian sparing me that defeat at the teeth of Aeskerat's last grandsire so that we both still live to play this little game tonight."

Elias falters, wiped off the board once again.

Gregori grins, fangs sharp in the candlelight. "Would you like another go?"

Gregori leaves on another hunt for better needles. The moment he's gone, one of Julian's scouts returns, and she's not alone.

Elias could recognize the mountain of ill-fitting furs anywhere. They've captured a clansman, though from which cave he can't tell from the tower windows. The mystery doesn't last long because Julian's soon ordering him outside to meet the man.

He's bloodied and flecked with ice crystals, wrists and ankles chained and mouth gagged. Elias still recognizes his squinty features beneath the grime. "Chief Yarren?"

The man's eyes widen and he gives a muffled yell through the gag. The vampire scout holding his chains keeps him standing right where he is. "I guess he wasn't lying."

Elias looks between his chief and Julian. "What is this?"

"This," Julian goads, "is my new leverage."

"Wha—"

"Do you want to go home, pig?"

Elias's jaw slackens. Home? Home to the cave?

Julian chuckles and smacks him hard on the back. "Of course you do! Yvette found your cave, all of them. As much as I'd love the fresh blood to feed my coven, your inbred kin taste disgusting and aren't worth the effort it would take to fix all your sickly, starving bodies. So!" Julian props his hands on his hips and beams. "How about we make a deal?"

"I don't want to go home." What's left for him there? What's left for him in the North now that Tanarang won't accept him? "I want to go to the South."

Yarren garbles in alarm. Elias looks away.

Julian shrugs, lips downturned in surprise. "South, eh? That can be arranged, *if* you do this one little thing for me."

As if it's all so simple. Elias shakes his head. "This is a trick. I agree and you tell Gregori and he mounts me on the wall."

Julian waggles a finger. "Aeskerat keep their promises."

"I'm not—"

"And Gregori isn't here." Julian smiles cruelly. "You help me dispose of our dearly beloved leader, and you get a seat on the first ship headed south once the ports open. Your chief and all your filthy cave rat littermates get to keep living in peace."

Elias's laugh is almost hysterical. "He's near a thousand years old and you think I can, what, sneak up on him? You want him gone, kill him yourself."

"That's exactly what you'll do. Or... Yvette?"

The scout kicks out Yarren's knees and bares her fangs, fist in his hair.

"Stop!" Elias skitters in his socks—they're not chains, but they might as well be. Warm enough for the frigid stone floors inside the castle but useless out in the elements if he tried to run. Another reminder that he's on a leash, even if it doesn't look like one, because Gregori doesn't trust him with shoes. Shoes matter little, however, when the vampires would catch him anyway. "He knows you want him gone, he's not stupid. What happens when I fail?"

Julian shrugs. "We wait for another opportunity, I suppose. We have time, pig. And *you* have the perfect motivation to not fail. Yvette? Take him away before he stinks up the place."

Elias watches helplessly as Yvette hauls his chief up and over the back of the horse like a fresh kill and trots out of the gates to wherever they're holding him.

"I'll tell him," Elias threatens.

"And your clan will suffer the consequences."

"Why should I believe that you won't come slaughter us anyway? Your word means nothing if you stand here mutinying against your grandsire." This is—*oh* this is—Elias can't think straight. This isn't supposed to happen yet. Gregori will see right through him or smell his panic and kill him because he means *nothing* to a being one step away from godhood.

"Hmm, that's true," Julian ponders. "I could kill you now."

"He doesn't care about me."

"Neither do I, pig. You're convenient to my plans." Julian folds his hands behind his back. "Plans that will succeed with or without you. I'm being generous, letting you leave with your life. You'll have to be standing on the right side when it's over or all deals are off."

What if Gregori does lose? In solo combat, he wouldn't, but if Gregori's wrong about the support Julian and Jacobi can rally? If he overestimates his coven's complacency, if he's swarmed, then he loses, Elias right behind him. Clan Maewag next.

Julian backs off with a hapless shrug. "Think about it."

But what if Julian's wrong about his own support? If his mutiny fails and the coven stands behind their grandsire? Then Elias will have betrayed Gregori for nothing and still end up dead with the rest of his clan.

He drifts down to the kitchens and holds his head in his hands. What if Gregori's overconfidence gets him killed? What if he really is that good of a fighter? If everything goes perfectly and Elias warns Gregori and Gregori kills both Julian and Jacobi and can remain in power, then he'd still be protected by the vampire.

He'd also still be Gregori's prisoner with no chance of going home or fleeing to the South. But if Gregori wins and promises to not go after his clan, Elias would believe that promise.

A plate clatters gently before him. Fawn, with a warm roll and a mug. She sips from her own and frowns. Elias waves her off with a tired but grateful smile and eats even though he's not hungry. The absolute *second* Gregori returns, he'll have to pick his side. And maybe... maybe honesty with Gregori could earn him his freedom.

Elias watches for him from the tower windows, paranoid that every noise outside the door is a betrayer or assassin. *He's hundreds of years old and wicked smart*, Elias reminds himself. *He can smell a trap. He's not stupid.*

He worries himself to exhaustion, slumping in the window's alcove with the chill of the glass against his face.

Gregori's soft chuckle rouses him. "Were you that lonely?"

He's alive. Elias trips over himself crashing into the vampire with an embrace. "Julian's trying to kill you. He has my chief as a hostage and threatened to kill him unless I cooperate and will let me go south if I do but I don't trust him."

Elias says it all in one breath and Gregori doesn't move, arms still extended in shock at the hug. He looks up, hoping for a healthy, productive, protective rage. What he finds is reserved contemplation. "I see."

Stern hands unwind Elias's arms. Elias steps back, then slams the door shut. "You see? How about you *act*? Kill him for insubordination? Make an example of him?"

"Have you considered that his actual intent was for you to warn me so that I go and attempt exactly that, walking into his trap?"

Oh.

Gregori unclasps his cloak and drapes it over the bed. "I did not expect him to grow this bold, I admit."

"Can you beat him?"

"You saw me beat him even when poisoned." Gregori paces quietly, without the urgency Elias hoped for. "It's not Julian by himself that concerns me."

There is a third, ludicrous option. "You said you didn't attack Tanarang so you wouldn't throw away your coven's lives. You owe Dorian your place as grandsire so if you don't want to fight, you can run."

Gregori *hmphs* indignantly. "I do not owe Dorian. Dorian did what he did for his own selfish benefit and I took the opportunity in the power vacuum and earned my place in combat."

"Fine!" Elias shouts. "Die here in a mutiny!"

"You seem certain I'm going to lose."

"You're not inspiring much confidence that you won't." Elias crosses his arms and drops down on the bed.

Gregori picks up one of the little game pieces, a pikeman, and smooths his thumb over the figure's shield. "Running would cost me any confidence still held for me by those who remain loyal. Aeskerat does not *run*."

"*Waste not*," Elias mocks. "Shouldn't that include your lives?"

Gregori cocks his head and leans against the foot of the bed.

"Are you worried for me?"

"I'm worried that when you die, I'll follow shortly after," Elias snaps, crossing his legs too for good measure.

"Is that all?"

"Yes, *Master*. I have the lived experience of a fly compared to you, you've ingrained that small fact in me quite well." Gregori lowers himself beside him and tries to turn his face. Elias stubbornly tenses against the touch, shoulders squeezing his ears. "My ability to worry for you as anything more than an immortal vampire shield might grow if you stopped calling me piggy."

"Elias."

His name sounds funny with Gregori's distant accent, a string of syllables foreign to his ears after months of never hearing it. He lets Gregori turn his head this time, those dark eyes searching.

Kymiria told him that vampires only show interest in the living when they're fledglings, or when they're so old that the distance doesn't register anymore.

Elias doesn't know what to do pinned by a stare tens of times his age. The divide is so vast it's invisible, gone beyond the horizon. He blames life growing up in a cave for his pendulum swing between violent monsters that keep bowling him off his feet. Whatever this is or could be is still chained to the power Gregori has over him.

But that is *want* in those eyes. It's possessiveness, ownership, bratty, spoiled *need*. Elias... did his job too well. He got Gregori to want him, and this is what it looks like—fingers that could crush his windpipe without a thought delicately touching his chin. A whole kingly suite of treasures yet desire only for him.

If that means Gregori will shove him face-first into the furs for a whole different reason, for a whole different claim... Luni got off easy as an unremarkable trifle. Elias swallows hard, mouth suddenly dry, skin cold and clammy. What does the millennium-old Grandsire of Aeskerat do to lovers who scorn him?

"And the *master* talk stops," he adds, softly but firmly. "I'm not your pet or your food. I'm a person." Another leap. If he's miscalculated, it's too late to climb back up so high, the ledge out of reach in a blink. He's back in his fishbowl, a refracted face on the other side that could shatter the glass on a whim and replace him with an identical fool in an instant.

The hand drops from his chin and Gregori shifts away from him. "Find me something to write with."

The frantic flurry of anticipation collapses in on itself with a pang. Not agreement, not denial, not a mote of consideration. Elias works his jaw and resists bringing a hand to his chest to check that his heart still beats. "You don't have any pencils and paper in here. I've looked."

"I have books."

"Nothing to write on them with besides the chalk."

Gregori stands and drifts to his wardrobe, rooting around until he comes back with a skinny ceramic case all painted delicately with fluffy birds. "A gift from some Southern lord," he says, and lifts the top. Resting on a bed of velvet is a glossy black pen painted with more birds. "Write on my behalf, please."

Elias doesn't take it immediately. Gregori leaves it beside his leg to rip the mostly blank cover page from the milling ledger.

"Do you have any ink?"

He huffs and flips his hair back over his shoulders. "So much tedium. No, any that I might've had would have dried up by now." He bites into his hand and blood wells in his palm. "Use this."

Elias holds the stone tablet for support and smooths the ledger page onto it, resting the pen at the top of its blank back. "What do you want me to write?"

"To Amaranth of Tanarang," Gregori begins primly. He waits impatiently for a stunned Elias to write, watching him dip the pen every few letters. "I release my claim on Elias of Maewag."

Elias almost drops the pen.

"Write, please."

"Why are you doing this?"

Gregori moves his hand back to the page. "*Write*."

Elias hurries as neatly as he can.

"The incident with Janneah was an accident. Grant him amnesty and a seat at your table, as you have other Aeskerat who earned their freedom." He bounces his foot, watching over Elias's shoulder. If he notices Elias's hand quaking, tracing out shaky letters, he doesn't comment. "Signed, Gregori of Aeskerat."

"Do you want to learn how to sign your name?"

Gregori wells fresh blood in his palm. "We don't have the time."

Elias signs for him and gently blows the letter dry, fingers numb where they grip the edges.

"You still have to make it to Tanarang—"

Elias's eyes sting and his throat clogs. Why does this feel like freedom?

"—and in that I can only help you so far. Regardless of what happens here, Amaranth will accept it. She knows my scent. That letter is your life. And this is yours as well." Gregori offers him the pen and its case. "You have more use for it than I."

Elias sets them both on the game table. "Mas—"

"Gregori."

"...Gregori. Come with me. Use your mind and not your muscles and recognize a sound retreat."

The grandsire stands gracefully and waves to the game board.

"You never win *King of the Hill* once you retreat. All you do is delay the inevitable."

"This isn't a game!" What *is* this? Gregori doesn't need to waste effort taunting him, he must mean it all. Freedom, and for what? Is the whiplash allure of the living that powerful? What a waste to throw it all away over some stupid throne. "Please."

"Elias." Gregori pulls a silky purple cloth from the wardrobe, another gift from some other Southern lord no doubt, and dries his tears with it. "If I run, Julian and Jacobi win. But if I stay? I might live, and even if I don't, I will thin our numbers so they can't attack another coven, and theirs will be a Pyrrhic victory."

"Tanarang has the numbers," Elias protests. "You could form an alliance with them and save whoever's still loyal to you."

Again, Gregori shakes his head. "This is an Aeskerat matter. I can't invoke another coven to save myself. When the dust settles and I'm standing at the top, I might consider a pact. Not before."

Elias drops his head on Gregori's chest. "I was waiting for this," he admits, because whatever attachment Gregori feels toward him is as warped and mangled as Elias's own. "I was waiting for someone to get annoyed enough with your fits to start a fight so I could escape to the ports in the chaos. You're supposed to be a monster. This was supposed to be easy."

Gregori laughs, arms loosely folding around him. "I am a monster, Elias. I'm about to slaughter my own coven in the name of another and a little piggy who chooses his words too well. I'm eight hundred years old, and still I hunger for a few years more."

Elias sniffles and the purple cloth appears back in Gregori's hand. He rolls his eyes. "Do my tears offend you so?"

"No." The cloth presses insistently and Elias takes it from him, stepping back. "I want to kiss you, and I refuse to do so with snot coating your skin."

Gregori isn't like Dorian—they might as well be wholly different species. And yet. Elias's eyes flick down to his lips and back, a terrifying thrill sparking up his spine. Gregori is about to take on his own coven, for *him*. The same Gregori who collects his little game pieces and sulks in his bathwater and invested such eager interest in the needle project.

In *him*.

Elias's mother told him he should try his luck on the surface just once. He tries to picture what melted-wax horror would afflict her face if he told her how far he got spelunking among immortals. *He* did this, and by Takkha, an insane part of him wants to know what it feels like to freefall.

Elias cleans up faster than he ever has before, rubbing his nose raw. "Good enough?"

"Good enough," Gregori concedes, and the kiss that follows isn't done with any flair, like he's studied paintings of still-life and can only replicate the form. Elias doesn't care. He wants to fall back on the bed and tangle his hands in all that silky hair, make a proper mess of everything. It's the taste of freedom talking, of respect, of more than he ever dared to hope for handed to him in a little painted porcelain box. Of knowing there's a high chance he doesn't flee this castle alive in the next few minutes. Gregori only allows the one kiss and muses after that such acts remain bland, then folds up the letter and presses it to Elias's chest. "Do you know how to ride?"

"Do I—" *Horses*. He means horses. He absolutely means horses. "Y-yeah."

"Good. You will need shoes." In the rush to find proper riding attire and flee to the stables to saddle the steed Tanarang stole, Elias forgets the pen.

He's astride the horse Gregori re-claims to follow his orders, trying to memorize the directions Gregori is throwing at him, when Julian reveals himself.

Julian, and six other vampires.

"Well, that didn't go as planned."

Elias grips the reins in shaking fists, sizing up the group and all their weapons. Gregori didn't bring anything with him to the stables.

"You were supposed to feed him, piggy," Julian taunts. "That's what the tea was for."

The tea...? *Fawn.* Fawn and the tea and the sympathetic bread roll. It was drugged.

Gregori snaps off a wrought iron bar from the stable fence. "It's hardly an honorable or respectable victory, poisoning your opponent before the fight."

Julian smiles unhappily. "You're one to talk, seeing as how a blood slave did your own dirty work. You're an opportunist."

"And you're not?" Gregori smiles determinedly up at Elias and pats the horse's neck. "Go, Elias. You won't be followed."

"Are you—"

"*Go.*" Gregori strikes the metal rod against the horse's flank. It rears back and nearly throws him and then he's left the castle. Elias hangs on as he passes through the gate but then pulls the reins up short.

He can't *not* watch, can't not see the reason for the screams and wails of pain.

Beyond the gate, Gregori wields the short iron bar like a sword, skewering his fellow vampires and delivering no mercy. One loses their head in a blink.

He's got this, Elias thinks. His horse skitters and Elias pets her neck, begging for a few seconds more. When Gregori isn't performing for a crowd, he's brutally efficient, but he's still alone. Other shouts ring out, more voices crowding the courtyard. Julian screeches, flipped head over heels in the same move that waylaid him in the fighting pit.

This time, Gregori doesn't give him a chance to rise.

Elias gawks, about ready to rush back in. But two vampires skirt past Gregori and break for Elias on his horse. His signal to run. No hesitating, no looking back. If he reaches Castle Tanarang and everything turns out fine, then he'll at least know he wasn't a deadly distraction. His vampire horse can move as quickly as it dares, in the dark, on unknown land, as snow clouds block out the moons, but not if he dawdles now.

Go.

Chapter 11:
Nineteen Miles Out

Elias would have crashed into a glacier steering a living horse. The wind burns his eyes and face, whips numbness into his hands holding the reins as he hunkers down and trusts the animal beneath him to know the way.

It's snowing hard, but the horse hasn't slowed once, sprinting at full speed deftly across the valley toward a gap between the mountains. Behind them, Elias hears the nightmarish whinnies of his pursuers.

Pursuers don't mean Gregori lost, only that he couldn't stop everyone. *He's still alive*, Elias repeats in his mind. *He's alive, he's alive, he's alive.*

If it weren't for the fresh snowbank that's deeper than the horse anticipates, they might've done it. She sinks up to her shoulders and chuffs in panic.

Elias is yanking the reins, shouting at her to listen to him when their pursuers catch up. A spear flies past them, grazing his calf.

His horse backpedals and bowls the snow aside to free herself, back on solid ground when an arrow pierces her flank and another skewers Elias's side. He gasps, almost crushed when she falls over, trapping his leg.

"Piggy, piggy!"

Jacobi.

No! Gregori would not have let Jacobi past him. So if he's here, then...

His horse limps to its feet only to be wrangled by the Aeskerat riders. Jacobi's on him in an instant, yanking the arrow free. Elias screams, numb hands fumbling to press on the wound. Jacobi's boot rolls him over and he groans.

"Good try! I mean that sincerely." Jacobi kneels, streaked and splattered with blood, and holds up something small and bloodied between his fingers. A tooth, a fang. *Gregori.* "But not good enough."

Elias curls in on himself and glowers. "I don't see a body."

Jacobi barks a laugh and spreads his arms. "Yes, nor do I! If he were able to come save you, surely he'd be here."

It's a ruse. That tooth might belong to anyone. Gregori might be alive but injured. Too injured to come after him. What matters is that he isn't here. Jacobi is. "I'll beg if you promise it'll be quick."

Jacobi laughs again and casually rests his arm on his knee, studying the stolen tooth. "If I wanted you dead, that arrow would have hit your heart. No, I have a proposition."

"What could you possibly—"

"We still have your chief," he warns. "And after the massacre of my coven, we're going to need fresh livestock. Fresh, fat, *healthy* livestock. You're going to get it for me." Jacobi's smarmy smirk sours and he fists Elias's hair. "You're going to get me Castle Tanarang. I don't care how but do make haste. Your chief and clan are a far easier meal even if sickly and disgusting vermin."

"It's not their fault you can't take care of your blood slaves," he snaps. "Or that your mutiny got messy."

Jacobi casts the tooth into the snow, bites his own wrist, and smothers Elias with it. Warmth floods his bones, washing away the numbness in his extremities. Elias loves and loathes the sensation, spitting it back in Jacobi's face.

Jacobi's hackles raise, but he doesn't bite. "I don't like Tanarang. No one likes Tanarang. They've strutted around long enough, pretending they know best."

Elias pants and holds his side. How many more vampires will pass him around like property? How many different masters will he have to answer to, just for being alive? Jacobi might kill him and end this vicious cycle, if Elias enrages him enough. "'Cause they prove you wrong about your slaves?"

But Jacobi lets his hair go. "Because that entire castle is full of spoiled children who don't know what it's like to be hungry thanks to us."

Elias frowns and would ask, but black stars dance in the sky and his ears ring. "They won't trust me," he hisses instead. *Just let it be over with.*

"You seduced the Grandsire of Aeskerat, piggy. You'll figure it out. Tell Amaranth that, on my honor, no Tanarang vampire need perish. We're hungry, and they have plenty to go around. We only want half and"—he shrugs, flippant—"Dorian. Have her send him home, as a peace offering. Do this, and I swear on my immortal soul, I will send you south the first chance I get."

Elias hates that he hesitates. South, where all the wildflowers grow, where there's sunlight and a sky that turns blue. Where it's warm and there's no snow and all the paintings he saw in that old keep pale on their canvases. Home? In the cave in the dark, the only sky above his head the stone, no wind on his face, no space to run? That's the last place he wants to see ever again.

If the South is still within his reach, well, Dorian is the only Tanarang who cares about him. The only one. Elias owes the rest of them nothing.

"They won't lift a finger for my clan," he mutters, as Jacobi whistles his horse back over, yanks the arrows free, and lifts Elias easily into the saddle. He hunches, fisting her mane with his arm pressed to his side. She whinnies in protest but doesn't try to throw him at least. "I'll bleed out before I get there."

"What say I heal it for you?" the vampire offers, sickly sweet.

Ugh! "No."

Jacobi ignores him, hawking spit into his palm. He's not gentle, fingers digging at the wound. Elias almost faints, gritting his teeth so hard he's shocked one doesn't crack.

"There." Jacobi dusts his hands off. "They might not care about your clan, but they care about theirs. Amaranth can submit in peace, or she can draw this out, long and bloody."

Elias manages his own laugh. He's afraid to look at the wound, but he no longer feels fresh, warm blood soaking his leathers. "You didn't have the numbers before. You definitely don't now."

They'll all slaughter each other in a bloody streak across the North. Maybe his clan's story of the Great Freeze being brought upon them by genocidal vampires isn't so far from the truth. Not a single moon in power, and here Jacobi stands, ready to eradicate a coven to tickle his own ego.

"Don't I?" Jacobi smacks his horse's flank. "Make haste, piggy! You don't want to die out here and turn all alone."

Can he turn from Jacobi's blood and starve? Elias hadn't

considered that. Trapped, lost beneath the snow, too weak to free himself and hunt down a meal, unable to die? He nudges his horse a little faster, as fast as he can tolerate with all the jostling.

"Just get us there," he mumbles into the horse's mane. "Just get us there."

It's Markus's idea to invite Kymiria on patrol with them. It's also Markus's idea that Kymiria ride with Dorian so they have no excuses not to talk. She's left the castle grounds but has never gone far enough to lose sight of it. Kymiria almost falls off Dandy as she twists to stare at the eastern slopes of the mountains and the wide-open plains. Dorian keeps her steady but still doesn't know what to say to her beyond pointing out landmarks as they go.

They're supposed to be out assessing the damage from hopefully the last blizzard of winter. The sun never returns in spring, but the warmth does, a black blanket pulled over the sky.

Winter's end comes when the rivers begin to melt, but River Tammen is still frozen. Ibir Pass will still be blocked, along with all the main avenues connecting one coast to the other. Another month delayed, then, before he can escort a party south and bring back much needed food to replenish their stores.

"Well, this is disappointing." Markus tests the ice's thickness, bouncing fearlessly. Aeskerat land starts at the eastern bank, and even though some scout won't pop out of the snow to attack, Markus's carelessness has Dorian twitchy.

Kymiria tuts. "We will have to fish. Migration patterns don't care about the weather on land."

Dorian wrinkles his nose. Fish stinks—worse than when the kitchens get creative with the plentiful kelp. Kelp flour, kelp wraps, kelp salads, kelp stews.

"We can't fish if the seas don't calm," he points out. "Unless we venture to the Catanz floodplain." Which is… a trek. All they have left is crab traps, and with the heaving waves tossing them about, he wouldn't be surprised if many didn't survive the winter.

Kymiria sighs and throws her hands up. "We're not out of food yet."

"Ooo! Snowberries!" Markus darts across the ice to snag the rubbery nuts that manage to grow by moonlight alone. They produce good ink, a metallic blue for the fanciest of missives. Dorian catches himself smiling at Markus's glee, at his complete ignorance of the fish predicament.

Kymiria's stare bores holes in the back of his head and he dismounts, offering a hand to help her down although she doesn't need it. "So." He clears his throat. "I'm not mad. Haven't been mad. I just… don't have anything to say."

"I suppose in some ways that's worse." She tucks her cloak tighter around herself. "Time isn't of the essence when your clock has stopped. Two months is a blessing."

Already this conversation feels lost. He hadn't meant to cut her out entirely, just… recenter what they have. "Kym."

"You were never mine to lose," she says simply. "If I had the chance to do it over, I'd choose the same. I love you, even if you don't love me—"

"I do love—"

"—the way I want you to."

He'd be lying to both of them if he pretended he does, but that's no secret. She's too young, not so much in years but in maturity, in worldly experience. That weird pocket of vampires, still so *alive*, still chained to the lives they used to lead. It doesn't help that Kymiria still has living relatives and descendants he constantly sees her face in.

Had they been closer when she was still alive and growing, this relationship never would have happened. As it is, he missed most of her life, away on scouting missions or caught up negotiating with the port towns. He'd missed twelve years without much thought, and when he came back, she'd already turned.

"Besides," she says, smiling bittersweet, gaze settled somewhere beyond him, "you're not much of a romantic anyway. Markus is much more to your taste."

"I have my moments," he defends in a pout. "I... dote."

"On children, not me."

... Yes, but on Kymiria, too. Just... not as frequently.

Kymiria hums and pats his cheek. "We have eternity ahead of us. If you get bored"—she wiggles her brows—"you know where to find me. And I, you. I hope?"

He scoffs and gently moves her hand. "Surely there's someone else in that castle who can give you the attention you deserve."

"Surely," she agrees, then pokes his nose. "But this is a face that will never bore me." Her hands fall away and she folds her arms. "Are you certain you're not mad about the y—about Elias?"

He shakes his head. "I would have done the same. Doesn't mean it's okay, it's just... I understand."

Kymiria puffs her cheeks like a weight's been lifted off her chest. "Thank you." She turns his cheek-kiss into a real one and toys with his lip, then laps up a bead of blood with a grin.

Dorian rolls his eyes. "*Kym.*"

"What?" She shrugs all nonchalant, then her gaze slides past him.

Markus has his head cocked, studying them like a funny new equation. "Can I try that?"

They're supposed to be taking notes about the snowfall. To be finishing their rounds and reporting back. Building a nest of cloaks in the snow and trading nips and nibbles simply won't do.

But it's—well, it's *fun*. It's fun having the wall lifted between him and Kymiria, it's fun ignoring duty to throw mushy snowballs at each other, it's fun wrestling Markus onto his back while Kymiria whistles coquettishly. She knows not to bite harder than teasing nibbles and Markus never asks why when she reminds him so Dorian doesn't have to. It's the most childish glee he's had in centuries, nestled between them both.

Until the wind shifts. It stops Kymiria mid-giggle and has her aiming an arrow eastward in a blink.

Blood. Living blood. Old, stale, and a lot of it.

The horses shift hungrily, ears turned into the wind. He knows that smell. Musty wood. Sweat.

Seershrooms.

"Elias."

"Clover, too."

They mount up without a word, clopping across the frozen river into Aeskerat territory. Clover, when he spots her, is covered with frost and smeared entirely in blood on one side. Muzzle to the ground, she noses at a motionless lump of furs.

"Elias!"

He slips off Dandy, dragging Elias away from Clover's hungry teeth as Kymiria leads the wayward horse aside.

"He's not dead?" Markus joins him, peeling away the blood-stained Aeskerat furs from a ghastly wound in Elias's side. He'd been cognizant enough to protect his face from the wind and wrap his belt around a wad of fabric dressing the hole, but how long has he been out here?

"Jacobi," Kymiria snarls, smelling him as easily as Dorian can. Jacobi's blood crusts Elias's lips. It isn't the only scent clinging to him, though. Jacobi isn't the vampire who claimed him—Gregori is.

Kymiria keeps her bow drawn. "If this is a trap, they're hiding well."

Dorian's not sure what this is. Jacobi's too good a shot to miss, and had he, he would have run Elias down to finish the job. No, either he let Elias go or Elias somehow got the jump on him and fled for his life. Dorian yanks his cloak off to wrap Elias in it, but one layer isn't enough. "Markus, your cloak, please."

Dorian checks his body for other wounds or bites and a paper crinkles, tucked tight against his chest.

"We're out in the open," Kymiria warns. "If they wanted to ambush us—"

"This isn't an ambush." Dorian stares at the blood-inked words on the paper, oozing of Gregori. "*I release my claim...*"

An Aeskerat never releases their claim. They run it into the ground, sucking it dry until it ceases to exist, and move on to the next plump blood bag in line.

"Kymiria, cloak. You take Clover." He and Markus bundle Elias as thoroughly as they can without suffocating him, then sit him awkwardly sidesaddle in Dorian's arms without another means to secure him.

It's a straight shot back to Castle Tanarang, Gregori's letter shouting in his mind over and over again the entire ride. Elias did not escape on his own. Gregori let him go. So why is Elias half-dead and reeking of Jacobi's scheming?

"Dorian," Markus calls as they slow to approach the gate. "We will get answers when he wakes."

Once they're inside, Markus splits off with Gregori's letter to go find Amaranth, and Kymiria helps him get Elias to the baths. Even with Jacobi's blood to warm him, Elias was out in the elements too long.

They can't shock his body with the heat of the water, instead working him out of all the furs and layers and wrapping his limbs in warm, damp towels. Kymiria grimly lifts Elias's blackened fingertips, and if he wasn't half-dead, Dorian would feed him more to try and save them. He won't take Elias's choice to turn away from him.

"Do it," Kymiria insists. She'd said nothing about his reappearance in their lives the whole ride. Now grudging pity pinches her face. "He made it this far."

Elphaba and Castor rush down moments later with a flood of their own questions. Kymiria fields them all as Elias remains unresponsive to fresh blood at his lips. Amaranth strides in, letter in hand.

"Jacobi is behind this, no matter what that letter says," Dorian utters before she can speak. "For all we know, Gregori's dead and Jacobi used his blood to toy with us. Double the guard on the wall and keep everyone else inside the castle and away from the windows."

She nods to Castor. "Dorian is correct about the guard, please spread the word."

Castor runs off, leaving the four of them surrounding Elias's body.

Amaranth pinches the bridge of her nose. "Is it possible that Gregori fell?"

Dorian gives up on feeding him and wipes the spilled and dried blood off his face. Elphaba frets and adds more warm towels. "Gregori is formidable, but Jacobi and Julian are honorless."

"Do we have the medicine to spare in case the ports remain inaccessible?"

"Yes." Elphaba rises. "I will have it brought—where, Master Dorian?"

"My room." Elias's hair is shorter, his face a little thinner, but he's not littered with unhealed bites or any flagrant brands of his claim. It's not Gregori's style to flaunt, though. He doesn't need to. "Would you let him take the oath, Amaranth?"

"If this is Gregori's word and not a ruse by Jacobi, as you suggest, I would accept it." Amaranth folds the letter into a pocket of her dress and links her hands behind her back and it's only because he knows her so well that Dorian sees the guilt in her eyes.

"And if it means conflict with Aeskerat?"

Her expression hardens as much as it can with her youthful face still round and soft. "We protect our own, Dorian. Jacobi clearly wants war. Whether I accept Elias or not won't change that. I will not sell a being to that slimy cur twice."

Dorian slumps. "Thank you."

Amaranth leaves to assess their offensive capabilities should Jacobi get his way. Kymiria helps him move Elias up the floors to Dorian's room, his bed already arranged with plush furs.

"Can I do anything?"

"Keep me from going out there to take Jacobi's head myself," he growls. For that smug arrogance, for his warmongering, for his insufferable face and grating voice, for Gregori not doing it himself in the decades he's had the ample opportunity.

"I can do that."

Kymiria leaves, and Dorian tucks the furs around the prone lump in his bed and crawls in to help keep him warm, at least until Elphaba comes with the medicine.

Cowards survive, he thinks, *so you'd better not die on me.*

Once, in the cave, Elias got drunk on a bad distillation of seershroom *schninir* and peered for hours into the flames of a bonfire. The visions he had, swirling in the flickering orange and yellow, he thought a curse by the gods themselves. After, he didn't remember what he saw, only the frazzled foreboding it left in his mind.

He could remember, though, the horrific heat sitting too close to the fire, remembered the dizziness from the lacking air in the cave, remembered coming in and out of awareness, the shapes of his kin warbly as if drawn by toddlers and granted life by some capricious celestial.

That feeling, as he tosses and turns, hot and freezing and nauseous and numb, haunts his body once more. He understands Gregori's desperation for cleanliness acutely, soggy with his own sweat and filthy with congestion and the acidic taste of bile gumming up his throat.

Wrinkled and warped outlines take care of him, but he can't tell who or how many or when they're nearby and when they're not, and half the time he thinks they're talking only to realize he's the one babbling to himself.

He's hungry then has no appetite, is freezing then boiling. His head pounds, stuffed so full it should crack like an egg. He's parched. He's drowning. He's rolling over himself like he's rolling down the world's tallest mountain in a tumble that never ends.

It does end.

Elias rouses slowly, snuggled against solid warmth, earthy and clean. He buries his nose against it. Something silky and bumpy. The thing moves, expanding and shrinking in his arms and... and...

Elias cracks his eyes open, getting a faceful of brown braids. The silk he'd been nuzzling is the collar of a deep red satiny robe, the bump his arm, thrown over a chest.

"*Dorian?*"

The name comes out in little more than a hoarse squeak, stretching and pulling Elias's chapped lips.

It *is* Dorian.

This is Dorian's room, Dorian's bed.

This is Elias's bare chest to Dorian's back, only the satin robe between them.

Dorian.

Elias made it. Or Dorian came and found him. The last thing he remembers is staring into the snowy wind, the horse's mane whipping.

And *oh* the sheer warmth in this room. In the plush furs but also the colors… Gregori's chambers held the only displays of decadence Elias had seen in Castle Aeskerat. Dorian's room might not have windows, but he's got tapestries of whales and vineyards, half-finished whittling projects all over the desk, a pile of books atop the wardrobe casually curated from their library that dwarfs Gregori's paltry collection.

You did come to save me, he thinks. *But why am I in your bed?*

He squeaks again, arm too heavy to move.

Dorian rolls sluggishly away from him and yawns. "Are you going to puke again?"

No? Elias's throat feels like sandpaper as he swallows so he can reply a raspy, "Why am I in your bed?"

Dorian blinks and huffs in surprise. "Well, there you are, finally." He yawns again and leaves the bed to bring Elias a tiny cup of water. "You needed to be warm. Your infection inspired delirium. And clinginess."

"And my clothes?"

"You kept getting sick and sweat on them. This was easier to clean."

"And *your* clothes?"

Dorian gives him an offended look like Elias did this on purpose. "Sick and sweat. Small sips," he orders. "If you keep it down, you'll get more. Let me check your wound."

Even lifting the little cup awakens a sharp ache in his abdomen. Elias, struggling to hold onto the cup with his hands bandaged so heavily, almost spills the water over himself. The shape of the mitt around his fingers looks *off*. Elias shakily raises his other hand to confirm he's not still hallucinating.

Dorian gently takes the cup from him. "We couldn't save all of them, I'm sorry."

All he can manage is a raspy, "Oh." As far as he can tell, he lost most of the two middle fingers on his left hand and his entire right pinkie.

"You still have all your toes." Dorian smiles sympathetically. "Will you still be able to draw?"

He'll have to learn a new grip to hold his pencils, but... Elias nods. How long was he asleep in the snow to have lost them? He doesn't remember arriving at the castle, only riding and riding, only staring at the horizon that seemed to grow farther and farther away.

"This might hurt," Dorian warns before he tugs at the bandages wrapped around Elias's abdomen. Pain doesn't strike until the material sticks to the healing wound. Elias groans, tensing automatically, worsening the sting. "You can look. The infection's gone."

"I'd rather not."

"I'll be quick."

Elias stares up at the ceiling, trying to breathe evenly and not flinch away from him. "How long has it been?"

"Almost two weeks."

"And I'm already healed?"

Dorian doesn't answer, looking away when Elias drags his gaze down.

"Is that a *You're now missing a kidney* silence?"

He huffs an awkward laugh and reaches for new bandages on the side table. "No. Um. Let's just say we gave you medicine to speed up the process."

Elias's brows raise. "You licked it."

Dorian drops the bandages on the floor with a full-body cringe. "No!"

"You *did*! That's so gross." *So, so gross.* Elias lurches and his side spasms. He gasps and locks up, hissing through his teeth.

Dorian sighs and helps him ease back down. "I didn't. Markus says it stimulates cellular division or something—I don't know or care—but I don't have to do that for it to work." No, that's right. Jacobi didn't either, thankfully.

Still, Elias whimpers and slowly exhales, uncurling his fingers from their death grip on the furs. "Saliva as medicine is disgusting." If he never turns only so he never has to *lick people*, that's a good enough reason for him.

"Yeah, well, without it you might've indeed lost a kidney," Dorian dismisses, and refills his water. "Now hush and let me work."

"Wait." Elias shifts and holds up one of his deformed hands. "Would it bring these back?"

His shoulders hunch and Elias knows the answer before he

hears it. "I would have if I could."

With great effort and mostly Dorian lifting him, Elias eases upright. He finishes the water without throwing it up, and Dorian slinks off the bed to order whoever's closest outside to bring him something substantial and leafy green. The robe reaches past his knees but a gap opens over his chest with his movement, letting something silvery, like snail-slime on his skin, catch the candlelight before it's covered again. A tattoo? It's the least-dressed Elias has ever seen him, and Dorian seems aware of that fact with how stiffly he moves now that Elias is lucid enough to notice.

"Here." Dorian holds a little jar in his hands containing something that smells like honey but looks like lard. "Beeswax, for your skin. Sit still."

Taking a minuscule amount onto his fingertips, Dorian works the soft paste around his raw nose and if Elias's hands weren't clumsy bandaged mitts, he'd do it himself. The last time Elias saw him he'd been an impulsive fool and *still*, though the vampire is trying his damndest to keep this clinical, it's *not*.

"D—"

"Shhh." The paste is amazingly soft on his chapped lips. Elias closes his eyes and bears the methodical little touches until he is permitted to smear the rest around himself.

"You were Aeskerat." The name, said as softly as he can, still seems to frighten the candles, flickering in a phantom wind. "A blood slave. Gregori told me."

The jar hits the side table with a tinny *clink* and Dorian holds his neck, shoulders up. "He treated you well, I see."

"What if it hadn't been him?"

Dorian drags a hand down his face with a sharp huff. "I didn't have any authority—"

"You could have turned me. I asked you to."

"You would have died anyway, either on the battlefield or over and over and over again in the fighting pits." He cradles Elias's deformed hand. "I'm sorry."

"You said you'd come after me."

"I said I would *try*," he defends hotly.

"What, Amaranth didn't let you?" Elias isn't even mad—not at Dorian. Life's too short to be bitter—that's what Gregori had said, and he's right. Dorian's just *here*, and it's all flooding back. He's missing *fingers* from trying only to stay alive under the teeth of all these vampires. "Her attempt to keep the peace turned out well."

"If I'd gone after you, I'd have gone alone," Dorian snaps. "I had nothing to offer Gregori except myself—is that what you would prefer? Both of us in his servitude? I wouldn't have been with you, wouldn't have been able to comfort you. You never would have seen me again, and we both would have died when Aeskerat and Tanarang went to war."

No, Elias scowls, *I just wanted you to fight for me.*

"I'm sorry, Elias. No buts, no excuses, no justifications. *I'm sorry.*" Dorian brings a hand to his chest and waits, eyes shiny.

Vampires can cry?

It's not his fault, but something else is. Something that Aeskerat now dangles over his head. "My chief isn't dead," Elias whispers. "You missed."

Shock ripples across his face. "I—" Dorian cuts himself off and thinks, fist beneath his nose. "You distracted me. I knew I missed, I was going to finish him off, and you stabbed me. Then you let me up and..." He slumps in wry astonishment. "And I forgot. Wait—did you reunite with him? He's at Aeskerat?"

Elias shakes his head. "Later. I'll tell you everything." None of it matters, even if Dorian had done it to be cruel. "I forgive you—for all of it. Life's too short to be bitter. You were right in the end. I didn't break."

Dorian laughs wetly and nods to him. "I can see that."

"Were you his?"

"Gregori's?" Dorian clears his throat and shakes his head. "No, I wasn't." A gentle knock at the door, and he's up to fetch Elias's food. It smells fishy and salty and about the most divine meal Elias could imagine, a dark broth with dark leafy chunks floating in it. *Perfection.* "What did Gregori tell you?"

"He said there were two vampires in his way to become grandsire and you took out one of them."

"Eat, please. Carefully."

Finding a grip for the spoon takes a few tries and more effort than Elias expects, but he's drawing his line at asking Dorian to feed him. He sits back, propped up against all the pillows. The leafy bits are chewy and the salt stings his sore mouth, but he doesn't care.

Dorian smooths over the wrinkles in the robe once he's sure Elias can keep the soup down. "You asked me once why I turned."

"I did." But now knowing what he knows, Elias isn't so sure he wants to hear the rest. "You don't have to tell me."

Dorian shifts on the mattress, letting one leg dangle. "They only came because Mount Inai erupted." His pitch lowers as he speaks, eyes drifting from the soup to the wall past Elias's head, to the bed frame on his other side. Never at Elias's face. "Lava, fire, ash everywhere. Much of the island died that day."

Dorian bites his lip and balls a fist in the blankets. Elias doesn't want to interrupt, not even with the *clack* of the spoon against the bowl.

"My sister lived. We thought we'd survived it, miraculously, but the ash cloud blocked out the sun for days and then the raiders came. They had her, Amelie, kicking and screaming bloody murder, fighting hard as her little body could. She was strong for a fishbone." He smiles proudly and folds his arms in his lap so his nails don't tear a hole in the blankets.

Elias can figure out the rest. "You don't have to finish."

Dorian shakes his head. "I offered myself in her place and they asked why they shouldn't take us all. And I looked at Amelie, knowing what awaited her if she left the island. So I told them I'd kill her to save her, but that if they took me and left, I wouldn't fight because I knew they'd come back if I did." He works his jaw and shrugs stiffly. "The last time I saw my sister, she was screaming that she'd never forgive me."

Dorian tucks his hair behind his ear and Elias isn't sure how he never noticed the little black stone looped on a ring through the curve of the cartilage. Once he lowers his hand, the braids fall back into place and hide it again.

"You were all she had left," Elias says, and then doesn't know how to finish that. *Of course she never forgave you? Why didn't you take her with you?* Dorian's no doubt plagued himself with those thoughts long enough.

"She was just a kid," he whispers. "I didn't want her growing up away from the sun or watching whatever would happen to me."

Elias almost tells him what it was like growing up without his brother, but there's no room for mourning in the clan. *We're alive and they're not.* Nothing will help Dorian feel better, like how nothing can change how Elias doesn't remember what Misha looks like or sounds like. But Misha didn't die a blood slave, and Elias thinks he's glad he was spared witnessing Misha fall, staring at what remained of him, out of their reach.

"I think she would have forgiven you when she got old enough to appreciate what you did," he says instead.

"She must have, because she wrote me letters. I believed Grandsire Tammen would keep to our agreement, but the vampire who owned me?" He purses his lips and contorts a rueful smile. "Tammen designed the rules but Eldelaire enforced them, and Eldelaire was her champion in every contest during her rule. No weaknesses, a perfect warrior."

Dorian nudges the bowl, insisting that Elias keep eating with a look that threatens to spoonfeed him if he doesn't. Despite his painfully empty stomach, Elias stirs the soup around, not all that hungry anymore. *No*, he thinks. *He took care of me. I have to take care of myself now.*

His slurping is painfully loud as Dorian continues. "She did have vices. All it took was a few longing glances at beautiful Tammen, and Eldelaire's insecurity did the rest. She took me to bed, and I made her fat and happy and engorged on nearly every last drop I had to give. While she slept it off, I killed her. And then myself."

Dorian says it so flatly, Elias thinks he's misheard. "They didn't immediately stake you for that?" The blood slaves he'd met would never have dared dream of such a desperate move.

He shakes his head. "Eldelaire fell to her own hubris, no cheats, no tricks."

Elias furrows his brows and tries to be delicate when he asks, "Sleeping with her to stake her wasn't a trick?"

Dorian sags and sweeps his hair back, only to pull it forward again to wring in his fingers. "Eldelaire wasn't exactly a romantic. I didn't poison her, didn't tie her down, didn't trap her. That she didn't think anything suspicious about her slave suddenly wanting to bed her? That's on her." He tuts and waves flippantly. "I didn't expect Gregori to kill Tammen in the chaos, declare himself grandsire, and pardon me. I stayed, gave my word, swore the oath, then my sister stopped sending me letters only forty years later."

Forty years… Elias knows in the grand scale of Dorian's life, forty years is nothing, but it's doubtful it felt like nothing as he lived it. "Gregori let you go?"

Dorian snorts an unhappy laugh. "The world ended with the Great Freeze a few decades later, and with no collateral left against me, I had my chance. Gregori challenged me to a duel for my freedom, painted the walls of the fighting pit with my blood, then said if I found any coven to take me in before I starved, he'd not hunt me down."

Not the first to arrive bloodied, frozen, and delirious at Amaranth's doorstep, then. Elias sips the last of the broth and Dorian clears the bowl away, setting it outside the door for someone else to take away.

"I can go back to my room," Elias offers, "or any room. So that you can have yours back."

"I don't mind. You're not healed yet anyway." Dorian tucks the blankets up to his chest. "It wouldn't have been the worst way for you to turn, and you came close a couple times."

Elias eases back onto his uninjured side and frowns. "What do you mean?"

"Turning only heals what kills you," Dorian says as he blows out a candle that had melted to nothing. "You are frozen in the state you died for eternity, and whatever wounds you sustain in dying stay with you."

"I… hadn't realized that. Haven't seen any vampires with it obvious." Gregori's puffy silvery-pink scar… it could have been a weapon or a piece of tree that did him in.

"They hide it well." Dorian presses the backs of his fingers to Elias's forehead. "Fever's broken. Clear skies from here."

Elias goes cross-eyed staring at Dorian's wrist where the sleeve of his robe brushes his cheek. Either he's shockingly modest, or… "Dorian?"

"Yes?" Too quick.

By the light of the fresh candle in the corner, more silvery snail trails shimmer on Dorian's neck that would normally be hidden by his cloak and jerkin. Elias can't touch them with his hand all bandaged up, but Dorian shies away from his reach anyway. "Like I said," he mumbles softly, "how you die stays with you forever."

Fair's fair, Elias wants to argue. Dorian has seen all of him, twice now. He scoots away with a muttered, "Sorry."

Silent, Dorian loosens the tie of the robe enough to slip it off his shoulders, sleeves pooling around his hands. Dozens of marks litter his skin. Silvery bites from Eldelaire, faint purple bruises surrounding them. Other bruises, shaped like fingers, trail his skin.

"Do they still hurt?"

"Sometimes. When I'm hungry." Dorian ghosts the pads of his fingers over a razor thin line down his wrist, its twin mirrored on the other. "Forever is too long to stay bitter," he whispers, "or ashamed."

Elias doesn't know what to say, if there's anything *to* say when an *I'm sorry* seems paltry. He spreads his arms in silent invitation, but Dorian doesn't accept, fixing his robe.

Instead Dorian asks, "Did you only come around to liking me out of a desire to survive?"

The question scalds. Elias's arms drop. His immediate thought is *No*, but that wouldn't be completely true. "You didn't do anything wrong," he settles on. "Survival was part of it, I think, but you're the first person in my life to be unabashedly kind to me."

Now Dorian moves, tucking up the furs as a buffer between them and curling up atop them. "I owe you an explanation—"

"No, you don't."

"Yes," Dorian insists, "I do. Or, I need to say it and I want you to hear it."

Elias lies back down to relieve the tension on his side, close enough to count Dorian's eyelashes. "Say what?"

"That I'm bad at this." He sighs wearily. "Showing I care. Whether that's you or Kymiria or Markus or anyone else."

"I don't think you're bad at it." Elias's face heats when he mumbles, "That you don't reciprocate is another matter."

Dorian smiles in sympathy, not denying it, and folds his arms across his stomach, knees bent. "It's the transient nature of what we are."

"Transient?" Elias scoffs. "You're immortal."

"And nothing else is." He's quiet, eyes on his thumbs as they massage the embroidery on his sleeve. "We don't get to go peacefully in our sleep. We don't get to see the twilight closing in after a long and fulfilling life. When we die, it's fast, violent, and unpredictable."

He sounds like Gregori, and how different they are, Dorian looking up at the ceiling of his room with regret, Gregori lording over his chambers with pride. Elias wants nothing more than to card those brunet braids through his fingers but he can't because of the stupid bandages so he frowns and patiently waits for Dorian to continue.

"Nothing is permanent when you live forever. Nothing is yours. This room won't be mine forever. My clothes won't last forever. Love doesn't last forever. So..." He heaves a shaky sigh and toys with one of the ties of his braids, firmly looking not at Elias but skyward. "So when someone becomes your friend or your ally or your confidant, your lover, your partner, it's always only *for now*. And I'm not old enough to appreciate the beauty in fragility yet."

Elias clumsily brushes those braids off Dorian's shoulder anyway and *hmphs*. "That might be the longest *It's not you* I'll ever hear." Dorian deflates, but it's not that Elias doesn't understand. "Kymiria explained this to me already. Why are you telling me now?"

"I'm trying to tell you that it's not that we can't care, it's the inevitable grief when all the care in the world can't stop the march of time, so it's easier to... pretend, I guess." Dorian sits up, arms around his knees. "Pretend the love isn't there, isn't real, isn't honest. That's the curse of vampirism, Elias. *Pretending*. I should have taken you back to your cave instead of dragging you into this, and for that decision, I'm sorry."

"But then I never would have known you." Elias scoots forward and noses his cheek. "And it is real."

Dorian pulls away, leaves the bed entirely. "For now."

Chapter 12:
The Oath

Dorian prepares Elias to face Amaranth and the entire host of Tanarang in the Grand Hall once Elias's strength returns enough to stand on his own feet five moons later. With big talk of this oath he must take to remain protected by their walls, Elias expected it to be a lot more intimidating and involved.

"If Amaranth weren't stuck in the body of a child, I wouldn't be surprised if the oath was sleeping with her." Elias stops up short when Dorian doesn't immediately answer, busy laying out fresh Tanarang leathers for him on the bed. He'd gotten his room back reeking of essential oils, and Dorian stubbornly did not explain where it all came from, too busy blushing and stuttering out that he had nothing to do with it.

He still doesn't answer about Amaranth. "It's not, right?"

"I didn't think I had to dignify that with a denial."

Elias hadn't gotten to sit for five seconds and appreciate being back in his company before Dorian pressed him to take this stupid oath, but *gods*, he'd missed him. Dorian has been doing a fantastic job at pretending their conversation never happened. Elias can't snag his attention much amidst battle preparations, and when he does, Dorian's polite but distant. He ensures Elias is eating and that the curious children leave him be and gives his excuses to be elsewhere. Or, like now, stands halfway across the room as if the humid air of the castle is some impenetrable wall.

Elias decides to try once more. Dorian wasn't this cold even when they met. "I told Kymiria that you aren't afraid to tell me how you feel. Are you embarrassed or something? Worried you said too much?"

Dorian puts even more space between them and folds his arms tightly. "We have more prescient crises to deal with."

Elias smacks his lips and smiles thinly. "Right. This oath that I don't even want to take."

Dorian sighs and pinches the bridge of his nose. "Please don't say that."

"Why?" Elias laughs humorlessly. "Would it be better for you if I'd died out there?"

"No!" Dorian balks and scrunches his face. "No, of course not."

"Then talk to me."

Still, Dorian refuses, looking constipated every second Elias refuses to avoid this conversation until, "I overstepped your boundaries and I'm trying to fix that."

Elias frowns. "You—what?"

"I should have given you your room back," Dorian explains without explaining anything. "Should have given you a bed to yourself, should have been presentable when you woke up, shouldn't have pushed about trying to explain myself. I gave you the wrong idea."

So he is embarrassed. Elias sets his jaw and nods. "What wrong idea would that be?"

"Whatever you think is going to happen between us, it won't."

So matter-of-fact. Dorian already said no once, but that had been under duress, hadn't it? He'd said no because he couldn't stop Amaranth from selling him to Aeskerat.

He has to feel *something*, doesn't he? Or does it still not matter because Elias is a fragile yearling and not worth the risk? Elias turns away and fiddles with the stitching of his new shirt. "Because I'll be dead soon."

"No, it's—" Dorian searches the ceiling. "You can't want me but reject everything that comes with me."

"I don't care that you're a vampire." *In fact, I don't mind at all.* Now if Dorian would let him in, they could discuss Elias's newfound appreciation for immortals.

"I'm a Tanarang and proud to be one," Dorian amends. "You owe this coven nothing, I know that. I know the oath is restrictive, but you're either here, with me, with all of us, or you're gone. My whole world is right here. I can't leave it for..."

"For me."

Reluctantly, Dorian nods. "You wouldn't have to take it if you left, but you're a liability and would never be allowed back," he says softly.

Pity is the last thing Elias wants. Whether it's Gregori or Dorian or Amaranth calling him piggy or yearling, he's never going to escape the centuries between them. They're never going to stand on equal ground.

Dorian gestures toward the door. "I can take you to Panolin to ride out the rest of the winter right now if you want. But I can't stay with you. You can't ask me to do that."

Panolin. One ship away from freedom and the sun and all the colors he saw in those paintings in Olimaunt. One ship away from a place without Dorian. "They sold me to Aeskerat."

Dorian quiets. "I know."

"What if I'd been given to an Eldelaire? Should I even bother expecting an apology from Amaranth? She still doesn't think what she did was wrong."

"I need you to decide. Stay or go? Right decision or wrong, she's my grandsire and has been for three centuries. She's kept us thriving for this long and did what she thought was best to keep our people safe."

Elias *hmphs*. This wasn't the reunion he'd expected while dying from blood loss and the cold. "I can understand her logic while still hating that I'm the only one who suffered for it," he mutters.

Dorian gives a sympathetic smile and drifts over, then thinks better of it and leans against the bedframe, arms folded tightly.

"Would you have me if I forgave and forgot?" Amaranth is the problem. The children aren't. Castor's been kind to him. Elphaba is stern but fair.

Dorian tilts his head. "Would you mean it?"

Probably not. Elias runs his hand through what's left of his hair. His handful of months with Dorian won't ever compare to three centuries of loyalty to Tanarang. Is it so selfish a notion, though, to want Dorian to fight for him like Gregori did? But Elias is all too aware of the last time he tried to get Dorian to go against his coven's wishes.

He'll end up dead, too.

Such a waste. Eight hundred years and then *gone*. Over something so trivial.

Dorian is still waiting on an answer. Elias shakes his head. "They can't protect me just because it's the right thing to do?"

"It needs to be official."

Elias spreads his hands. "Then claim me."

Dorian gives a tedious sigh. "It's not Aeskerat you have to convince your loyalty to, it's us, and we don't recognize the claim. You have to prove you're worth dying for, and the oath is how you do that."

And they're back here again. Elias groans and slumps back on the bed. "Coven politics are going to get me killed."

"Only if you break your oath."

Elias squirms, staring at the house sigil of the breaching whale on the leathers.

"Is there something else?"

The only person who cares about him in Tanarang is Dorian, and if Jacobi gets his hands on Aeskerat's wayward vampire, there's nothing protecting Elias from Tanarang teeth either. Would Jacobi keep his word? Would he bother escorting Elias to the port towns to send him south if Dorian can't? Because if Gregori's dead, there's nothing else left for Elias beyond the wall of Castle Tanarang. Not even his clan.

"What exactly does a betrayal of the oath look like?"

Dorian steps back, hands on his hips. "Selling secrets, slaying your own kin, conspiring with the enemy. The usual. Why?"

Elias swallows thickly. "Something happened. Something that might muddy the waters."

"Might it have to do with that little letter pleading amnesty?"

"Gregori kissed me." Elias rushes through an explanation of how he only planned to survive, to have enslavement feel a little less awful. The books and the urchins and Jacobi and Julian's scheming. *King of the Hill* and Gregori's last stand helping him escape and Jacobi's smoke and mirrors about his grandsire's demise. When Elias details Julian's demise, Dorian frowns and looks away.

"I expected some relief," Elias ventures curiously. "He was an ass. One less Aeskerat to worry about."

"Julian..." Dorian shakes his head. "Nothing. You're right."

Elias gives him a flat look. "Stop doing that."

"It's nothing," Dorian repeats. "He just wasn't so careless when I knew him. An inglorious end is all."

Whatever Julian Dorian knew wasn't who Elias met. He can't picture them in the same coven, much less as friends. Inglorious it may be, but he brought his end upon himself, and at least Gregori made it fast.

"I don't..." Elias huffs. "Emotions aside, Gregori is honorable, he kept his word. He fought his own coven for me and to prevent a bloody war between your houses. He said he couldn't run to Amaranth or anyone else to save him but if he's alive and it's between Gregori and Jacobi, would an alliance not benefit you both?" Elias raises his hands, then takes the Tanarang jerkin and clutches it to his chest. "I'm not saying I'd betray my oath, but is it still conspiring with the enemy if he's not actually your enemy?"

Two weeks removed from Gregori's company and in some ways, Elias can't separate it from his fever dreams. "Is it really that intense?" he asks Dorian when he hasn't said anything. "This—this whatever you'd call it that happens in older vampires that makes them care. Is it even real?"

Dorian sits at the edge of his bed, knee drawn up to his chest. "I think it depends on the vampire," he says softly. "Is it *real*? It's real enough that it's not some compulsion he couldn't resist. But *real* as in *love* and not just *want*, I don't think even Gregori would know."

Elias huffs again and pulls his new shirt on, painstakingly

tightening the laces on the jerkin as much as he can. "I know with him it's the survival talking," he says. "I don't *want* him. He's just... he's not the hungry monster I thought he was." *None of you are.*

Dorian sighs deeply and turns around to let him swap sleep pants for proper leathers. "He remains an Aeskerat even if he has lost the grandsireship to Jacobi. His views on the living and your place as livestock remain at odds with Amaranth's, and if he hasn't changed in eight-hundred years, he won't change tomorrow, even given his treatment of you. You are his exception."

Elias can't tie the laces on his new boots without his missing fingertips. He glares at the clean black leathers and the white-spotted cloak, both happy to be blanketed with it again and too confined by its weight. "Can you...?"

Dorian does them up for him and Elias tries to catch all the elusive feathers of his argument in one fist. "The enemy of my enemy is my friend. You're all vampires of the North."

"*If* he lives," Dorian begins slowly, "and *if* he indeed wants an alliance, he will have many concessions to make. That is assuming he can reclaim his place atop Aeskerat and keep his coven in line. Gregori is Aeskerat first, he always will be, and won't kneel to Amaranth to save his own life." Dorian pulls Elias's cloak around his shoulders and secures it, smoothing the furs. "If you're imagining racing out into the snow to hunt him down all by yourself, or him showing up in the eleventh hour to kill Jacobi for us and slaughter the rest of his coven, you are mistaken. They're hungry, and it's his duty to keep them fed even if that means taking our food for themselves."

Oh, how did I get tangled up in all this? Elias drags his feet, still achy and stiff from Jacobi's arrow but whole again. "If I go South, I want to study art." If Jacobi doesn't come to slaughter them all. Amaranth sold Elias without pause before to prevent a war, and Elias will likely remain her lowest priority to protect, oath or no oath. He wouldn't be surprised if Jacobi *accidentally* lets one of his new underlings kill him in the heat of battle. "I'd want to paint those wildflowers."

"You will."

The walk down to the Grand Hall is tediously long. Elias has to hold onto Dorian down the many stairs and stop more than once when the walls start to spin. "Are you sure it's safe to bleed more for Amaranth and Hyacinth *right* this second?" he jokes while catching his breath against a warped window.

"You're the first living soul to take the oath in the history of the castle," Dorian says, solid arm keeping him upright. "No special treatment, I'm afraid."

"Ooh, what an honor."

He'd rather walk under his own strength into the Grand Hall and its piercing stare of hundreds of eyes, but hanging off Dorian is better than crawling. Once again, Amaranth and Hyacinth stand before the head table.

"You have to kneel," Dorian reminds him in a murmur. "Can you get back up again without me?"

"I'll manage."

Dorian lets him go at the bottom of the steps to go stand with Kymiria and Markus. *It's short*, he thinks. *It's a couple words and a few drops of blood.* He drops into a kneel with far less grace than he wants, steadying himself with a hand on the steps. Neither grandsire smiles, but Amaranth does take a shuffle-step forward in what he hopes is encouragement.

She had to protect her people first, he reminds himself. She thought the best way to do that was by giving up one soul they'd only known for two months. The North is bitter and pitiless, and if this oath is this serious, Elias can forgive her. Now she'll have no excuse to not fight for him again. This is her apology.

"I, Elias of Clan Maewag, swear my blood, my body, and my immortal soul to Tanarang, House of the Whale, until its stone crumbles to dust, the sea withers to a desert, and the stars fall from the night sky."

Perfect, he thinks, bandaged fist balled on the step. Amaranth offers a hand, palm up and fingers curled. Elias sets his hand in hers and braces for her teeth. Instead, a single sharp prick sticks his index finger. Amaranth drags the needle against her lips.

Her eyes glitter as she gives him the tiniest of nods, then she passes the needle to her brother. They hand it back and warmth unfurls in Elias's chest with only a drop of Hyacinth's blood. "May you have a place at this table and sanctuary within these walls. Rise, Elias of Tanarang."

Amaranth and Hyacinth agree to see him privately about Jacobi's threats in their chambers and neither is thrilled with the news.

"I can't confirm if Julian found my clan, but I saw my chief with my own eyes."

"The same dead chief that Dorian killed?" The three of them sit around a woven wicker table inlaid with a map of the North. Or, Elias sits. Hyacinth looms over the map with little figurines of whales and bears like she's at Gregori's game board.

"Apparently he lived."

"Are you sure he lives?" Amaranth fiddles with one of her braids beside her brother. "He hadn't turned?"

Elias hesitates, thinking back to the way Yarren looked all filthy in chains. "He never would have willingly. Julian and his scout were still disgusted by him and his smell."

"That could be another ruse. Jacobi is fond of his tricks."

"It was him, and living or dead, he'd never give up our—*his* clan." Elias still can't find their cave on the map. He folds his arms on the tabletop. "I know you don't care about them. I know they hate all vampires and see no shades of grey. I know they'd never respect your ways. They're still people who don't deserve to be caught in the middle between you and Aeskerat."

Hyacinth flexes his fingers and taps one of the whale figures. "What would you have us do? We don't know where your clan is, we don't know if Jacobi was bluffing, we don't know if Gregori lives. Sending our scouts out to drag them to a sanctuary they don't want, even if we did know these things, risks Tanarang lives that we need here, not out in the open vulnerable to ambush."

"You're right," Elias mutters, as much as he wishes to believe otherwise. He holds his head in his hands, hair snagging on his remaining bandages. "I watched Gregori take out at least four of his own when I'd thought he'd had Jacobi outnumbered. Jacobi wouldn't resort to threats if this were a lost cause, would he?"

"Have you ever been starving, Elias?" Amaranth asks. "I don't mean an empty stomach. I mean, your body eating itself, every joint exposed and raw and aching. You can't sleep because your head pounds and your dry veins grate against each other with every breath."

"No, my Lady."

Amaranth hops up onto the table and removes two of the Aeskerat bears. "Jacobi and Julian would not have acted without confidence that they could win against Gregori. They would have promised their constituents better lives than Gregori's conservative nature provided."

"Those who survived the coup would have bled their blood

slaves dry healing themselves," Hyacinth adds, knocking over another bear with a flick of his finger. "Their pride is wounded, they're thirsty for vengeance. If Jacobi wants to remain in power, he needs to keep his promise to his hungry people, and that means taking ours or dying in the attempt. And he is, unquestionably, in power." Hyacinth waves Elias's letter and casts it onto the map. "Or Gregori would have sent a messenger saying all is well by now."

So that's it, then. Jacobi will attack because he must, and Elias's clan is beyond their reach. "All this over one dead fledgling?"

"I'm sorry we can't help your kin, Elias." Amaranth's small hand falls heavy on his arm. "You're right, they don't deserve to be caught in the middle. Perhaps they lied and your chief is all they found."

"Maybe," he mutters, hollow. "Jacobi said he wanted half of your people to avoid a fight. And Dorian. Do you believe him?"

Amaranth scowls frostily. "That usurper is in no position to negotiate."

"What if he finds another coven to align with?" Elias recalls the bitter disdain on Jacobi's face when he sent him on this fool's errand. "I take it that every other coven hates you because of how well you treat your people, but how did you get here?"

It should not be a question that has both grandsires sharing a cautious look, minute flickers of warning and doubt passing in silent conversation, until Amaranth sighs. She taps Tanarang on the map. "Of all nine covens, what do you see here?"

Elias frowns and stares blankly at the map—the same nine covens that had been in the atlas. Little fox and wolf figurines pile up over Geltmon and Houlind on the other coast. Son Kir's moose lie in the ocean to the north. The map doesn't give any other helpful information like castle size, population, or terrain beyond the artsy feathering of vague mountains and hills. He sits back and studies the map as a whole, the southern edge bordering at a thin line labeled, in frilly script, *Tropic of Chrysanthemum.*

Oh. "You're the closest to the South." Not by much, but the three on the other coast, deep within their own mountains, look far harder to reach on foot.

"There aren't many old vampires left," Amaranth says. "In the War for the North, they elected Chrysanthemum to lead the united covens. Her coven, *our* coven, was the flagship, and we took the steepest losses."

Hyacinth sits back and crosses his arms, looking like an old man in a child's body with the darkness in his glower. "They didn't understand that it was a lost cause, and they resented her for refusing to blanket the entire world in an eternal night."

Elias scrunches his face in confusion. "Dorian told me what would have happened if the sun disappeared completely. *Everyone,* and everything, would have died."

"They didn't see it that way," Amaranth mutters. "So when all was over and Hyacinth and I became grandsires in her memory of peace, those who survived thought their families died for nothing and left. We rebuilt with fresh blood, and they've never forgiven us."

"*First Dominion* vampires," Hyacinth mocks. "We lost all but four."

"And gained one," Amaranth reminds him with a lopsided smile. "But no, Elias, as long as we keep to ourselves, historically, the other covens have left us alone. Jacobi forging an alliance this fast is a slim possibility at best."

"Jacobi is no Gregori," Hyacinth dismisses. "The price for an army to fight on his behalf would be far steeper than he's willing to pay when he has only proven himself an honorless betrayer."

Amaranth summons Dorian to escort Elias back to his rest so

he can continue rebuilding his strength, but then stops him on his way out the door. "You're a Tanarang now. You're permitted a single braid to show your camaraderie."

She glances at Dorian and dips her head, then closes the door.

Elias bunches up his cloak, a shiver running through him. "We're going to war?"

"We'll win."

"That's what Gregori said."

"C'mon, let's see about your hair and get you more soup." And without a response, Dorian offers to help him down the steep stairs of the tower.

Elias runs his hand through what hair he has left, long enough to braid a tiny lock over his temple. "Does it have to be seaweed soup? It's getting kind of old."

"You need the iron and it's the only green we have."

Elias wrinkles his nose. "Even I know the seaweed isn't green. Not really."

Dorian shrugs.

"Can I have dessert after?"

Dorian winks. "I'll see what I can do."

Dorian paces a brand new ditch into the ground outside the wall. They're as prepared as they can be with the gate fully blocked and barricaded. The only way past the wall now is up and over.

Stake pits of Northern ice litter the battlefield for any cavalry. He doesn't expect more than half a dozen horses with how much blood they require to sustain, but Elias was of no help when he asked for an estimate. Tanarang's hundred and thirteen vampires have only Lily, Dandy, Rose, and Clover since he lost Poppy.

He counts and recounts their stock of arrows—two hundred for each bow—and their barrels of whale oil to spill and burn. The doorway into the Holdfast has been locked and barred, and in case of catastrophe, they have their escape routes.

Dorian nods to himself, then goes back to restart the whole count because he can't rest otherwise.

Elias had gawked at their lone sailing ship, the *Peony*, docked in a cove below, and asked why, then, they cross the continent to reach the Eastern ports instead of sailing south outside their front yard.

"The seas are treacherous up here," Dorian had explained. "Us and Son Kir are the only settlements on the western coast since the Great Freeze. No merchant wants to risk their ship, their crew, or their time sailing all the way up here for two castles without many valuables to trade." That they're only two covens and Son Kir is one of them also doesn't help. They're ambivalent toward Tanarang at the best of times, outright hostile otherwise—harsh slavers gritting out a bleak existence in their icy castle. "We used to have a little fleet of three."

Piling the entire host onto one ship to sail to sanctuary is their last resort. Dorian finds himself staring at the *Peony*, defenses checked and rechecked and still insufficient.

No matter what, Jacobi isn't getting Elias back. He'll make sure of that. Elias has a perfect excuse to avoid whatever fight is coming by resting and healing and regaining his strength. He'll be fine.

They'll all be fine.

"Afraid it will float away?" Markus's boots crunch on the snow, a skip in his stride. He might be the peppiest vampire in Tanarang convinced that they'll win for simplicity's sake. That victory is fact and they need not fret.

If only it were.

"Aeskerat never had the numbers. We don't know how many Gregori took out before he fell, but now they have even less."

"Is that not a good thing? Simple math."

"Jacobi won't fall on his own stake. He's going to find reinforcements from somewhere." Elias's suggestion that he could align with another coven, spitting fire and venom about the scourge of Tanarang if he promises them their share of the spoils, isn't without merit. "It's not the battle that scares me. It's who we'll have to mourn when it's over."

"Kymiria thinks you're going to do something stupid." Markus casually toys with one of his arrows. "Does she have to snap your neck again to keep you safe?"

What does she expect? They're vampires. Who they were in life is exacerbated in death.

Markus twirls the arrow and rises up on his toes. "I have a new experiment I want to try."

As wonderful as that sounds on the never-ending eve of battle, "I'm not in the mood, Markus."

"I can respect that." Markus nods and stows the arrow. "But the defenses haven't changed since the last dozen times you checked them, and we need you of sound mind when they arrive."

He's annoying when he's right. Markus does have a backup offer that involves himself, Dorian, and Kymiria all piled in the latter's room for blood pops and snuggles.

To this, Dorian agrees.

Kymiria can't stop complimenting Markus's ingenuity, crunching the ice crystals loudly with every bite. She's deposited herself in Dorian's lap, hanging off him and trying to steal his once she devours hers. He halfheartedly threatens to dump her on the floor if she doesn't let him nibble in peace.

Their new arrangement leaves Kymiria a little less eager to shed clothes, whether for his benefit or Markus's comfort, he's not sure. She's still handsy where Markus isn't, touching Dorian's shoulders, his arms, his hair. What can he say? He likes the attention.

"You've outdone yourself," Dorian whispers against Markus's neck once they're all sinking in the bed's fluffy furs. "I know this is outside your comfort zone."

"That's why I brought relief." Markus nudges Dorian off him and onto Kymiria instead, scooting away to prop himself against the wall as they meld together. He stays close enough to keep their legs tangled but doesn't cuddle. Dorian doesn't push.

This is... nice. Better than marching ditches into the snow. Sleep at least lets him turn his brain off and stop thinking about tactics and strategies and wherever Jacobi's going to get his extra forces and what if he does manage to outnumber them—

"You're thinking too loud," Kymiria whines. "Hush."

"As you wish." He dozes curled against Kymiria and eventually feels Markus dip the bed on his other side and smiles.

It's new, being in the middle, and he thinks they shift around four or five times because Kymiria's bed isn't meant for three. At some point he ends up using Markus's thigh as a pillow, Kymiria curled up loosely in his arms. Markus undoes Dorian's braids and methodically runs his fingers through his hair and if this is the best it will ever get, he's okay with that.

He looks up at Markus's honey brown eyes and shushes the voice whispering that this, too, won't last forever. Markus must see it on his face, because he dips his head, fingers stilling at his temple. "What's wrong?" he whispers.

Dorian refuses to ruin the moment. He dons a dopey smile and whispers back, "Do you want to switch?" He's been itching to get his hands in that golden fluff.

Markus shakes his head. "I'm happy right here."

Quinn comes to drag them out of bed far too soon. "Storm blew in," she says. "Left a mess of the stairs down to the ship. We need help shoveling."

Kymiria groans. "There's a hundred other vampires in this castle you could have recruited for grunt work."

"A hundred vampires who would complete a task that takes three hours in ten minutes." Quinn crosses her arms. "Those stairs have to remain clear."

"Indeed they do." Dorian shoves his boots on and follows Quinn to the wall. The blizzard must've come fast and hard, dumping snow up to their ankles in every direction. Other vampires brush snow off the walkway that runs along the wall and through the courtyard as wind fights them in gusts.

He drags a shovel that scrapes on the rocks, shuffling after Quinn when they both smell it: rotting carrion. Not fish, not whales. Terrestrial animals.

People.

Quinn drops her shovel and races with him to the wall amid shouts for arms. Jacobi's not out there, but it doesn't matter. Jacobi found his reinforcements, unburdened by the snow, immune to pain and exhaustion and any instinct for self-preservation.

Withers.

Markus could burn through his entire quiver without denting the battery of withers below. The gusting wind blows his every shot off course, and even when calculating for it and hitting true, the creatures slow for nothing except an arrow through the brain or the heart, even then rousing themselves shortly after and pulling out the weapon and resuming running.

He counts nearly fifty racing raggedly through the snow, drawn to Tanarang by all the living blood behind their walls. They answer to no one, rabid dogs unleashed. So few roam the Northern wilderness and here they gather so conveniently at their gate.

Where did they come from?

"Markus!" Dorian shouts, enkindling an arrow as Neire rolls a barrel of oil over the wall. "Light the oil!"

"That won't slow them down—"

"It's what we have, and if they're dry enough, they'll catch." He races off to spread the word.

The withers still have to scale the wall. Markus cuts into his wrist, letting it drip over the ledge, and readies a barrel with two of his kin. They'll bunch at the base and become easy targets, no minds for forethought or strategy. Only blood.

They screech and snarl and as they approach. He throws the barrel over, dips the head of his arrow in pitch, and ignites the oil below. And then Markus recognizes the tawny colors of their leathers.

"Dorian!"

Where'd he go?

He leaves Vick and Henri firing arrows straight down into the fray. Dorian is already back in the courtyard, commanding their kin to ready spears and swords and reminding them to go for the head, to decapitate if they can.

"Dorian!" Markus skids down the stairs. "Dorian, they're the Aeskerat blood slaves."

He falters, gaze snapping to the wall. "Jacobi truly has gone mad."

"He's also not here."

"Not yet." Dorian runs off and Markus loses sight of him again and returns to the wall. It's a couple dozen of them at least and they don't stop even as they burn, losing fingernails to the stone as they scale the wall. They have plenty of arrows but if even one gets over, it'll pull defenders from the wall, open a hole, wreak havoc until they can put it down.

Someone has to go down there.

He restocks his quiver and grabs two Northern ice swords. "Vick," he calls, standing on the ledge overlooking a clear space below. "Don't let them over."

"Where are—Markus, *wait*!"

Markus jumps, aiming for a softer pile of snow. It's still a rough landing, the drift consuming him so swiftly that he drops hard on his ankle. His bow snaps on impact and *damn* he should have thought about that.

Two stakes came from it, at least. He rolls to his feet and tosses the useless bowstring aside. He whistles at the horde to his left and bites his lip hard enough to draw blood as he holsters the stakes on either hip. "Buffet this way!"

Swords drawn, Markus skips backwards, whirling them in arcs to get their attention.

Come and get it.

Kymiria has her arms full escorting Gilan and his mother from the baths and into the kitchens with the rest of their family. Gilan wriggles in Tannys's hold the whole way while Kymiria tries to keep the other children from lagging behind, demanding that he can fight, too, that he knows how to shoot, that he's not afraid.

"That's why we need you protecting all your cousins and siblings, the last line of defense," Kymiria says, "You'll be brave for everyone, won't you?"

He puffs his little chest with pride at that. "Yes, Master Kymiria!"

Hyacinth is already down there with them as Tokh distributes furs, weapons, and emergency packs in case they have to run. He stands on a table, calmly explaining the plan to evacuate to the dock.

Tannys has Gilan hop along to find a bow his size. Kymiria kicks the kitchen door shut. "Hyacinth, do you need me down here?"

"No, we have this."

Dorotea stops her from peeling out into the fray, offering a tie for her hair. "Should we not load up the ship now before we're cut off? At least with Mother and the younger children?"

Elphaba looks ready to dual-fist swords and wield a third between her teeth to protect her brood.

"It's not as defensible and the seas thrash still with the wind." The last thing they need is a tipping boat and people overboard, or a rogue wither sniffing them out and alerting the mass of them with a single bite. "Hyacinth and Tokh aren't leaving you. They will know when it's best to run."

Kymiria doesn't often like to remember that Dorotea is her grandniece, that more than half the vulnerable faces gathered all in one spot are not only her charges but her blood, her kin. She never regrets her choice to turn. She's still here, still youthful and strong, and now better able to protect her family's legacy even three generations later. But it is a vulnerability itching hot beneath her skin.

Dorotea's already turned away fixing cloaks on her own children and nieces and nephews. The only face not present is Castor's. If she knows him, and she was there the day he was born, he's out there playing medic and hero to any vampire who needs his blood.

Elphaba, too, notices his absence and finds Kymiria over the crowd. Kymiria nods. She'll bring that brash fool back where he belongs, where it's safe, even if she has to break his bones to do it.

"Kymiria!" Elias elbows his way through, a determined set to his features. "I'm going out there."

"You're a shit shot, Yearling, and—"

"I know that!" He gets in her face, bow limp in his pinkie-less hand. "I can't hide when I brought them here."

She still doesn't like him, and still recovering from getting shot once, he'd be a fat, juicy target out there. What a time to decide to shed his cowardice. "Jacobi would have come whether you survived or not."

"I'm going," he insists, "either with you or after you."

Kymiria bares her teeth in a sneer. "I'm not dying for you."

"Nobody is dying for me," he argues.

Fine. "When I find Castor, you see that he comes back here and you *stay,* or I knock you on your ass now and you sleep the whole battle." Kymiria slams the door behind them and leads the way, barely slowing up for him.

Castor isn't so easy to find once she hits the courtyard. She hefts an axe and lops the head off a burning wither that got over the wall and tried to peel the skin off Lucius. He gives her an exhausted groan of gratitude as she runs past. She shouts back at Elias to find Castor and prays he has a single modicum more self-preservation than the withers to do as she says.

Not many scaled the wall successfully, but they don't relent even when missing arms and impaled by arrows like porcupine quills. Those on fire melt the ice over slick stone, and Kymiria almost slips twice in the puddles running past a wither that wriggles uselessly, burned black to bone. Best not let that one heal.

Two more leap thoughtlessly to the courtyard, straight from the upper walkway, and crumple on the ground only to rise again. Their grey skin bulges with rotting blood, the whites of their eyes gleaming sanguine red. Kymiria snarls in disgust. Aeskerat blood slaves, likely drank to the brink then fed deliriously by whatever sadistic Aeskerat vampires remained, made to die from the fever and turn into... *this*. No souls remain in their hearts, no emotion, no thought. Only hunger.

She puts the pair out of their short-lived misery and spins around again, searching for her grandnephew. *Castor... Castor... Where are you?* The fighting tapers off; the courtyard quiets.

Was that it? Is that all Jacobi has to throw at them?

"Vick!" She bounds up the stairs, glancing over the wall at the scattered vampires picking off the stragglers. A sizable pile of at least a dozen that have burned and melted into each other still twitches. "How many are left?"

Vick pants, singed, hands on his knees and carnation pink bites on his arms. "That's it down there."

She lowers her axe. "Jacobi?"

He shakes his head. "Don't hear, see, or smell him or any other reinforcements."

"Did we lose anyone?"

Vick jerks his chin over the wall. "Markus jumped. Saw him down there, haven't seen him since."

Kymiria scans the snow for him, squinting into the light flurries. "If that's the end of it, we'll clear the gate and go out looking for him and anyone else unaccounted for."

Vick nods and shoves off his knees with a haggard sigh. "Dorian said to use the ladders still, just in case."

"Then do that."

"Care to assist?" He drags one over and Kymiria hoists the other end. "Hold it steady, yeah? One—"

An arrow pierces Vick's back. He stumbles and chokes, ladder dropping with a heavy clatter. With a bemused frown, he grabs weakly for the tip protruding from his chest. His face goes ashen and he drops like a stone.

A wooden arrow.

Up on the gables of the castle, an Aeskerat archer readies another. Kymiria searches above them, up the sharp cliff face the castle was built into. Ropes dangle in the wind, rappelling the archer's kin down from above.

"Aeskerat!" she screams, shielding her chest with her arms and sprinting for cover under a barrage of pine.

Where did they get so many wooden arrows?

She's never seen her kin drop so fast, those limping from their injuries picked off like lame cattle. There's a dissociation between deadly weapons and reckless behavior when they can bounce back from any of it, even getting shot. Northern ice does not kill.

Kymiria ducks into the stables and fires back three arrows of her own. They can't have that many between them all. Wood is rare, invaluable this far north under the grip of winter. They'll run out. Have to climb down and face her coven in close combat.

Her kin have scattered, the courtyard clear of all except the dead.

And Amaranth.

Her grandsire marches out into the open, skirts sweeping about her legs in the wind. A sword rests at her hip and she grips her bow, glowering unflinchingly at the invaders.

"Jacobi!" An arrow sails at her head. Amaranth leans away, stoops to retrieve it, and nocks it in her own bow. In a blink, she fires. The archer rolls off the roof and splatters before the front doors. She backs up for cover behind the whale ice sculpture, pulls another arrow from the battlefield, and nocks it. "All Aeskerat, hear me now. Lay down your arms, turn over this cowardly usurper, and you will survive this night. You've slaughtered all your food, you have nowhere else to go, and you will deplete your quivers before you strike me down."

Neire *pssts* at Kymiria from the other side of the stables, and Kymiria crawls over, watching her grandsire the whole way. "I got six circling around," Neire whispers, "but if they came from above, there's a lot of unguarded windows."

Kymiria didn't consider them sneaking in. She counts eight archers within her line of sight, none of them Jacobi. "Castor? Dorian?"

Neire shakes her head. "Aeskerat doesn't know this castle like we do, but it only takes a couple."

"I'm not leaving her out there alone."

"Of course not." Neire glares out at the courtyard. "If things get hairy out here, don't expect backup. We're spread thin through all the corridors."

"We'll manage."

Neire scampers off and Kymiria scowls. Vick's up there with an arrow embedded in his chest that she needs. Thirteen of her kin have joined him around the courtyard. *They'll run out eventually,* she thinks. *Faster if they think they can hit me.*

She hesitates, trying to figure out how to signal Amaranth of her plan to snag all the arrows without distracting her.

Wait—that's—*damn.* Across the way, hiding beneath a horseless sleigh, lies Elias. Kymiria begs every god and goddess beneath the moons and beyond that he stays there out of the way and out of sight.

Amaranth shoots another Aeskerat down. "Jacobi!"

Chapter 13:
Blood-Bound

Every time Dorian resolves to return to the courtyard, an Aeskerat intruder bars his way. Castor is still stuck with him—exactly where he shouldn't be, even if he does come in handy with his stake—from their attempt to reach the kitchens where he belongs.

Castor drives a wedge of wood between the shoulder blades of an unsuspecting Aeskerat that Dorian doesn't recognize and yanks it back out. The intruder is yet another to stain their rugs tonight, but as far as Dorian can tell, no withers slipped past the courtyard. "Should we try for the *Peony*?"

"We can't defend the ship and the castle, and we're too scattered to get everyone on before we'd have to cast off." Once they leave and Aeskerat banners hang over their ramparts, it'll be that much harder taking it back. "We haven't lost yet." Though, the prospect of having to leave some behind to rendezvous at Chryssy Point is quickly proving inevitable.

He detours to the lounge for hidden stakes, nursing lacerations from close calls with every vampire except Jacobi because that bastard will send everyone else to die before himself.

Castor offers his wrist. "You need to heal."

"I'm fine." Dorian crouches, pulling stakes from beneath the couches and chaises. Only three, but that's three more than they had before. "You might need it more than me."

He stakes another Aeskerat in the lung on their way out and slams her to the floor. "Jacobi," he says, spitting the name in her face, "where is he?"

She chokes and wheezes and still sneers defiantly.

"He'll run out of meat shields eventually."

She dies, and he doesn't know her name, how old she was, how many other battles she'd survived, only to die in Jacobi's crusade for power.

"They can't start abducting people back up the cliffs," Castor says. "They'll have to leave on foot, and the only exits have been barricaded." Unless they missed a godly battering ram destroying the front gate, he's right. But his face turns grim, and they're thinking the exact same thing. Jacobi murdered all his food and marched his starving coven through the mountains for this fight. "Unless... he's desperate enough to try and take the castle for himself?"

"He's not taking the castle while there's even one Tanarang left defending it."

They finally reach the kitchens, doors barred up tight. Dorian bangs on the ancient wood. "Hyacinth, open up!"

Whalebone table legs screech on the other side and Dorian bounces anxiously. Tokh pries the door open a crack as the table scrapes out of the way. "What's going on out there?"

"I'm about to find out, just take Castor."

Castor shifts his weight, pulse racing loudly in his veins. He doesn't argue, though. He glowers and squeezes through the gap. Yes, Jacobi surprised them. Castor going out there blinded with rage would get him killed and he must know that. Fortifying the kitchens is the safest task he can do, out of the way and untouchable.

"He'll die slowly, won't he?" Castor asks.

If it's up to Dorian, Jacobi will die quickly, painlessly, and without ceremony, dumped and forgotten and unspectacular. He's not worth a mote more. "Just stay in here. We'll come for you when it's clear."

Tokh turns to look over his shoulder and moves out of the way for Hyacinth. "How many have we lost?"

"I don't know. I've killed four Aeskerat myself, but there's at least sixty out there from what I've heard in the halls and seen up on the roofs." The shameless cowards, turning their own blood slaves and sending them to the slaughter while they watched idly from above.

"Jacobi?"

"Haven't seen—"

Hyacinth gasps and shouts. "Dorian!"

Pain explodes in his shoulder, and he smacks into the door as hands yank him through the gap. A bone arrowhead pokes out beneath his clavicle. The Aeskerat archer readying another arrow is yet another he doesn't recognize. Dorian loses sight of them behind the door as it slams shut between them.

Every brush and bump of the arrow sends fire shooting through his shoulder. It's not an ice arrow; the shaft is wooden, and it splinters and frays like it was carved in a rush.

"Move the table back," he grunts, shoving Tokh aside to pull the arrow clean through. Hair-thin splinters scrape and stick, and he grits his teeth, and *oh* are those going to be a pain to dig out.

He tests his arm, hissing through the gritty tear of the splinters. No, they'll have to come out before he heals over them if he wants to shoot at all accurately for the rest of this battle.

Around him, children and parents panic. Then the door shudders under the sharp *thwack* of an axe.

The hall's too narrow for an entire army. Even if they break the door down, they'll meet faces full of arrows and stakes. Still, Castor and Dorotea order their family to upend the remaining tables for cover.

Tokh lays Dorian on the floor, ripping at the laces of his jerkin. "How many splinters?"

"I don't know, a lot?"

Hyacinth skitters backward with every *thwack* of the axe, twitchy fingers ready to loose through the first opening that appears. Tokh disappears from his side to grab a paring knife. "I need a light!" he shouts. "Try not to move."

Dorian squeezes his eyes shut, biting into the soft wood of a stake as the knife digs and Tokh's fingers pry. Tokh hisses, his *sorrys* running together in a slurry of panic.

That door won't hold, Dorian thinks as wood buckles and snaps. *It's too old*. It's not the only way in and out of the kitchens, but it's the most obvious. Unless they've found the false walls and hidden servants' passages, they'll come only through the front.

"Almost done, almost done, almost done…"

The door cracks. A vampire on the other side wails from Hyacinth's arrow.

"Done!" Tokh's knife clatters. "Done?"

It feels like Tokh tore a hole the size of his pinkie into one as wide as his fist, but yes, the splinters are out. "'Preciate it," he grunts, staggering to his feet. "Cera? Do you mind?"

She emerges from the crowd, swinging his good arm over her shoulder to drag him behind the shield of tables. "As much as you need."

He doesn't have the resolve to be gentle, biting down to bone on her thin wrist. Cera flinches and whimpers through an assuring nod that it's okay. The arrows stop flying and he pulls away from her.

Is that it?

Dorian sits up and stretches to see over the table. The door has several missing chunks, but it's still barricaded. Hyacinth doesn't lower his bow. "I believe," he says, "it's time for the backup plan. Elphaba, do not wait for us. Dorian and Tokh, please take the front and the rear of the group."

Dorian gnashes his teeth but nods. "What about you?"

"I will be your decoy." Hyacinth's voice cracks no more than it usually does, but his face betrays him.

"I'll be the decoy," Dorian decides. "They need their grandsires."

"I will not flee until I am the last, should it come to that." Hyacinth raises his wobbly chin with pride. "None of us is irreplaceable. Take the group. That's an order, Dorian."

Hyacinth never earned Dorian's respect for his finesse in a fight or his way with words, but he's a noble little bastard who asks nothing of his people that he wouldn't do himself, and it's going to get him killed.

Dorian gives him one of his stakes and Hyacinth keeps smiling bravely as he tucks it into his belt.

Tokh attempts to drag away the table blocking the door by himself and Dorian huffs, awkwardly lifting the other side one-handed. A bottle of alcohol sails inside between them through the new hole in the door, a burning cloth shoved down the neck. It shatters on the kitchen floor, splattering liquid flames and shards of glass in every direction.

In an instant, the crowded kitchen devolves into pandemonium. Tokh and Hyacinth attempt to smother the flames while another bottle sails in, landing even farther, catching aprons, rags, towels, dried spices, and wooden tools.

The damage is done. The fire spreads. The neat, orderly retreat splatters like an egg.

Dorian flips the table sideways to get the door open, narrowly missing an axe to his chest. Children sprint past him, parents chasing after, all scattering three different ways.

The Aeskerat with the axe lunges again, scraping sparks on the hallway stone above Dorian's head as he ducks. He tackles them to the floor, teeth tearing at their throat. Hyacinth gapes, bow arm limp.

Dorian drags his sleeve across his mouth, done with merciful efficiency. The Aeskerat gurgles at his feet and should be glad that Dorian doesn't throw her body into the fire they started.

He keeps their axe for himself and skirts around the flames to help whoever's left. "Get to the *Peony*," he orders, tossing people into the hall. He loses Hyacinth and Tokh as they chase after their scattered kin, their distant shouts and screams echoing through the halls.

Jacobi's vampires still have to take the main gate to escape—that's where they'll go, toting their living armor to protect them.

But first, the fire. The barrels of icy water in storage will have to suffice. They're heavy, even for him, and he coerces his lame arm into dragging and rolling them and splitting them at the seams with the axe. Smoke and steam billow, filling the kitchens with an orange-grey haze.

He soaks tablecloths and runners, slapping them over flames climbing columns and licking rafters.

Another shrill, childish scream of pain—Gilan.

Someone else will see the fire and deal with it. Gilan can't wait.

"Gilan!" *Where'd he go?* Toward the upper floors, the stables, the courtyard? The *Peony*, like he was supposed to?

"Help me!"

Left. The Holdfast.

"Gilan!" There he is—thrown over the shoulder of an Aeskerat running for the open door. Dorian nocks an arrow, aims low for their calf. The vampire grunts and falls flat on their face, Gilan flailing to the ground with them. Gilan yelps and pounds little fists against the body pinning him, cursing like a sailor for them to let him go.

"*Move*." Dorian stakes them and hefts Gilan into his arms.

The boy clings to his neck, left arm bleeding and broken. "I missed," he blubbers. "I missed, I missed."

"Shhh, it's okay. You're okay. We'll all be..." He trails off, face-to-face with the instigator behind this whole mess.

Jacobi smiles hungrily, aim casual like he's cornered a bunny in a snare. "No, you won't be okay." By the gods, he's still treating the world like his stage. Whether Gregori survived or not, allowing Jacobi to live to orchestrate this carnage, to be so smug about it, is a grave oversight that Dorian will never forgive him for this.

Dorian shushes Gilan, who's gasping and yanking on Dorian's braids. "You've finally deigned to show your face. I'm surprised your own coven hasn't yet slaughtered you for how many you've gotten killed tonight. Your blood slaves? Really?"

"They served their purpose." Jacobi juts his chin. "How about you join me outside?"

Gilan wriggles in his arms. "Dorian?"

"Don't look, just close your eyes and hold on, okay? As tight as you can, don't worry about me."

Gilan hides his face in his neck, grip trembling in his jerkin. Jacobi walks them out, backing carefully down the steps to the Holdfast. Dorian contemplates kicking him over the side, but it would be for naught.

Elphaba's down here, a knife to her throat. And Castor and Zeon. No Tokh, no Hyacinth. Twenty-three of their people held by Jacobi and twelve of his vampires.

Dorian adjusts his grip on Gilan. He eyes the Northern ice stalactites above—Liar's Ice.

"You wanted me?" he recalls. "I'm here."

He's here and Elias is not. He wasn't in the kitchens, he wasn't anywhere. Had he been stuck up in his rooms? Out in the courtyard?

"I believe my demand indicated I get you and half your slaves." Jacobi spreads his arms. "This looks a paltry half."

"Oh, yes. Half. How generous of you." Does anyone else in the castle know this is happening? Surely, the fire didn't go unnoticed. Anyone looking for the *Peony* will figure out it's missing too many people. They'll come running and... and do *something* to get them out of this.

"Generous, no. This way, you've reason not to hunt us all across the North. If I took all of them, you lot would have nothing left to lose coming after us to reclaim your pets." Jacobi shakes his head, loving the sound of his own voice. "But half should do."

Dorian toes toward the table. "You wouldn't slaughter them all."

"Slaughter?" Jacobi has the gall to look horrified. "Who said anything about murder?"

Oryn, the vampire holding Castor, shoves him down onto the alcove's frigid ground and chuckles salaciously, getting handsy. He's older than Dorian, older than Jacobi, and he puts up with this? Was Gregori that awful a grandsire?

"That one reeks of you." Jacobi sniffs and wrinkles his nose at Castor. "Oryn doesn't need to use his teeth to lay a claim."

Panicked whispers flutter through the Holdfast. Resolute,

Castor remains statue-still.

"Enough, Jacobi. You want something, or you would have shot me already."

Jacobi shrugs. "I was hoping the little piggy would show himself trying to save you, but it seems he's hiding well." He raises his bow again. "On your knees, please. You can let the kid go now."

Dorian bites his hand and slaps the stone table. *May every word spoken at this table be true.* "You can have me. Only me."

Gilan wriggles in his arms, bumping one of the stakes shoved in his belt. Dorian squeezes him tighter and eyes the many restless Aeskerat in the room. The tired, hungry, desperate Aeskerat who betrayed Gregori for Jacobi. Jacobi, who stands perfectly unbloodied, who hasn't earned his title the Aeskerat way.

Jacobi *hmphs*. "Found a new little sister to die for? I don't intend to become another Eldelaire underestimating you."

"Eldelaire? Eldelaire would have been the first boots on the ground tonight." Silent, Gilan eases a stake free from the folds of his little cloak. "She was a true Aeskerat."

Jacobi smiles mockingly. "And look where it got her."

"She loved me, you know," he says, the most ridiculous claim he can come up with.

Jacobi's smile curdles in revulsion. "*What?*"

Above, Northern ice crackles and gives way.

Gilan drops from his arms and scrambles away. Dorian leaps over the stone table and misses staking Jacobi's heart by a hair. Jacobi gasps and bucks him off, and around them, Aeskerat's hostages break for the table and start belting lies.

Jacobi, for all his bark, was still Gregori's lieutenant. He snarls and bites, yanking at Dorian's hair and clawing at his eyes. Dorian wrestles him back over and slams Jacobi's head against the stone.

Ice falls all around them and he hopes their little army is holding their own—he can't look away to check. Jacobi wheezes out garbled orders no one hears, and if Dorian can kill him and *end this*, they can all rest easier knowing a more sensible Aeskerat grandsire leads.

Dorian's stake skittered away, but a shard of ice works well enough. He aims again for the heart, wrists caught in Jacobi's fists. Jacobi sneers, hissing through his teeth. Dorian's shoulder burns from the strain, from throwing all his weight and strength into shoving down, and *still* it's not enough.

Is there any ice left above them? Can Dorian take them both out like this?

Castor screams, shrill and agonized. The scent of Zeon's blood explodes in the air. Dorian stiffens and twists, chasing the source. Oryn stands above Zeon's headless body. The vampire's face slackens, body frozen in resigned horror. The rest of his gathered coven stalls as if standing still will glue Zeon's head back to his neck.

Dorian has been hungry, has been impulsive when blinded by it. He's never been this monumentally stupid. He locks eyes with Oryn and silently promises a swift death.

He forgets entirely about Jacobi until ice spears through his stomach. Dorian lurches, body seizing from the sudden cold. He paws at the shard, muscles stuttering, and chokes out, "You missed."

Jacobi sets his jaw. "Somebody shoot him. This is over."

In his periphery, a bow raises. Then everything goes dark.

Kymiria has shot one Aeskerat dead and caused two others to slip and fall off the roof by the time she smells the smoke. She, Amaranth, and Henri alone couldn't stop them all from swarming the courtyard, but now they've started retreating.

Kymiria sees red, itching to run inside and rip her teeth into every Aeskerat in her way. Amaranth warns her not to give chase, that they still have to hold the courtyard and guard the wall in case a third round of reinforcements shows. They leave Henri to watch both above and below to pull arrows out of their kin and sort the dead from the dying.

"Amaranth." Elias crawls out of his hiding space, wringing his hands as he approaches. "Who can I help?"

Almost all the dead are older than her, all slate grey and still. They can wait until it's finally over. Kymiria drags Elias along with her to tend to the wounded suffering all manner of burns and wither bites and bleeding arrow holes.

"Only enough to get back on their feet," she warns. "This isn't over yet."

Elias helps without complaint as bedraggled bodies creep outside, escaping either fire or Aeskerat invaders blocking their path to the ship. They move in a frightened daze, and Kymiria directs them to empty stable stalls for now.

Neire finally reappears, bloodied but whole. "They're retreating," she says. "We put out the fire in the kitchens and got people to the ship, but there're many missing."

Missing? Kymiria would have seen any Aeskerat trying to scale back up the cliffs with person-shaped baggage.

"Amaranth!" Henri shouts from the wall. "It's Jacobi!"

Kymiria races for the stairs, grabbing a fresh bow and quiver on her way to stick that spineless *twat* through both eyes. There he is, down there marching through the snow and past the dead withers, herding all their missing people, lugging Dorian whose blood-matted head lolls listlessly, and...

"Zeon?"

Elias curses beside her, holding his head. "What do we do?"

Zeon's decapitated body, hauled front and center. They must've come from the Holdfast. Kymiria pounds her fist against her thigh. She'd shoot straight through Dorian to hit Jacobi and she knows he'd be more than okay with it.

But he's not the only hostage out there.

"Amaranth," Jacobi greets roughly from below, "lovely to see you again. Sorry about the mess and your old man."

Elphaba, Castor, Patrick, half the children. It's not one vampire to each of them, but it doesn't matter. Jacobi brandishes a stake against Dorian's back, and one of his lackeys puts a knife to Elphaba's throat.

"I know that piggy delivered my conditions for surrender. I want half, Amaranth, and I know this isn't it. Your little man here"—Jacobi waves to Castor with a wide smile—"tells me there's seventy-eight of them. That means thirty-nine come with me. Thirty-nine volunteers, preferably strong, healthy ones. They walk out, I let the little ones and the elders go. Unless you want Elphaba here to join whoever that was." He kicks snow at Zeon's corpse.

"You expect me to watch you march all the way back to Aeskerat dragging my freezing, exhausted people, and do nothing?" Disgust sours Amaranth's voice.

Kymiria tries to get Dorian's attention, for all the good it will do. He sags in Jacobi's hold, unresponsive.

"As I suggested to Dorian, there's plenty aside from death I can do to them if you give chase. They're called hostages for a reason."

This *sick, twisted*—

Kymiria raises her bow. Amaranth knocks her aim off as she looses and it sails harmlessly into the snow.

Jacobi prattles on. "And I won't be dragging them. I want sleighs and horses and whatever food hasn't burned. Unless you want your people frostbitten and starving. And the piggy, too. I see him up there. I wonder if he'll volunteer?"

"I do," Elias spits. "With me, that's seventy-nine. One less of yours who has to go."

"No one is volunteering," Kymiria snaps. "Amaranth?"

Her grandsire doesn't answer.

"Amaranth."

"Open the gate." Amaranth ducks her head, eyes closed. "The coven would survive another fight, Kymiria, but everyone down there would suffer the consequences. Dorian, too."

"Becoming an Aeskerat blood slave is a far worse consequence! Especially with Gregori gone!" Kymiria shouts, and Elias nods gravely in agreement. He tries to volunteer himself again and Kymiria stops Elias in his tracks. "You aren't going anywhere."

His gaze flies every which way, like Kymiria's the enemy and not Jacobi and would he get *over* it already? "I don't think Jacobi—"

"Damn Jacobi. You were the last person inside that castle. You now know it better than anyone here. If we're going to save our people, we need you *here* to help us do that."

Amaranth hesitates, then nods resolutely. "Kymiria is right. We need to know everything you know—"

"No." Elias balls his fists at his sides. "I need to be down there."

His heart hammers and Kymiria crosses her arms. "You don't care about our people, not enough to enslave yourself to Jacobi of all vampires."

"And you don't care about me enough to send someone else in my place." His pulse quickens. Stress-sweat reeks as it beads at his temple beneath his lone, stubby braid.

While that might be true, Kymiria blocks her grandsire with her arm. "What did he promise you?"

Elias blanches. "What?"

"Jacobi. What did he promise you? I'm telling you that your grandsire and your people, whom you swore an oath to, need you here, and you're all too eager to run off." Did he...

No. No, he was in the courtyard most of the battle. He wouldn't have been able to clear the door to the Holdfast by himself unseen, unheard.

His voice rises in pitch when he lies. "Nothing."

Too quick.

"Nothing you—you're losing most of your healthy donors. You need me to feed you as much as you need what I know. Don't lie and pretend you don't."

Too quick, little yearling. Kymiria's hackles rise. "You selfish coward, you—"

"Yes!" he yelps. "I am a coward. Dorian is the only one here who cares about me, and he's down there. What happens to me once I serve my usefulness? What happens to me if Dorian can't be saved?"

"What did Jacobi promise you?"

Amaranth steps up to Elias, hands clasped behind her back. "You swore an oath to this house. That means forfeiting your own desires for the survival of us all. I'm releasing you from it, but don't expect to find sanctuary here again."

Elias balks, stricken. He looks between them helplessly and Kymiria *hmphs*. "I didn't ask for any of this," he utters, as if something as trivial as wishes matter now.

As badly as Kymiria wants Jacobi dead, the idea of Jacobi double-crossing Elias is too good a punishment to pass up for him. Only by Amaranth's command and Henri holding her back does she let him go.

She still wants to rip the yearling's throat out for continuing to shove their kindness back in their faces. Yes, he would have had to bleed for them. Yes, it would have been uncomfortable giving more than was strictly safe for him. How many ways must they prove such a sacrifice is more than returned? At least thirteen vampires died tonight while only one of their living kin fell.

"I hope, for your sake," she says, "that Jacobi keeps his promises better than you do."

Elias scurries off with his tail between his legs and Jacobi is right there all smug and satisfied that he's gotten everything he wanted. *Right there.* Kymiria can shoot him with a wooden arrow. Dorian is on his knees. *He'd* survive it even if she missed.

"Let him think he's won," Henri whispers.

Amaranth orders, "Open the gate!"

"You swore to protect Dorian." Kymiria can't bite back all her ire at Amaranth. "Jacobi wants him because he's the one that got away. It doesn't matter if he's a vampire now. That only means Jacobi can do whatever he wants, be as cruel as he wants, as violent as he wants, and Dorian must endure it."

"I know." Amaranth's voice is barely a whisper.

Kymiria doesn't want to hear it. "Volunteer yourself, Amaranth. Send your brother in his place if Jacobi wants a hostage so badly." Hyacinth had, at some point, lost half an arm in a skirmish in the halls. There he is helping anyway, leading horses to their sleighs.

"He doesn't want me, he doesn't want a different hostage. This is personal."

"And you're letting it happen."

Amaranth bristles but doesn't deny it. "They will endure."

Kymiria refuses to help with the exodus, standing by up on the wall as what's left of the castle regroups and word spreads of the need for volunteers. She doesn't ready the horses or load up the sleighs, wanting to stab out her own eardrums as children swap for their fathers and older brothers and wail hysterically.

Jacobi can't kill them. He can't torture, beat, and bleed them and waste all the healthy bodies he's stealing. He *can* frighten them, turn their dreams to nightmares, rip hope from their chests, threaten the family they leave behind if they disobey.

But they'll live.

Kymiria gives Henri her cloak to help wrap Zeon's body—she can't bear to go down there herself. She can still smell drops of Dorian's blood in the snow. Thirty-nine living souls departing, one to bury, and one that can't die from Jacobi's cruelty.

Elphaba returns with her head high and eyes shiny, her son and nephews ripped from her. Kymiria watches them all go, thinking, *We could have taken them.* How will Son Kir coven react when they learn how easily Tanarang gave up? What of all the other covens, who wouldn't have surrendered for their blood slaves? "We're a joke now," Kymiria warns. "I hope you know that, Grandsire."

"Gregori had the respect of the North." Amaranth lingers outside the gate. They still have kin to recover out in the snow from after the wither attack, Markus among them somewhere. "The other covens don't appreciate our ways, but what Jacobi has done here tonight will not stand."

"I know." Kymiria never doubted that, and Jacobi surely must know it, too. "But will it stand long enough that there's nothing left for us to save?"

Amaranth doesn't have an answer.

"I'm going out to find Markus."

She spots Cera dragging her feet in the courtyard as the pile of dead withers to dispose of grows. Kymiria doesn't have to ask if she's able enough to join. The woman perks up when approached, fists balled and ready to act, to do *something*.

Kymiria offers her wrist so she can brave the snow for however long it takes. Cera's own is wrapped in a dish towel, matted and sticky from Dorian's teeth. "We'll get Dorian back."

"We will."

"Are you okay?" Elias whispers from the sleigh, trying not to be obvious even with an Aeskerat sitting at the head watching them all. The sleigh's skis smooth the ride over the snow, leaving only the whistling wind and the creaking harnesses of the horses.

Dorian, though awake, doesn't answer, hands bound by a rope leashed to the sleigh, the only one of them Jacobi forces to walk. Elias tries to offer his wrist, only to be yanked back by the stern Aeskerat.

Castor's with him, hunkered down and sullen. Brigs, too, the smith who repairs the blood needles. And Patrick, who bakes the fancy pastries for the lavish parties. Beside Elias sits a woman whose name he never learned. They didn't have thirty-nine able-bodied men to volunteer.

Jacobi won. He got exactly what he came for and still leads a couple dozen survivors home. He has his title, half of Tanarang's people and food, and Elias can't imagine the strain put on those who remain with Elphaba to shoulder double the burden feeding the coven. More than double if they still refuse to feed from children. Jacobi didn't have to kill them all. He's left them to die or risk turning into monsters like himself.

Amaranth has a plan, she must. Uniting the other covens to take Jacobi down. And staying with Tanarang? With all the children, mothers, sisters, daughters who would have loathed him for being free while their family bled? A stupid oath wouldn't mean anything to them.

Elias can't help the ones around him either. He'd be branded as a Gregori sympathizer, and he doubts there's anything he could say or do for Jacobi to convince the vampire he's happy to bleed.

They'll be fine on their own. Castor will lead them. Jacobi will have to fight tooth and nail for control and for respect every second of every hour, and if nothing else, then they'll annoy him to the brink of insanity and guarantee his regret of every last choice that earned him their wrath.

Elias isn't paying attention to their journey until they stop well before they should. They've rounded a bend in the foothills of the mountains, icy spires spilling into the valley below that remind him of the petrified forest.

Lights up ahead—lantern lights.

Jacobi hops off his horse with a happy sigh and struts his way down the caravan. "Piggy, you're needed." He beckons with his fingers and yanks the unnecessary rope around Dorian's hands. "You, too."

Dorian stiffens. "Jacobi—"

"Ah-ah-ah! Don't ruin the surprise."

Elias hesitates, one leg swung over the edge of the cart. *What surprise?*

"Piggy!"

Elias climbs down and drops into the ankle-deep snow, a stitch tugging at his side and his knee complaining, still sore from

Quinn's kick even all these weeks later.

Dorian drags his feet and Jacobi simpers, whaling him with a sucker punch that knocks him flat on his back.

"Stop!" Like an idiot, Elias gets between them. "We're coming, we're coming."

Jacobi shoves him out of the way and wraps the end of the rope around Dorian's neck. "Before I send you off, how about a parting gift?" Jacobi's slimy tongue licks up Dorian's cheek.

Castor shouts, and Jacobi pulls the rope tighter. "To anyone plotting to mount a stubborn little rebellion in my house, I am above *nothing* to quell it."

Jacobi pulls even tighter and Dorian claws at the rope.

"Jacobi, please," Elias begs. "Please!"

The Aeskerat cackles and lets Dorian go with a kick of snow at his face. "You have no idea what I'm capable of, piggy. Save your begging for when it actually matters."

Elias could faint but instead drops to his knees to unwind the lax rope. Dorian coughs and hacks and still doesn't give Jacobi the satisfaction of looking afraid. Elias's terror was enough for the both of them.

Jacobi tugs the rope, jouncing Dorian's hands. "Get up."

Dorian shrugs off Elias's help in silence and shakes his head in warning. As if it matters. What more could Jacobi glean that he doesn't already know?

They round the front of the caravan toward the lantern light. A shaggy, antlered animal built like nothing Elias has ever seen is hitched to a waiting sled, its lead in the hands of Chief Yarren, Loric beside him.

Elias stops up short. "Chief?"

Yarren says nothing and Elias considers that Amaranth might've been right, that he did turn, until Jacobi forces Dorian to kneel. "This the one you wanted?"

Yarren squints and huffs, "Don't remember what it looked like, only its voice."

Jacobi whaps the back of Dorian's head. "Well, say something!"

Dorian glowers, teeth gritted. "It was me."

"See? I can deliver. One guilty party for the loss of your hunters and the abduction of this one here." Jacobi waves at Elias flippantly. "And the abductee himself. Both as promised."

Elias can't breathe. Jacobi struck a deal with... Yarren? For Dorian? Where did they even get that bull or buck—whatever it is? Aeskerat has no living stables and he's certain his clan wouldn't keep the animal fed given the amount of blood it would demand. "Chief, what is this?"

Jacobi postures grandly. "The man knows how to negotiate! He gave us the wood we needed for our arrows, along with a disgustingly convincing argument for how nasty your clan's blood tastes, and asked only for justice. Behold—*justice*."

He spears an arrow through Dorian's back and breaks the shaft, leaving the arrowhead deep inside him. Elias screams. Dorian arches and chokes, face scrunched in agony, then slumps.

"He's harmless now." Jacobi hands the rope to Loric. "Oh, relax, he's not *dead*. It was Northern ice, not wood. Though, I'd leave it in if I were you."

Loric gags him and hauls him to the sled.

"This is you keeping a promise?" Elias shouts. "Actual backstabbing? Selling out your prisoners? What's an Aeskerat's word worth now?"

"Buck up, piggy," Jacobi chirps. "You asked to go south and away you go! *South!* Away from all us nasty vampires and back to your little cave." He mounts his horse—no, not *his* horse. Dandy. Freshly stolen and no doubt re-claimed for Aeskerat. "My word is gold."

"What happened to being petty? Aren't you selfish enough to want this revenge for yourself?" Elias spreads his hands, spitting venom for all the good it will do. The only soul here that seems even marginally sympathetic is Gregori's third mutinous lieutenant and Elias still doesn't know her name. She sits astride her horse in silence, glowering at Jacobi only behind his back. She won't do a damn thing to stop any of this.

Elias shakes his head at her and turns away. Gregori might not have been perfect, but now they're stuck with Jacobi. They deserve an eternity with him.

"Your chief told me all about your last vampire blood slave, and what do you know, I knew him!" Jacobi's voice drops, hackles raised. "Twenty years, piggy. That's how long it took him to die. What more fitting demise could I imagine for an Aeskerat deserter?"

The caravan moves on without them, leaving Elias in the snow with his chief, someone he once considered a comrade, if not a friend, his only real friend trussed up on the sled as a gift to his clan.

Elias stays rooted exactly where he is as Loric nicks Dorian's hand for a lick of blood and Yarren follows suit. Everything is all mixed up and backwards now. Black is white, up is down, right is wrong.

"Elias, you need to stay warm. We have a long walk ahead." Yarren offers the knife, edge glinting red.

He couldn't take either of them at full strength with all his fingers. He'll be no help to Dorian if his chief doesn't trust him, and Elias is getting them out of this, even if he dies in the process.

"You came to rescue me?" he asks, pouring all the horrified

disbelief into his voice and distorting it into shock and awe. The clan never sends rescue missions.

Yarren claps his shoulder with pride. "I thought you were gone. Then I saw you with those leeches and couldn't abide that."

"And they—they're really letting you take me?" No, Jacobi must have a plan. He's sure of it. Some scheme beneath the grander scheme.

Yarren pulls a face. "They seemed more interested in the slaves owned by this one's coven."

What, his blood isn't good enough for Jacobi now?

Yarren carries on. "I wasn't keen on questioning them. We'll get you home to see your mom, and everything will be like it was."

"Home. I never thought I'd see it again." Elias accepts the knife and dips his head in gratitude to hide the panic in his eyes.

Chapter 14: Monsters

"Markus... *Markus!*"

He hurts. His head hurts, his limbs hurt, his chest hurts, his throat hurts. About the only thing that doesn't hurt is the middle toe on his left foot. Cera's split wrist presses to his mouth and even the protraction of his fangs hurts.

"C'mon, easy does it."

Weight starts to fall off him, and Markus sighs. He's cushioned by snow and rotten bodies and he's deeper than he expected when he opens his eyes. Cera kneels at the edge of a hole uncovered in the snow, stretching toward him.

Kymiria shoves the rest of the dead withers off and hoists him up under his arms. "How many did you take on exactly?"

"A lot." Where'd Cera go? She smells *divine.*

"Markus." There she is. He hopes she doesn't mind if he leans into her for a tick. Those buggers took more than their fair share of bites out of him.

"How'd we do?" he asks, head heavy in satisfaction as the fresh blood flows to all his open wounds. The castle's still lit—brighter now than usual—and people mill about in front of the wall. "Was that it?"

Kymiria's face turns stony. "Um." She swallows roughly and blinks rapidly. "Jacobi came and made a mess of the place. He killed Zeon and took half the clan and Dorian back to Aeskerat."

She's joking. She's... not joking? A terrible thing to joke about but why else state such nonsense? "Huh?"

"It's true, Markus." Cera looks waxy pale, eyes red-rimmed and nose raw from more than the cold. "There was a fire and everybody scattered. They picked off whoever they could reach."

... Oh. "How many did we lose?"

"Nineteen of the coven confirmed. Zeon from the clan."

"... and when you say half, you mean?"

"Thirty-nine." Kymiria tugs him to his feet. "C'mon, we gotta do a headcount for whoever's still missing."

There's less destruction than he expects from a battle that somehow cost them half their people. Smoke still thickens the air from the kitchen fire and the burning withers. Vick tops the pile of those they'd lost, Tokh right beside him. Markus slows up, asks if it was withers or Aeskerat, and moves on. Tokh went out with honor against a stake. At least it would have been quick. Zeon is by himself, wrapped up in layers of white that don't stop his open neck from bleeding through.

Inside the castle, everyone gathers in the Grand Hall—everyone being all the women and children who weren't able to volunteer—wrapped up in blankets and furs in one small huddle on the floor. Sniffles and quiet sobs echo. Baby Lidya gurgles in her mother's arms, perfectly oblivious.

There'd been a fight in the Holdfast, he learns, and no one noticed.

How did no one notice?

Markus checks himself present and accounted for and takes a seat at a table. Kymiria sits right beside him and he draws away. "I would like to be alone right now, please."

She crumples, and he knows she wants comfort, he just... can't. He's aware of her leaving and finding Quinn instead and hopes no one else thinks he's lonely and comes over. He props his head on his hands and stares at the shallow engravings across the tabletop.

Why do people do this? This—this *love* thing? It sucks, it hurts, it rots the wound it carves. He wants to slice it out like a burst appendix, useless little flesh nugget of pain that it is, except he can't slice away what's already gone. Things were fine when they were simply friends, and now...

Now Dorian had to go and martyr himself.

Love is an awful, wretched, all-consuming affliction. Love, Markus decides, is an unwelcome and uninvited weed growing interminably through the cracks in all the fine stonework he's built. Even if the little flowers that bloom from it boast beauty.

Amaranth announces their losses at the head table. Twenty-two vampires dead and one abducted. With them they took down seventeen Aeskerat. She goes down the list of those who fell to withers and those who fell to the Aeskerat invaders.

Hyacinth's voice squeaks and catches more now than ever when he says, "We will not let them have died in vain. We will get our people back, all of them, the moment we have the strength and opportunity to strike."

Vengeful murmurs arise. Markus can't bring himself to join, only twisting around on the bench to face his grandsires properly.

Amaranth laces her fingers and sighs softly. "Winter still isn't over. We lost half our people, yes, and most of our already dwindling stores of dried goods. We do not have enough medical supplies to treat everyone's injuries, so I need someone to ride to the Houlind Coven and offer candles, lanterns, and leathers in exchange for rations and other supplies. Dorotea, is inventory complete?"

Dorotea hands her a rolled-up parchment. "I'll go along as the living ambassador."

"Amaranth," Quinn cuts in reluctantly, "we don't have any horses left."

Amaranth doesn't miss a beat. "Then sail up to Son Kir instead. See about bartering a mule at least from them."

"That trip will take weeks—"

"Then walk," Amaranth snaps, and then droops. "I'm sorry. You're correct, it is too far."

Markus crosses his ankle over his knee and leans back against the table. "There's an emergency stash at Chryssy Point. I don't know how much, how old, or in what condition. I can be there and back in four moons." Anything to stay busy and not lurk around a castle filled with holes and scorch marks and melancholy.

"Doesn't Clan Catanz use dog sleds to get around?" Neire asks. "We can trade them the fish and lanterns for one."

Amaranth shakes her head. "They're on the coast like we are and can fish for themselves. That sled won't be cheap."

"We have dried fruit, my Lady." Tannys's hand shoots into the air. "And one honey pot and some spare tools. I can have it all packed immediately." She runs off before Amaranth gets her approval out.

Neire juts her chin. "I'll take it there. Catanz is only an extra day south from the Point. Markus?"

Sure, why not? He shrugs.

"Leave immediately, please. Even if they only accept a loan until spring." Hope creeps into her voice, wrought with a spark of determination. Markus rocks to his feet and Amaranth nods him over. "See about bartering blood off them, if nothing else."

Of the forty living who remain, twenty-one are neither too young nor too old to keep sustaining the coven. Twenty-one, for ninety vampires. Amaranth should be glad they don't also have to feed their horses, even if they're effectively stranded without them.

"Showing up asking for blood will hint quite clearly that something happened." Not that he expects a fishing village to jump on a moment of weakness, but they can't go looking desperate around Catanz's persnickety chief. "If they suspect our dire circumstances and refuse? We're bygones, but those dogs are worth more than gold to them."

"So are our people. Convince them. We only need them until we can fix this with Aeskerat."

If they can fix this with Aeskerat. Markus suspects they only lost so few because they know their home so well. They can navigate its halls in pitch blackness.

He splits with Neire the load of the wares to trade and suggests sweetening the pot with a jar of blood from them both, costly as it is. Dorotea's all bundled up in her furs waiting for them with her own food and drink supply that he takes off her back immediately.

"Are you sure you want to come?" he asks. "We must be quick, and Neire and I won't rest."

Dorotea ties a thick knitted scarf around her ears and bunches it up over her nose. "They'll be less threatened if I'm with you. If anything goes wrong, I can keep both of you fed and you'll keep me plenty warm."

He'd already accounted for a trip, prepared with a little

concoction of concentrated blood jerky, as close as he could get to fruit leather from the South.

Then they're off, set to miss the funerals and however Amaranth and Elphaba plan to address the blood shortage. Markus has been around a couple centuries now and never once felt the compulsion to participate in politics. A three-moon hike down for supplies? Sign him up. Losing sleep over inventory and how to keep his coven from falling apart at the seams, how to cheer them up, how to maintain morale? No. Leave that to more empathetic minds.

Maritime wind blows in, salty and clean, and the smell of smoke and death fades behind them.

Yarren has them set up camp at the same shallow cave where Elias saw his first shades of true blue. His knee aches and his abdomen pulses angrily with every step.

Both Yarren and Loric seem convinced that Elias has been seduced by the wiles of vampirism. While they don't blame him for his attempts to check on Dorian's well-being, they certainly don't let him get close to the dangerous monster bound and gagged on their sled. He only wants to know if Dorian's still conscious with that icy arrowhead in his heart. If he's awake and in pain and paralyzed by it. Or if it's like the sleep-death that happened when Kymiria snapped his neck.

Elias hopes it's the latter. That this is all a senseless, dreamless sleep for him, but he doubts it. More pressingly, now that he can rest and prop up his knee, Elias has other questions.

Namely, "Chief? I thought you were dead."

"I felt dead." Yarren pulls his mask down, revealing more of his nose missing, a ghoulish, permanent sneer formed by cracked and discolored lips. "Tracked down that calf," he mutters. "By the time I did, it was too weak to flee. Lived on it, healing, until those leeches found me."

"You really think they'll leave us alone?" he tiptoes. "Jacobi doesn't strike me as the trustworthy type."

Loric grunts and tears at a strip of jerky. "Got us this far keepin' its word."

How did it come to be that his prejudiced clan decided to put their faith in Jacobi of all vampires? "All they wanted was wood? And you gave it to them?"

Loric snorts. "No, they attacked the cave. Threatened to seal us in, make meals of us all."

Yarren pats the bull's neck with pride. "Can't say we got off that poorly."

Yes, a single bull and no female to mate it with. A bull from a species they've never come across before and one they have no idea how to care for or feed or find companionship for. A bull that can't even give them milk, only meat when it dies. A splendid trade.

"Did they tell you where they got it?"

Yarren waves dismissively. "Some other coven."

"And they just gave it to you."

"Said it can't breed." He shrugs. "It's well-behaved and healthy, far as I can tell. I wasn't going to say no."

Uh-huh. Jacobi just giving away priceless animals isn't at all suspect. "Did you give them the whole stockpile of wood?"

"Didn't have much of a choice." Yarren drops himself down. "But they did tell us Clan Hogul's gone, also courtesy of *that* one." He spits in Dorian's direction but it doesn't make it halfway to him. "Told us whatever supplies remain there are ours, if we can dig it out. Another hunting party is there as we speak. With any luck, we'll all be home with fresh meat, furs, and firewood before the next storm blows in."

Elias draws his good knee up and hugs it. His body's exhausted, but his mind won't let him sleep. If he pretends, they might let him, so he adjusts his furs and pillows his head on his arm.

No such luck.

"What was it like with them?" Loric asks, picking at his teeth. "You still got lotsa meat on your bones. Seem well taken care of."

Oh, how he wishes he could tell the truth, convince his clan to pack up and leave their home behind to go join forces with Tanarang who are not the monsters his whole lineage believes them to be.

"It was... different," Elias mutters.

Yarren isn't impressed, grumbling gravely. "That bitch who held me for weeks told me all about them. They're worse than leeches, they infect your head, convince you to like it, *need* it. Depend on them. Desire them." He scoffs in disgust and regards Elias piercingly. "That one didn't try anything, did it? Better not have."

"Could chop its prick off." Loric snickers to himself and scrapes his knife against the ground in messy scratches. "Wait for it to grow back and do it again." He props his chin in his palm and hums sourly.

"No wasting precious resources," Yarren warns. "The more we bleed it, the more we have to feed it."

Waste not hammers in Elias's mind. If he weren't wearing gloves, he's sure his nails would have bit into his palms with how tightly he clenches his fists. "He didn't. They think we're dirty," he mutters. "Like lying with a pig." *Piggy, piggy.* "It's not worth their time."

Yarren harrumphs and waves dismissively. "Good, then. I'll take first watch."

Elias rolls away from them, facing Dorian on the sled in a lump obscured by the bull's legs. All he has to do is get Dorian free and healed enough to defend himself. Dorian won't make the mistake of sparing Yarren again and Loric is no match for him.

But *how*?

His window's closing. Once they're in the cave, one narrow way in and out and the rest of his clan to deal with, it'll be that much harder. He needs time to dig the arrowhead out, time to feed him, time for Dorian to gather his strength. Yarren and Loric haven't given him more than a minute away from the sled to relieve himself.

If Elias waits until it's Loric's turn for watch, could he stab him? The noise would wake Yarren. In the heat of the moment, Elias could do it, but not by lying here contemplating it, thinking about every minute detail of what happens if he misses. Of what happens if Loric doesn't die fast enough. If he fails entirely and Yarren, convinced Elias is under some spell, punishes Dorian for it.

He misses his opportunity by falling asleep, and his new plan is to limp so badly that they get annoyed enough to suggest he ride the sled.

"No, no, I'm fine," he assures, hopping along after them. "I can do it."

He pitches forward and crumples, apologizing profusely.

"Just get on the damn sled, by Takkha." Loric watches his every move, spear in hand. Elias feigns disgust and throws a scowl Dorian's way, sitting at his feet.

Elias waits and waits and waits for Loric to find better things to do than keep pace with the sled and watch him be unspectacular. When finally he starts sharpening his spear blade on a whetstone and humming to himself, Elias scoots up the sled, nudging Dorian's bound feet aside to lean subtly over him.

He looks asleep, eyes closed and face smoothed of any pain. That's something at least. Not that silent scream of agony when Jacobi stabbed him in the back. That buried arrowhead probably sits deep and snug. Elias would have to take off his gloves and dig with his fingers inside a wound that's likely healing around it, feeling for Northern ice that would burn his skin with every brush of contact.

No way Loric wouldn't notice.

I'm sorry, Elias thinks, voice in his head projecting it futilely where Dorian can't hear. Elias squeezes Dorian's leg, trying to convey that he's here, that he's not giving up, that he's going to get him out of this to wherever Dorian is in his mind.

They cross a frozen river and reach the cave and Elias is sick to his empty stomach. He's out of time.

Yarren carries Dorian over his shoulder like fresh game, welcomed home a hero by his clan. Loric whines about how he helped, too. The only soul who notices Elias in the shadows is his mother.

She parts the crowd to crush him to her chest. "Oh, my sweet, baby boy," she whispers. "I never thought I'd see you again."

Elias bears it and doesn't shove her away. He knows she hasn't mourned. She didn't mourn Misha. She'd toiled in her garden not talking about him until Elias figured out he should stop asking about it. She didn't miss Elias. She had most of his life to be a mother and couldn't be bothered.

She doesn't deserve this.

None of them do—standing here praising their heroes and clamoring for fresh vampire blood. It takes everything in him to not retch. They're his people, his clansfolk, the only family he's ever known for his whole life until a few months ago. But it's *because* he knows these faces that he's so sick.

We're monsters. You're a monster. I'm a monster. The only soul here that isn't a monster is about to be hung like meat off a butcher's hook.

His mother cups his face, fretting with concern. "Elias?"

"It's just overwhelming," he croaks. "Can't believe I'm here."

This, naturally, calls for celebration. Elias, veritably back from the dead like their chief, isn't allowed one foot outside the main atrium, asked the same questions a hundred times by his skeptical clan. How'd he survive? What does their cave look like? What filth do they live in? What hedonism do vampires enjoy?

They didn't miss him. He's alive, and their better, more competent, more useful kin are not. They want to know why. Why does Elias deserve a second chance, but Lalo and Minira, Netto and Ulric, hundreds of others, never get one?

Elias ignores them all.

"Can I see Dapple?" he asks his mother. "The calf?"

"Oh." She laughs uneasily. "Oh, *bimpet*, she didn't survive without her mother. I'm sorry."

He hates every note of pity in her voice. "Right. Of course. I should have guessed."

The raid on Clan Hogul's remains is a success. A modest bonfire burns and shots of vampire blood spread about the cave. *We're alive and they're not*, the fire revels.

Elias drinks only because he can't siphon it back into Dorian's body. *Waste not.*

He throws it up later when the rest of his clan is drunk on alcohol pilfered from Hogul's stores. In a way, it reminds him of the lavish parties thrown in the Grand Hall. Life is too short to wait for a perfect occasion to drink the good spirits and eat the good food and use the good cutlery.

But the debauchery that follows shatters any similarities in animalistic fervor.

Elias disappears to the seershroom garden before he throws himself on the remains of the bonfire, and cries into his knees. He prays to whatever gods exist, to the sun and beyond, for a way out of this.

Maybe Gregori lived and he's on his way to kick down their door as a one-vampire army. Maybe Castor and the others escaped and overthrew Jacobi and they're marching an assault on the cave this instant. Maybe Dorian was pretending to go belly-up in his bowl and plans to free himself.

Elias's old drawings have since been smudged by the dew from the river, but he still recognizes Dapple's face and floppy ears.

Who is he kidding? He can't save anyone, and the gods don't care.

Clan Catanz is a village of rounded canvas-and-ice huts at the mouth of the River Tammen where it spills into the ocean. They stay on their land and don't travel north of the lighthouse, and Tanarang allows them to live. Markus doubts Amaranth would send anyone to carry out threats should they cross the border, but he has also never heard of Catanz acting up.

He, Neire, and Dorotea observe the clan milling about within their village, hauling in fresh nets of fish. He spots three sleds and enough dogs running around to pull each of them, which hopefully means they're willing to part with a spare.

Dorotea had wanted to be left at Chryssy Point to sleep and rest her feet, conceding he'd been right and had told her so and that their brutal pace overspent her. She'd guard the Point's meager rations—old lanterns and a couple thin blankets they could tear into strips.

Markus had instead passed their packs to Neire and carried Dorotea on his back, ignoring her complaints that she's a grown woman for gods' sake. She fell asleep clutched to his neck.

Now she's wide awake, lying on her belly between him and Neire on a hillside. "It's a loan," she mutters, "they'll have to accept."

"They don't *have* to do anything unless we threaten to eat them," Neire points out. "And we can't guarantee our intent to give the dogs back."

"Why don't we give them the benefit of the doubt?" Otherwise they'll stay stretched in the pine needles contemplating what-ifs. This far south, the sun does shine distantly for a few hours but only in the peak of summer. In winter, the sky's a little more grey than black, a false twilight. It's enough for twiggy trees to grow, a strange sight to see. Imposing village guardians of sap, moss, and *green*.

Dorotea insists on leading their little parlay. The dogs smell them immediately, ears perked and hackles raised. One aspect they didn't consider is how readily the dogs will obey them, strange vampires or simply strangers holding their leads.

Sled or no, they might at least hike back with fresh supplies.

Chief Fadehier, a wreath of furs around her face, heels her dogs. Her whole village stands in a cautious crowd, scrutinizing their approach. "What brings you so far south, Tanarang?"

Wary, ill-impressed, grumpy. *Not good.*

Dorotea steps forward. "I'm Dorotea, daughter of Elphaba,

Head of House at Castle Tanarang. We come to barter, Chief."

Fadehier's gravely voice drips with skepticism in a single syllable. "For...?"

"Medicine. Pain relievers. And a sled, if you're willing to part with it temporarily." Murmurs erupt immediately, but Dorotea stands her ground.

The chief bats them all aside. "You ask for much, Dorotea. What do you have to trade?"

"Dried fruits, honey, candles, two oil lanterns, and"—the bundle of tools clinks and clatters as she wrestles it from the pack—"metal tools for fishing equipment and home repair."

Markus nudges her shoulder, glancing meaningfully between himself and Neire.

"And a jar of vampire blood."

Fadehier purses her wrinkled lips and turns toward the largest hut, beckoning them with her back turned. "Come, let us see the state of these tools." She's flanked by two of her clansfolk brandishing spears curved like the jaws of a shark, teeth and all.

The hut's roof has a small open circle in the center for smoke to escape. Fish and turtle skeletons hang from the ceiling, coral and shells spiral up the reedy support columns. Markus has grown used to thick, stone castle walls. The huts seem so fragile in comparison.

Markus finds himself stopped by an invisible wall at the entrance, Neire in the same predicament.

"We're still protected by Natzothele," Fadehier explains as if it's an afterthought. "You must be invited in."

Some sea god, he recalls, detailed as a footnote in one of his books. "The gods still care about thresholds?"

"Ours do." Fadehier sits on a small throne of furs and wood.

"You may hand your packs to the lady. She is safe to enter here."

Dorotea might be, but Fadehier's two clansfolk stand too close to him and Neire with their weapons. Markus slides his pack off, handing it over to a sheepish Dorotea. He supposes that he owes her a *You told me so* as well.

Dorotea drags both bulging packs in and presents the tools: a hammer, a flathead screwdriver, pliers, scissors, and a hacksaw. All in perfect, rust-free condition.

The chief examines them critically, face impassive. "Doesn't your castle have a stable of undead horses?"

"We do. We still ask for the sled."

"And medicine and pain relievers. Suffer some complications with another coven, have you?" Fadehier tosses the hacksaw back into the pile with a clatter and laces her knobby fingers. "Come to throw your weight around my village?"

Markus bites his tongue. If he steps in, he'll undermine Dorotea's image, but *really*? They let bygones be after the Great Freeze. Tanarang asks nothing of Catanz and lets them carry on, far kinder than any other coven who might have caught wind of a village of food so exposed. Why the attitude?

"I came to barter," Dorotea repeats, "as your neighbor. You owe no fealty to Tanarang and we request nothing we can't pay for."

Fadehier shrugs, her blasé attitude reminding him of Elphaba. "I haven't named my price. You're asking to borrow our means of transportation and eight of our family members to pull it for an unspecified amount of time. What happens when your loan becomes a promise you can't keep? Then all I will have gotten to compensate for my dogs is a handful of sweets and metal."

Neire growls, so softly only Markus can hear it. Her lip curls enough so one fang pokes free.

Dorotea's back is to them, but Markus hears the polite smile in her voice when she asks, "We've given our offer, what's your counter?"

Fadehier sits forward, dark eyes agleam. "How old are you, my dear?"

Dorotea balks. "Excuse me?"

"You heard me."

"Um... thirty-one."

"Oh, do you look young for your age," Fadehier praises, still managing to sound insulting. "Have you borne any children?"

"Three."

Markus figures out where this is going unfortunately faster than Dorotea does.

Fadehier claps. "Excellent! You have experience."

"In...?"

The chief wrings her bony fingers and nods to Neire. "You want my dogs, Tanarang, fine. I'll take this one here for safekeeping until they're returned to me."

Neire sneers and half-lunges but is blocked again by the threshold. "No deal."

Fadehier shrugs. "Why not? I'm about to lose eight working dogs. She's a working woman and you may have her back when I get my dogs back. I see no problem."

Markus wrinkles his nose. He doesn't meddle in politics, but the Catanz chiefs have gotten quite self-important of late.

"Chief, can we have a moment?" Dorotea waves stiffly. "I'd like to discuss logistics with my advisors."

Fadehier grumbles and shoos her away. Dorotea trips over herself fleeing the hut.

"We're not leaving you here," Neire snaps, ushering them away from prying ears.

"I wasn't about to leave my boys," Dorotea huffs, cheeks pink from either the cold or indignation.

Markus raises a finger. "Fadehier wants a hostage. Can't we take our own and demand the sled?"

Neire scowls and crosses her arms. "This is supposed to be a diplomatic mission."

"I didn't say we had to hurt them. I simply suggest we negotiate with terms Fadehier understands. If she wants to barter people, she can stomach bartering her own." Like that lanky guard who probably hasn't seen too many winters.

Dorotea shifts her weight and grimaces. "I don't want to be mean."

"She was mean first."

Neire sets her jaw and studies the clan. "These dogs are loyal to them. If we pick a fight, there's no guarantee they'll happily accompany us, and I don't like our chances against the twenty dogs I see prowling around."

He and Neire could handle the dogs, they'd just all be dead and no one would get them. "We can leave instead?"

"We came all the way here," Dorotea hisses. "We need the ability to reach another coven for help."

"There's no guarantee anyone else will help either," Markus points out. He doesn't think there's been a solid alliance between the covens since the War for the North, and that ended poorly.

Dorotea scoffs. "We can't sit on our thumbs and hope Jacobi returns our people. Every day we do nothing is another that my brother and everyone else suffers at his hands."

Neire pinches the bridge of her nose. "Medicine is what we

need the most, and Markus, you need to be there to treat your patients, not traveling from coven to coven begging for scraps."

"Me?" Markus points to himself. "I studied dead bodies, not living ones."

"You're the best we've got," Neire huffs. "We'll figure something else out for Castor and the others. I'm sorry, Dorotea."

Dorotea blinks hard and turns away. "You'll come rescue me if Fadehier breaks her word?"

Neire startles. "What?"

"I'll stay," Dorotea decides.

"No, you won't. Your boys need you."

"I need my brother back," Dorotea insists, fists balled at her sides. "He'd figure something out if it were me out there."

"You give him much credit. But you must understand that he wouldn't want this risk. If we can't get back to you, you'd be on your own down here."

Markus can't get a word in edgewise as Dorotea continues to attempt her justifications. As far as he knows, there's not another clan within walking distance, much less one with draft animals. "Neire is right. You aren't staying."

Neire nods, foot tapping impatiently. "Tell her we'll take the supplies and be on our way."

Dorotea crumples.

Neire softens and dries her face with her scarf. "We aren't abandoning Castor. He knows we're doing all we can to bring him home."

Dejected, Dorotea nods and blinks rapidly, and marches back toward the hut.

Neire curses under her breath. "We're too soft on these people."

"Their dogs mean as much to them as our people do to us."

She scowls again. "This is a time for commiseration, not logic."

"Oh, is it? Then they're despicable."

She gives a tired snort. "Never mind."

Dorotea emerges from the hut and waves them over, a fishnet bag over her shoulder. Fadehier's guards disperse, piling fish and crabs in a crate.

They got what they came for, mostly, and no bloodshed. Castor, Dorian, and the rest of their people will have to hold out a little longer.

Chapter 15: The Starless Skies Above

lias can't sleep unless it's in the seershroom garden. His entire clan gossips behind his back, and sometimes when he's looking right at them, that it's some vampire-related trauma.

He still wears his tailored Tanarang leathers because throwing them out on the grounds they don't match would have been a waste, but standing in his black and grey ensemble, its little whale emblem over the heart, among his kin in their shapeless, russet furs, only reminds them that he's not one of them anymore.

He has his Keeper job back because everyone else thinks it too tedious, and it remains his convenient excuse to avoid everyone and everything and to hide in the garden. His insomnia is a wholly different matter.

After an entire life in the cave and only a few months breathing fresh, clean air, Elias can't stand it. It's stuffy, it's stale, it's mildewy and sour. It reeks of sweaty bodies and he's never far enough from anyone that he can't smell their breath.

The rocky ceilings and the rocky walls suffocate him. He got used to the pitched rafters of Castles Tanarang and Aeskerat, to the colorful tapestries and paintings and the windows. The *windows*. He got used to seeing stars and to feeling wind in his hair and on his face and to having space to run and jump and walk in a line of his choosing, unbound from the fixed dips and curves of the tunnels.

Maybe it is trauma, because he suffers more than one claustrophobic panic attack in the garden, heart cracking through his ribs, lungs filling with broken glass.

The only person who doesn't ignore him enough is his mother. She's incessant, monitoring his eating and drinking, asking if he's warm, keeping him busy, trying over and over again to yank him into the circle, into reconnecting with his clan.

It would be sweet and thoughtful of her if she didn't also ignore all his protests, his insistence he's sitting out because he's more comfortable sitting out. She wants to compensate for lost time, but her come-to-Takkha moment when she thought he'd died and left her doesn't suddenly mean she's a better or more understanding parent.

Morjanot is, however, the only soul he can even think about trusting with the truth.

He's sitting in the gardens drawing on the rocks so he can think. It's the only piece of the cave that was always his and it still bears the echoes of his old musings. Rocks are a far cry from sketch paper and sharp pencils and scented candles and a million other luxuries, but this at least strikes a familiar chord.

His mother tends to their lone bull, glancing over at him every now and then as if he might vanish into mist.

If he can get her on his side, then they, together, can start convincing the others one by one to consider aligning with Tanarang. If they need a blood slave so badly, they can pick a different vampire. Preferably Jacobi.

Convincing them to pack up and leave the cave will never work. Starvation didn't convince them, siege by Aeskerat vampires didn't convince them, freezing to death hasn't convinced them, and neither has living like moles afraid of their own shadows.

He needs to prove that not all vampires are monsters. Dorian wasn't the one who chained up Yarren like a dog for weeks. Dorian didn't lead the raid on their cave. He needs to convince them that Dorian was, and still is, a person, too.

... But Dorian *did* kill Minira and Lalo and leave Yarren for dead. Dorian did abduct Elias and not return him to his family.

Elias crumbles his charcoal, mashing it against the rocks. Soot cakes his hands and clumps under his nails. He's getting used to his missing fingers even with the nubs still bandaged. They ache sometimes, and the feeling whenever he props his face on his hand without all his digits digging into his cheek still surprises him.

Their loss simply pales in comparison to everything else in his life. He hasn't had headspace to panic about a few fingers along with his worries about Dorian and Aeskerat and getting traded around like a cut of beef.

But the soot on his hands snaps an image of frostbite into his head, and he sits staring at it, unaware of all other sights and sounds, until his mother is right in his face. "Elias?"

A soggy wet sob escapes his throat, and he fists his mangled hands in the furs at her back.

"Oh, baby," she whispers, cradling his head. "I'm here."

He can't tell her he didn't miss her, that Morjanot's newfound love for him is cheap and asphyxiating and all he has down here.

He can't tell her that he misses the stars and the clouds and all the colors, all the *blue*. He can't tell her that he misses clothes that fit, tailored for him alone. He misses fresh-baked bread and even seaweed soup. The smell of the books in the library, their soft leather binding, all the shiny metallic ink in their margins. Warm baths.

Laughter, forks scraping on plates, tankards hitting the table, all echoing in the Grand Hall. He misses Rinn's last performance on stage, Amaranth's dresses and how they swirled around her feet, everyone's glossy braids in shades of gold and red and brown he didn't think possible. The untapped strength in his arms drawing a bow, the sting of string-burn, the *thwack* of hitting a target semi-accurately for the first time.

Waking up with Dorian in his arms and nuzzling into that satin robe. Losing to Gregori at *King of the Hill* over and over again. Desperate kisses in the library and the grandsire's chambers. Dorian tending to his wounds, the beeswax balm on his lips. Gregori speaking the words of his freedom over his shoulder as he wrote that letter in his blood.

He can't tell her that he weeps because he threw it all away for Dorian, the only vampire he wants to bleed for. That he weeps because he can't do a damned thing to save him.

It's all nothing more than the soot blackening his fingers.

Elias's whole body heaves with grief unleashed. He exhausts himself of tears and all the strength in his muscles to stay upright, head pounding with clogged sinuses.

Help me free him, sits heavy in his throat. *I love him.*

Even if he can't articulate what kind of love he means, Elias is as certain of his feelings as he is that the stars don't disappear when he can't see them in the cave. If his mother still thinks he's under some beguiling enchantment, if he spills everything and she believes it's all a monster speaking through his mouth, he'll never get to see Dorian again.

His mother dabs his face and lets him twist around to slump

against her shoulder, nestling in the crook of her arm like an overgrown babe. "I saw colors you'd never believe," he says, to give some reason for the deluge of tears, "and they're gone."

For once, his mother doesn't try to coax him to sleep with the others. She lets him stay in the garden wrapped up in his furs, and when he says he's not hungry or thirsty or cold, she doesn't push.

Elias still can't sleep, but now he stares at the trickling stream in the garden concocting a plan, one he's finally confident will work and that he's ready to put into motion, starting with distracting his kin all at once.

Elias runs the inventory and, as Keeper, has access to every pocket of the cave network except Dorian's hold. He likes to think it's Gregori's voice in his head whispering, *The strongest plans have the fewest variables.*

They have one full jug of *schninir* from Clan Hogul, and several empty jugs lying around for better use. Elias takes one that he's filled with water from the river to the bull's pen, adds a smidgen of manure, seals the top, and buries it in the dirt with the seershrooms to fester.

He waits until Bini's on guard and starts asking her casual questions. *How's Loric? Oh, you're official now? Trying for twins, eh? Boys or girls or one of each?*

She's no more a monster than her ignorance, and Elias can't blame her for it. Dorian and every other vampire and all of Elphaba's children and grandchildren didn't blame him for his insulated life. She'll fight for her clan without question, though, thus she's in his way.

The hold's door still doesn't lock. It's not even a door, it's thick woven strips of furs in an out-of-the-way corner of the tunnels. He's never seen inside the hold, but it must be excessively fail-safed with only one guard.

Elias attempts no sly maneuvers to enter, not yet. He leans against the opposite wall of the tunnel to chat with Bini and doesn't even let his gaze slide away from her. "Is this boring?" he asks casually. "It must be."

Bini shrugs and smiles unhappily. "Yes, it is."

"Does Yarren let you do anything except stand there?"

"Like what?"

"Hobbies. Whittling, carving, filing your nails."

She shrugs again. "We're mostly here listening for escape attempts."

He hums and shoves off the wall. "Well, that's disappointing."

He leaves without giving her the chance to interject and busies himself learning their rotations under the guise of the comings-and-goings nascent to Keeper duties. Bini, Loric, and Kelso are the only guards, and all of them do the job seeming bored out of their minds.

They don't always stand alone. Bini sneaks time with Loric whenever either of them is on duty. Kelso falls asleep more often than not. Still, if they're listening for escape attempts, Dorian will need be silent as the grave.

Elias approaches Bini again with an offer. "I can multitask," he says. "I can do my numbers here, if you want. I'm sure you've got better places to be." He leans in and whispers loudly, "Loric misses you."

She smirks and tells him it's not her he has to convince, it's Yarren. "Why do you care if Loric misses me?"

"His pining is annoying."

She hums and, when Kelso comes to relieve her, joins Elias to convince Yarren to give her shifts to him instead. Yarren is not so easily duped, even occupied as he is sharpening all their pointy sticks because that bull won't last forever.

Yarren pins him with a mighty skeptical stare. "You've never been interested in the guard."

"I'm not interested in the guard." Elias jabs a thumb at Bini. "I can't stand these two and their woe-is-me longing."

"Guilty," Bini admits. She props her fist on her hip and waves the other hand. "It's not hard, Chief. Something happens, he screams. You want the legacy of this clan to live on? Give me more time with Loric."

"Gross," Elias volunteers.

Yarren sets the spear aside. "I don't trust you alone. You're still too fresh, it could trick you into freeing it."

Elias shrugs casually and looks to Bini. "I can shadow you?"

"Can he?"

"No." Yarren stands. "He can shadow me."

Elias doesn't get the chance until conditions are established—he must balance his Keeper duties with the guard, he's not to be left alone until Yarren clears him of suspicion, and he's not allowed to complain. One utterance of boredom or exhaustion or discontent, Yarren will find someone else in a snap.

Elias's only saving grace is his desire to do the job. Yarren's already annoyed enough by everyone else he picks for guard duty and their endless badgering to be let go, even if they're all far more competent warriors than he is.

Warriors, right. The brave and the bold naked cave rats.

Soon. A few more pieces to set on the board, then he'll strike.

Castle Tanarang felt the strain of Jacobi's theft within hours of his departure, but it becomes impossible to ignore when Dorotea's party returns all but empty-handed. Kymiria, who had been helping with the repairs in the kitchen, drops everything to sprint for the courtyard to greet them and sniff out the Catanz blood that they don't have.

Markus, Neire, and Dorotea bring some hope with supplies and medicine, but it's a fleeting relief. They still don't have a way to reach the other covens for aid. Markus works himself to delirium treating the wounded all while insisting that he works on corpses, not beings who can feel pain.

He's also the only vampire who can work around open wounds and not lose his composure. Kymiria tries, at first, to help, but her body betrays her, and she loses control of her strength, shattering a ceramic bowl of soup all over herself.

Kymiria is *hungry*. They all are. She can last a week before her skin starts to itch, no special feat among vampires of any age. The emotional strain exacerbates it at every turn. She couldn't organize their new medical supplies without her stress pitching her into a tantrum about asinine issues like how they don't stack perfectly symmetrically. Henri devolved into hysterics when he couldn't get a stain out of his leathers. Lucius cried over a cowlick in his hair that wouldn't stay flat but never has.

She drops her head in misery and stoops to pick up the shards. Markus looks up from breaking and resetting a broken tibia on his unconscious patient. Blood stains his hands up to his wrists. "You can go, Kymiria."

"I can help."

"You really can't."

"How do you do it? Stay so calm?"

Markus blinks. He finishes bandaging the leg and lifts his bloodied hands. "I can't put this back in my patients."

They can't put it back and Markus can't stop the wounds he fixes from bleeding, but it still feels like stealing. She's too exhausted to try and scrape the blood off his hands so she doesn't have to lap at it like a dog, but her hunger wins out.

There's no dignity in this, Kymiria thinks as she licks his palm. Over a century old and here she stands, in a makeshift hospital of their wounded, sucking up crumbs. She tries to comfort herself with the knowledge that at least it's not slurping off the floor, but it feels as depraved no matter how satisfying it tastes. Worse, it dulls only the hunger for blood. Beneath that is the hunger for revenge, for Jacobi's head on a spike, for getting their family back.

Any attempt to talk about Dorian is shut down and redirected, or flat-out ignored. Kymiria knows Markus has no interest in her, physically or romantically, but they can still commiserate, can't they? Markus seems determined to block her out, passively letting her take her crumbs in stiff silence, then returning to his work.

"Thank you."

He allows the rest of the coven to scavenge what's been spilled from his patients under heavy scrutiny and with Elphaba's permission, and then finally there's no more wounds to treat.

Amaranth, Elphaba, and Dorotea talk extensively about how to address the shortages compounded by burns, lacerations, and broken bones that needed strong, heathy bodies to heal properly. Gilan marches right up to their table with his little brigade of children both younger and older than himself to offer their blood to the cause. His lip wobbles as he talks. "Use the needles," he argues. "We can lose a little, right?"

Markus, for his part, assures them that, medically, they wouldn't suffer lasting consequences with tiny donations here and there. Nicky, the oldest boy who remains here, too young to volunteer, crosses his arms hotly. "See? And it's temporary. Can't the rules be bent this once? If our moms get too sick feeding you, everyone suffers."

"This is not your failure to answer for," Amaranth decides softly. "The coven will survive on quarter-rations for as long as we must."

"Because you're too proud?"

Kymiria smothers a smile at Nicky's obstinance. Now isn't the time to encourage him.

"Because it's never one rule that bends." Amaranth sits on the steps and has to look up at them. "We lose our senses when we get hungry, Nicky, but we all know the consequences of breaking the rules. Tonight it's a few drops from a needle. Tomorrow, hunger could justify a bite. Next week, something worse." She smiles sympathetically. "Thank you for your bravery, but the decision is final."

Quarter-rations keep the manic headaches away and never satisfy. They'll bleed the fish they catch as a salty, stomach-churning last resort, its effect as diluted as drinking from other vampires. Kymiria wrinkles her nose at the mere idea of the fish. She'd barely kept it down last time. The gods can't let circumventing the curse be too easy, can they?

Physical activity doesn't burn through blood like healing injuries, but even seeking out a partner for something quick and fun leaves her unsatisfied. Drinking from each other is like trying to drink her own saliva—they're recycling the same dwindling supply.

She almost joins the short list of vampires who decided to hibernate and sleep through starving, but her hunger's too strong to lie still enough for it by the time she tries. The castle becomes quieter than the wind howling through the broken windows. Conversations become snappy and short, those who chose to remain awake left with the repairs and guarding the castle against other opportunists.

She glares at a burning kelp log in the lounge with her measly dribbles of blood in a bowl and her arms around her knees. If she drinks it slowly, it almost tricks her body into thinking there's more of it.

Watching the flames, she goes over the battle again and again, wondering what she did so wrong to end up here. Alone. Markus buries his head in his books and dissects fish and whatever else they haul in, so bogged down with activity that he doesn't have time to think about missing Dorian like she does. Quinn hibernates. Kymiria considers herself friends, if not chosen family, with more than half the coven, but they offer paltry sympathies, too engrossed in their own miseries to distract her from her own.

"Master Kymiria?" Gilan toes into the lounge and drags her eyes from the fire, flickering flames burning her retinas as she blinks. His arm is in a sling, the worst of his injuries beyond scratches and scrapes.

"You can drop the *master*, Gilan."

"Can I call you auntie?"

She sips from the bowl and lets it linger, thick on her tongue, fangs achy with need. "If that makes you happy. What do you want?"

"Can I sit with you?"

"Aren't you supposed to be in bed?" She has no idea what time it is or what meal is up next for them. No one has entered the Grand Hall since the aftermath of the battle.

"Can't sleep." She scoots over and pats the cushion. Gilan crawls up beside her and hugs a pillow to his chest. "I miss him, too."

"That why you can't sleep?"

"Yeah," he admits, eyes on his lap. "Are you mad at him? You look mad."

"A bit."

Gilan sniffles and pouts. "Well, you shouldn't be. He didn't mean to leave."

"Pretty sure he did. I know he volunteered first."

"No. He got shot because I was in the way." Gilan tells her about the fire in the kitchen, forgetting about the ship as he ran and getting separated from his mother. He tells her how the vampire who grabbed him and broke his arm appeared out of nowhere, how Dorian had to save him because Gilan missed with his stake.

"He could have run away, but he was holding me and couldn't." Gilan lets the pillow fall and hugs his knee, dragging his eyes across his cloak there and sniffling. "It's my fault."

Kymira pulls him into her lap. "It's not your fault." Jacobi wanted Dorian from the start and would have gotten him one way or another. He would have traded any one of the children for him. Elphaba.

Gilan blubbers and sobs and Kymiria leapt off the path of parenthood decades ago, but she still remembers what it's like to be small and young and afraid. In a blink, he'll be as old as she was when she turned, then older, and even all those years from now she'll be a living portrait of the exact same face he's crying to tonight.

She sings him to sleep with the same lullaby that once comforted her, that he might one day sing to his children and grandchildren. A funny little song about the river of clouds and stars that arcs across the sky and all the spacy, glittery fish that swim within it. He doesn't rouse as she carries him to bed, but his fingers catch in the laces of her tunic. She gently disentangles them, then debates on moving his arm from the sling, unsure if he's meant to sleep with it on, and ends up leaving it.

Kymiria tugs his blankets up to his chin and pads out of the room he shares with five others. A canvas shade on a lone lantern spins slowly in the rising heat, constellation cut-outs casting stars of light over the walls.

Kymiria hasn't seen the state of the Holdfast and wanders there now, finding the entire place in shambles. Henri had spared her from retrieving Zeon's head. His blood is still there, a frozen puddle. More blood riddles the ground, the walls. Living blood, but also vampire blood, and she smiles to herself despite the carnage. They'd tried, and that's more than Amaranth can say of herself. Kymiria ensures the Holdfast door locks behind her, the knob smeared with dried Aeskerat blood and more staining the stone floor. She walks right past it with a mind for her grandsire.

Amaranth is wide awake, sweeping up snow that blew into the castle through one of their many broken windows. Kymiria marches up to her.

"We didn't get the dogs," she blurts, too strained to pretend at politeness. "Are we going to just sit here now, waiting for a miracle?"

Amaranth had traded her velvet dress for working leathers, braids all held back in a knitted wrap. She looks like a lowly servant's child, not their glorious leader. "Even if we had obtained the sled, I'm not sure that using it would have been wise."

"Fadehier thinks we're a coven of degenerate fools. Why bother asking if you never intended to use them?" They all agreed to follow Amaranth and Hyacinth despite their age because they're idealists—and their vision came to fruition. They proved that sustenance doesn't have to come from blood slaves, that they don't have to lord over the living, threatening their short, frightening lives. That there can be peace.

"I had intended to, at the time," Amaranth explains impatiently, grip tight on her broom. "I don't trust that Grandsire Kota wouldn't take advantage of our vulnerability and strike. Or that she wouldn't alert Jacobi to our attempt to forge an alliance."

"What, then, was all that talk about the other covens not letting this injustice stand if you didn't believe that?" Kymiria is her junior, but in some ways, Amaranth's curse of being frozen as a child limits her. Her age betrays her mettle against the other coven grandsires. Gregori lived for eight centuries, and it wasn't his belief in Amaranth that kept Aeskerat from wiping them out, it was his reluctance to get his coven killed fighting an unnecessary war.

Now it's necessary. They burned twenty-two of their kin, held Zeon's funeral without Castor, and for what?

Amaranth stoops and sweeps the last of the snow into a dustpan to toss out the window. "What I don't believe is that they won't seize the opportunity to rid themselves both of us and Aeskerat once they learn that we've both been weakened."

"What about Houlind, then?" Son Kir is… temperamental, Kymiria can attest. "Geltmont?"

"We would have to cross Aeskerat land to reach either quickly."

"Perfect, then Aeskerat will face a battle on both fronts."

Amaranth's face pinches and she shakes her head. "And if you get caught? You'd be slow on foot."

"I'm no tactician," Kymiria mutters, "but even I know there is no way out of this without a price. Aeskerat has too much land and now not enough scouts to patrol it all. If Houlind or Geltmont want to attack us, they'll have to deal with Aeskerat first. An army is a lot harder to hide than a lone scout."

If the alternative is waiting around in vain, walking there at least shows that they haven't given up.

Amaranth rubs her eyes, then leaves her fingers steepled in thought. "If Jacobi rightfully suspects we're trying to circumvent his claim or indeed start a war on both his fronts, our people will pay for it."

Kymiria raises her hand to interject but comes up empty.

"I'm sorry, Kymiria," Amaranth says softly. "I am leading us down the best of all paths I've been given and am no more proud of my actions than you are."

"What if a miracle never comes?" Kymiria slides down the wall and crosses her arms. "We're at our strongest right now. The longer we wait, the more we starve, the more we lose hope." The more strain they put on the rest of their people to sustain them. The more Jacobi's prisoners suffer.

Amaranth leans on her broom. "My brother is still healing," she says. "If Jacobi isn't overthrown by his own mutineers or our people can't rescue themselves, we can discuss a march on Aeskerat when we truly are at our best. There will be consequences, and Dorian will be one of them."

A gust of wind whistles in through the cracks in the broken glass. "What's worth fighting for, if not this?"

Amaranth nods gravely and gives a hapless shrug. "Save your strength. We will need it."

If she was worth anything to Jacobi as a blood slave, she would have volunteered. Still, she runs over the disastrous battle in her mind yet again. If she hadn't lost sight of Dorian, he'd still be here. If they'd considered Jacobi attacking from above, they could have killed him and been done with it. If Amaranth had let her shoot Jacobi through Dorian when she had the chance, they would have lost more than Zeon, but Jacobi would have been dead, unable to steal away half the clan.

"We had plenty," Kymiria mutters. "You just didn't want to use it."

She leaves Amaranth in the hall and digs an apron out of her wardrobe that Elphaba had stitched her name into with crooked pink embroidery when she was a child. The castle needs repair, blood needs scrubbing off walls and out of rugs, linens need washing, bread baking, fish gutting. She's not about to let the fire in the hearth go out.

Elias braces for the worst when Yarren *finally* lets him in to see Dorian. Or, more accurately, Yarren tests his loyalties by seeing how Elias reacts to witnessing his former captor in chains.

Dorian's about as lifeless as a gutted pig, hung upside down by a rope lashed tightly around his ankles. His hands, tied to a bolt in the floor, don't scrape the floor like his tangled mass of hair. It's lost its sheen as has his skin despite being upended.

With Loric's slimy attitude, he expected them to have stripped Dorian of his Tanarang leathers, but the only component missing is his boots. Either Yarren didn't care or they didn't want to risk freeing him long enough to strip or cut everything away. His mouth remains gagged—probably because they didn't have the means to smith a muzzle.

Yarren observes unblinking. Elias keeps his face impassive, shouting *It could be worse, it could be worse, it could be worse* over and over again in his mind. The cavern is small but steeply pitched, room enough for three glorified blood bags if they ever find themselves so fortunate. It's utterly empty now except for a little concave table with the tools for bleeding and the rig for the ropes, both well out of Dorian's reach. Elias pokes at his side. It's not hard enough to move Dorian, but Yarren still twitches.

"How did the last one manage to kill th—itself?"

Yarren folds his arms tightly, his permanent grimace making his face hard to read. "Sawed at the ropes with its fingernails and dislocated both its shoulders. Reached a knife someone left behind and carved its own heart out."

The determination to die, the fortitude it must've taken... Would Dorian have that? Or would his yearning to return to the hamstrung Tanarang supersede it?

Elias swallows dryly and hides his shaking hands under his arms. He rounds Dorian slowly, noting the dried blood on his shoulder, his stomach, down the center of his back, but the black jerkin hides the worst of it. "This one doesn't seem strong enough to lift a finger."

"No, whatever the other one stabbed it with was very effective." Yarren's voice cuts like steel. "Do you know what it was?"

"Didn't it say something about icicles?"

Yarren *hmphs*. "No ice I've ever heard of that doesn't melt."

Elias cracks a wry grin. "Is this a thinly veiled interrogation, Chief?" Yarren doesn't answer, and Elias steps away. "Have I passed the test?"

"I haven't decided," Yarren replies stiffly.

He puffs his cheeks in a scowl. "What exactly are you waiting for me to do? Sneak an entire vampire past the whole clan and hope no one notices? My mother's life depends on keeping this leech right where it is."

Yarren still doesn't look convinced. "You still haven't told me what happened. You're remarkably healthy given how long they had you."

Elias scoffs and pushes through the wall of pelts. "What happened? They're not like us, Chief. They live in luxury and they eat luxury. I look healthy 'cause they fatten slaves up for the harvest, but thank you for your continued skepticism. Really feel welcome now."

"You screamed for that *leech* like they'd killed your mother."

"Yes!" Elias hisses. "Yes, it got in my head. They have this—this *spell* they do." He didn't prepare the words flying out of his mouth and can't take them back now. "A beguiling. Honeyed words and satin promises to convince you that you like being their food. That you need to be their food."

"By Takkha, I knew it, I knew you—"

"But it wore off." Elias lets his voice catch and blinks rapidly, dragging his sleeve across dry eyes. "It wore off," he repeats, softer now. "I'm free, finally, yet here you stand second-guessing me, as if I *actually* liked being *food*. You want to know why I wanted Bini's shifts? So I could claw back some semblance of power over this *monster*. I need you to believe that I'm not lost or it's all going to feel like a lie."

Yarren arches away from him in shock.

Elias sniffles and curses. "Forget it. I'll go back to doing your inventory and staying out of your way." He storms off and shoulder-checks Loric in the tunnel.

He's almost to the garden when his chief stops him. Elias imagines knocking an ebony pikeman off the board.

"I'm sorry," Yarren says, the words sounding foreign on his lips. He grips Elias's shoulders like he means to shake the sadness out. "You can have the shift, and I will battle my own worries that this beguiling hasn't worn off as well as you think."

"What have I done that you believe that?"

Yarren heaves a long-suffering sigh, as tired with the direction of this conversation as Elias is. "Shadow Loric. The leech has been quiet, but it might try something to win your pity."

More time wasted. "Thank you."

His shadow shift can't come fast enough, and once Elias does sit across from Loric, he supposes he doesn't have to scrap step two of his plan entirely. Loric might be the most understanding on that front, so long as he goes about it delicately.

"You keep glancing at the door like it'll move if you look away." Loric isn't at all thrilled about his new side-job babysitting Elias.

"If I tell you something... do you promise to keep it to yourself?"

Loric arches a brow and folds his arms on his knees. "Oh? Finally weaving a strand in the web of gossip?"

"I lied about why I wanted to be on the guard."

"Ha!" Loric springs to his feet. "I knew it. You're infatuated—"

Elias squirms and waves at him to sit back down. "I thought you would understand."

"We're not friends."

"That's why I know you won't talk me out of it."

Loric glances between him and the door, absently twirling his spear. "Talk you out of what?"

Elias raises a finger to his lips and scoots closer. Warily, Loric lowers to a crouch. "The claim," he whispers. "That's how they work. A vampire bite shows every other vampire what's theirs. It's degrading and humiliating. Like we're possessions, trophies. Not people."

Loric lurches in disgust. "And?"

"And they're manic clean freaks. They don't lie with the living because they think we're filthy pigs. That one in there," Elias jabs his thumb, "threw a tantrum over an infant's spit-up."

Loric snickers and sits back, kicking his feet out to rest his spear across his thighs. "They eat people to survive. How does that even work?"

"Beats me." Elias shrugs. "But I can't get it out of my head."

"... the baby tantrum?"

"No!" Elias smacks at Loric's chest. "Showing it how it feels to be owned." He lets hunger slip into his voice, gesturing emphatically.

"Four hundred years old. Taken by *me.*"

Loric leans away from him and gives an uncomfortable laugh. "You're serious."

"I am. Yarren wouldn't understand but I knew *you* would. Don't you? You understand who the real animal here is. Act like an animal, get bedded like one." The words sound ridiculous to him, and Elias is immensely proud of himself for not fudging his speech or stuttering over this flagrantly hideous persona.

Loric drums his fingers in thought. "I admit, I never expected this from you."

"I didn't either, but I can't stop thinking about it. I can't sleep because of it."

Loric laughs again, a giggling snicker at his expense. "It really did a number on your head, didn't it?" He purses his lips. "It's unnecessarily risky—"

"I don't intend to remove the ropes or the gag. That's part of the appeal. He's the animal, remember?"

"Uh-huh." Loric licks his lips and gives Elias an appraising once-over. "I assume you want me to stand guard while you have your fun?"

"Could you?" Elias laces his fingers under his chin. "I don't want Yarren finding out."

"No, no, best not. But"—Loric regards the door again—"I'd like a piece for myself for my troubles."

Unlike Elias, Loric's interest is genuine. He turns his shudder into a shrug, prepared for this even as he'd hoped even Loric wouldn't stoop so low. "If you want to take the risk. I know you're trying for a kid with Bini, and I heard there's a chance of... performance issues after the fact."

Why? Damned if Elias has an answer—he's making this up as

he goes. It doesn't have to make sense, it has to scare Loric. And scare him it does. Loric grimaces and scoots away. "You sure you want to do this?"

"I don't have anyone to impress."

"Hmm, how much time you think you need?"

"More than we have right now." Elias hangs off every second of lingering deliberation. *Agree. You have to agree, you sick pig.* "I'll sneak you extra shares of *schninir*? Off the record?

Loric smiles to himself and finally nods. "Deal."

Chapter 16:
Too Far Gone

Elias keeps dropping the pliers he stole from the stable as he practices using them with his limited grip. His hands are too sweaty to squeeze securely, no matter how many times he dries them on his furs.

Loric will likely grant him the chance to sate these horrible fantasies he's concocted only once. He has one chance to get that arrow out without any sure idea of how to do it. If Dorian's healed around it, if there's no easy purchase and it's sunk deep into his body, if it's stuck frozen to his flesh like a tongue to an icicle, he's not sure what he'll do. He doesn't have the resolve to start carving at another body, not when he'd have to keep up appearances, and he has nothing to practice on.

He refuses to let Dorian wait any longer, and now that Loric's invested, if he tries putting it off, he'll look suspicious. He hides the pliers, his mother's work gloves, and a knife in his boots, psyching himself up among the seershrooms.

Loric smirks at him when he's late for his shadowing shift. Elias shoves the little flask of stolen alcohol at his chest, a wordless excuse. "What if someone comes looking?"

"Do try to be quiet. I'll figure it out."

The amount of noise he expects is exactly why Elias went with this ridiculously disgusting farce. He parts the furs and wishes for a door with a lock. This entire plan depends on Loric having zero interest in watching, on him staying committed to guarding from anyone else sneaking up on them. If Loric changes his mind...

Well, Dorian had better heal fast enough to break them both out.

Elias lowers Dorian to the floor as gently as he can and loosens the ropes. The vampire still looks dead, skin still ashy. "Dorian?" he whispers, backs of his fingers to his face. An unsettling pit opens in Elias's stomach as he considers that the corpse-grey body is actually gone.

Dead vampire blood is poison, though, so he can't be. Elias watches his chest for movement and holds his fingers beneath his nose and sees nothing, feels nothing. There's no pulse at his neck either. He can't be dead, but he *is*.

Elias presses his ear to his chest and waits and waits and waits.

Ba................. bump................... ba...................

If he's this far gone, maybe he won't even feel Elias digging out the ice. A small mercy, then. Better this way.

Dorian won't notice the gag loosen either, but Elias can't bear to leave him like this. He tugs the cloth free, stained with dried blood from the empty pockets where his fangs used to be. Elias startles and recoils. Jacobi didn't do that. Jacobi didn't have time to do that.

The Aeskerat steal teeth for prizes all the time but knowing either Yarren or Loric did this purely to be cruel has Elias swallowing back bile. It's not like Dorian can't bite down like anyone else and leave a bloody mess behind, so they can't use caution as an excuse.

They did it for no other reason than to mutilate.

Elias's eyes sting and he turns around, fists balling on the dusty floor. There's surviving, there's being wary, there's being careful. Then there's this monstrousness. The clan doesn't need to do this—any of this. They didn't have to stay after the vampires took the sun away. They don't have to hide in this cave, stubbornly clinging to a pile of rocks simply because they were here first. They don't need to feed on vampires to survive.

His clan does this because they want to, because they think they deserve to.

Elias almost walks out to stab Loric and let him die choking on his own blood. Loric and everyone who gets in his way. They aren't his to kill, and reminding himself that is the only thought that keeps him in the hold to gently roll Dorian over to get this over with.

Elias tips his head back and breathes until the threat of tears recedes and he can focus on what he came here to do.

First—some padding. Elias shrugs off his coat and folds it up on the floor, then nods to himself.

Step one, done. *Deep breath.* He can do this.

Roll up the jerkin and the shirt beneath and ignore all those silvery snail-trail scars and don't retch all over Dorian at the sight of the wound.

It hasn't healed. It's black and frozen around the edges, blotches like mold creeping across Dorian's back, skin burned from the sheer intensity of the cold. The broken arrow shaft isn't buried too deep, luckily.

Elias nods to himself again and tries the pliers, tiny metal teeth slipping on the ice. He tries again and again with each sharp *click* of failure, then rakes back sweaty flyaways from his face.

I'm so sorry for this.

Between the knife scraping out room and his gloved fingers digging in and a fair number of whispered curses, Elias digs the broken arrow free with a moist squelch that sends horrible shivers across his body.

Dorian doesn't move once, doesn't even bleed where it's been taken out.

Before Loric can come in wondering what's taking so long and why it's so quiet, Elias pockets the arrowhead, fixes Dorian's clothes as they were, and cuts shallowly into his own wrist.

"Take as much as you need," he whispers, and nothing happens. "*Please.*" He hauls Dorian upright, mashing his wrist against his teeth. *Please.*

Is he too far gone? Too deep inside whatever death-adjacent netherworld starvation sent him to?

Afraid Loric will walk in and see something Elias can't explain, because this wasn't at all how it was supposed to go, Elias gives up. He resets the gag, ties off his cut, and pulls his coat back on, leaving everything appearing exactly the way he found it.

Loric probably expects some self-satisfied dishevelment, some suave swagger. Elias goes through the doorway on wobbly knees, waves off concern that he's hurt. Loric can go see for himself. Let him think Elias simply couldn't do it, that he sat in there at war with himself.

He goes to the garden, chucks the arrowhead into oblivion, and throws up in the stream. The rest of the plan can't delay. He'd wanted to give Dorian time to heal up enough so he'd be able to stand on his own in case escape got ugly, but that's not going to happen.

Elias rinses bile from his mouth and scrubs away the evidence on the rocks, eyeing the dirt pile concealing the catalyst for their escape. Then he flops over to pass out.

Elias hadn't thought bulls could die from depression, but it passes in silence and its body barely stops breathing before the clan busts out the butcher knives.

He sits alone and away from everyone and everything, there only to maintain his already questionable profile. Loric hasn't ratted him out to Yarren or spoken to Elias about what he didn't do with Dorian, but he's also got a mind for Bini and nothing else.

Elias eats without a thought for what's being served to him, meat tasting of dust. At one point, his mother comes to join him and he doesn't have the energy to give her more than one-word answers. This feast was the perfect opportunity to poison his entire clan at once, and he passed it up, the jug still buried.

What if Dorian can't be saved? Elias still doesn't know the way to Tanarang even if he'd go only to deliver Dorian's body to Kymiria and offer her closure. Vampires are supposed to be immortal, invulnerable to every means of killing a mortal soul except fire, sunlight, a wooden stake to the heart, and a beheading.

Neire told him Northern ice can't kill them, it just hurts. Therefore, Dorian can't be dead. But if he also can't wake up and give Elias directions and walk on his own feet so Elias doesn't have to drag him on that sled, Elias might as well put him out of his misery.

When shots of blood begin to disperse around the cavern, Elias takes his and can't bring himself to not waste it, letting it dribble and splatter at his feet. He'll use his next shift to check if Dorian has at all improved, try to force feed him if he can figure out how and if not, then put him down. Consequences be damned.

Yarren notices him wasting the blood and sits heavily beside him. "They choose this, Elias," he says. "They choose to become what they are, choose to become monsters instead of leaving this world when their time comes."

Amaranth didn't. Hyacinth didn't. Chrysanthemum tricked them. Dorian turned to protect his sister. *Gregori did. Kymiria did.* "Have you ever talked to one, as equals?"

"They will never see us as their equal." Yarren sighs. "I—"

"Draw me a monster, Chief." Elias pulls a bit of charcoal from his pocket. "I'd draw you a rapist. A slaver. A murderer. None of them would have fangs and all of them choose to be evil."

Yarren accepts the charcoal but doesn't do anything with it. "But all of them *could* have fangs. They could rampage for a dozen mortal lifetimes."

"Or they could be good for a dozen more."

"It's not natural, Elias. It breaks the circle."

Elias grits his teeth to keep his lip from trembling and still fails. "I know you think we have to hate them, that we have to be enemies, but we don't. Your blood slave has a name, and you haven't given him a chance."

"It shot me and killed Minira and Lalo without giving us a chance."

Elias drops his head in his hands. He stares at the fire and sets his jaw. All around them, shadows flicker over the finger paintings from generations past. "They see us as animals. Pigs and frightened little deer. Animals never grow, never change, never learn. Do you want to prove them right, Chief? Or do you want the chance to be the last chief unmourned in this gods' forsaken cave? Don't you want to be the chief that leads our people to the surface—forever?"

Yarren observes the clan partying around them, oblivious to their conversation. He offers the charcoal back and smears black from his palm onto his knee. "You think this vampire would listen, after what we've done to it?"

"Yes."

"And this isn't the beguiling talking?"

Elias shakes his head. "He doesn't need enchantments. Aeskerat Coven knows where this cave is, and our last living meal just died."

He's not saying any of this expecting Yarren to agree. When Elias escapes, either with Dorian or after explaining why he put their blood slave out of his misery, he'll remember Yarren's refusal to cooperate even at this point and won't look back.

"Very well."

Elias gapes. "What?"

Yarren sits up into a crouch, poking a log closer to the flames. "If we can wake it up, I will let it speak."

"You're serious?"

Yarren arches a brow. "Should I not be? That coven and our starvation are serious threats."

Elias flounders for an answer, tripped up over how to explain that Dorian might not wake up and he knows exactly why and may have already deceived them all to try.

Yarren stands and winces, holding his stomach. "Later," he decides, "once I have a clear head." He's interrupted on his way out of the cave by other clansfolk, and Elias panics.

He jerks to his feet and skirts around his clan. He needs to talk to Loric—needs to make sure Loric doesn't tell Yarren about his lies before he can come clean himself. *Where's Loric?*

Probably with Bini, trying to make that dream of twins come true.

A rowdy Kelso blocks his escape, drunkenly asking how he

enjoys the guard, if he's bored out of his mind like the rest of them. Elias peels Kelso's arm off him and ducks out of his reach.

"Aww, where you goin'?" Kelso croons after him. "Lighten up and have some fun for once."

Elias contemplates knocking him on his ass as a particularly fun endeavor. When he turns to offer that because his sense of self-preservation shriveled up and died in the snow, Kelso coughs blood all over his face.

Elias sputters and backpedals. "Kelso?"

Kelso lurches and gags, spitting up red chunks of his meal. He's not alone. A gory menagerie of drunken clansfolk drops like flies behind him. No one is spared, falling over each other in a bloody delirium.

Did... did Elias poison the dinner and wipe the incident from his memory?

Kelso slumps at his feet and starts seizing, frothing at the mouth.

Elias can only gawk. He ate, too, and he's fine. He's fine, right? He touches his face and holds his throat, his stomach, nauseous only from the sight and stench of the scene before him. The only thing he didn't—

Dorian.

But he's not dead. And dead vampire blood doesn't do *that*. It causes a nasty case of hives and nausea, like bad meat, and it passes.

Elias runs for his cell anyway.

"Dorian?"

He's still not moving.

Elias cuts him down. Dorian's skin is still ashen, but he's breathing, short and shallow, eyes flicking rapidly beneath their lids. Outside, the cave has gone disturbingly silent. Elias leaves the cell, creeping back toward the main atrium.

The only sound is the crackling fire. Yarren lies on the ground in a puddle of bloody sick. Loric and Bini, too. All of them.

Elias holds his throat, breathing in staccato gasps. *What is this?*

If... if they wake up and think Dorian poisoned them on purpose, they'll have him begging for death. Escape can't wait.

He sprints back to the cell.

"We're leaving. Right now. Just stay with me." Elias loops Dorian's bound arms over his shoulders and hauls him onto his back. The sled should still be by the door up the stairs. All the way up all those stairs.

He fights his way to the surface, Dorian an anchor. The sled is right where it's supposed to be, and Elias dumps his deadweight onto it.

North—that's all he knows. And west toward the coast. He doubles back for food and water for himself, the rest of the firewood, a couple weapons—anything he can carry in a single trip.

He's reached the first step on his way out when a series of wet, groaning growls echoes in the cave. Shadows flicker dimly from near the feast. He frowns, listening to the uneven shuffle-steps of someone approaching.

Whatever state they're in, they won't be stopping him. Elias readjusts the load in his arms to grip a spear.

The shuffle-steps belong to Kelso, lumbering along like he drank three bottles of *schninir* all at once.

"Kelso?" He reeks of blood, bile, meat, and alcohol.

Kelso moans that same wet, sticky growl and turns toward Elias's voice.

"Kelso."

Blood still stains his chin, and his eyes... cloudy white and vacant. Kelso snarls, hackles raised and fangs spilling from his gums.

He—*oh, gods*. He died. He's dead. They're all dead. He died with Dorian's blood in his body and it—it—mutated?

None of them drank enough to turn into withers. None of them died from fever. This is something else.

Kelso snarls and gives chase.

Elias squeals and sprints up the stairs before the rest of his clan can converge on him, dumps the armful of supplies onto the sled with Dorian, and slaps on his snowshoes. Finding purchase in the snow with his awkward feet, pushing a heavy sled laden with an entire person and supplies, Elias is panting after the first couple of laborious steps.

The door doesn't need to hold them forever, only long enough for him to find a way to cut them off. He searches ahead over the flat plains of the Great White Waste—

The river. Frozen, but not after he's done with it.

He pushes the sled with renewed vigor, hearing Kelso and the rest of his clan spilling out of the cave and not daring to turn around. They're downwind and they can see him and they're hungry. That's all that matters.

The skids of the sled slide easily on the ice. Elias pushes it clear to the other bank and grabs two chunks of wood, stopped in his tracks by the sight of his undead clan far closer than he expected.

His mother's there, hair and spittle flying in the wind. Yarren, too. Possessed by something unrecognizable.

He kneels and sets the narrower end of one of the wood chunks against the ice, hammering it straight down with the other.

"C'mon, c'mon, crack already." It's thick, strengthened by winter. Elias keeps hammering until it starts to give and frigid water spurts up from below. He scrambles back and kicks the wood one last time with his heel.

Kelso does the rest. He falls through with a sharp *crack*, fissures webbing. Elias flattens his body and distributes his weight as the rest of his clan fall in one after the other. In a blink, his mother vanishes.

He didn't let himself think too hard about the part of his plan that demanded a distraction so he could escape. He'd wanted to get them all sick enough to not give chase but still survive it. If they died shortly after from the cold, that would have been their fault.

But this... Elias chokes, hands cupped over his mouth in horror. *The last chief unmourned. Lead our people to the surface.* Did he do this? Have the gods finally answered his prayers in the cruelest manner possible?

The last of the snarls fades as they sink and the current carries them away. Elias rests his head back on the ice, staring up at the hazy sky. If he lets himself think about it, blame himself for it, he'll lie here and never get back up again. Dorian needs him. "I'm sorry," he says to the stars, then eases himself onto the shore.

He peels away the hasty bandage over the previous cut on his wrist and tries once again to coax Dorian back to the realm of the living. "You're all I have left," he rasps, "so take it."

Dorian groans lowly, brows knitting. A dry tongue prods at the sensitive scab, and Elias sends prayers of gratitude up to any god left listening. "There you go, take what you need."

He bites rather hard with his remaining teeth, but Elias can forgive him this one instance if it means he gets his friend back. Apologies clog Elias's throat, and he doesn't know where to start. "I'm sorry I didn't get you out sooner" feels reasonable. "I'm sorry for that stupid fledgling who started all this. I'm sorry for fighting you at every turn when you were far nicer and more forgiving than I deserved."

Dorian squirms in his arms and bites even harder and Elias can't hold back a hiss of pain. Dorian says nothing, and maybe the roughness is his answer to Elias's apology, but while he's not forming any words, he is making plenty of other noise.

"Dorian?" Elias tries to pry his wrist free. "Okay, you can be furious and I know you're starving, but we're out in the Waste."

Another harsh suck and nibble, more ignoring him.

"Dorian."

Dorian snarls, looking up at him with the whites of his eyes gone blood red, pupils overtaking the irises, skin ashy grey with rot. The same skin he'd seen on those slaughtered during the wither ambush at the castle.

Elias tears free and falls back into the snow. "Dorian?"

The wither snarls again, no recognition on its face. Its hands, still bound, are useless in stopping its fall from the sled into the snow. Elias kicks away and keeps calling Dorian's name, cradling his wrist to his chest.

The thing that was Dorian can't get to its feet, wriggling like a worm. Elias stays out of its reach and that it's so easy is the only thing that gets him upright. He hiccups, tears burning in the wind.

There's still wood in the sled. He should grab a piece and end this but crumpling in the snow and letting the monster haunting Dorian's body finish him off sounds like a fairer way to go.

Elias falls to his knees and looks away. Distant clopping reaches his ears, but maybe it's the wind.

Just let it end, he thinks, *I have nowhere else to go.*

The clopping grows louder, and Elias sniffles, hearing the harsh snuffling of a racing horse before he sees it—a black streak against the white wasteland headed straight for them. The rider has a sword, long and meant for horseback, reared back to—

"No, don't!" Elias screams, bodily shoving Dorian out of the way and nearly getting trampled himself.

The rider dismounts. They're not alone, another horse not far behind. Elias doesn't care, putting himself between whoever it is approaching and the wither as it tries to bite at his leg. "Don't, please. It has to be me who does it, *please.*"

The rider draws up short and Elias blinks bleary tears away. A bear fur cloak, a belt of stolen teeth and a choker to match. The sword drops in the snow and wiry arms haul him into an embrace.

Elias locks up. Maybe he's already gone hypothermic. This is some vivid hallucination, a gift from the gods, as he dies blissfully unaware of his final moments.

"You're not dead yet," Gregori whispers.

"You are."

Gregori has to be, otherwise he would have stopped Jacobi's raid on Tanarang. He would have stopped Jacobi's deal with Yarren. He would have come to rescue Elias from his clan before catastrophe struck.

Gregori sets him back on his feet, guilt wracking his face. "Not yet."

The other rider slows beside them, the third lieutenant who likes knives. She dismounts in a huff and hefts the wooden end of a spear.

Elias gets back in front of Dorian, hands raised. "Don't!"

Puzzled, she looks between him and Gregori. "Is he sick with the cold?"

"Elias." Gregori eases around him, purposefully slow with his movements. "I'm not killing him, not for good. Understand?"

Elias understands nothing of what's going on right now.

Gregori doesn't wait for his confirmation, stopping Dorian's low snarls with a sickening snap. Elias watches numbly as Gregori deposits him back on the sled and drags it over with ease.

"Are you back with Jacobi?" Elias asks, floundering for an explanation. "Our cave is on Aeskerat land, isn't it? He never actually killed you, and you're here to take us to him?"

The lady vampire gives a derisive snort. "Hardly."

"Yeah? I saw you with Jacobi. You stood by and watched him sell us to my clan. You were there, at the castle," Elias snaps. "I don't even know your name."

"Veronique," she says proudly, like it's a fancy title bestowed on her. "As far as my grandsire and I are concerned, we are the last true Aeskerat in the North."

Gregori dusts his hands off and strides back over, then his shoulders slump. "Veronique convinced Jacobi that I had fallen with some clever sleight of hand and has been spying for me."

"Sleight of hand?"

"A wax-dipped stake," Veronique gloats.

Elias doesn't care if she negotiated with gods. He glares at Gregori. "Where were you?"

Gregori smiles grimly. "Healing. Regrowing arms, legs—most everything, it felt like—with only fish as feed. I'm sorry I couldn't come sooner."

Yes, terribly guilty, isn't he? He should have run with Elias when he'd begged him to, and none of this would have happened. Nevertheless, what's done is done. He nods slowly and folds his arms but his wrist protests. Gregori holds his hand out for it and Elias lets him take it, refusing to look at the damage. "How did you know where to find me?"

"I was at Jacobi's meeting discussing the raid on your cave," Veronique explains. "His maps weren't all that accurate, but we smelled you and the horde behind."

"Well done with that," Gregori praises though his face wrinkles with disgust at the state of Elias's bite. "This will need tending, but we should get out of the wind before someone else smells you. Veronique? Please pull the sled."

"There's a shallow ice cave between here and the petrified forest," Elias suggests. "Our hunters would stop there to rest."

"I know it," Veronique says. "It's not far."

Gregori mounts up behind him, chest to Elias's back. "Are you warm enough?"

Elias snuggles into the bearskin cloak. "I'll manage."

Then they're off.

"They started seizing and I didn't stick around to watch what came after. I just know they died and then they turned." They've made camp beneath the swirls of blue ice, burning a fire entirely for Elias's sake with the last of the wood. Gregori has practically glued himself to Elias while Veronique watches Dorian, bound now to the sled itself.

"I know they turned because of Dorian, but even dead vampire blood doesn't kill you like that." Elias winces at Gregori's touch on his arm. The bite burns now, angry red lines streaking all across his skin. "And this has never happened before either. Did I do all of this?"

"You've never been bit by a wither before," Gregori mutters.

"And that's what happens to the living who turn on wither blood. They're barely even withers themselves, something more... base." He sighs and rests Elias's arm on his knee. "And no, Elias, you did not do this. He would have turned without your intervention."

Veronique toys with a set of wide leather bracelets on her arm decorated with little bird skulls. "I thought only the living could turn into withers," she says. "That once you're a vampire, you're a vampire. I didn't know you could revert."

"It can happen. Now sit still, this will hurt." Gregori's solution to the infection in his arm is to suck it out, and he's right, it does hurt. Elias swears and does his best not to yank away from him. His inflamed skin is hypersensitive to every minute touch and scrape of Gregori's teeth.

Elias can't imagine it tastes or feels good on his palate. He doesn't take much, instead teething around the wound and healing it as he goes with that magical mystery medicine in vampire saliva.

Gregori pulls away with a shudder, gagging with all the grace of a yakking animal. "Oh, that is vile."

Elias's arm has already healed over, an angry pink. He tugs his sleeve back down and hugs his legs.

Veronique kicks Dorian's sled. "What about him?"

"Theoretically, he's savable."

"Theoretically?" Elias asks.

Gregori sighs and sits back. "I have never seen a wither recovered. Withers are born from people who die from too much vampire blood," Gregori explains. "A reverted wither chases that same insatiable hunger from a place of existential starvation. It's not just many moons without a meal, it's pain. A wounded animal limping on its last legs."

Elias hugs his legs tighter. "Wounded like having a Northern ice arrowhead stuck in your chest?"

Gregori shrugs sympathetically. "It would have killed him over and over again, stopping and restarting his heart until his body gave out. Jacobi's sadism will not go unanswered for, I promise you this."

"Jacobi knew this would happen?" Elias didn't consider that all this could have been Jacobi's plan. He'd seemed tickled pink thinking Dorian would be aware of his own suffering for the next twenty years. Had he anticipated Dorian turning and taking out Elias and his clan in one fell swoop? Maybe Jacobi actually wanted some twisted sense of justice for his clan's last blood slave. As if Jacobi could care about anyone but himself.

Gregori frowns and shares a glance with Veronique. "It would have been convenient for him to punish Dorian and your entire clan all at once by letting them poison themselves with wither blood," he muses carefully, "but I can't say if that was his intent."

Elias cocks his head. Gregori sure doesn't seem all that fazed by Dorian turning. "You've seen reverted withers before."

"Once. She'd been pinned inside a sunken ship, drowning ceaselessly." Gregori heaves a sigh and shakes his head pityingly. "We tried everything to reach the part of her soul that remained and it all amounted to nothing. Any blood we gave her soured from what resided within her, and bleeding her dry to start fresh failed because always a little remained."

"And you think Dorian's different because...?"

"No, I don't think he's different at all." Gregori waves to Dorian's sled with another mournful frown. "But now the tools exist that I did not have before, namely the needle devices at your castle."

Elias startles. *The needles?* "What difference would that make?"

"I have been toying with the design you provided." Gregori

smiles softly at him and fiddles with one something in his hand—one of his game pieces. It's not polished white or black, not part of the old set. It's as if he'd found something to carve a new piece from in the wilderness. "My hypothesis is that if he's completely dried out, the rot will die. He'll be catatonic and unable to feed, but those little devices can go straight to the heart where fresh blood is needed the most."

Elias ghosts his fingers over his healed bite, still not convinced that this whole thing wasn't a massive ploy. Gregori happening to wait just long enough that Dorian could only be saved by him and his knowledge. A valuable bargaining piece to buy himself a new alliance.

Or he really did race southward as fast as he could as soon as he was able, and the gods really haven't forsaken Elias.

Veronique settles down and huddles in her cloak, nodding at the gathering clouds in the distance. "We should wait to move out until the storm rolls in. Scouts will be taking cover."

A chance to rest and sleep after everything should be a blessing. Elias can't stop imagining what it must feel like to drown, or to have his heart give out over and over and over, waking up in agony and dying again, an endless cycle.

He crawls over to the sled and doesn't care if the act is pointless—there's a spare cloak beneath Dorian and Elias wriggles it free to tuck around him, protect his feet. "Here we are again," Elias whispers.

This time, there's no hiding that Dorian's not asleep. He's dead, by nearly every definition of the word.

Gregori toes over and lowers to a crouch, still giving him his space but close enough to speak softly. "I'm sorry I wasn't there."

"Do you actually care about Dorian, or is this just politics?" Elias tries to muster hurt in his voice, but Gregori's old. That he cares about Elias is a fluke, a byproduct of the curse of vampirism. Gregori not caring about Dorian and only seeing his salvation as a tool wouldn't surprise him one bit.

"You care," Gregori says quietly, "so I care."

Does he, though? If Gregori wants Elias for himself, letting Dorian die would remove any competition. If it's real, then Gregori has to show more for his efforts than gambling with coven politics.

Whatever Gregori's intent, no matter how altruistic his desire to help, Elias isn't about to squander his best chance at getting safe, getting warm, and getting a real cure for the only vampire to respect him without pageantry.

Keep him talking, he thinks. *Keep him interested.*

Elias settles closer to the fire in his blankets and scoots over to leave room for Gregori in silent invitation. Gregori joins him all too eagerly under the furs, and it's almost cozy. It's a little silly if he thinks too long about it—Gregori pillowing his head on his arm and looking at him like he's no older than Elias beside a corpse-like Dorian.

"Is it me?" Elias asks. "Or is it the novelty?"

"You are fair to ask, and to be honest, I don't know." Gregori moves like he wants to touch him but aborts the gesture and tucks his arm back against his side. "That this is possible at all is a fascinating novelty, but that it's *you* is not."

"You barely know me." Most of what he does know came from carefully constructed manipulations to earn a looser leash.

"I would like to," Gregori admits, far more earnest than Elias can handle right now. "Or is it someone else you want?" The *someone else* is spoken with a deliberate glance at Dorian.

That is also too much for Elias to handle right now. "He's taken," he mumbles. "Even if he weren't, he doesn't see me the way I want him to."

Gregori shifts closer and tucks the furs over Elias's neck, nails grazing his ear. "Those of his age find it difficult to ignore the distance. I'm afraid by the time he grows out of it, you will be but ashes and dust."

"Would you mourn me?" Elias asks, trying to shake all these nebulous feelings that slip like smoke through his fingers. They're untethered and uncoordinated and it's exhausting. "Or move on like I'm a toy that broke and became obsolete?" A dead fish, replacement nigh indistinguishable. What exactly does Gregori see in him beyond a lowly piglet that dared surpass his low expectations?

Gregori's eyes, brown gone black in the dwindling firelight, flit between his. Elias's disfigured fist tucks against his chest and Gregori's gaze catches on it, jaw setting, but he doesn't ask. "I don't know."

At least he can be honest. Elias nods to himself. If Gregori doesn't have the answers to his most important questions, he can't expect Elias to have any either. If all else fails and Elias's last hope for sanctuary is utterly solitude with Gregori, they'd have work to do. Reckonings to meet. Far more than he's prepared to face right now.

Elias rolls over and draws his knees up.

"Would you like me to leave?"

"You don't have to."

Elias sleeps until the storm blows in to give them perfect cover. Cover, at least, for unbothered undead horses that ride hard and fast. He closes his eyes and hides his face in the furs, and it's eerily similar to his first ride to Tanarang.

Gregori's arms around him holding the reins tight keep him steady. He imagines galloping through the gates in triumphant return, all of Tanarang singing his praises for bringing Dorian back.

You haven't done anything, a traitorous voice whispers, *and the only soul there who cares if you live or die is already gone.*

Chapter 17:
The Pyre

Markus and Quinn have the approaching party in their sights, and Elias's scent wafts up from below.

"We come in peace," the lead rider shouts. "Please open the gate."

Something rotten clings to them. Quinn narrows her eyes. "Gregori."

They'd be extraordinarily idiotic to try and attack an entire castle, just the two of them and Elias. Markus shrugs and Quinn orders the gate open.

Just in case his nose is lying to him, Markus leaves the wall to greet them with an arrow nocked.

The little yearling who refuses to die or remain an Aeskerat prisoner drops heavily from his horse, steadied by the Aeskerat behind him all decorated like a macabre tropical bird. He doesn't say anything nor does he meet Markus's baffled gaze.

A crowd gathers of everyone who's still awake, Amaranth and Kymiria shoving their way to the front. Amaranth draws up short.

"Gregori."

At the sound of Gregori's name, bowstrings creak, a semicircle of arrows aimed at his head.

He's not all that scary, if Markus is being honest. Quite skinny, if imposingly tall. And isn't he supposed to be dead?

Gregori and the other Aeskerat raise their hands in surrender. "We come in peace," he says again, wearily, "and we can explain. We're not associated with Jacobi or the attack on your coven."

"No?" Kymiria growls. "What are you doing back here, Yearling? Did you cross Jacobi, too?"

"I wasn't with them," the little yearling mumbles. "Jacobi... he bartered with my clan for me. Me and—and Dorian."

Hyacinth elbows his way through the crowd, dutifully at his sister's back with a sword. "Then where is he?"

From the sled tethered to one of the horses, a mass beneath a pile of furs wriggles and snarls, wet and predatory. Gregori's smile strains, and he tries to step between Markus and the sled, only for their archers to threaten once more. "Withhold your judgment and remember that Jacobi is the guilty party here."

Guilty for what?

Markus prods the pile of furs with the tip of his bow. The wither beneath it—because that's what it is—snarls again and jerks. Kymiria marches over and rips the furs away, and a familiar face rages against its binds.

Markus can pretend it's not Dorian because that's impossible. He can pretend the volcanic pearl earring is a coincidence. The wither's hair isn't as glossy or warm in hue, even if that is Dorian's arrangement of braids. Those aren't his eyes—there's no brown left, no soul, no intelligence. That's not his face, all skeletal and discolored with grey and red. That vicious hunger mutating his expression isn't compatible with the vampire Markus knows as one who's always so collected and poised and kind.

It's not him. It doesn't look like him, it never was him, it never could have been him. It's not, it's not, it's *not*. Withers are born from depravity and idiocy, and any living body that can't feel the fire burning them from the inside out and *stop* before it's too late deserves their fate.

It's not him.

The cry that tears from Kymiria's throat shatters the illusion in Markus's mind. "What did you do?"

It's him.

Markus stands there staring at the snarling wither, ignoring the shouting and the screaming and the accusations and the fight that nearly breaks out. The not-Dorian struggles to reach him. It smells the blood within him and wants to consume it all.

It must still be weak from starvation. Markus stills its head in his hands without much trouble, tangling fingers in hair that's still blood-stained from the battle for the castle. The earring catches on his finger, and despite the struggling and the snarling and the rot of its breath, Markus closes his eyes and presses their foreheads together.

Now, who has a stake? Cera should always have hers on her. He lets go of the not-Dorian to seek her out of the crowd.

"I can fix him!" Gregori bellows, cutting through the din like a scythe through grain. "Amaranth, a word, in private."

"Absolutely not," Hyacinth scoffs.

"More private than before your entire coven, then. You can have guards, a stake at my back, whatever you need to feel safe." Dorian's the only body left making noise, and Gregori huffs, waving at his lieutenant to do something about it. "Shut him up, please."

Her snapping Dorian's neck in front of his entire coven doesn't appeal the Aeskerat any more to them or serve Gregori's whole coming-in-peace claim, but once the snarling ceases, it does lift a weight from the air.

"Fine," Amaranth permits, then juts her chin at Elias. "He's not welcome here."

"He's with me."

"You're not welcome here either." But she's already turning toward the Grand Hall, the coven parting around her. "Kymiria, Markus, Hyacinth, with me. Quinn, watch our guests and the abomination with which they've graced our doorstep."

"Yes, Grandsire."

A crypt-like stillness has settled over the Grand Hall in its stint of disuse. It's cold and grey-blue in the absence of lit candles and sconces and all the laughter that echoed off the walls.

Amaranth still isn't level with Gregori standing at the top of the short stairs to the head table, but she tries. Markus drifts over to an empty table, arms crossed.

Amaranth demands, "Explain."

Gregori's reason for his absence seems sound even though he can't prove it. Vampiric regeneration leaves no scars and his only evidence that he didn't simply let Jacobi act out his violent fantasies is the universal hatred they all share of that smug sadist.

"It's still your fault," Markus argues. "You didn't kill him when you had the chance."

"I didn't." Gregori sighs deeply. "I underestimated him, and it cost me dearly. My pride, those of my coven who were still loyal to me and died defending me, the respect of the Aeskerat name, and likely the legacy of our house."

"You're here because you have nowhere else to go, nothing to offer anyone, except Dorian," Hyacinth accuses.

"I don't deny the convenience," Gregori admits. "I owe Dorian nothing, but he did serve me well, and I grow weary of adding names to the list of those I've lost this winter."

Gregori looks quite defeated and humbled from behind. From the stories Markus has heard, though, Gregori is supposed to be a formidable tactician. Reminding Dorian's coven of where he came from and of the kinship the two share is a trick.

He shakes his head at Amaranth and she presses her lips together. She knows. Good.

"You said you could fix him." Kymiria sits on the edge of a bench, fingers drumming against her bicep. "Withers can't be fixed."

Gregori's hypothesis isn't as ridiculous or unfounded as it could be. Vampires don't devolve, not that Markus has ever seen, so that impossibility is equally matched by the impossibility of reversing it. "Dry him out how? Slice open every vein and artery and wring his limbs?"

Somebody, or several somebodies, could drink him dry, if they could stomach the taste.

"No, you won't get every drop by bleeding him." Gregori dips his chin and smiles unhappily. "Fire is the only way."

Kymiria shoots to her feet. "You said you could fix him!"

Amaranth's face contorts in horror. "You're mad."

"It will take finesse," Gregori admits. "I'm happy to practice on volunteers. I've tried every other way, Amaranth. If this fails, he is dead anyway."

Kymiria calls him all manner of colorful names, and Markus thinks up several himself. Burning Dorian alive is cruelty at this point. If Gregori hopes to teeter between burns a body can and can't revive from, they could have saved some of Jacobi's withers for him to test first.

The only insult that lands is Kymiria's accusation that he wants to see Dorian suffer for successfully escaping his rule. "Might I remind all who stand here that I have but one loyal soul left to my name and that my ability to return your scout to you is my only avenue toward retaking my home *and* returning your stolen people to you. I am under no illusions about how precarious the ice is upon which I stand."

Amaranth lowers to sit on the top step, hands wringing in her lap. "You need more from us than good faith."

"An army would be helpful, yes." He huffs and ignores all their twitchy holds on their weapons to pace in an agitated circle. "It is not easy for me to admit my weaknesses and ask those so younger than myself for help. Slaughter is not my goal. I need those surviving under Jacobi's boot to see sense in surrender, and they won't surrender to me alone."

Amaranth shakes her head. "I'm not granting pardons to those who killed my kin. Twenty dead, Gregori, not counting those who died to the withers."

"They were following orders, nothing more."

"I don't care. I gave them a chance to lay down their arms. They refused."

Gregori gnashes his teeth and turns away from them. "Can we discuss punitive terms at a later date? I agree that you deserve justice, but I owe my coven a chance to defend themselves and attempt amends. They were *starving*, Amaranth," he implores.

Markus bounces his foot. Eternity would provide quite a long time to have souls work to right their wrongs. Killing them would be a waste of potential. He's not the decision-maker, though, and maybe this is another one of those situations with the nuances that elude him.

"A trial, then," Amaranth decides. "Juried by Tanarang and Aeskerat—to determine not their guilt but how severe their sentence."

Kymiria glares daggers at her grandsire.

Gregori buckles to Amaranth's terms with relief and the ghost of a smile on his face. "Agreed."

From all the horror stories Markus has heard over the years, he expected Gregori to be a lot less emotional and transparent—unless it's an act, pretending at being vulnerable, pretending to care about his coven and not simply the power to lord over them.

"All of this is moot if you can't save Dorian. You may use all the tools at our disposal to create your contraption, but if you want test subjects, you can go out and find your own beings to murder. My house will volunteer no more sacrifices." The meeting ends and his coven disperses. Quinn leads Gregori up to whatever room he'll be allowed to borrow. Amaranth sweeps through the Grand Hall, Hyacinth at her side, and orders that Gregori be watched at all times but given freedom to work properly. He's not a prisoner, not yet, and neither is his lieutenant.

Elias, however, is. The yearling has demonstrated quite clearly that whatever loyalties he has don't lie with Tanarang, and there's nothing Gregori can do to save him. Elias must save himself. By the nasty face Kymiria throws at the mention of Elias's name, Markus suspects she'll be all too eager to toss him in a cell and let him experience the madness of starvation.

Markus retreats to his room to gather some of his anatomy books for Gregori's perusal and passes Dorotea on his way. She and the other fragile living were kept at a distance when Gregori arrived, left to decipher the exchange on only rumor and hearsay. Markus fills her in on the truth. She asks, "Do you think it will work?"

"Gregori thinks it will work, and for his sake, it must."

Dorotea takes it upon herself to prepare something warm and nutritious for Elias because he's not her prisoner to punish. Markus agrees to bring the clear broth and chunk of bread down to him, but she stops him at the door. "We must help Gregori even if he can't save Dorian. We still need our people back."

"Amaranth is aware, I'm sure."

She nods mutely and tends to the dishes. He doesn't have anything more to comfort her with.

Elias's cell is, all things considered, cozy. He's not chained, he's got a thin bed of furs and a candle outside the bars, and there's space to move around in and a bucket for doing his business. He looks up from the bed, arms folded on his knees, and frowns. "You're... Markus, right?"

"I am." Markus sets the meal on the floor. "You're the yearling with more lives than a cat."

Elias frowns again. "Huh?"

"Never mind. Would you like something to keep busy? I heard that you like to draw and read. I can bring you a book." Folktales or something academic? Maybe he'd like a children's story with lots of pictures. Or one about cats.

"A book would be nice." Elias stares, either waiting for him to leave or to say whatever else keeps him there.

On a technicality, by serving himself at the cost of the coven, he broke his oath. Markus understands his coven's frustration. What he doesn't understand is why Elias was so eager to jump ship in the aftermath. No one attacked him, no one tried to force him to bleed for them. Did he fail to understand the value of an oath? All he had to do was hide with the others and help them rescue their kin from Jacobi. Their kin and Dorian—well, assuming Dorian had been there to rescue.

"You know, if you hadn't broken your oath, you would not have been there to save Dorian." His clan would have died unbeknownst to the rest of the world, and Dorian would have spent an eternity down there with them.

Elias *hmphs*. "I don't think Kymiria would accept that argument."

"Likely not." Markus cocks his head, giving up. "Why did you? Break the oath."

Elias curls in on himself. "I didn't want to take it in the first place."

"Are we that nasty?"

He sighs and drops his head on his arms, then flops onto his back. "I have been passed around like livestock since Dorian found me out there. I'm a bargaining chip, owned by whoever sank their teeth in me last. Jacobi promised me the South, and it's the first thing I've actually wanted since... since *ever*, and I believed him. I wanted out."

"Dorian promised you the South first."

"Yeah, well." Elias throws his hands up to drop them back on the furs. "He wasn't going to be here to fulfill that promise. I never wanted to be food, never wanted to compromise in the same way all your people have. The only vampire I—" Elias cuts himself off and his pulse flutters.

Ohhh. "I heard you kissed Dorian. I didn't think you meant it."

Elias jerks upright, face red. "That got around?"

"Should it not have? He's kissable, I don't blame you."

Elias hides his face in his hands and gives a miserable, mortified groan. "This is a unique and unexpected form of torture."

"I will find a book for you." Markus steps away from the cell, then turns back. "You will not get a trial. Kymiria will present a very strong argument for your head."

"I ran away," Elias sighs. "Is that really as damning as betraying you?"

He didn't let Jacobi through the Holdfast door, didn't spy for him, didn't give them any unreliable information. He's not their enemy, he's a scared little kid with the worst luck in the world. If he'd been a little nicer when Dorian saved his life, they would have fought for him. The yearling happens to be the perfect target for all their starved frustrations.

"They are looking for someone to blame, and Jacobi is out of reach. You may not wish to be food, but if you wish to live, I recommend thinking long and hard about the plight of choosy beggars."

"Yeah," Elias rasps. "I am."

Markus checks in on Gregori's work on a syringe he probably thinks he himself brought into existence. It's larger than any they have in their medical stores and better for one big dose, but it's nothing special. Markus won't dash the elder vampire's dreams, though. What Gregori came up with is crude, but it only has to do its job until Dorian's fixed.

"Do you need assistance?"

Gregori wraps up the syringe in a protective sleeve of padded leather and stows it in a pack. "With?"

"I know a thing or two about dead bodies." He's mostly curious as to how Gregori plans to know at what point exactly Dorian is dead enough so that the rot burns away but so that he is still revivable. His anatomy books haven't been touched, remaining in their stack by the door. "I was a mortician's apprentice when I lived."

Gregori wrinkles his nose. "Mortician?"

"Mhm."

Gregori shoulders the pack. "If you'd like to take Sascha's place escorting me to find withers to practice on, be my guest." Sascha would be better suited. He's their best scout second to Dorian, even if he complains ceaselessly about the cold.

"Do you know where to find any, or are we picking a random direction to ride into the wilderness?"

"Oh, you're a funny one." Gregori smiles unhappily. "I have a direction in mind."

Sascha is more than happy to give up the task to Markus instead but does warn him against any attempt by Gregori to turn him into a test subject once they're alone.

How would he? There's no time to existentially starve him.

He rides the spare Aeskerat horse, and Gregori doesn't tell him where they're going as they ride unwaveringly southward. Gregori says nothing at all most of the way, pushing his horse so fast that Markus might think he were trying to lose his escort if he didn't know Gregori needed this to work so badly.

They pass Chryssy Point far faster than he, Neire, and Dorotea did on foot, taking only several hours instead of moons and slowed only by the difficult terrain. They leave Tanarang land for the flat plains of the River Tammen delta and Catanz, and Gregori finally slows.

"There are no withers here; the clan would have complained," Markus advises.

"Oh, I know." Gregori moves his horse in Markus's path. "Best stay up here and out of sight if you wish to preserve Tanarang's relationship with them."

Gregori thunders over the plain, splashing through the river trickling freely as winter's hold finally loosens its grip on the North. Markus can't see too well from afar, but the screams, the dogs' howling and snarling, travel unimpeded.

Gregori rides back, blood splatters streaking his face, the bodies of three clansfolk piled on his horse. Better Catanz than other Tanarang. Markus wouldn't put it past Gregori to accidentally let them burn too long.

"Quite fickle, their god, no? They can stop me from crossing a threshold but not running the home down on horseback."

The bodies he stole squirm and groan. One looks up and recognizes Markus, pleading for mercy. Gregori sighs and pulls him off, letting his horses feast, and takes the second for himself. He hums at Markus, waving at the third.

Markus dismounts and cocks his head. He's never turned anyone and wishes he'd brought a notebook to detail his observations. The clansman is reluctant at first, thrashing deliriously in Markus's hold. As he drinks, his face flushes, sweat beads on his skin, his pulse gets faster and faster.

The clansman pulls off gasping and paws at his furs, writhing in the dirt. He nearly strips naked, crustacean red and twitchy, as wheezy as the other one. "Please," he whines, stretching to grab for Markus's ankle. Markus kills him before the rapid fever can make his heart give out, but his eyes have already gone pink. Blood trickles from his nose and ears. By bleeding them and turning them at the last second, Gregori hypothesizes they'll revert much faster once woken and killed again.

They load up, intent to reach the castle before any of them turns and starts wriggling. "If you don't want Amaranth or anyone else noticing where they came from, you should know their furs will be recognized."

Gregori tuts in surprise. "You weren't going to tell her?"

"They're not my people, and their chief has an overinflated sense of immunity."

"I have nothing to hide, then." They race back on freshly fed horses and the fledgling vampires rouse only once the castle gate has already come into view. Others are less than enthused about the dead Catanz clansfolk, but none grumbles too loudly about it.

Gregori stabs them all the same way Jacobi did, by Elias's account, leaving Northern ice arrowheads in their chests. They're strung upside down in the dungeons, exactly as Dorian had been, experiment replicated to the closest of degrees. Elias's story had been damning enough, but the entire coven witnessing exactly how Dorian was brutalized nearly gets him eaten.

Markus studies the dead clansfolk, idly tapping his chin. "You might have a problem."

Gregori dusts off his hands and props them on his hips. "What problem?"

"You've got six centuries on me, you know best," Markus placates, "but I don't think they were vampires long enough. They didn't even feed. You stabbed them all before they fully woke."

"One need not feed to complete transition," Gregori says, dripping condescension. "And you Tanarang refused to volunteer seasoned vampires."

"We don't trust you." If the method were solid and tested and verified, Markus would have volunteered himself. But then volunteers wouldn't have been needed at all. "I'm only saying that from my studies and experience, fresh fledglings don't compare to Dorian." Fresh fledglings are irritable, impulsive, erratic, and only focused on sating their hunger. And whether or not feeding is necessary to complete transition is nebulous as well.

"It's what we have," Gregori huffs.

"If reverted withers are born from existential hunger," Markus argues, "your fledglings won't have the fortitude that Dorian does to resist it."

Gregori draws an arrow and offers it to him, fletching first. "Then be my guest and join them."

"No, thank you." He's confident that fledglings will produce an unreliable experiment, not that Gregori's methodology will produce satisfactory results.

"Then get out."

Markus shrugs and keeps the arrow.

When it is time for the flames, none of them want to watch, smell, or listen to the undead bodies burn. Gregori takes his withers outside the wall and places them on a slab of granite jutting out of the melting slush. Amaranth brings oil and dried kelp to burn, lingering beside Markus. "I need to see this," she says though keeps her distance.

Gregori doesn't leave the first one awake to burn, snapping her neck instead. "Dorian'll have to be awake," he mutters.

"What? Why?" Amaranth props her hands on her hips.

"I think," he says, exuding such confidence, "that I'll need to listen to his heart."

Markus almost offers his stethoscope he keeps mostly for play to the cause, but the fragile implement would likely melt against the heat of a burnt body anyway. "Maybe you won't. We know what burned withers who still survive look like."

"We'll see." Gregori lights the small pyre of kelp and oil, and the body burns as still and unflinching as any other corpse. The smell's identical, and Markus shields his nose with his furs. They'll need a deep soak after this ordeal.

Gregori has a pile of wet furs and a bucket of melted ice at the ready to smother the flames, and when he says *Now!* they all spring into action to stop the burning. Meat still cooks on the inside even after it's been taken off the heat, and Gregori wastes no time, plunging the needle through blackened skin, straight to the heart.

"I need more."

Markus offers his own arm to the warm metal surely crawling with little gremlins of disease. Blood is blood, and withers aren't picky. She heals, slowly, remarkably. Like an insect shedding its exoskeleton, the burnt skin falls away. Hair regrows, muscle takes shape.

"More." Markus donates three more syringefuls, and they all stand on their toes, waiting to see if it's worked.

It growls, low and guttural, healthy pink flesh turning sour right before their eyes.

Well. Gregori did revive a burnt vampire from the brink, but can he bring back a soul? He tries again and again, pushing the body ever further. "Maybe it hasn't burned long enough," he muses aloud, tapping his hip restlessly as the wither revives yet again.

The second one, Gregori burns alive, and the clansman returns to consciousness as soulless as the first. Gregori curses, and the crowd of those watching from the wall continues to grow. He tries over and over again until they're dead for good, burnt too long. Markus has to sit, dizzy and lightheaded.

Kymiria steps up to take his place. "Use me for the third one."

The third burns too long from the start. Their skin never changes color, their hair never regrows, their chest never rises with renewed breath. They're dead.

Amaranth *tsks* and holds her face. "You could turn all of Clan Catanz and not succeed."

"A sacrifice I'm willing to make," Kymiria snarks.

"I am not. They've done nothing to deserve this, to suffer only because they're unfortunate enough to live so close." Amaranth sighs heavily and stares at the burnt shell of the last dead Catanz. "He's dead anyway," she says softly. "It's time."

Dorian will be different, Markus tries to reason with himself. Dorian's a proper vampire and has been for several centuries. Gregori has ample data now on how bodies burn and whereabouts the limit lies for survivability. If Gregori cuts it too short and Dorian wakes up still a wither, they'll try again. They have nothing else to lose.

He'll be different. He has to be.

Kymiria isn't granted a soulful goodbye because the wither inside her beloved won't sit still and act properly mournful for her to speak. Markus has nothing to say that he wants to waste when he knows Dorian can't hear him. Such words' first utterance should mean something, should be able to be said back.

When they're all ready and waiting for him, Markus finds Gregori dawdling beside the stables. He didn't seem too assured before, and he certainly dawdles now.

"Cold feet?"

Gregori has his eyes closed, seemingly at prayer. "If I fail, your entire coven will demand my head."

"You fear a thwarted alliance more than losing my friend." Markus crosses his arms and leans against a support beam. Gregori might not be indebted to Dorian on a technical level, but he still owes his life to his former blood slave. "Perhaps that's the problem."

Gregori laughs humorlessly. "I stand by what I always have. We are all vampires of the North, and squabbling over our differences only distracts us from the real threat."

"The real threat being...?"

"The living? Clinging to existence on the edge of the world?" Gregori scoffs. "There were thousands of us once. Chrysanthian vampires will never know what it used to be like."

"Of course we won't. We weren't alive yet."

Gregori balls a fist and punches the stone wall behind him. "You're irritating, you know that?"

"And you're late for your appointment." Markus steps aside and Gregori marches out like a man bound for the gallows.

He can't watch, can't be out there when it happens, because he won't listen to that body scream. Somebody else can donate— Kymiria, Amaranth, Hyacinth. Markus hides deep inside the library, Dorian's earring in his palm because it wouldn't have un-burned with his body.

He holds his hands over his ears. Him and Dorian. It was supposed to be an experiment born from boredom with someone he trusted. It wasn't supposed to sink claws into his chest and never let go. The salty taste of tears on his lips isn't a sensation Markus has experienced since before he turned. It's as awful and upsetting now as it was back then.

Kymiria comes to get him eventually, crying herself. Big, fat tears.

Then she gives a wide, wobbly smile and crashes into him.

Arms full of Kymiria, Markus can't breathe.

Dorian misses the grey void. Comforting in its emptiness, deprived of all sensation. The red void stretches him, painfully so, pulling at his hair, his skin, his teeth. It stretches him like straining leather that's ready to give and rip apart. In the red void, not being able to touch the walls or the ceiling or the floor is maddening. Dorian can scream all he wants. No one hears.

Sensation bleeds slowly back to him. Fingers in his hair, nails tracing his scalp. It's too raw and sharp and he flinches no matter the pressure. Wherever he is, he's beset by extremes—ice so frozen it burns, water so hot it chills.

Even the voices whispering hurt too much, gravel in his ears. The bed, too soft, suffocates him, individual strands of its furs impaling his back. If he's broken every bone in his body, if he lies here skinned like a deer, the pain might make sense.

Something marginally cold and abrasive dabs his face and he wants to burrow back down in the grey void, a snow hare, until all this noise goes away, but the void won't accept him. Wherever he is, he's not allowed to die.

So *fine*. He'll see what all the fuss is about.

Two faces blur into focus. Markus and Kymiria. He's... in his bed, in Castle Tanarang, and they're so close the two of them knock heads. Dorian manages an undignified *Uh?* with an uncooperative tongue.

Both descend like hug-happy vultures.

Every scrape and slide of their clothes stings. The squeeze of their arms, the jut of Markus's chin into his clavicle, Kymiria's hair falling on his face—it's all too loud and overwhelming and they will not let go.

Markus notices first and peels away. "Too much?"

Is he crying? Even his tears hurt. Dorian nods, and Markus pulls Kymiria off him. "What can we do?"

Dorian gestures vaguely at the furs, trying to explain that they hurt but not knowing how. Kymiria, bless her, brings over his robe. They have to ease the sleeves onto his arms and slide the fabric between him and the bed because standing is not an option.

It's too bright, too, the lone candle in the room. Markus blows it out.

Damn the bed, it's still too much. Can he...

"—ath?" Gods, what happened to his voice? "B—th, —ater."

"Bath?" Kymiria's already trying to help him up. "We can do that. We can do that, can't we? C'mon."

The motion and the swinging is too much to comprehend. Dorian hides his face in her neck and holds on for dear life, missing pockets of the journey down to the springs and—*no*. Not hot water. No more burning.

"Wait, maybe not those baths." Bless Markus, too. "I have an idea."

Kymiria still leads him into the caves, but they have a smooth tub brought in. The vampires who bring it won't stop staring at him as they fill the tub with spring water and ice from outside. His joints bang into the sides, aching, as he settles in, but *oh* is it worlds better than the bed.

"Better? Better, right?" she asks.

He nods and slumps against the raised back of the tub, still wrapped up in his robe. Bless that, too. His hair doesn't pool around him, doesn't snag on the metal seam of the tub, doesn't anger the back of his neck—and how? Dorian pokes at the fuzzy fluff growing from his scalp, all curly and wispy and what in the world...?

"It's growing back," Markus assures. "Slowly."

Yes, of course it grows back, to the exact length it was when he'd died and no longer, but why is it all gone?

Kymiria sends for Cera and Tannys, and Dorian sluggishly tries to protest that Tannys isn't his partner.

"Shhh, you need it and Cera can't give it all." If they're sure. If Tannys is sure.

They come rushing in, shrieking his name too loudly. Yes, hi, wonderful, now *hush*. The first taste of Cera's blood gags him.

Dorian lurches and coughs it up onto the floor.

Way too much.

"Here, let me." Markus swipes his fingers over the open wound and offers it like that instead.

Better. Much better. Feeding like this takes forever, the buzz of hunger vibrating under the cacophony of every other sense taking center stage.

Dorian doesn't care if it's Cera or Tannys or Markus, he needs *more*.

"Okay. Okay, I got you." Markus is probably for the best. He can't die if Dorian takes too much, and he left his self-control somewhere on the floor of his room.

Tannys only takes over once the sharp edge of starvation smooths out, and still he feels guilty for being rough. The oversensitive burning sensation across his body fades with the hunger. Soon he can think. He clutches onto the edge of the tub, forgetting why they brought it down when there's plenty of perfectly good warm pools.

"What happened?"

"It can wait until you're feeling better," Kymiria assures. "Are you feeling better?"

"I'm cold. Why the tub?"

She chuckles softly and moves him to the nearest pool with Markus's help. "You asked for the tub."

"I did?"

Markus presses something delicate and metallic to his palm. "You probably want this back."

His earring, *what...*? That thing never comes out.

Neither is forthcoming with answers, Kymiria busy hugging, Markus busy staring. He keeps touching Dorian's face like it's a mask he'll find the seams of. They both join him in the water, and the all-encompassing embrace is wonderful but weird.

"Did I miss much?"

Markus finally regales him with disorienting bluntness. Losing to Jacobi—that, he remembers. Getting staked with Northern ice and shot after Zeon's death—he remembers that, too. Getting stabbed again and traded to Elias's clan is fuzzy, and everything else is black. By the looks on their faces, not remembering being withered is a scab he shouldn't pick.

He does let himself enjoy the bath, until little feet pad swiftly, pulling up short and on their toes at the cave's edge. Gilan peeks around the corner of the archway. Kymiria chuckles softly and floats away from Dorian. "Somebody else missed you, too."

Gilan takes that as permission, running over so fast it's a miracle he doesn't slip and crack his head. Dorian's not prepared to catch him, fully clothed, arm in a sling, jumping straight at him. The force knocks him off the pool bench, and they both nearly go under without Markus's help.

Gilan sobs, little fist trembling with how tightly he holds onto Dorian's robe. "I knew you'd come back."

Kymiria lifts herself out of the water and nudges Markus to give them room.

Dorian is careful of Gilan's cast, soaked along with all his clothes, and moves them back to the bench. Gilan's heart pounds, and he holds on like if he relaxes even a little, Dorain will slip through his fingers.

Gilan is the second child he's promised that everything would be okay, only to leave them watching as he got dragged away by Aeskerat captors. This time, he keeps his promise.

"Of course I came back."

Chapter 18:
Twelve Minutes to Midnight

Gregori is not dead. Gregori is very much alive. He stares at Dorian in the Grand Hall like Dorian should be dead. Of all the information he had to play catch-up with, finding out Gregori not only survived the mutiny but is responsible for Dorian's also not being dead is the strangest pill to swallow.

Until the knowledge that Gregori only did it to save his own ass, which fits like a final *puche* stone clicking into home.

"The Catanz weren't full vampires yet," Markus says, continuing his summary of Gregori's experiments. "They hadn't fed before they devolved into withers, so there wasn't much to save."

Amaranth calls a meeting, having woken up every hibernating vampire to prepare a raid on Castle Aeskerat. He misses most of the strategic part of the meeting, still getting reaccustomed to his own body, regrown hair up in a messy bun to be dealt with later. All the flickering candles and the fire in the tiny hearth in the corner and the jumbling voices grate on his irritatingly raw nerves.

Gregori's goal isn't to terrify his remaining coven into

surrendering, but to offer them a better future than Jacobi can, hopefully by challenging the usurper to a one-on-one duel. Jacobi will refuse because he'll know he'd lose, spitting in the face of their oldest traditions, and the rest of the coven will buckle. Anyone who sees a chance to take him out shouldn't hesitate. No blaze of glory for the slippery bastard.

Amaranth will hold up her end of the new alliance—if and when all surrender, accept Gregori back as their grandsire, and hand over all their stolen people. Something that doesn't seem to thrill Gregori.

Things don't get heated until the question arises of what to do with Elias. Elias, a prisoner with no leave to attend the meeting, never gets the chance to defend himself as the coven bickers back and forth and around in circles. Kymiria wants his head, as so does the majority of the coven and Elphaba's host, what with much of their family suffering under Jacobi's boot.

Gregori is Elias's only defender, and Dorian never expected to side with him again on anything, but here he goes, standing to temper his coven's bloodlust. Everyone quiets at the sight of him.

"This whole mess with Aeskerat started when a fledgling attacked Elias as my charge on Aeskerat land," he begins. "Jacobi argued that since I didn't claim him, he was fair game, and since I couldn't face punishment for the fledgling's death, Elias would in my place. Even if Elias had killed the fledging, Aeskerat doesn't entitle the living with the right to self-defense. They're livestock, pigs, cattle. We're better than Aeskerat, aren't we? Elias deserves a trial at least."

Gregori looks miffed by the slights against his coven's reputation, but he must lie in that bed. He says nothing, leaving Dorian with the floor.

"An oath is sacred," Quinn argues. "No one gets a trial. Everyone knows the consequences of their actions well before having the capacity to betray."

Murmurs arise in agreement.

"What good would he have done here?" He waits and no one objects. "You wouldn't have used his knowledge of Castle Aeskerat, and he likely feared that he'd suffer death next, oath or no oath. What's more, Jacobi might have come back to finish us off. He stayed here, he would have been a target. A wrongful one." Dorian spreads his hands. "What about exile? Send him south so we never have to deal with him again."

It's what Elias wants anyway, Dorian tells himself. He's been clear that he'll never be at home in the North, never be at home with vampires.

"No charity, no patronage, just dump him with the clothes on his back at some random Southern harbor. What he does with his life after that is his own responsibility."

"We can't control what happens to him in exile." Neire shrugs with cold indifference. "He might luck into luxury. No, he must bleed for the time lost and the innocent blood spilled of our kin."

That's not an argument for his head, at least. A step in the right direction. Whether they wanted a trial or not, here it unfolds before them.

Elphaba stands and smooths her skirts. "That boy has never wanted to stay here for any reason other than catching your fancy, Master Dorian, and sending him south would be a gift, yes, but I'd rather be rid of him than waste more energy punishing him. He gave the oath under duress and, knowing that my son, my grandsons, and my nephews suffer as we speak, I don't hold Elias's choices against him."

When they come to a decision, Dorian goes to deliver the verdict.

Apparently, no one told Elias that Gregori's experiment succeeded.

He flies to the bars of his cell and squawks Dorian's name in disbelief. Dorian can't get the door open fast enough before he has an armful of a greasy, bawling prisoner, wailing *I'm sorry* so many times it stops sounding like words. Elias's knees give out and then they're both on the floor, snot and tears soiling Dorian's new furs.

He might be more upset if he remembered anything after saving Gilan with any clarity. The last real moment he remembers between them is when Elias asked him about the *Peony* before Dorian went to check the defenses around the castle.

That he'd gone and turned on his entire clan… it was never supposed to be like this. *He's leaving. Don't get attached. Don't make this harder than it has to be.* "I forgive you," he says, Elias's face squished between his hands so he stops blubbering and *listens.* "Are you being fed and watered?" Dorian checks him over for injuries and malnutrition. "Warm enough?"

"Yes, yes, and yes." Elias hiccups. "Why aren't you more upset?"

"Because I'm not." Dorian coaxes him back onto the threadbare bed. "Do you want to tell me what happened after Jacobi sold us out?"

"No." Elias mutters the word into his knees. He tells the story anyway, unintelligible at times, particularly surrounding his plan to get in with Dorian alone. Face aflame, Elias assures half a dozen times that he'd never, and that he'd never let Loric touch him either, and that it was the path of least resistance, and that Elias doesn't want that in any way, shape, or form. "Just… next time you shoot someone, be sure they're dead."

Oh, he will not be making that mistake again. "Promise."

"I was going to let you get it over with," Elias utters, voice raw and hollow. "Once I realized you were gone. I deserved it and I had nowhere else to go."

Dorian bumps their shoulders, lacking a proper response. *I'm glad you didn't* sits wrong in the back of his throat. *A terrible way to go out. A waste of your life.* "They, um, we had a debate over what to do with you," he says instead.

"Oh." Elias sniffles and pulls his furs tighter. "And?"

"You're going to join us in the raid on Aeskerat to get our people back." On the front lines, when he has zero skills with a sword, when he's already a novice and shooting a bow with the wrong grip? It's a death sentence. Dorian will make sure it isn't, damn whatever Amaranth says. "If you survive, you'll remain long enough to join a party to Panolin and be sent to the South. We'll give you no money or aid or connections. You will be on your own, and barred from ever returning to Tanarang."

"I'll never see you again?"

Of all Elias's possible concerns—how Dorian expects the battle to go, how likely he is to live through it, how he can possibly survive destitute and clueless in a strange land—this is what he asks?

"It's not forbidden or impossible," Dorian answers slowly. "I still expect to be the guide across the continent and you could find passage back to Panolin, but that's as far as you'd be permitted."

"But..." Elias stares in brittle disbelief. "Oh."

Dorian tips Elias's chin to kiss his forehead. "In another life, perhaps." Elias's face still tints. He still stares like every time is the last time he'll ever see him. Dorian stands and shakes his head.

"Wait." Elias stumbles between him and the door. "Just—what if you came with me?"

"With you?"

"South." Elias rises up on his toes, hands clasped. "We can just go, you and me. Take one of the horses, skip this whole battle, leave behind all the coven drama, and just *go*. I know the sun will be a problem, but only during the day, and—"

Dorian stifles a sigh. "I already told you, I'm not leaving my home behind."

Elias doesn't move from the door. "You never gave me a straight answer on if you feel anything at all toward me."

No, because Elias would deny his reasoning until he turned blue in the face. "What I do or don't feel doesn't matter—"

"Because I'll be dead soon."

If he wants to hear it so badly, fine. "Because I don't want to take advantage."

Elias frowns. "Take advantage?"

Dorian coaxes him away from the cell door and holds his hands. He thumbs over sore knuckles split from the cold. There's a dozen reasons why they won't work, and that Elias is so fragile can't be ignored, but even if he weren't...

"I'm your only friend. It's not about your mortality or the centuries between us. I'm worried about your dependency on me."

Elias's frown deepens. "I know what I want. You're not manipulating me to get it."

"Gilan has experienced more of this world than you have." Dorian lets his hands drop. "You have no idea what you're missing out there, Elias, and when you see it, you won't want to be chained to someone who can't participate in life with you."

Elias doesn't skip a beat before denying it, voice tight. "Yes, I would, I l—"

"Let me rephrase." This is why he never said it before. "You want an answer on if I feel anything—*yes*, I do." Before Elias can go giddy with glee, Dorain cuts him off. "*I* wouldn't want you to be stuck with me when there's a whole world out there. And if you found somebody else who's not four hundred years older than you? I'd want you to be able to pursue that."

Elias scoffs wetly and clears his throat. "If I recall, you have two partners. Why can't I?"

"Two partners you'd be asking me to abandon."

Elias goes to speak, winces, and throws his hands up. "They can come?"

Oh, yes, the four of them trying to carve out a coexistence in the South. Elias wouldn't last the voyage without Kymiria trying to kill him. "If you got caught with me in the South, it wouldn't end well." He'd be a social pariah from the moment they set foot off the boat. He'd never be safe. None of them would be. "I already did my time in a cage. Living half my life hiding from the Southern sun would be no different."

"Then we stay here, I don't care."

He's missing the point entirely.

Elias backs up and rakes back his hair. "I understand what you're saying, I do. You're worried that I'm too attached and couldn't survive without you." He nods to himself. "So if I find friends and start hobbies and get myself some aspirations, what about *then*?"

He should want to do those things for his own sake, not to please his partner. Likely, in doing so, Elias would find someone else he can stand on equal footing with, leaving all of this moot. "If I said yes, would you give up going south to stay here? Up in the cold, miserable, sunless North?"

"Yes."

Damn it, Elias. "How about a deal? You spend one summer, minimum, in the South, studying whatever you want and living life to the fullest," he parses carefully. "You try your hardest to like it there. And *if* you would still rather be up here, we can resume this conversation."

Elias huffs, blinking rapidly at the far wall. "What about this exile?"

"We can revisit that, too."

"You promise?"

Damn this mortal. "If you want me, you have to want all of me, and that includes this coven."

"Of course."

"Then, yes. I promise." He's still never tried to pursue a relationship with someone who lives such a short life. Someone who ages and wizens with it. Elias will move on, he's certain of it.

And if Elias can't learn independence and thrive without him, then feelings or no feelings, Dorian won't let anything happen between them. "May I go?" he asks gently. "I'm still recovering."

A mistake to admit. Elias thrusts his arm out. "Oh, here."

Dorian nudges it aside. "Not what I meant."

"Oh." Elias steps stiffly aside, then snags Dorian's arm on his way out the door. "Can I... just in case something goes wrong?" His heartbeat skitters and a flush rises in his cheeks.

He's being purposefully vague, but Dorian knows. "Don't waste the present mourning a future that isn't set in stone."

Elias balks and blushes harder. "Well, I—can I do it anyway?"

It wouldn't be just a kiss, though. It would be a fulfilment of a request Dorian already declined because Elias's feelings toward him are still too tangled up on an unbalanced seesaw of genuine emotion and survival instinct. And it's... not something Dorian wants to do. Doing it would still feel icky and like he's taking advantage.

"No, Elias." He knows it's the right answer, whether Elias realizes it or not, because Elias straightens, takes the rejection with grace, and nods to himself.

"Good night," he says, and leaves.

All this is exhausting. His relationship with Kymiria has lasted for so long because she's not glued to his side. She seeks out other people whenever she wants for whatever she wants. Markus, too, likes his independence. They all have their space to think. A relationship with Elias promises to be suffocating. Trying to evenly split his attention between three people without one feeling underloved? It's hard enough balancing two.

Dorian shakes his head. They can revisit all this after summer and by then it might not even matter. Elias might simply move on to brighter horizons.

He heads to his room without any detours; he can't be bothered with any more talk of back-up plans or escape plans or what to do if Jacobi does this, that, or the other thing.

Markus is waiting for him, perched in the middle of his freshly made bed with a book in his lap. It's... nice. Markus is different.

"You smell like the yearling."

A weight lifts off his shoulders at the sound of Markus's voice.

It's so, so different.

"Someone had to tell him the news." Dorian lets the door close, half-expecting Kymiria to be lurking behind it in the shadows. He rolls his neck. Is sleeping until they have to leave too selfish an ask?

"You are upset."

Dorian works out the crick and winces. "Not upset, just spread thin. He's too attached to me. I worry about him." He yawns and notices the new candle sitting on his wardrobe, dyed snowberry blue. It smells like the ocean and Dorian smiles. "Did you make this?"

Markus laces his fingers beneath his chin.

"Yes."

"It's beautiful, thank you." He kicks off his boots and hangs up his cloak. Markus stops him before he can lose anything else.

"Can I ask you something?"

"You just did."

Markus thumbs his book, pages whispering against each other. "Do you want him, too?"

Today really won't let dead horses lie. "I want him to be happy," Dorian says, "and that won't be with me."

Markus swings his feet. "I'm happy with you."

Even something so simple sends a pleasant tingle down his spine. Dorian catches himself grinning despite his exhaustion. "You're very different people. Now can we either sleep or talk about anything else? I'm tired of thinking."

"I want to try something." Markus leaves something shiny among the furs when he slinks off the bed and undoes all Dorian's laces and ties with both ease and a fervent concentration.

"It's not an exam. You don't get bad marks for doing it wrong."

"This isn't the something," he says, tossing the jerkin aside and Dorian's shirt somewhere else. If Dorian didn't know better, he'd say this was Markus's first time seeing a half-naked body with how reverently and delicately he touches. "Close your eyes."

Dorian does, then hears a soft click and rattle from the bed. The touch of not-fingers to the center of his chest startles him, and he jumps. It feels like metal and... canvas, perhaps, or parchment.

"Breathe."

"I am breathing."

"Deeper."

Dorian does, and with each exhale, the metal moves around. Markus walks behind him and starts placing it all over his back, and curiosity wins out. He opens his eyes. "Markus?"

Markus comes back around, a contraption hanging from his ears and connected to a little metal drum between his fingers. "You're alive," he declares mischievously. "As alive as an undead vampire can be."

"Thank you for that astute diagnosis. Is it my turn?" Dorian smirks and holds his hand out for the contraption.

Markus's face falls a little, a degree of seriousness and determination appearing, and he leans forward on his toes. "I love you. You don't have to say it back, I just want you to know."

Oh.

Dorian rocks forward and brings their foreheads together. Markus smells like paper and ink and... marigolds, if Dorian recalls correctly. He could get lost in it standing here. He doesn't throw around the L-word very often and while he can't say he means it to the degree he thinks Markus does, this, he thinks, is what love is supposed to feel like. Peace.

It's just... "Give me time," he whispers. "I'm not there yet."

Markus beams, then urges him toward the bed. "There's more to the something!"

His back hits the furs and Markus crawls atop him, peppering kisses all over his face. They're wonderful, and may or may not earn a surprised giggle, but Dorian pushes him back by his shoulders. "You don't have to do this to make me happy."

"I'm doing it to make *me* happy." Markus bats his hands aside and kisses him hard and mumbles something that sounds suspiciously like *erasing the scent of that yearling.* He doesn't ask about all the bruises that will never fade, doesn't give them any special attention by tracing them, doesn't even seem to see them. Either Markus asked somebody else or he doesn't care.

Markus's *I love you* sticks like a splinter in his mind. Here, like Kymiria, is another whose candle burns brighter for him than his does for them. He'd mean it, saying it back, but... he can't. Even as vampires, love rarely lasts. Of the whole of Tanarang, Quinn and Blane might be the only two committed for eternity, and eternity with Blane was Quinn's whole reason for turning. This is temporary. Why invest when it's never going to last?

Markus looks up from trailing a studious path of kisses down to his stomach. "Okay?"

He'll try. Even if it doesn't last, right now, it's happening. "Yes, it's okay."

Dorian never cared all that much for sex when he lived and Eldelaire's stains on his skin don't improve his opinion of it, but the attention? The softness, the chance to not think about the stressors of the moment, the trust between him and his partners, *that* helps the little discomforts here and there seem worth it. It's temporary, but Markus is trying so hard, it's impossible to not enjoy the moment.

Then the little drum contraption comes back, square over his heart. "Now then," Markus says, all coy and giggly. His other hand travels lower and when Dorian's pulse jumps, Markus grins in triumph. "Interesting rhythm you have there."

"Is this the rest of the something?"

"Maybe." Markus kisses his chin. "Now make music for me."

Of Tanarang's remaining ninety vampires, they will leave Hyacinth and nineteen others behind. Twenty vampires can't hold the castle should more withers or some other coven attack, so those left behind will await their people's return at Chryssy Point. Kymiria, as much as she must want to watch Elias squeal in battle, will remain behind with them, and he couldn't be more relieved to hear it.

None of them has the shiny metal armor Elias has seen drawn in books, and he asks Dorian if they can't afford it.

"It gets so cold up here in the dead of winter that Northern ice arrows crack straight through," he whispers as the armory behind them empties of everything except armor. "It's loud, too, and cumbersome, all the mail and creaky plates."

Coven armies don't stand in opposing lines slashing each other with swords, he also explains. They aim, too, for the joints, where no armor can protect.

Still, Elias thinks, it'd have to be better than thick leathers alone.

As they load up all the wooden arrows left behind in the courtyard, Elias isn't as nervous as he should be. Amaranth basically sentenced him to die in whatever ugly fight erupts. It's unavoidable, though, and panicking about what might go wrong won't shake him from this path. Whatever happens, happens. Or perhaps the prospect of imminent death is so terrifying his brain decided not to deal with it at all.

He hovers in the back of the crowd as they see off the *Peony*. Every candle has been blown out, the hearth fires smothered, the ovens left to cool. Tanarang will be silent and empty for the first time in centuries. Elias never wanted it to be his home, but now, staring up at the dripping icicles on the gables and the mighty ramparts in what might be the last time he ever sees them, he thinks, even if this is it, it's better than the rocky ceiling of the cave.

Elias hangs near Gregori's horse, impatient to get moving if only so boredom doesn't shatter the placid calm he's found. He's being permitted to ride with him only because he'd be too slow and cold trudging through the snow. Veronique is all ready to go beside him, equally antsy to reclaim her home.

Now, where is Gregori?

Elias tugs his cloak—Gregori's cloak—tighter, and wanders off to find him. Neire catches him stretching to search over everyone's heads and points toward the armory.

The armory is only bare shelves and racks now, the perfect place for Gregori and Dorian to talk unbothered. They must hear or smell him approach, but Gregori carries on anyway.

"...just save you to save myself."

Dorian's not having it. "I thought I was the one that got away?"

Gregori sighs like a tired parent. "You can deny your Aeskerat roots all you want, but they will always be part of you. Once this alliance is solidified, you will be less of a stranger to our house, won't you?"

"If my grandsire wishes it so." Dorian leaves it at that, brushing past Elias in silence.

Elias shakes his head at his departure. "Convincing myself he's no better than you is what stuck me in the middle of your covens. You may have waited centuries for your throne, but you still had one within your reach."

Gregori fixes his sword, Northern ice like every other except for the metal hilt, specially carved and gilded, on his belt.

"You're all vampires and you were all living once, but you've never lived without. That's why Tanarang's different, and you'll never understand that."

"Perhaps." Gregori guides him back to the courtyard with a light hand at his back. "But in the end, it will be all of us against all of you, and who we were in life will matter no more."

He sounds so certain, like he knows something no one else does from some third eye that sees six moves ahead on his game board. Elias can't even let himself contemplate this battle, much less whatever lies after it, likely long after he's dead and gone.

It will still take several moons to reach Castle Aeskerat. Once they move out, they don't break once. The vampires marching beside him walk no faster than a living body, but they don't know the meaning of fatigue in the bloodless fight against the cold and the soggy terrain.

Elias is thankful for the horse and Gregori ensuring he doesn't fall off. He sleeps, either slumped back against Gregori's shoulder or over the horse's neck, in quick, uncomfortable bursts. His legs grow sore from sitting astride a saddle, even as the constant rocking of the horse's gait lulls him.

The grip of winter loosens, leaving behind slushy snow. White-capped mountains glow purple in the ever-present starlight. River Tammen isn't frozen solid anymore and so they must detour through the ruins of a town little more than the remnants of foundations and chimneys to reach a bridge of stone, sticks, and dirt that looks as old as the mountains themselves. The moons shine bright, a nebulous aura of light arcing overhead. It's so... peaceful, and their army is marching right through it.

Tanarang Coven may still not trust Gregori, but they stop to camp after an unlucky herd of caribou crosses their path, two stragglers bled for breakfast.

Quinn stops Gregori cold when she asks, "Jacobi murdered all your blood slaves. If we take all of our people home, how do you expect to feed your coven?"

"Spring is upon us," he answers smoothly. His voice is

commanding but soft, speaking only as loud as he must. "The port towns and borderlands aren't deserted. We will take what we need, or find another clan to rehome. Aeskerat keep their promises, my fellow warrior, and your people will be returned to you. All of them."

Whether they believe him, Elias can't tell. Gregori keeps his promises, but he's not grandsire yet, and Jacobi won't let his food go without a fight.

Gregori then explains every weakness of Castle Aeskerat to his new allies in case things get ugly. Elias can't corroborate any of it, the subtleties of above-ground architecture an enigma to him. He could tell them what support beams and columns risk collapse, which walls will drop upper stories if knocked out, but Gregori probably doesn't want his home back in ruins.

Elias stares eastward, where he thinks Castle Aeskerat might lie beyond the horizon. They're close. He's been given a sword with no idea how to use it beyond swinging it blindly, and twists the frozen blade in the starlight. Dorian approaches, boots crunching on the melting slush.

"You told me cowards survive."

"You will have to go in there with us," Dorian whispers. "You don't have to fight. Pick a spot and hide, and Amaranth will never know."

Elias shakes his head. "I took that oath knowing I'd break it if Jacobi won. Amaranth wants me to fight, not hide, and if there's any chance at regaining her favor, you aren't covering for me or protecting me anymore."

Dorian hums and takes Elias's sword hand, fingers ghosting over his missing digits. He should learn to fight and draw and do so many other things with his right hand, missing only a pinkie, but it won't matter for this battle anyway. "Then I guess you aren't much of a coward anymore."

Something's wrong.

As they approach Castle Aeskerat across the griddle-flat land, sentries would have seen them coming now for half an hour, and yet there's no one up on the walls, no shouts in response to the army marching on their gates, no torches or lanterns or candles to be seen.

They're still in there—Dorian can smell them all, living and undead alike—so they haven't abandoned their home. He grips the reins of his borrowed horse tighter and Amaranth peers around him, eyes narrowed. Gregori *hmphs*, and with Veronique behind him, the four ride to the main gate. His voice rolls across the field. "Jacobi!" he all but sings. "The consequences of letting other hands bloody themselves with your atrocities now stand before you. I invite you to respect the traditions of our shared coven and face me now. One on one."

Amaranth's pitch is comically high compared to his, but her voice carries as far. "I offer this again to all Aeskerat who lay down your arms: Surrender, and you will survive this night."

A beat passes, then two. Wind rolls over the field and low wispy clouds froth. The ripe scent of Tanarang's people is too pungent, as if they're right on the other side of the gate, waiting.

The gate rumbles, chains squeaking and old iron and wood creaking. On the other side...

Castor. Patrick. Brigs. All of them, bundled in their furs and shivering in one big mass. They start shuffling as one, and Dorian dismounts, baffled. Amaranth follows hot on his heels.

"Castor?"

Castor smiles weakly and hobbles over. "We're okay. Cold, but okay."

Dorian nips his wrist and insists Castor take as much as he needs. Others waddle stiffly out like they can't believe the gate's really open. Patrick collides with Quinn and breaks down in her arms.

They're not okay in the slightest.

"Amaranth, they're letting us go," Castor says, licking his lips with an exhausted sigh. "The new grandsire wants to talk."

"Which new grandsire?" Gregori asks, and goes ignored.

Beyond their group, Aeskerat vampires load up their stolen food and their stolen sleighs hitched to their stolen horses.

None of them are armed, none move like this is a trap aching to spring. Dorian shrugs at his grandsire helplessly. Amaranth whistles and waves, and the rest of their coven swarms their freezing kin. "Get them out of here. Dorian?"

He wavers between his bow and his sword, and nocks a wooden arrow, a safety measure only.

Ionia and Oryn, both his elder, wait beside the sleighs above a body on the ground, skewered with arrows like a porcupine. Ionia stands with her boot on the body's shoulder.

Jacobi's shoulder.

"A peace offering," she tells Amaranth as they pass in through the gate. "He's not dead yet. Justice is yours to take."

Jacobi, motionless and temporarily dead with seven arrows impaling him, isn't as satisfying a sight as Ionia likely hopes he is. That he won't get his shot at a redeeming fight leaves Dorian miffed. He's not going to risk Jacobi slithering out of justice by letting him heal back to his full strength for an honorable match, but he's left wanting something more than this. The chance to skewer him with all those arrows himself, at least.

"If you were going to betray Jacobi from the start," Dorian says, "you could have done it in the Holdfast, Oryn." He aims loosely at Oryn's chest. He's the Aeskerat who beheaded Zeon. He doesn't get to offer peace.

"We weren't." Ionia raises a protective arm, as if he won't shoot through her to hit Oryn. "Dorian, I'm sorry. We were hungry. You've been hungry. You've been shortsighted and desperate and did what you thought was necessary to survive, too."

"I didn't slaughter an innocent old man," he snaps. "I staked a warmongering rapist who none of you challenged or mourned."

"She didn't—" Oryn doesn't get to finish. Dorian's arrow embeds in his chest.

"Yes," he mutters, "she did."

Ionia startles but doesn't move to avenge her kin. The whole rest of Aeskerat stills when Oryn's body hits the ground, but no one does a damn thing about it.

Maybe they really are surrendering.

Ionia holds up her hands and nods. "I'm not Eldelaire, but I am sorry."

"You're only sorry because you've lost." He nocks another wooden arrow.

Amaranth gently tugs on his arm and shakes her head. "Please help the wounded into the sleighs and secure Jacobi."

"... Yes, Grandsire." Dorian hauls Jacobi up by his armpits, and Quinn appears beside him to help. Elias, bemused, toddles over to watch them tie Jacobi down.

"Aeskerat," Amaranth shouts to the loitering coven, "this is your last chance to join us on good terms."

Dorian counts eleven Aeskerat sheepishly abandoning their kin for the open gate. Cowards, the lot of them, even if braver than the vampires who remain. They'll have a deluge of amends to make.

"Is this it?" Elias asks him. "No fight?"

Dorian laces his fingers as a step for the sleigh, easing exhausted bodies in among the barrels and crates of food. "We came to take our people back and kill Jacobi. Nothing else is necessary."

"Glad to see you alive, Master Dorian."

"Patrick." Dorian shrugs in question. "What happened?"

Patrick sniffles and bundles tighter in his furs. "We think they came to their senses when Jacobi sold you to the clans. Didn't matter that you're Tanarang, a vampire's a vampire, and a fate as a blood slave is a fate worse than death."

Dorian crosses his arms. "Then why did we have to forge an alliance with Gregori and march all the way out here for them to give you up? Why didn't they turn around and take you home to begin with?"

Patrick shrugs and sneezes. "They were hungry. We're okay, though. Some of us got sick, but no broken bones."

Yes, yes, it could always be worse, but this is still terrible and, more than that, unbelievably frustrating.

Dorian lets him rest, and Quinn leads the sleigh out, the last of their little caravan leaving a near-empty courtyard behind. Elias idles about because Amaranth hasn't yet told him he can leave, and without the fight meant to take him out, Dorian can't imagine what other punishment she'll devise for him.

She's busy accepting Ionia's surrender, the Aeskerat prostrate on the stones. Amaranth's terms are loud and absolute: Aeskerat scouts are henceforth forbidden from Tanarang land under penalty of death, only messengers and refugees may cross into it.

Tanarang scouts will enjoy free travel over Aeskerat lands with no tax for parties journeying to and from Panolin. The last of their wooden arrows, too, now belong to Amaranth.

Ionia looks ready to kiss Amaranth's boots, agreeing easily to spare more death to her kin. It's not punishment enough for the tragedy they wrought, but Amaranth won't line them up to bear their necks to an executioner's sword. It's not worth another fight, their reputation is finished, and… they were hungry.

It's their own damn fault that they were hungry, their own damn fault for mutinying on Gregori and ending up with Jacobi. But if it means he gets to go home and not burn anyone else's funeral pyre, then so be it.

Ionia's surrender seems to rankle Gregori, though. To him, Ionia doesn't get to negotiate for Aeskerat. "You're not in charge here," he growls.

Ionia squares her shoulders, meeting him head on. "Neither are you, Gregori."

Veronique sneers and calls Ionia a coward, but it's trampled without a thought by the new grandsire. "You lost, Gregori. You ran. You're not Aeskerat anymore."

Gregori laughs unhappily. "You mutinied. There's no honor in your victory."

"Elias," Dorian mumbles, "get out of here. Find Markus."

"But—"

"Go."

Elias scampers off, and if he's smart, he won't look back. Dorian draws his sword and lets it hang limp in his hand, retaking Amaranth's side.

"If Jacobi were alone in his misgivings about you, Gregori, he would have stood and died alone." Two others Dorian doesn't know flank Ionia, unarmed and expressionless. "We're done allowing you to keep pretending you lead by divine right."

Gregori wheels on Amaranth. "If they want a fight, so be it. You swore."

Amaranth doesn't cower. "You're not grandsire." She shrugs and dips her head to indicate Ionia. "I swore to help you take your coven back from Jacobi, and that task has been done for me. I did not pledge my kin's lives to meddle in your in-fighting after his defeat."

Gregori's hackles rise.

Dorian tugs Amaranth toward the gate. She can back-talk vampires like Jacobi, not Gregori. Her competency in battle hasn't been tested against the likes of him. She'll get herself killed. "Your coven, your problem," Dorian says to get the attention off his vulnerable grandsire and onto him. "Eight hundred years doesn't have to end tonight."

"Maybe not, but I don't like you." Gregori ignores him entirely, sneering at Amaranth. "I don't like your little dollhouse. I don't like your continued poaching of my kin, of vampires who break their oaths to me and should not be shielded by you. I don't like how you run your little gag with your needles, your people too soft to abide the sting of fangs. Show some respect to your elders who had this figured out centuries before you were born."

"Jacobi stole my people because they were healthy," she snaps back. "Not just physically—emotionally. Mentally. They thrive in my house, and because I take care of them, they take care of me. If you had this all figured out, you wouldn't be bathing in mutineer blood."

"Amaranth," Dorian hisses. "Let's go."

"We can't," she whispers. "There's nothing stopping him from raising a new coven and starting this whole mess all over again.

This has to end here."

Kill Gregori? "That is not within our power."

It doesn't look like it's in the remaining Aeskerat's power either. They have no food left to heal from another battle, and Gregori doesn't lose.

He's not stupid, though. Dorian nudges Amaranth behind him and tries a different tactic. "You started this when you didn't kill Jacobi," he calls, still edging them toward the gate. "All this, all the Aeskerat blood that's been shed, this is on you. You want your title back? Reckon with your own coven, not us."

He glances back, and the caravan is thankfully on the move, only Neire lingering for her grandsire. Neire, and stubborn, *stubborn* Elias, ignoring Markus trying to drag him away.

Elias must think himself immune to Gregori's ire because when Markus loses his grip, he rushes back in, right up to Gregori's toes. "The real enemy's out there, right?" Elias tries. "It's the living. Not other vampires."

Gregori nods. "Aye, so how about we renegotiate this little alliance, Amaranth? You want me leading Aeskerat, or Ionia?" He jabs his sword at the other vampire, who is quickly retreating. "Ionia didn't save your scout here. Ionia wouldn't have known how."

Elias wisely backs up. He doesn't leave but hides behind Dorian and Neire, who has also joined in the fray. "Elias, get out of here."

"I can talk him down."

"No. You can't."

Gregori eyes the two of them and his face contorts with jealousy. "Elias."

This isn't a competition for Elias's affections! Even if it were, Dorian didn't have to buy them nor does he want them.

Elias shakes his head. "You didn't spare me or save me selflessly. You didn't help Dorian just because either. It's always a move on your board." He shrugs, a defiant scowl pinching his face, and Dorian would be proud of him but this is absolutely not the time to spit in Gregori's face. He can do it after they have a solid wall between them. "I hope the hill is worth it, Your Highness."

Gregori leans back and *hmphs*. "Veronique."

Above them, already on the wall, Veronique slashes the chains of the gate. It hammers down in freefall, cutting off their escape and Markus on the other side.

Gregori is on him in an instant.

Elias scatters. Dorian barely deflects in time, slivers of ice chipping off both their blades. Neire attacks Gregori from behind, and he dodges as if he's got eyes on the back of his head.

Neire almost hits Dorian instead.

The elder vampire rips an iron bar from the stable's fence and fends them off with ease. He's been doing this for eight centuries and it's all Dorian can do to block and not get in Neire's way.

"Neire, back off," he grunts, ducking a blow.

A wayward arrow sails between them from above and Gregori snarls up at his lieutenant. "Do not interfere."

Amaranth readies her own bow across the courtyard and Veronique changes targets. He can't help his grandsire but Neire can—if she'd *move* and wait for an opening, he'd have one fewer distraction. "Neire!"

Gregori doesn't care about her or Amaranth. Amaranth will be easy. Dorian is a nuisance, and Gregori is only toying with him. "You threw the first stone by killing Janneah. Did you even give her a chance? Tell her who you are? Or did you decide from the moment you saw her that she would die?"

Just keep talking, Gregori. Neire finally listens and relents. He has a plan, a stupid plan, but a plan nonetheless. There's only room enough for one martyr in Tanarang, and it's him.

It's a dance, a game, as Gregori lunges wide and Dorian skitters back, blades squealing and sliding off each other. "I didn't decide to kill her until she decided my ward was meat for slaughter. Not a person."

Gregori laughs, shoulders shaking. He moves like a snake, aware that Dorian's not his only opponent even as Neire waits impatiently and Veronique keeps Amaranth distracted.

Not yet.

"You have always been, and always will be, an Aeskerat at heart, reborn in this world after staking a sleeping vampire in the back. Really, Dorian, you're no better than I am."

"Maybe so." Dodge. Block. Parry. *Not yet.* Dorian gets in close, locking Gregori's blade at the hilt. "But my family is loyal to me."

Hackles rise. Gregori's arm trembles from the strain.

Now.

The last time they dueled, Gregori fought for showmanship, serving him up as an example to the rest of their coven. His goal was to shed blood more than cause pain, stretching the fight out for the spectacle.

That Gregori is gone.

Dorian almost falls to one hit, tripping over loose stones and empty pockets in the courtyard. As he feints, Neire sneaks in. She takes Gregori head-on, and Dorian manages a slice at the back of his calf, carving through sinew, and Gregori howls and buckles, cleaving the air where Dorian's face was a second before, and none of this feels like enough because it doesn't matter if Gregori's angry.

Veronique chases Amaranth in his periphery. The whole

courtyard is too open. If they could get the gate up, get back-up, get the rest of Aeskerat to bother lifting a finger to help instead of hoping their enemies slaughter each other—

Gregori pummels down and Dorian's sword shatters under the force. White-hot ice slashes across his chest. He flinches and turns away and a boot kicks him across the courtyard to smack the far wall with back-breaking force. Cracked ribs, surely, and probably a vertebra or two, his lungs wrung like wet linens and refusing to cooperate. His head smarts, vision melting into black wax.

The slash he took isn't deep, but it's long, collarbone to hip. He looks up, expecting Gregori to appear and finish him off. Veronique falls, and Amaranth's bow lies broken. She bleeds from her temple, drawing her sword to help Neire.

It's not enough.

Gregori is too strong. They weren't prepared for this, and Ionia isn't going to help them. Gregori was right. He would have been the better choice as grandsire. The vampire they know intimately over Ionia's untested mettle.

Then Elias is at his side. "What's broken?"

"Get back," Dorian wheezes, shoving at him.

"He won't hurt me."

Don't be so sure.

"Can you use this still?" Elias shoves an Aeskerat bow at him. His own lies among the splatter of his blood on the stones, string severed.

The strain on his muscles even nocking an arrow burns like lava. He can draw it, barely, enough to stick a pig and anger it. Several of the arrows in his hip quiver snapped on impact and he pulls one with bent fletching. It'll have to do. He shoves again at Elias to move his ass to safety, *now.*

"You need—"

"I need you to *move*."

Elias had better have scurried back upstairs or even inside the castle because Dorian can't look away from the frenzy long enough to check if he's gone.

Gregori laughs through his pain, toying with Amaranth and Neire, dodging every attack like it's all a match he's allowing them to finish. Amaranth nearly stabs Neire as often as she misses Gregori and if they'd all stand still for two seconds, Dorian can end this.

Amaranth's opening comes when Dorian misses, arrow flying wide. Gregori's head swivels like an owl. She stabs him in the thigh.

He backhands her with the guard of his sword and Amaranth drops. Neire screams, diving between Gregori and her grandsire.

He takes her head in a single blow.

Neire's body falls, her head rolls, and Gregori doesn't give them a chance to breathe before he chucks his splintered blade at Dorian's head.

He rolls. Behind him, Elias chokes.

Gregori's withered snarl falters, eyes impossibly wide. Dorian turns slowly because Elias was supposed to run. He was supposed to be hiding anywhere else but *right there*.

The fragile little yearling stares dumbly at the hilt askew in his stomach, then slumps down the wall.

"Oh no," the Aeskerat rasps. "No, no, no."

Dorian stares blankly in the deafening silence. Neire's dead. Elias is almost dead. Amaranth will be dead. Gregori roars and *now*, he thinks, this is the closest a vampire gets to seeing the end come upon them.

Gregori stomps forward a single step and an arrow impales his eye. He drops like a bag of rocks.

Markus is there, racing down from the wall. He throws his bow aside and cracks Dorian's bruised spine further in a crushing embrace. "Neire was in the way. I didn't want to distract her or you and then she was gone and it all happened so fast—"

"You did your best." Dorian pulls back and can't get his limbs to work properly to crawl over to Elias. Markus has to help him. "Elias?"

Elias isn't dead yet, his stuttered, shaky gasps the loudest sound in the silence. Dorian crawls over and tears at the leathers around the wound. Blood spurts and trickles and freezes on contact with the stuck blade. He yanks it out, knowing the consequences, and lets it clatter behind him.

Elias coughs and paws at his wound. "S'my own fault."

"Yeah, it is." Dorian moves Elias's hands away. Markus lowers beside them and shakes his head as if Dorian doesn't already know. "I told you not to be a hero."

Elias smiles deliriously, then it crumples in a trembling frown. "M'gonna die?"

"I can turn you." Dorian bites into his wrist and offers it. "Let me."

Elias shakes his head, eyes squeezed shut.

"I can turn you and give you time to decide with a clearer head if you want to stay a vampire?" Already, Elias's face is clammy. He wouldn't get to find whatever afterlife may or may not exist, but Dorian hasn't heard him once pray for his gods to save him.

Aeskerat vampires slowly spill from their hiding spots. Ionia approaches And Dorian snarls up at her. "Where were you?"

"You brought Gregori here," she says gravely. "We already tried deposing him. As far as we're concerned, he's Tanarang now.

And your mess to clean up."

"You couldn't send out even one archer to shoot him while his back was turned?" Dorian wheezes, undercutting any venom in his shout. His nails scrape on the cobbles, black spots like ash clouding his vision.

"We had one, in case you lost."

He hisses a laugh. "We won't forget this."

"We're not friends, Dorian. Bygones at best, never allies," Ionia says simply. Now that she doesn't have to kiss Amaranth's boots. Now that she has power and Dorian's unarmed. Aeskerat never changes. "You alone killed eight of my kin since this started."

And I'd happily stake a ninth.

Ionia turns away, headed for his motionless grandsire.

Markus tilts his head toward Amaranth and Dorian lets him go but stays. Elias is more important, looking at him with pity. Damn Ionia for interrupting them. "I suppose that didn't make a grand case for joining this eternal, bickering feud?"

Elias's hands tremble, voice all gummy and shredded. "Can't."

Dorian smooths sweat-stuck hair from his face. "If you hate being one that badly, I won't force you to stay one." He can only change his mind later if he accepts it now, though. Dorian won't lie, there's no sunshine and rainbows to be had, but if every waking moment of eternity were misery, the vampire species would have died out a long time ago. "Please let me do this."

Tears trail down into his hair. Elias sniffles and shakily grabs for Dorian's hand. At first, he thinks, for something to hold until he's gone, but no. Elias drinks, only a drop would be enough, and the deed is done.

"U-use m-me," he stutters. "While st-still mortal. Heal."

"We'll be fine without it." Fine enough to catch up to the caravan, at least.

Markus carries Amaranth over, nose broken and cheek scraped to bone. Alive, and soaked in Neire's blood.

Elias dips his fingers in the red pooling over his stomach and smacks Dorian with it, smearing streaks across his jaw. His eyes plead, burning with it.

"Damn it all, Elias. Okay. If that's what you want, okay." Dorian tries to be gentle with his wrist even as he doubts Elias registers such an insignificant pain anymore. His sore ribs and split skin glue themselves back together. His spine re-aligns.

Markus only takes what's already spilled and makes sure Amaranth has her fill, too. Elias doesn't last long enough to notice. Dorian has ended lives quickly and slowly, sat with the late members of their own little clan when old age came for them. Watching the light fade from the eyes of the dying never gets easier. Elias is still looking right at him, but in a whisper, he's not there anymore. His skin is still warm, the stars still reflect in his pale irises, but they're empty now. Dorian closes his eyes for him, then notices the tip of the stake sticking out of Elias's boot.

"Markus, please figure out how to get the gate open and find us transportation home. I'm finishing this."

Markus frowns and shakes his head at Elias's body, a heavy hand offering his sympathies, before he's gone to find a spare mount.

Despite everything Gregori has done, despite Neire lying headless beside him, Dorian still hesitates to kill him forever. Eight hundred years. Eight *hundred* years of history no one wrote down, knowledge lost with each generation, songs and stories and legacies remembered only by Gregori.

"Please." Veronique, missing an arm and an eye. "Please don't."

"We can't rest easy if he lives." Gregori didn't let a mutiny keep him away; he won't let a second defeat stop him either. Such is the curse of vampirism. "And he deserves it."

"I know he does." She gets to her knees. "You owe me nothing, but please. I will make sure he knows that he owes you his life. I'll take the Tanarang oath to council him in your favor and warn you if he tries to scheme. You're going to need him when the real fight comes. You needed him to save your life when no one else thought it could be done."

Amaranth hobbles over and leans on Dorian for support. "Take the oath, then, Aeskerat."

Veronique does, repeating the vows as Amaranth speaks them.

"Someone must answer for Neire now that I can't kill Gregori to avenge her." Amaranth sniffs and cocks her head at Ionia. "What do you suggest?"

As his grandsire negotiates, Markus returns with a horse no one had better dare complain about them taking to transport Neire. Dorian wraps her body up in her furs and loads her carefully onto the steed's back.

"You didn't do this," Markus says softly to Dorian while the cowardly Aeskerat fix the gate chain. "Gregori did."

He nods, not able to answer. They never should have trusted him. Alone, surrounded by the entire Tanarang host, they could have taken him, and Neire would still be alive.

Ionia and his grandsire finish their negotiations and Dorian can't imagine what Aeskerat had left to bargain. "Grandsire?"

"The House of the Bear has fallen," Amaranth declares. "Veronique and Gregori are exiled."

"We can't trust Ionia," he mutters. Veronique, maybe. Loyalty like hers is rare outside his chosen coven.

"We can't," Amaranth agrees. "But she'll have us and the other seven covens to contend with if she wants to pick a fight after this ordeal."

So Ionia stays grandsire. He can't say he's looking forward to it. She's a schemer—the whole coven are schemers—but it only matters if her schemes don't align with Tanarang's interests.

Amaranth sighs and smiles pityingly at Elias's body. "I'm sorry."

"He shouldn't have been here." He should have been safe in his room waiting for them all to come home. "He was just a kid, Amaranth. You're supposed to lead, not cave to the whims of hungry vampires who wanted to see him punished. What does any of this accomplish?"

"He needed to bear witness. I said he had to be here, I didn't say he had to fight."

No, she didn't, but she's being vindictive. Elias is his friend, if nothing else, and didn't deserve this end. He will turn, but he will do so frozen in the state he died. Dorian still doesn't know how old he was. Most who turn by choice do so in the prime of their life, after they've had time to think about the consequences, get their affairs in order. This was no way to go out, whether he was twenty or fifty or anywhere in between. "He died helping me. You know that, right?"

"I know."

Dorian shakes his head. "Now he's your problem for eternity."

Markus interrupts before Dorian can say something he'll regret. He nods at the castle around them. "So Aeskerat's... done?"

Amaranth nods, shoulders set. "I can't kill Gregori, but I can kill his legacy. Aeskerat is no more."

Dorian spares Ionia one last look, reminding her exactly who fell tonight, which new bygones she did nothing to aid, and turns away. Markus helps Amaranth up into the saddle and they turn west, toward home.

Chapter 19:
Thrall of the Morning Sky

When Elias wakes, Dorian is the first thing he sees. It doesn't hurt as much as he thought it would. Dying had, but coming back...

Everything about Dorian is sharper. The browns and coppers in his hair, the faintest of freckles that vanish if Elias looks at them head-on, and his *scent*—earthy like the watering caves, metallic like iron, and bitter like... wine? Something sour but fruity that he can't place.

"Hey," Dorian says softly, and even his voice is richer, as if Elias lived his whole life with mud in his ears. His voice, and his strong, steady pulse. Distantly, too, heavy footfalls echo from running children, doors closing too hard, warbled chatter.

The cave was never silent, but the constant parade of sensory overload for eternity isn't something Elias anticipated. Will he get used to it?

He doesn't want to be aware either of the stitching of his new shirt or all the individual furs touching him or how intensely bright even the smallest light shines. Elias closes his eyes and groans and even that's too loud and weird, as if his own voice is being spoken back to him.

"You're hungry," Dorian says, even softer now. "That sensitivity kicks in to help you hunt."

Hunt.

Right.

Deep breath. When he does take one, his chest tightens like there's a rope wound around his middle—a very real one. Elias blinks and sits up, lifts his shirt. No rope. Only the ghastly scar from Gregori's sword hilt.

"Oh."

It's silvery, like every other vampire's, but all rough and discolored around the edges. Wrinkled and ugly. He touches it and can't feel his fingers, only the pressure of his touch. Elias puffs his cheeks and nods, and lets the shirt fall. He's alive… but also not.

Dorian swallows—*so loudly*—and offers Elias a chalice of fresh blood. "It's Castor's," he says, as if it helps, as if Elias wants to know. "My ration of Castor's. We're still figuring this out."

Blood, too, smells different now. Not literally, but in his mind? It's like Castor's name is signed in his scent, the knowledge imprinted in his brain. Elias can't begin to untangle what that means or what he's supposed to do about it.

"Oh."

Dorian balks when he doesn't take it. "Elias, you need to eat."

Elias numbly shakes his head. He wants one of Elphaba's bread rolls. He wants the cake he never got to try. The fish, the jerky from his clan that's all gone anyway and will never be made again. He wants to try the honey from Olimaunt. He wants that damned seaweed soup.

He—

The sun. He'll never get to see it.

The chalice clinks on the floor, and Dorian's clothing rustles against the furs, and a wrist or a knuckle pops, and he doesn't see any of it, eyes squeezed shut and burning and *why* can he still cry? He's *dead*.

Dorian hugs him, crushing. "I'm sorry."

Not even crying feels the same. Tears come but snot doesn't. He doesn't get stuffy and his voice doesn't gum up. Like an imitation of hurt meant to trick would-be prey. Dorian lets him let it out, Elias knows he will for as long as he needs to, but he's staring down eternity now. How long is too long?

They rock gently, Dorian humming some slow, somber tune as he runs his fingers through his hair. The rest of the noise of the castle melts away and Elias can focus on the vibrations against his chest and the warmth in his arms.

He's staring down eternity, but he's not alone.

He can still smell the blood sitting there in the cup on the floor, but his face is buried against Dorian's neck and that earthy-fruity-irony scent is intoxicating. Elias hiccups and shudders at the slide of new fangs extending and—

Elias yanks away and slaps his hands over his mouth, almost shoving Dorian to the floor.

"It's okay." Dorian offers the chalice once again. "You need to eat."

The blood glistens invitingly in the candlelight. Elias only stares.

Neire's funeral takes with it the last snowfall. They light her pyre in the courtyard as the ice sheets that grew over nine months of snowstorms thaw from the castle walls. It won't ever be warm enough for the children to shed their furs, but it might rain if they're lucky.

Lying in the grass and catching raindrops on his tongue used to be Markus's favorite pastime. It was senseless, unproductive, and left his clothes stained green and muddy. When everyone else ran for cover from the lightning and the thunder, Markus had the world to himself.

Gilan will like it too, he hopes. The child sniffles now and clings to Kymiria's leg, face turned away from the dying fire. He's not alone in his grief, but it's a feat that dies with the living—the ability to love with an entire being because there's only so much time to devote to precious things.

Kymiria loves, more like the living than Markus ever did or will, but there's still a vastness to her soul, a sterility, when short lives come and go as surely as the wind erodes stone. She can't devote her life if her life never ends. Being loved, like Neire was by all her students, is a sacred thing.

Dorian loves, in confusing and overwhelming ways sometimes. When they'd chased down the caravan in the wake of Aeskerat's demise, Dorian had pulled Markus aside and crushed him back to his still-healing chest.

"I'm sorry," he'd kept repeating. *I'm sorry, I'm sorry.* Sorry for almost dying again, sorry for what almost happened, sorry for almost leaving Markus alone and robbed of a goodbye *again.*

He'd started babbling a tempest of weak justifications. That it had to be him because Amaranth is still little and would never win against Gregori. That it's who he's always been, a trait amplified in death, and that he can't help it and understands if it means Markus wants nothing to do with him.

Markus had cut him off. "If we were frozen as who we were in life, I wouldn't be in love with you."

The words had seemed to shake him to his core. Dorian had no response.

"So it's not *just who you are*. You *can* help it, and I can help you do so." He'd given Henri the task of riding Dorian's horse and guarding Elias, and sat with him in a sleigh, sharing a cloak, the whole ride home.

The symbolic death of Aeskerat isn't enough for some of them. They want Gregori dead, but they still have Jacobi to punish in his place, and he is more than guilty enough on his own.

The only member of the castle who doesn't join to watch Jacobi's sentencing is Elias. Markus had come to get both him and Dorian before they missed Neire's pyre and found Elias curled up in a ball on his bed and Dorian still trying to persuade him to eat.

"Just go," Elias had muttered. "I need time alone right now anyway."

Actually getting Dorian to leave his side had taken quite a bit of nudging and tugging. "Be there for Neire," Markus had said to finally coax him from the room. Elias never came down.

Amaranth and Hyacinth force Jacobi to watch his ex-kin, who betrayed Gregori for his cause, betray him now for Tanarang's. Eleven of them take their oaths but are permitted no braids and will be given the worst jobs in the castle until they prove they deserted for more than just a lesser evil. Markus hopes it's scrubbing chamber pots or carving up bloating whale carcasses. Those odors tattoo themselves inside his nose for weeks, and he's rarely elbow-deep in the messes.

Throughout, Jacobi remains stubbornly silent, scowling at his feet. Either he still thinks they're too proud and noble and merciful to actually hurt him, or he thinks himself too proud to even beg for mercy.

He's silent even as Amaranth reads his punishment. She stands on the back of a sleigh over Jacobi, chained and sad on the ground, reading off a parchment Markus suspects is purely for spectacle.

"Jacobi of no House," she begins primly, "you sought to enslave my scout, my kin, my family, in the deep darkness of a clan's cave, suffering a perpetual death and revival until he withered. Witnesses claim you intended to let this atrocity endure for twenty years. I sentence you to the same fate."

Not in the deep dark of some clan's cave, oh no. They all board the *Peony* and chain Jacobi to an unused anchor, sailing into the bay deep enough to host pods of whales two-hundred strong in summer.

Then, and only then, does Jacobi start screaming and begging. He kicks and writhes against his bindings, calling them every name under the moons and the stars, vowing vengeance all in the same breath.

Quinn kicks him overboard and his pale head vanishes in a second.

"We didn't attach a chain," Markus muses. "How are we supposed to pull him back up in twenty years?"

Amaranth purses her lips. "It must've slipped my mind. Pity."

Dorian stares ruefully at the lapping waves where Jacobi sank until Markus tugs him away. "I don't remember being withered," he mumbles, "but I don't think I'd wish it on anyone, even him."

"Maybe the sharks will eat him first. Or he'll sink so far that the weight of the water will crush his body." Markus taps his chin, now wishing they really had attached a chain so he could pull it back up in a bit to check if he's right.

Either prospect seems to put Dorian's mind at ease. "Maybe."

Kymiria joins them at the bow for the trip back and Markus still stands by what he said when this started, that if Dorian wants something Markus can't give, he should get it from someone who can. If Kymiria is that someone, then all the better for it. Or Elias, now that he's turned, though Markus hopes not, because Elias seems to him too much hassle to be worth it.

"I don't know what the three of us have," Dorian says, "but it's unequal. I want it to be fair."

"Who said it wasn't fair?" Kymiria throws her arm around his shoulders. "We discussed this by the Tammen. Nothing's changed."

"I believe there's a Southern expression related to bicycles and three wheels?"

Markus frowns. "You mean a tricycle?"

Kymiria socks them both gently in the arm. "See? Balance! Maybe the wheels don't all match, but it rides, doesn't it?"

Dorian doesn't have a rebuttal. "Just... communicate, if it does change."

"If you will, too." Communication is easy. When doesn't Markus ask for what he wants? Like now, for instance, standing against the railing and leaning into the wind. "Come here, please?"

He climbs the prow and throws his arms out, Dorian at his back even though the wind isn't strong enough to knock him over. Strong arms around his hips keep him steady until he's had his fill, salty sea spray making a mess of his hair.

He had turned so that he could answer the ultimate question of life: What happens when it ends? It's moments like this one, though, that make eternity worth it.

Loving something that intends to outlive even the wind that erodes the stone is an impossible promise to keep. Markus can't cement the future even if he's as certain of its arrival as he is that the moons will keep rising on their journey around the sky. One night, inexplicably, they might not.

He can promise the present, and the present right now is Dorian beside him on the deck and Kymiria sprawled across their laps like a house cat from his stories, and it's perfect.

Elias misses the funeral and Jacobi's dive, as badly as he'd wanted to witness both. His head pounds, his gums ache, and there's a cold hunger in his bones. He didn't want to draw attention away from Neire and Jacobi.

Elias grew used to the snide comments at his back long ago, but the smug satisfaction of someone having to feed him after he'd so long insisted that it's wrong, that he'd *never*, keeps him up in his room. Dorian hadn't taken the chalice. There it still sits, probably undrinkable now.

The darkness is even brighter now, innocuous sounds sharper and more irritating, and his sense of smell, *eugh*. Has his own sweat always stunk this badly? He rubs his temples and is aware of the approaching footsteps in the hall but hopes they continue past his door.

"Elias?" Dorian, his attempt at a gentle knock a hammer banging. "Did you eat? I brought more."

No thanks, he thinks as his mouth betrays him and says, "Door's unlocked."

Dorian's not alone, but he leaves Markus at the threshold. Great, more witnesses to his pity party. The new blood in the chalice smells *divine*. Tangy and spicy and familiar. Elias lurches, body seizing as he resists ripping the cup from Dorian's hands. If he clawed his own nose off, how long would it take to grow back?

"What is that?" It's so different.

"Mine." Dorian shrugs and picks up the forgotten glass of Castor's blood. "*Waste not* applies even here. We're on rations, Elias. You can't start eternity here like this. You need to eat." He makes a point of giving the cup of his own blood to Markus and shoves Castor's back in Elias's face.

Markus hums and takes it happily, running his finger around the sides to get every last drop. Already, Elias mourns not tasting it.

Elias sinks to the floor and *thunks* his forehead on his knees, which doesn't help his headache. "Everyone's going to…"

The metal base of the old chalice clinks on the floor beside him. Dorian's leathers rustle as he sits. He smells now like smoke and sea salt. "Pride? Really? I'd let you drink from me, but the sooner you can accept this and move on, the better off you will be."

"I'm not biting anyone." Licking another person's arm or neck to seal the wound? His lip curls.

"You don't have to. We still have the needles."

Yes, the needles. Can Elias permanently skip the whole oral process altogether and inject himself whenever he gets peckish? Must he put blood to his mouth at all?

His fangs protract at the thought and he hisses in pain, slapping his hands over his mouth. "When will this stop? I feel like a child having to face maturation all over again." He can't even speak properly around them, always mucking up his consonants.

Dorian picks up the chalice with a tired sigh. "When you eat. Vampirism is a curse, remember? Enjoying it, or even tolerating it, takes practice and discipline." He pinches Elias's lip with the rim of the chalice. "Drink. We have measures to train fledglings."

"Oh, I've graduated from yearling to fledgling." Elias closes his eyes and takes a deep breath and he knocks it all back in one go because at least he doesn't have to be creepy by savoring it.

Immediately, his headache begins to clear and the yammering of his stomach ceases. He drags his hand across his lips, smearing them red.

Dorian's brows rise. "Better?"

No. "Yeah." If better includes the urge to lick the chalice clean.

"Good." Dorian hops to his feet. "Get dressed. You and I are going out."

"Out?"

Markus leaves, saying he'll ready the horses. Dorian throws a mismatched pile of clothes at Elias. "Yes. Out. Now get dressed. You might not need the warmth anymore, but we do still care about public decency around the children."

What, his frumpy nightshirt isn't suitable for horseback riding? Elias slips it off and picks through the pile of clothes and his eyes drift to the puffy pink-and-silvery scar beneath his sternum. It's ghastly compared to the jagged stitch from Jacobi's arrow, the pale teeth marks on his wrist, and Elias *hmphs*, thumbing at the indentations.

Dorian smiles sadly. "Most vampires don't turn by choice, much less with death looming near. I'm sorry that couldn't be healed."

"I'm not complaining." Elias dresses and watches his uneven fingers tie the laces. With eternity ahead of him, maybe he can carve himself false fingers and paint them all ornately. Have an entire box filled with detachable digits instead of silver spoons. "I do wish I'd died with my hair longer. I can't even pull it back and it'll be like this forever."

"Oh, I'm sure we can figure something out. Weave in donated hair or whatever other material you want."

Is that how every single Tanarang has hair long enough for all their braids?

"I can't decide if I'm going to hate the permanent stubble or not." It doesn't itch, thank the gods, but forever with this exact shape and leanness to his not-beard? Forever with the red bumps along his jaw and whatever other minor bruises that now tattoo his skin?

Dorian snickers and holds the door open for him. "You can still shave, it will just grow back with every meal."

He doesn't surrender wherever they're riding to, only that it's south. Already the landscape looks wildly different. The snow hasn't all melted away, but waxy tufts of black and purple grass have grown through the slush like whiskers. Elias could stop his horse right now and flop onto the ground to admire the muted colors for hours.

Dorian doesn't let him; wherever they're headed is quite a journey yet. Bears unfurling from hibernation scatter when they near. Deer and other antlered animals whose names he's unsure of cross their path, as do molting hares and foxes. He sees the snowy owls and eagles, as Dorian points them out, that survive on fungi and the fish in the rivers. He slows up before the crest of a hill and lets Dandy slip into stride with Lily. "Okay, either hop on behind me or hand me your reins so you can close your eyes."

Elias tosses the reins over, legs tense with anticipation. He can't see but he can feel the elevation changes as they ride up and over the hill.

When the wind shifts, the smell hits him all at once. Earthy and light, sweet but not sugary, and woody. "Dorian?"

"Almost there."

The sound of the horses' hooves shift from the clop and crunch of rock and gravel to the squelch of mud then to something soft and muffled, that strange scent sharpening. Lily lumbers to a halt.

"Okay. Open."

As far as Elias can see, wildflowers bloom. Pinks and yellows and blues and purples, so thickly knitted, they blanket the ground. Walking atop them might be the closest he gets to flying through the clouds. A shallow river winds toward the ocean and in the distance...

"Are those trees?"

"Look behind you."

"I—*oh*!" Dorian had brought them out into the meadow, but twisted, black-barked trees guard the foothills at their backs. Elias slides off his horse like melted wax, wishing for eyes on the back of his head so he can capture it all in one view.

He can't stand on the tips of his toes without crushing flowers but squashes all the more beneath his shins. If the nectar stains his pants and furs, he'll never wash them again. The petals, so thin they're translucent, are softer than silk, than that red satin robe. Pink pollen dusts his fingers.

Elias falls forward and bathes in it.

"You can pick some, if you want. I've seen them pressed between book pages and stuck to canvas."

Oh, an entire wall-sized landscape of real flowers? Elias would never leave his room all winter long, but... "It would kill them, though, wouldn't it?"

"It would. They will come back next year."

Elias sniffles and stares up at the wispy clouds in the night sky, warming toward day. He sits up and looks eastward for the sun, hungry for it. Curse be damned.

"Elias." Dorian dismounts, and from a saddlebag, pulls an oblong steel disk, a shield about the size of a serving platter. "Do you want to watch the sunrise?"

"What—can we?"

"Reflected, imperfect. But yes." Dorian sends the horses to make themself scarce beneath the furry canopy and props the shield against one of his boots.

The shield is scratched and hazy, reflecting their blobby forms back at them. Elias doesn't care, scooting sideways to block as little of it as possible. The purple-grey sky fills the disk, growing brighter, brighter, brighter still. Wispy clouds turn pale pink and orange.

It takes everything, every drop of willpower, to not turn around. Elias's fists twitch on his thighs as Dorian ensures he's protected by his furs, his hood, his gloves. Will the light be strong enough to warm his back through the layers? Does it make a sound? Oh, he still hopes it roars.

Yellow glows like a candle that can't flicker, silently.

"You can look," Dorian says softly, "but only for a few seconds. It mesmerizes."

Elias twists so fast his spine pops. If there is a god above all others, the pale rays brandished like lances cutting through the sky, the burning ball of gold, the halo, must be what they look like.

A capricious god that begins to burn his eyes, his cheeks, his nose. Dying like this, staring at the sunrise, doesn't seem like a bad way to go.

But *no*. It's seared to the backs of his eyelids now. He may only ever see this once, but he can draw it and paint it ten thousand times, and maybe one of them might come close to the real thing.

He turns back around, afterburn black over the meadow. "How long does it last?"

"Only an hour or two this time of year."

So *short*! "Can we stay?"

"Well, we'll have to stay. Dandy and Lily won't be going anywhere until it's dark."

It's the best news Elias has heard in his entire life.

"So... we get to sit here in the flowers, doing absolutely nothing, until sunset?"

Dorian shrugs. "You got somewhere more important to be?"

"No." Elias tips his head back, counting the sparse stars still bright enough in the blue-grey sky. "No, I don't."

About the Author:

Anne Bellows is a fantasy and sci-fi author from Tampa, Florida. She runs the "Writing Tips Blog of Many Colors" for character creation, story structure, and worldbuilding. She also designs fantasy maps and book covers. She lives in Orlando with her two cats, Loki and Hella.

See Anne's website below for more about the world of *Northern Skies*.

www.annebellowsbooks.com